A Threat from the Past

Paul Cude

DEDICATION

To Rachel, Jaina and Poppy – the best family anyone could ever wish for. Thank you so much for your love and support, without which this book would never have been possible. The three of you make me feel like the luckiest man alive.

And to the real Alan Garrett - thank you for letting me use your name, and for your friendship throughout the years.

A long time ago, through a stroke of luck, I was introduced to the sport of hockey. It changed and shaped my life beyond measure. Those of you who play any sort of team sport will undoubtedly know what I'm talking about. Those of you who don't, should try taking one up - you might like it! To players of all team sports everywhere... this book is dedicated to you. Hope you enjoy!

Paul Cude

CONTENTS

1 DRAGON SLEIGHING
(AND YES, IT'S SUPPOSED TO BE
SPELT THAT WAY)

Mystical power and pure, unadulterated magic have long since infused our world and those that reside there. All this has been going on since at least the prehistoric. Speaking of which....

Plumes of dark smoke billowed into the air across the broken and battered city as the sickly smell of death wafted on a gentle breeze across the market square, tugging at the canvas of the overturned market stalls scattered haphazardly amongst the raging fires and ruined buildings.

Off to one side stood the giant archway, which for hundreds of years had been regarded as the main thoroughfare to the city. Normally a giant monster of a retractable drawbridge with a thick steel portcullis hung, attached to the weathered archway, providing a reassuring air of safety to all the residents within. Fifteen minutes ago, that illusion had been shattered forever. All that now remained was the splintered outline of a ferocious beast, where it had casually walked through both drawbridge and portcullis, as a knife would slice through butter. Darkened steel had melted in places from the heat that it had radiated, the metal now looking like wax running down the side of a candle. It was odd that the creature had decided to do this; after all, it could have just flown over the walls and landed with ease anywhere it had wanted to. Currently the citizens had far too much on their minds to worry about details like that.

Steam rose from the dark cobbles of the square, the occasional one or two glowing bright orange from the heat. A faint trickle of water could just be heard from a pile of debris that not ten minutes ago had been an ornate fountain. Despite the burning buildings, the casualties and the corpses, those left alive were all mesmerised by the sight before them.

Near what was left of the drawbridge and portcullis, surrounded by piles of smouldering wreckage, hovering a few metres in the air, a gigantic, menacing dragon surveyed all the damage it had previously wreaked. Matt black all over, it seemed content enough with its progress to let snaking lines of flame dribble down both sides of its colossal jaws.

In spite of its size and formidable presence, it was clearly agitated, roaring occasionally, raking its talons along the top of the surrounding rubble and banging its tail into the ground with such force that the shock wave could be felt over a quarter of a mile away, terrifying residents trapped inside quaking houses and shops. The object of the dragon brute's agitation stood on the opposite side of the colossal square: out of breath, clad from head to toe in chainmail armour, clutching a rusty shield in one hand and a rather large, ordinary, dull blade in the other, the knight was sweating profusely. Random parts of his armour were blackened from fleeting encounters with the dragon's flame over the past few minutes. Onlookers couldn't decide if both were either having a rest, or had indeed reached a standoff. It didn't seem possible for that to be the case, but most would have said that for the knight to survive as long as he already had was nothing short of a miracle. Fear and terror gripped most of them, having lived through the nightmare that had come out of nowhere only a short time ago. But macabre as it may have seemed, they desperately wanted to witness the outcome of the most one-sided fight in history, despite knowing that the knight yonder had absolutely no chance at all.

His armour feeling mighty hot in places, the scorched knight seemed to have spent the last few seconds deciding on a course of action and, in one swift motion, dropped his rusty shield and pulled off his helm, tossing it far off to his right, revealing long, straggly, dark locks of hair. As if an almost everyday occurrence, he casually removed his gauntlets and the armour around his feet. Stifling a gasp, the entire crowd were unaware the best was yet to come. Waving his heavy sword around his body with such speed and athleticism that the blade was a constant blur, silently he mouthed a challenge to the, by now, very disappointed scaled monster. Impossible as it may seem, the beast appeared to understand the knight's whispered challenge from over four hundred metres away and with one huge flap of its wings, propelled itself forward, creating such down force that dust, stone, wood and even dead bodies scattered into the air in its wake. At exactly the same time, the knight started sprinting towards the dragon, with most of his armour removed and just his two handed sword for company. City folk collectively held their breath.

Time slowed as the speeding dragon travelled towards the knight, just above the ground, emitting a thunderous cone of fire out in front of it. Everyone was of the same opinion: the knight would be obliterated by the mighty dragon.

As the inevitable drew closer, the sprinting knight, arms and legs pumping, face full of anger and passion, managed to find just a little more speed, and at the split second before hitting the tip of the fiery cone, dived headlong towards the cobbles. Miraculously the knight's extra speed had caused the dragon to miscalculate and as the knight rolled underneath the dragon's exposed belly, he managed with all the dexterity and agility of an Olympic gymnast, to thrust the heavy two-handed sword into the beast with just one hand.

An almighty gurgle reverberated across the square as the flames instantly died away and the dragon thudded awkwardly to the ground, its massive body narrowly missing the exhausted knight. City dwellers covered their ears as the BOOM from the impact shuddered across the city. Massive cracks in the cobblestones rippled out from beneath the beast's body as a low-pitched holler echoed from the depths of its very being. Painfully the knight hauled himself up from the ground, visibly panting as he did so. Slowly, he strode along the side of the dragon as if inspecting it, only stopping when he reached its head. Kneeling, he started to recite the words of an ancient tongue, so that only he could hear.

Meanwhile citizens appeared to be recovering from the shock of the dragon having been defeated, rushing to the aid of the wounded, putting out fires, rescuing animals and comforting those mourning the loss of a loved one.

From out of a darkened alleyway between two of the remaining shops on the far side of the square, a small group of people led by the mayor, headed towards the knight, meandering through the burning rubble, the pillars of thick black smoke and the numerous cadavers. As they approached, the knight finished uttering the mysterious words, words which had caused a soft purple glow to spread from its head to the tip of the tail, finally encompassing its entire body, barely noticeable against the space-like black of the dragon's scales, but it was there.

Ignoring the people heading towards him, the knight walked back to the dragon's belly. Crouching, he put two hands on the hilt of the massive sword, and yanked it free. A dozen tiny scales, about the size of a man's fingernails, clattered onto the cobbles from around the entry wound that the sword had been pulled from. With a sleight of hand any magician would have been proud of, the knight scooped up the scales and poured them into a silk bag that hung from his belt. Sheathing his sword, he turned to face the newcomers.

"Is it dead?" asked the mayor, nervously.

"It is," replied the knight, taking a deep breath.

"How can we ever repay the debt we owe you for what you've done here today? That vile beast would surely have destroyed the entire city and everyone in it, if not for you."

"You have no debt to repay. I'm sorry for the loss of

life and damage," the knight replied in a heartfelt manner. "I have companions who, as we speak, are on their way here to assist with what has happened this day, among them healers and engineers. I ask only that they are allowed to help as best they can."

"Of course, of course," mumbled the mayor. "May I ask your name, brave knight?"

"George. You can call me George."

Nodding in unison, the group of dignitaries told George that lookouts would be posted on the walls of the city to greet his companions, before hastily rushing off, frightened by the corpse of the twisted dragon.

Things started to come together over the next couple of days. Major fires were extinguished using water from the city's many surrounding rivers, with people forming giant human chains. Others helped the wounded, of which there were many. In fact barely anyone was left unscathed. Volunteers to help at the hospital, or with the collection of medicines in the form of herbs and roots from the nearby forest, were many. Every man, women and child chipped in. Copious amounts of corpses were collected and placed in huge pyres that had been erected outside the city's walls. Fortunately undamaged, the spire of the magnificent cathedral cast its long shadow over the city square, as if joining in the people's collective sorrow.

Throughout all this, George's companions started to arrive in dribs and drabs, some in small groups, others on their own. They were easily identifiable because they all wore the same tunic as George: white with a bright purple trident running diagonally across them. On arrival, the visitors were all escorted through the bloodstained boulevards to the overcrowded hospital, where George helped tend to the seriously wounded in a dark, dank, death-smelling ward.

Seemingly in charge, the dashing knight dished out assignments to the new arrivals straight away. Healers stayed in and around the hospital, while the planners and politicians worked closely with the mayor and the rest of the city's hierarchy to coordinate the rebuilding effort and temporarily re-house those who had lost their homes.

Meanwhile the engineers appeared to be achieving miracles. Working around the clock, they designed, built and maintained two massive conveyor belts spanning the entire circumference of the square, powered by an array of shire horses and ingenuity. They'd also taken the city's one decaying crane, reinforced it so that it could bear ten times the previous maximum weight, and made it mobile.

Citizens watched, in awe at the efforts of the newcomers. Some whispered in hushed tones that they were doing the impossible and that they must be using some kind of magic. This caught the attention of a few. Most couldn't care less, not with the amazing results that were being achieved. Repairs that should have taken years, looked now like being only a few days away at most.

Throughout all this, the giant, warped body of the matt black dragon lay broken in one corner of the square, eagerly avoided by everyone. Its magnificent wings lay at an excruciating angle, delicate flimsy arms tucked under its bulging belly, all having taken on a shimmering purple hue, not that anyone had looked closely enough to notice.

As the days passed, the progress in repairing the devastation was phenomenal. The crane moved around the square lifting debris onto the conveyor belt. Usable material was taken off at different points of the conveyor, while anything with no value was left until the very end, and then taken off out of the city by horse and cart. It was a little chaotic, but it worked. Planners had drawn up a blueprint of where new buildings should go, agreed it with the mayor and had passed it on to the engineers. It worked like a well oiled machine.

Everyone with a minor injury had been discharged from the hospital. Broken bones, concussions, burns and shock had all been dealt with swiftly, much to everybody's relief. Seven seriously ill patients remained, all but given up on by the doctors and nurses. During triage, these seven had been deemed to have no chance and their blood soaked bodies had been moved to a mouldy, shadow-ridden corner of the building. Each of the seven now owed their existence to the dedication and perseverance of one individual... GEORGE! He'd found them lying there, waiting for death's embrace. The doctors and nurses thought him insane for wasting his time on what they knew to be a lost cause, but he didn't give up on them. It wasn't in his nature, something that should have been obvious from his duel with the dragon. Having found them waiting to die, he'd tended to them personally. Remarkably, and much to the medical staff's amazement, one by one their conditions stabilised. It was just another of the miracles that seemed to be coming thick and fast these days.

Having done all he could at the hospital, George tasked himself with overseeing the rebuilding work, conversing regularly with the planners, politicians and the idiosyncratic engineers. As he moved through the streets from one part of the city to another, people would approach him, men shaking his hand, women kissing him on the cheek, all offering thanks for the seemingly amazing feats he and his colleagues had achieved, much to his ever increasing embarrassment. Everybody in the city remarked what a true and inspiring leader of men he was. If only they knew the truth...

In the early hours of the morning on the seventh day after the battle with the dragon, in the shadows of a partly rebuilt house on the edge of the square, George and his companions found themselves shivering with cold. Teeth chattering ever so slightly, he managed to ask the question.

"How long until everything here is complete?"

"Two full days from now the whole thing will be finished; the city will be as good as new, if not better," explained Hannah, the chief politician.

"What about the chamber?" whispered George. "Will it

be ready on time?"

"As far as we know preparations are at an advanced stage, and it should be ready when we get there."

"Have we procured any transport for Troydenn?" George asked, directing the question towards the eclectic group of engineers sitting silently in one darkened corner. From out of the darkness behind them stepped a short, fat, balding man with a great big, thick, grey beard, as wide as it was long,. Although nothing special to look at, this man clearly commanded respect, as well he should, for he was renowned as one of the best engineers that had ever lived. His name was Axus.

Shoving his way through his fellow workers so that he could address George directly, he did his best to answer the question.

"We've asked the mayor if we can have two of the massive freight sleighs that they use in winter to transport goods up the main road and through the pass. I don't think there'll be a problem, given the time of year and with everything we've already done for them. We know how to convert the runners on the sleighs to work effectively on grass, mud and road. Our biggest issue is Troydenn's massive frame. Both sleighs will have to be attached so that they run side by side and must be reinforced dramatically. I don't have what I need here to even begin to solve that problem. I've sent word back with a view to them finding the mantras that we need. Hopefully they'll have a hunt around and come up with something useful. If need be they can always head on over to Gee Tee's Mantra Emporium and see if he has anything that fits the bill."

George let out a long, slow breath that he hadn't realised he'd been holding in. It immediately froze in front of him as the portly engineer continued.

"All seven miles of the route have been checked for any obstacles that may impede the sleighs, and the two miles inside the cave have been reinforced and lit up. Guards have been posted discreetly along the entire length of the journey."

Letting out a sigh of relief, George addressed everyone.

"You've all done an amazing job. You should be really proud of yourselves. Be under no illusion though, the toughest part is yet to come. Continue what you've started here, finish the city to the high and exacting standards that you're used to. Give the citizens something that will stand for centuries, and help negate some of the pain that they're feeling. Given what WE'VE put them through, they deserve nothing less. Don't forget: be constantly on the lookout for anything unusual, no matter how insignificant it may seem, because if they get him back, this will all have been for nothing, and the consequences will be felt across the planet."

What little light there was in the half constructed building showed a solemn looking group of individuals who fully understood the consequences that George had outlined.

"Let me know if there's anything else I can do," George stated.

Without a sound, the assembled group slinked off into the night, careful to stick to the shadows, all making their way back to the lodgings that had so kindly been provided for them.

Axus remained next to the dragon slayer until everyone else had disappeared.

"Is there any word on how or why he's changed colour?"

"Not so far," replied Axus. "The Council are working hard to try and find out though. They believe nothing like this has ever been documented, but are having libraries across the globe scoured for the tiniest of clues. That includes Rome, and the king's private library."

That caught George's attention. The monarch's own library. As far as he knew, that was off limits to everyone but the king himself. Things must be bad if they'd got that far. But it was time to go. They'd already been out here too long, and George was worried about pushing his luck too much. So with a friendly slap on Axus' shoulder, the two of them slid out into the darkness.

The following day work continued at a frantic pace, with most of the buildings being finished by early afternoon. Intricate pieces of the totally rebuilt fountain, the square's magnificent centrepiece, were crafted expertly together in the glare of the afternoon sun. Signing off on the engineers taking the two freight sleighs, the mayor then, much to everyone's delight, announced that a feast like no other was to be put on that night, in remembrance of all those who had lost their lives, and as a thank you to their guests for the outstanding work they'd done. A muted buzz of excitement zipped its way around the city as preparations got underway.

Not long before sunset, a visitor arrived on a horse, asking for Axus. Guided through the hectic groundwork of the feast, the visitor dismounted on seeing the rotund engineer and handed him three large cylindrical objects from his saddlebags. Moving in to surround their leader, the engineers gathered, keen to see what had arrived. Axus opened the first cylinder, pulling a large sheet of parchment from it and inspecting the mantra for any irregularities as he did so. Hushed whispers ran around the rest of the group. From this point on, the engineers looked more like a gaggle of naughty school girls than the brains of the outfit. They remained huddled together, whispering, sighing and even giggling uncontrollably at times. This continued for the rest of the afternoon and evening, only pausing momentarily when they went to obtain food and drink from the superbly catered feast.

The celebration itself was a great success. Given the tragic circumstances of a week past, the variety and quality of not only the food, but the drink as well, was staggering and a credit to all of the craftsmen and women of the city and its surroundings. As the singing and dancing began against the backdrop of crackling fires and the tantalising aroma of every different kind of roasted meat, bands from all around filled the warm spring night air with an array of diverse sounds. Flutes, lutes, violins, guitars and tambourines played with unheard of enthusiasm. It was magnificent, and a night that no one there would ever forget. Towards the end of the evening, almost midnight in fact, the mayor gave an emotionally charged speech, naming those who had lost their lives in the attack, praising George's courage in confronting the dragon (much to the crowd's delight) and thanking the new arrivals for their part in restoring the city to its former glory. Before finishing he announced to everyone that George's entourage would be taking the dragon corpse with them when they left the next day.

As the sun rose the next morning, the city seemed to be a hive of activity, with the smell of freshly baked bread wafted down the streets and alleys as people cleaned up from the night before, some looking more the worse for wear than others. Stalls, marquees, and the bandstand in the centre of the square were all being dismantled. Some picked up litter, others were washing shop fronts, or the very streets themselves. It was good to see people take pride in the city that they lived in. George, a little fuzzy headed from too many glasses of beer, weaved his way through the streets, eager to see how much progress the engineers had made. Arriving in the main square he was confronted by a group beaming with pride, but looking very much under the weather after the previous night's merrymaking. Axus appeared off to one side of the group.

"Blimey, that wine was potent last night. My mouth feels like a badger's bottom."

Some of the newer additions to the group of engineers wondered briefly how he knew what a badger's bottom felt like.

Bedraggled, and with chunks of meat and bread littering his unkempt beard, he continued.

"Still, could have been worse I suppose. Poor old

Hopkins spent most of last night whispering sweet nothings to the two sacks of flour over there, even coming over at one point to tell us that he thought one of them might even be marriage material. Haaaa haaaa! I don't think he's going to live that down for quite some time."

Hopkins, having already thrown up at least half a dozen times this morning, skulked even further back into the shadows than he already was.

"Anyhow," continued Axus, throwing a small chunk of cooked meat from his beard into the air, before gobbling it down like a well trained sea lion at a zoo, "onto more important matters. It's done! One of the mantras sent out did the trick nicely. Both sleighs are as one, and look as though they've always been that way. We've been up all night testing them to make sure they're okay. Only a matter of getting him on there now."

A tiny flicker of movement from across the square caught George's eye as he listened intently to what Axus was saying. From between two shops on the far side of the square, a small boy appeared and started skulking towards the lonely dragon corpse. George stood riveted to the spot, having forgotten all about what his friend was saying. None of the city folk would go anywhere near the beast's carcass; most refused to even look at it.

As the boy got closer, he started to pull something from his belt. That was George's cue. As fast as was humanly possible (and maybe even a little faster) George moved to put himself between the boy and the dragon.

"Can I help you?" he asked curiously.

Looking more than a little sheepish, suddenly realising that not only had he attracted the attention of George, but everyone else in the square as well, the boy did his best to answer.

"Well... um, I, er... my name is Sam, Sam Smithers. My dad is Elron Smithers, the city's best known butcher. I um... thought it would be a waste, you know, what with some of the not so well off people in the city not having enough food and all. I thought it would save you the trouble of having to take it away as well."

"Let me get this straight," exclaimed George dubiously, "you were going to skin it!"

"To make sausages," added Sam.

The group of engineers, who had moved closer to back up George if needed, burst into laughter as one. Everyone else looked on in astonishment as Sam's face turned a deep shade of scarlet. George urged the crowd to quieten down.

"Sam, my young friend, you seem full of noble sentiment, which I admire greatly. But unfortunately there is a much bigger picture, which because of your age, you fail to grasp. Perhaps you'd like to take your knife and try and skin the dragon for me? If you succeed you can keep all the meat you like."

With the eyes of the entire crowd on him, Sam pulled a bright, shiny knife with a dull leather handle out from his belt and stepped determinedly towards the dragon. With the knife in his right hand, the muscles in both arms bulging and his left hand braced against the dragon's right thigh for purchase, he drew back his arm and, with all his might, thrust the knife towards the dragon's flesh.

At the first point of contact the knife buckled in on itself, the shock from the impact forcing Sam to drop the crumpled blade onto the cobbles. The clang echoed across the square as the onlookers and Sam all gasped in amazement at what had happened.

George put a comforting arm around Sam's burly shoulders.

"Sorry Sam, that was a bit mean of me, but I thought a demonstration would be more effective than anything I could say. One of the reasons we need to take the carcass away, is that it requires special measures to dispose of a dead dragon."

Sam gawped, open mouthed.

"I... I... I understand," he stuttered.

George smiled at the boy, pushing the lie he'd just told

far to the back of his mind.

"But since you seem to have ruined your best knife, you can have mine as a token of how sorry I am that your very worthy idea hasn't come off," said George, slipping a gleaming dagger made from white gold, tiny jewels embedded into the hilt, into the youngster's outstretched, quivering hands.

Managing to squeak a "Thank you," Sam rapidly slipped back through the crowd in the direction of his father's shop.

With the excitement over, everybody went back to their work with a quiet dignity, knowing they had all contributed to a job well done.

By early afternoon the building work was complete and the city's giant crane perched precariously over the body of the outstretched dragon, like a huge heron waiting to rip into the water to nab an unsuspecting fish. Leather harnesses crisscrossed the dragon's body, meeting in the centre above it to form a gigantic net. Horses that many of George's companions had arrived on had been tethered together and attached to the front of the double freight sleighs that stood off to one side of the square. Axus was busy co-ordinating the efforts of all of the engineers. Time ticked by slowly as the crane took up the slack in the gigantic net. Creaking and groaning timbers whipped in the wind across the city as the dragon corpse was raised a foot into the air. Collectively, everyone held their breath as they watched from the city's walls, hanging out of windows, perched on balconies, or caught up in the six deep crowds that lined the square. Much like the feast from the previous night, it was something they would never forget. With the dragon suspended in mid-air, the sleighs were guided very slowly into position underneath. Gently, the monstrous beast was lowered onto the makeshift transport, to a resounding round of applause.

Checking the sleighs to make sure they were secure before lining up behind them, the engineers, politicians and planners created two lines in front, to form a convoy facing the south eastern exit of the city. George shook hands with the mayor and took his place at the head of the procession, leading them towards the exit to a fanfare of trumpeters, high up on the city's walls.

A small familiar figure broke ranks from the six deep crowd lining the route and sprinted towards George. Those surrounding him stood ready to act, but it wasn't necessary.

"Sam, my young friend, whatever are you doing?" enquired George as the city watched.

Slipping off a heavy backpack almost as big as he was, Sam offered it out to the gallant knight.

"For the journey," panted the youngster, having run all the way from his father's shop.

George looked at the young man quizzically.

"My dad's best sausages. You'll need something good to eat."

The dragon slayer's smile nearly outshone the sun as he accepted the backpack, passing it back over his shoulder to one of the planners, before ruffling Sam's hair playfully and then offering his thanks. For his part, Sam sprinted back to the edge of the crowd where his father duly waited. Excitement over, the journey continued.

It took an agonisingly long time to reach the gate, but when George finally crossed beneath it, he reflected on all that had happened in such a short space of time. The good folks of the city waved him off believing he'd conjured up some sort of miracle to defeat the murderous dragon. It had been a one-sided fight, that was for sure, but not quite as one-sided as the citizens believed. Truth was far stranger than fiction, and not really ready to be disclosed to the humans that he'd spent so much time with recently. Briefly, he wondered if it would ever be revealed... you see he and his fellow travellers were dragons as well, only they were currently in their *mutatio* form.

Being a dragon in human form *(mutatio)* gave George

enormous advantages over normal humans. Superior strength, incredible stamina, off the scale intelligence, amazing agility and cat-like reflexes were just some of the many benefits. Those, along with his enhanced metabolism and a much higher tolerance for pain, made him tougher than old boots, very difficult to wound, and almost impossible to kill. That's not to say the battle of over a week ago was a fair fight. It clearly wasn't. A dragon in its natural *solitus* form is virtually impossible to kill. A normal human being would have no chance of killing a dragon in its natural state as there is only one spot on its entire body where it is vulnerable, and it would take a perfect strike to actually slay it. Even a blow to injure it would be remote, as generally the area of vulnerability is very small.

During the battle, George was able to discern exactly where Troydenn's susceptibility was because no matter what form they're in, dragons can always see another dragon's weak spot, as it's known. George very deliberately thrust his sword into that self same weak spot at an angle, knowing that a killing blow would have been avoided, but at the same time inflicting massive amounts of pain, and incapacitating his enemy for some time to come.

As he pondered all of this, the troop and the giant sleighs ferrying the matt black dragon passed out of the city and into the countryside.

For the next five hours they travelled, before finding a suitable place to stop for the night, just before sunset. Having not journeyed quickly enough to reach the spot they'd hoped to, they had to make do with a clearing near a small brook, off the main route, if you could call it that. As the horses were loosed from the burden of the sleighs and led to the brook to drink their fill, George told everyone what they needed to do.

"We need torches and lots of them. Plant them in the ground to form concentric circles all the way to the edge of the road with Troydenn at the centre. I don't want anyone sneaking up on us. If they're going to come for him, I want to see what we're facing. We will fight them here, and we WILL win. It's too important not to. Get used to this, because at our current speed, we're going to have at least two more nights in the countryside before we reach the cave's entrance."

It didn't take long for George's orders to be carried out. With guards posted all around the clearing, the horses fed and watered and a small fire set up in the middle of the ramshackle camp for cooking, some of the contingent settled down for rest, others to eat, while one or two sat together shooting the breeze. It was eerily quiet with everyone being so on edge.

As George sat off to one side, chomping on the best cooked sausage he'd ever tasted, Axus trudged past the fire to sit down beside him, sausage and bread in one hand, mug of water in the other.

"No bloody wine again," he moaned. "I know, I know. Need to be sharp and on the lookout. What's an old man supposed to do?"

George grinned at those words. He knew more than most just how ridiculous it was for the engineer to refer to himself as an old man. On two occasions he'd had the pleasure of meeting Axus in his natural form, and he was as colossal a dragon as he was an engineer. Just the thought of him being old and toothless made no sense whatsoever.

As they sat eating, Axus gave a nod towards the dragon at the centre of the camp.

"Slightly ironic that you were sent to bring him back I suppose, what with the two of you growing up in the same nursery ring and then being in the King's Guard together."

A very awkward silence fell over the two human shaped dragons against the reassuring sound of the fire crackling, roasted meat sizzling and the odd whispered conversation. Not normally one to worry about holding back for fear of offending someone, Axus started to have serious misgivings about the situation because of the silence that had now stretched into minutes. For his part, George just sat there with a faraway look on his face. After only a few more moments, the city's hero let out a deep breath, the look on his face having turned to relief.

"It was no coincidence that I was sent to confront him and bring him back. The Council knew after what happened in Panama that it had to be me. Not only that, but apparently there are prophecy mantras that predicted that all of this would one day happen, depending on who you believe."

Axus, visibly stunned, sat on the ground shaking his head as George continued.

"What I don't understand Axus, is how anyone is capable of what he's done. As you said, we practically grew up together. I've fought alongside him for decades on the battlefield, letting him watch my back, while I covered his. I would have laid down my life for him in the blink of an eye. Not anymore. Believing he was capable of that level of deception and those atrocities was never really an option for me, until I witnessed firsthand what happened at Panama. It had to be me that confronted him and returned him to the others. I never really believed it before, but I know it now."

The noise in the camp had died down, with only the sound of the surrounding torches and the dying embers from the fire for company. After finishing their meagre meal quietly, George piped up with a question, moving all thoughts of the past, very much onto the future.

"Can I ask about the area in Antarctica?"

Axus, clearly happier talking about something engineering related replied,

"What would you like to know?"

"I know it's a containment area only to be used as a last resort, but that's all I really do know. If there's a chance we might have to go down that road, I'd really like to learn all about it."

Axus stroked his dishevelled beard as he composed his

response.

"About fifty years ago, some of our top geologists were in southern Chile, scouting out new laminium deposits. They were looking at two volcanoes in particular, Monte Burney and the more southerly Fueguino. Although successful in finding the new deposits they were looking for, the state of the art equipment that they carried with them kept on giving off very strange readings. Instead of putting it down as a fault with the instruments as most would have done, the expedition decided to investigate and made a startling discovery. Running from southern Chile out towards the Falkland Islands, was a large underground channel. About half a mile wide, running approximately two miles under the ocean's surface, just before it reached the Falkland Islands, the channel divided, with one branch leading to a secluded surface entrance on the Islands themselves, while the other twisted sharply heading directly towards Antarctica. Staggered at the sheer size of the thing, the geologists had never seen anything remotely like it. Most bewildering of all to these highly skilled individuals was the fact that they couldn't tell whether or not the phenomenon was naturally occurring. Intrigued, the group followed the channel south and eventually came up against a problem they were not equipped, or prepared, to deal with."

"Of course," said George quick-wittedly, "the temperature."

Axus grinned wildly.

"That's right. And with low temperatures having such a detrimental effect on us dragons, sapping our strength, energy and stamina, as well as clouding our judgement and minds, wisely the group stopped before the temperature plummeted too low. At that point, they decided to set up camp, while two of them returned to collect specialist protective mantras. After discussions with all the leading experts (and more than one visit to Gee Tee's Mantra Emporium) appropriate mantras were found and were deemed most effective in human *(mutatio)* form. Once everything they needed was procured and the Council informed, the geologists set off into the channel in the direction of Antarctica, continuing for many days and nights, only able to survive because they were in human form, protected from the cold that would almost certainly have cost their lives, solely by the magical aura of the specialist mantras they had returned to get.

As the collective trudged on, temperatures plummeted even further and the channel became more precarious. Two of the team succumbed to frostbite in their feet and had to turn back, escorted by one of their healthy colleagues to make sure they returned safely. By now, things were looking really bleak, but their curiosity pushed them ever forward, determined to find out as much as they could about the phenomenon. Sitting around a makeshift fire, wolfing down the last of their provisions, they concluded that they could only travel for another day or so before having to turn back. Setting off early in what their body clocks told them was morning, quite quickly, the floor of the channel started to descend steeply into the darkness. Weaving their way around giant stalagmites growing up out of the floor and ducking down at times to avoid even bigger stalactites hanging from the ceiling, to the few remaining dragons left the entire route looked like gigantic jaws about to swallow them whole. At the point of no return, with defeat looming over them, the path ahead opened out into a vast cavern, like nothing any of them had ever seen before. This was as far as they got on that first expedition."

George let out a long breath that crystallised in what had become very chilly air, as he contemplated everything Axus had said.

"Any tales that have something to do with cold always send shivers down my tail, no matter what form I'm in."

"Aye," chuckled Axus, "but that's not the end of it. After that startling discovery, more expeditions, better equipped, were sent to explore and document the place. Six missions over a fifteen year period finally revealed all. The cavern that the original geologists came to the entrance of below Antarctica is believed to be the biggest of its kind on the planet. In excess of five hundred square miles, it has a depth in places of over two miles. Unusually it has half a dozen underground fresh water streams running through it, the source of which has yet to be determined. Another odd fact is that there is no geothermal activity whatsoever, with not a single trace of any known mineral deposit anywhere in or around the entire cavern system. Ideal for the purpose the Council has in mind, the channel appears to be the only entrance and the temperature never gets above -10°C."

Running his chapped hands through his long, matted, dark hair, George considered everything his friend had told him.

"It just feels so permanent, Axus. I understand the need to punish Troydenn and his followers for what they've done. I do. I really do. But I also hope it doesn't come to that and that the Council can find a more..." (he nearly said humane... that would have been ironic) "...suitable solution."

"Aye, I know what you mean son, but these are undoubtedly the darkest times we've ever faced as a race. Even all that trouble that went on in South America, pre Balfor, pales in comparison. None of this sits very comfortably with me George, but I trust in the wisdom of the Council, and so should you. Once they've made their decision, whatever that may be, we can be confident that the hard work of so many has left us well prepared. Should it be needed, the cavern is stocked with everything required to survive well into the future. It won't be easy, but it will be achievable. Starting at the exit of the cavern, going ten miles back into the channel at quarter mile intervals, the individual shaped charges have been laid and have been carefully tested so that they only bring the roof of the channel down and do not disturb the ocean above. If it's decided that Troydenn and his followers should be incarcerated then they will be, well and truly, in that cavern."

"I appreciate you filling me in on some of the details," George whispered to Axus. "Let's trust in the Council's judgement and wait to see what they decide."

With that the two parted company, George slipping off to guard duty, while his engineering friend headed for some well needed sleep.

As the bright morning sun cut through the early morning mist of the camp, those sleeping were woken, bread and cheese passed out, horses watered and fed, ready for the next stage of their unusual journey.

The next two days proved uneventful. Many people were passed as they made their way along the prescribed route, all shocked to come across the corpse of the massive ferocious dragon being dragged along by the giant sleighs. On occasion, sly hand signals or the briefest of telepathic touches were exchanged with passersby, those who were more than they seemed, anyway. All the cloak and dagger business showed that the way ahead was clear, something of a relief to those in the convoy.

In the middle of the afternoon on the third day, the convoy left the poor excuse for a muddy main road at the point where a purple trident had been inconspicuously painted onto a large boulder, and headed across an open field in the exact direction in which the trident pointed. Once through the field, they came to a coppice and noted the same trident carved into a tree, and adjusted their heading accordingly. This continued for four more hours, until they came over a rise and into a beautiful meadow full of tall green swaying grass, punctuated with gorgeous wild flowers. A large rocky outcrop could just be seen in the distance.

As the troop entered the meadow, hundreds of warriors and archers silently appeared from atop the outcrop and within the surrounding grass. Bows and swords appeared from nowhere in the hands of George's companions as they formed a defensive perimeter around the captured dragon. Those without weapons readied their magic. A tense silence enveloped the entire meadow; the only movement was that of the long grass rippling in the wind. George stood up from his kneeling position in front of Troydenn and sheathed his trusty sword. As he did so, a loud horn echoed across the surrounding countryside. One of the foremost warriors stepped forward from the long grass, stowed his sword and clasped George's proffered hand. Greetings were exchanged, magic dispelled and weapons lowered. Warriors in front of the convoy parted swiftly, forming a huge path straight to the rocky outcrop. At a snail's pace, the convoy crawled along the corridor that had been laid out for them, the soldiers in the meadow closing in behind them, forming a giant impenetrable ring.

As everyone gathered at the cave's entrance, the exhausted horses were untethered and led off into the meadow to graze. Meanwhile ropes appeared from the well-illuminated cave entrance and were threaded through a series of pulleys on either side of the sleighs.

After Axus was satisfied, the warriors in the meadow picked up the slack on the ropes in two lines as a large horn echoed deep within the cave. Slowly the rope in and around the pulleys began to go taut, pulling the sleighs and their giant burden forward through the cave's entrance and into the massive interior. All this happened at a funereal pace, with the daylight from outside gradually fading, being replaced by dull yellow lights from stony protrusions both on the cave's floor and in the surrounding walls that carried on down the winding slope, as far as the eye could see. Occasionally a hairpin bend would have to be negotiated, which meant that distance became measured more in inches, rather than miles per hour.

After what seemed like an eternity, but was actually just

over eighteen hours, the weary travellers reached their destination. Opening out into a colossal grotto, filled with dragons in both their natural and human forms, the same light producing protrusions lined the walls and the floor, fading up above, the ceiling some way off in the distance, shrouded in darkness. Far from being damp and cold, the chamber was filled with toasty warm air that tickled and prodded, washed and wavered, all the time carried on a subtle breeze. Brilliant red lava oozed down mineral laden walls sporadically throughout, in complete contrast to the countryside through which the convoy had travelled.

Shuffling feet could be heard in the dimly lit arena as the beings let the sleighs through. Those who had accompanied the sleighs drifted off to join the already gathered crowd, with the exception of George who stayed where he was. Little shapes scurried out of the shadows, surrounding and inspecting the sleighs purposefully.

After much whispering, George was asked to step back, which he duly did, while others surrounded the prehistoric arrival, chanting in hushed tones. Starting low, it didn't take long to reach a crescendo of raised voices, all in unison. Abruptly there was an almighty BANG, startling all of those not paying attention.

In the subsequent near silence, it would appear that instead of a scene of utter devastation and carnage which they nearly all expected, all that had happened was that the double sleigh on which Troydenn had been resting completely disappeared, leaving him lying on the cold stone floor.

Unexpectedly, huge stone doors swung in on themselves right in front of George and the captured dragon. Through them walked a tall, lean man leading twenty four other men. I say "men"... they were of course dragons in their human guises. As one, the crowd started to kneel and bow their heads, realising it was the king and his councillors.

In his *mutatio* form, the king looked nothing short of

magnificent. Standing seven feet tall with long golden hair flowing down past his shoulders, rippling muscles threatening to burst through his clothing, which was all white with a bright purple trident running across the tunic. Most stunning of all though was the real trident the king carried by his side. It was as tall as he was and appeared to be made of a bright purple metal that seemed to be constantly moving within the form of the trident. An eye-catching ring that seemed to be visible one moment and then gone the next, constantly phasing in and out of existence, decorated the king's left hand.

Abruptly the monarch thumped the trident's base onto the stone floor, the resulting sound hurting everyone's ears.

"Be upstanding," he declared. "You should know why we are all here. Let the proceedings begin."

One of the councillors strode over to Troydenn, pulled some parchment from beneath his robes, and began reciting the words from it. The purple glow on the dragon's body receded. Finishing the mantra and slipping the parchment back in his robes, the councillor addressed Troydenn for everyone to hear.

"Will you voluntarily turn back into human form for this trial?"

Gradually the dragon's mighty skull moved slightly from side to side, dragging its massive chin along the cold stone floor, while dribbles of flame squirted contemptibly from each nostril.

"I'll take that as a 'no' shall I?" fumed the councillor, stepping aside to let the king through. On noticing the king, a little quiver of fear ran through the defiant dragon.

Face contorted with rage, the king addressed the rogue dragon.

"Since you won't change of your own free will, I will force the change upon you, which unfortunately for you will be most unpleasant... something I'd hoped to avoid."

Shimmering beams of brilliant blue energy lanced out

from the tip of the trident as the king levelled it at Troydenn. Just as the first beam connected, the helpless dragon let out a YELP, much like a frightened dog. Onlookers in the shadows could barely watch something that hadn't happened in over three hundred years. History was quite literally unfolding before their very eyes. As the separate beams hit Troydenn's body, they formed straight lines all along it from head to toe, encircling the circumference of his belly. All the while he remained motionless, determined, resolute, apart from his eyes which flickered from side to side, betraying the fear coursing through him.

By now the lines of energy had started to crisscross each other, giving the impression of an all encompassing giant net. Without warning, Troydenn panicked and, mustering all his remaining strength, tried desperately to get to his feet, clearly sensing what was to come. Crackling ferociously, the shimmering net of blue energy surrounding him began to shrink, causing the captive dragon to let out a blood-curdling wail.

As the contracting lines of energy sparked, crackled and smoked, and Troydenn's pain echoed around the underground space, it became much harder to determine what was happening inside the energy net. Certainly a change of some sort was occurring because the area the net covered had diminished to about a third of its original size, and the howling and screaming coming from within now sounded much less like an animal, and much more like a human.

After a few more seconds, the transformation was complete. Lying slumped on the chilly stone floor, gasping for breath, a stocky, bald-headed man with a brown goatee beard and strange black tattoos on his cheeks and neck looked up menacingly at the audience before him.

A low murmur of disbelief rippled through the crowd. Unsteadily, the fully naked man before them got to his feet, taking in his surroundings as though he'd been asleep for many years. Gazing over the king's left shoulder, his eyes locked onto a pale blue pair he knew very well. George!

"Traitor!" he screamed, lunging towards his former brother-in-arms with a crazed look on his face, only to be stopped inches away by hulking great guards who had appeared as if from nowhere. Troydenn spat in George's face, all the time wriggling and kicking in an attempt to break free from the guard's vice-like grip.

Wiping his face with the back of his hand, George desperately tried to maintain an illusion of calm and serenity, even though every muscle in his body screamed at him to fight. With Troydenn's feet dragging along the ground, the guards hauled him back to the spot in front of the king that he had previously occupied. This time a red beam of energy shot out of the trident at the king's command, hitting the imprisoned dragon in the right foot before curling upwards and around his entire body, finally stopping at the top of his head, forcing him to stand bolt upright.

"ENOUGH!" roared the king. "You will stand and listen to the charges brought against you and your supporters."

From the darkness above the stone doors a balcony suddenly appeared, illuminated by an eerie green light. Dressed in scarlet robes, lined with purple piping and a matching hood over her head, the magistrate slinked into view, gavel in hand. Smacking it onto the stone balustrade in front of her, causing a distinctive THUD to resound around the cavern, she commanded everyone's attention.

"Troydenn, formerly of the High Council's Royal Guard, you are hereby charged with one of our race's gravest crimes. Your followers have already admitted that they murdered, maimed, kidnapped, stole, threatened and embezzled, all on your orders, all in your name. The one thing that is sacred to us as dragons, taught to us throughout our formative years in the nursery rings, is that we as a society are here to protect and guide the human race at all times because of their potential, and because of THAT prophecy. Throughout dragonkind's history, nearly all dragons have strived to obey this underlying principle laid down in our law.

I declare that you, Troydenn, are not only guilty of the crimes previously mentioned, but of the most heinous crime our civilisation recognises... manipulation of the human race for your own selfish purposes. Since nothing on this scale has happened in over fifteen hundred years, the punishment will be decided by the king and his Council," she announced, clutching her gavel tightly.

As the magistrate stood up, the eerie green light illuminating her faded away, making her indistinguishable from the stone walls behind. Simultaneously, the same green light appeared around the king and Troydenn.

With his long golden locks, backlit by the light, the noble features of the king's face turned from quiet contemplation to steely determination as he prepared to speak.

"Over the last two days the Council and I have discussed the sentence that should be imposed on you, Troydenn. I can honestly say that this has been the hardest thing I've had to do throughout my entire reign. I believe the outcome was reached in a fair and unbiased manner, considering all the relevant options and circumstances along the way, although it should be noted that the decision was not unanimous, but reached by a majority of twenty four to one. The Council hereby decrees that, YOU, Troydenn, and all of your conspirators currently in custody, will be transferred forthwith to our secure, remote detention facility, where you will remain for the rest of your natural lives."

A combined GASP from those looking on echoed around the chamber. A few feet behind the king, George stood rooted to the spot, absolutely shell-shocked. Not for a moment had he believed the sentence would be so harsh, despite his earlier conversation with Axus.

Throughout the proceedings Troydenn remained totally impassive with his jaw jutting out, his piercing eyes not moving from the king.

"Because of the natural constrictions of the detainment facility, you will all be extremely limited in using your magical powers. Provisions and equipment will be on hand to prevent any unwanted fatalities; however you will have to work hard and constantly manage the limited resources available to you, to ensure your continued existence. Life will be very difficult for all of you. If you have anything meaningful to say Troydenn, any words of regret or apologies you'd like to offer up, now is your chance to do so."

Instantaneously the red coil of energy holding the guilty dragon in place faded to nothing. Troydenn held his finely honed arms high above his head and turned three hundred and sixty degrees, addressing everyone in the cavern as the green light cast an ominous shadow over his malevolent face. Snarling like a rabid dog, he spat,

"We will break free from whatever prison you confine us in, and when we do, we will destroy your precious dragon domain and visit a terror like none other on all your little human pets. Whether it takes ten years or five hundred, we WILL find a way."

Having heard enough, the king, in one lightning fast swipe, knocked the over-confident dragon firmly to the ground with the end of his trident. Blood poured from his mouth and nose as the urge to get up and strike back overwhelmed the dark dragon. But it was too late. Six guards appeared out of the shadows, completely surrounding him. It was then that he knew any chance he might have had was long since gone.

"Sentence has been passed," announced the king. "Secure him for his flight with the rest of them."

The guards duly hauled Troydenn off into the darkness by his arms, the sound of his bare feet dragging along the ground gradually fading into nothingness.

A booming THUD reverberated around the chamber as the magistrate smashed her gavel once more against the stone balustrade in the darkness, high above them all, and declared,

"This tribunal has ended."

Dragons in various guises shuffled out via several concealed exits. George remained with a heavy heart, on his own in the darkness, tears streaming down his face. He struggled to understand why. Of course he understood that the crimes committed by his former comrade in arms and friend were amongst the most serious his kind had ever seen, and on a purely intellectual level he understood that the punishment was probably the best thing for dragons, humans and the whole planet in general. But somehow he couldn't help thinking that this was a sad day in dragon history, and something that could possibly have been avoided if he and others had acted sooner, to stop Troydenn's actions before they'd got so far out of hand. As he wiped away a few of the tears with the edge of his shirt sleeve, he couldn't help think that today's events might have repercussions well into the future.

Suddenly a well muscled arm appeared around George's shoulder. Instinct and training taking over, he became immediately alert and ready to fight. Dropping, he pulled away, turned and squared up to... the king.

"I'm, I'm, I'm sorry Your Majesty," he stuttered, caught entirely by surprise.

"George, less of the 'Majesty' please."

"Sorry," replied the forlorn knight, wiping his tear stained face on his sweat covered tunic.

"Listen, son, I know you have reservations about what's happened here, and you wouldn't be half the dragon I know you to be if you didn't. It's understandable, it really is. I also know what a wonderful job you did in bringing him in, keeping the carnage and loss of life to a minimum, and in repairing that wonderful old city. You are a credit not only to that uniform, but to the entire dragon race. It's no surprise that what's happened is affecting you so badly. It's nothing to be ashamed of. But try and think about the bigger picture. The pain will ease over time, and gradually fade altogether, but it might take a while.

You're a good dragon George, one of the best in fact. One day you will make it onto the Council and I think you'll go on to make a great king, mark my words. But tell anyone I said that and I'll have to have your tongue cut out, as I'm supposed to be entirely neutral in these matters," said the king, winking and smirking at the same time.

Finally breaking into a smile for the first time in days, George replied,

"Thank you Majesty," with the emphasis very much on the 'Majesty'.

Smiling back, the king said,

"That's more like it," before breaking into a great big belly laugh.

Over as quickly as it had begun, the light-hearted moment and the bond of friendship between the two immediately became concealed as one of the councillors approached.

"The flight has gathered with all the prisoners, Majesty, and is ready to take off on your command. A tracking station has been set up in the magistrate's main office so that we can all monitor their progress."

"Thank you for letting us know, Osvaldo. Give the order. George and I will be there shortly," replied the king.

The councillor nodded and disappeared back into the shadows, but not before giving George a disapproving look.

"Hmmm..." whispered the king. "There's something about that dragon that's always bothered me, but I just can't seem to put my finger on what it is. He's always worked tirelessly for those he's responsible for, helped others, been a model councillor in fact. But just recently, the way he's acted and some of the things he's said have been really out of character. You're not to mention this to anyone else, but Osvaldo Rosebloom was the one councillor that opposed Troydenn's sentence."

George tried to take in the importance of what the king had just told him, but there was no time.

"We'd better get moving youngster," whispered the king.

Fleet of foot, the two of them headed off in the same direction as Osvaldo, the king leading, in near total darkness, through a maze of narrow corridors. After a minute or so, the monarch stopped abruptly. Running his hands along one wall, high above his head, George could just make out the tiniest of 'clicks', before the wall parted in front of them to reveal a bustling, brightly lit control room. As they stepped forward, the young knight told himself that he had to get a secret entrance like that of his own.

At least the size of two tennis courts put side by side, the square office was gigantic. Huge long counters that acted as desks for the dragons in their human form ran the entire length of every wall. Taut, white, stretched canvases covered every inch of the walls above the desks. Dozens of dragons darted about, most either holding clip boards, strangely shaped tools, bunches of different coloured wiring, or an array of different dragon snacks. In the middle of them all, Axus stalked about, adjusting, double checking, and generally moving things along, his muted, gruff tones gave some idea of the stress he was under. Many dragons sat at the lengthy desks along each wall, only one per wall though, wore a shiny, copper coloured helmet with a dizzying array of multicoloured wires coming out of it. Wires ran in a big bunch, down the back of the chairs, along the floor and then up to an odd looking machine in the centre of each desk, lights flashed, parts whirred, while all the time a faint tap-tapping could be heard. It was unlike anything George had ever seen. All connected together by an even bigger bunch of wires thicker than a weightlifter's arm, 'advanced' didn't begin to cover the machines. George wondered if he was getting a small glimpse into the future. If only he knew.

In the centre of the room, two dozen leather clad stools had been scattered about for the councillors to sit on. Most chose to stand.

Axus, shaking his head and tutting, made his way across the room to the gathered councillors and the king. George listened off to one side.

"We have four dragons flying separately from the rest of the convoy, Majesty. They will transmit the images they are seeing directly to their opposite number in this room. Those telepathic images will be passed through the wires in the receiver's helmet, and then projected onto the canvas on the walls. We should have nearly real-time images from four different viewpoints, one on each wall."

Glancing around the room, George tried to get his head around what Axus had just said. The flying dragons would travel with the guards carrying the prisoners to the detention facility, but their job would be to transmit telepathically the images that they were seeing so that everyone here could make sure the rogue dragons were successfully incarcerated. Every dragon had telepathic abilities, but George figured these four were probably handpicked for the job given the importance of this mission, maybe from the pool of dragons that worked for the Daily Telepath itself.

The Daily Telepath was known to every dragon outside the nursery rings (because those still studying there were deemed too immature to receive it) as a daily news bulletin transmitted telepathically throughout the world. Remote or cold places might be the only exceptions. Reporters collated the news before it was then edited into a telepathic version of a broadsheet. Those that worked at the Daily Telepath were generally accepted as being exceptional in their chosen field of study, particularly if the field was telepathy. The Daily Telepath's offices were situated in the dragon domain, ironically directly beneath the Daily Telegraph's offices in Fleet Street, London. Dragons in their human guises worked for both, making sure news items from the dragon and human world were available to the editor of the telepathic news bulletin.

Once edited, the bulletin was broadcast at precisely five fifty eight am GMT daily, via humongous thought-amplifying transmitters located in the basement of the offices. On leaving Fleet Street, the information would flow freely throughout the underground world of the dragons, using massive crystal boosters on a local level, each individual one powered by geothermal energy. After it had been made available on that day, it was then stored in much smaller crystals throughout the land, so that those who had missed the original transmission through either sleep or work, could catch up. A typical Daily Telepath bulletin consisted of the main news story (either dragon or human, occasionally the same story but from the two different points of view) usually with a bold headline. Global weather warnings played a part... typhoons, blizzards, tidal waves, that kind of thing. Sport was also on the agenda. Not human sport of course... what dragon on the planet would want to know about that? None of course. No, we're talking about dragon sport, and in particular... LAMINIUM BALL! There also featured a letters section where dragons could air their feelings, as well as an obituary column where dragon death notices were placed. This was one of the most important functions of the bulletin as dragons rarely die, but when they do their kin, and of course their friends and colleagues, travel far and wide for the normally extravagant funeral proceedings. Coverage of the Council's activity normally featured high on the list of what the dragon in the street wanted to know, while the king himself normally took something of a back seat unless there was a special occasion of some sort.

It seemed to work quite well for the most part, with

dragons often being overheard in both their human and natural form discussing the day's events from the bulletin. Recently the Telepath had been experimenting with images and had tried incorporating them, with varying degrees of success. These experiments had taken the form of black and white pictures, but by the time the bulletin had reached the readers, information drop out had caused the pictures to become blurred and unrecognisable. They hadn't given up though, with dragons right at this very moment working on how best to incorporate pictures so that regular readers could get a glimpse of their favourite laminium ball players scoring, winning that vital point. The future was not that far off.

George's mind, having wandered off, was brought back to the room by hearing Axus finish off telling the king about the projection system.

"So you see Majesty, this was the only way to use the boosters in that area and keep the transmission secure. We certainly don't want every dragon in the world viewing the captives on their way to Antarctica, do we?"

"Not with some of Troydenn's followers still unaccounted for, no we don't," replied the king gravely.

Axus clapped his hands to get everyone's attention.

"Could you all move to the centre of the room please, as that's where you'll get the best view of all four projections."

Turning to one of his subordinates, Axus ordered,

"Dim the lights and start the projectors please."

Everyone gathered in the centre, most still choosing to stand. Osvaldo, though, was conspicuous by his absence. Abruptly the room plunged into darkness, before the walls came alive with moving images that took George a little while to process.

On the main wall, the one he thought of as 'in front', was an image from the middle of the pack, showing dragons left, right, above and below, all flapping their gigantic wings, propelling themselves along. It was just possible to make out the tightly fitting harnesses they all had strapped on, each able to transport one, two or three sedated dragons in human guise. Nearly all of the visible prehistoric beasts carried three unwilling prisoners.

On the left wall the view was clearly from a dragon flying at the back of the pack, high up on the right hand side. It showed all of the dragons and their cargo from above, moving at break-neck speeds through a large open cavern.

On the right wall the view was from a dragon skimming along the surface, underneath the left side of the flight. As this particular winged behemoth looked up, he could see giant underbellies with prisoners strapped to them, bones and muscles in the dragons' wings working furiously to keep them aloft, speeding them along at nearly five hundred miles an hour.

Behind, the scene showed the convoy from quite some distance back. The dragon projecting this image must have been trailing the group by about a mile and a half, with the group only really showing up as small dots, ones which appeared in corresponding shades and positions to those in the convoy. The carried captives weren't visible at this range.

Those gathered in the control room all seemed to have a different idea about which was the best projection to view the proceedings from, the majority watched the main wall, with a few looking at the side views, while even fewer flicked between the different images, just like George. Currently the limited light in the cavern made the convoy look like stars in a dusky night sky.

Progress was slow, but dragons were renowned for their patience and understanding. Even so, the events unfolding today were testing this, almost to breaking point. Everyone watching knew that this was only the start of the epic journey. The convoy's underground route involved flying south west from Europe, towards Africa's eastern coast. Once there, the dragons would head south under the coast until they reached the capital of Sierra Leone, Freetown. Turning south west again, they would then fly beneath the south Atlantic for about three thousand miles, before arriving under the outskirts of Rio de Janeiro. Following the coast of Uruguay, they would head towards Buenos Aires in Argentina, then turn directly south towards the Falkland Islands before joining the huge trench there, following it all the way to the containment facility. In all the entire journey was over eleven thousand miles and would take about twenty two hours in total.

"So far the convoy has flown under the Mediterranean and along the coast of Morocco," piped up Axus, tearing away the silence of the last few minutes. "They have just passed beneath Casablanca and shortly you will see from the projections, increased magma activity as the group skirt around the newly reopened geothermal power plant in the Canary Islands."

From his preferred view, the long distance one, George could see that the bottom of the cutting now being traversed by the party was growing increasingly bright. Giant slivers of molten lava weaved along the floor and lower part of the walls, making it look as though a massive spider had spun a mammoth fluorescent web.

Like all dragons, George knew everything there was to know about geothermal power; he had after all spent months studying it in the nursery rings. Subterranean dragon cities were all heated using geothermal power, and had been for many centuries. Vast underground areas had also been specifically heated to exacting temperatures, so that a diverse range of crops could be grown all across the world, acting as giant greenhouses. Although all of this was amazingly clever, advanced and interesting, most dragons' favourite part of the geothermal process was the HOT SPRINGS...

Ahhhhhh.

Just thinking about hot springs made George's tail twitch in delight, despite the fact that he was currently in his human form, a tail of course nowhere to be seen. That didn't stop the twitching though. Whatever form he was in, George remained convinced that a dragon's tail was like its soul, always there. So much so, that sometimes he even had to look behind him to check that he wasn't dragging it along the ground when he was disguised as a human. This thought, it must be said, was totally private and not something he would ever want other dragons knowing, for fear of ridicule.

'Hot springs,' he thought, 'are just pleasure personified, that, and chewing your way through a whole block of charcoal... totally the best dragony things to do on the whole planet.'

If there's one other thing that dragons like, it's gossip. They can often be found sharing the latest rumours and shooting the breeze about pretty much everything. Talk about the next big project was commonplace amongst groups such as the engineers. George had overheard some of them back in the city above ground speculating on rumours of a planet-wide transport system being built, harnessing geothermal power.

'Pure fantasy of course,' he thought. 'Just like the idea of different flavoured charcoal and that absurd rumour about each city getting its own automated dragon wash. Utter madness!!!'

With others in the room starting to get a little bored because of pretty much the same views on all the walls, George returned to his thoughts about geothermal power. It was widely hoped within the dragon community that with the right guidance and a gentle nudge or two, humans in the coming decades and centuries, as they develop, will become more advanced technologically and take up the mantle of geothermal power because of its abundance and pollution-free properties. Most dragons hark back to the Roman times and point out that the Romans themselves were subtly nudged in the same direction and achieved great success, especially at Pompeii, that is until the catastrophic eruption of Mount Vesuvius in 79 A.D.

One of the regular updates, once again interrupted George's wandering mind.

"They've nearly reached Freetown and will soon be changing to a south westerly heading," muttered Axus, with distinctly less enthusiasm than an hour earlier.

Over the course of the rest of the day, the prisoners and guards followed the planned route exactly and made relatively good time. Axus continued with the regular updates, with many in the room paying more attention than others; some closed their eyes and meditated, while others, chiefly Osvaldo, left for short periods, before returning later.

Once the convoy entered the trench at the Falkland Islands, the tension in the room ratcheted up another level or two. Some paced and held whispered conversations, dragon bottoms shifted on stools, betraying the nervousness they all felt. Even Axus was more agitated than George had ever seen him, something he would have thought impossible only a few hours ago. Not able to stand still for more than two seconds at a time, constantly berating the technicians for the smallest of things, and flitting in and out of the room like a headless chicken, the famed engineer was the total opposite to the cool, calm pool of radiance that was the king. The monarch seemed totally unaffected by the tension and pressure, standing next to the stools in the middle of the room, looking like he didn't have a care in the world: the calm centre of a hurricane raging all around him.

"Majesty," called Axus over the hustle and bustle of the control room, "the group are about five hundred miles out from the entrance and should arrive in approximately one hour."

The king gave the engineer a nod of understanding. Axus continued.

"The facility is fully provisioned for the prisoners; it should just be a matter of the guards releasing them from their harnesses, and then using the mantras they're equipped with to bring them round. There should be a short crossover period after the mantras have been used, between the fugitives waking, and being fully conscious and aware. During that time the guards will be able to make their getaway and blow the shaped charges beyond the entrance of the tunnel, sealing it with thousands of tonnes of rock and ice for all time.

George knew that the whole sorry episode was nearly at an end now, but as he glanced around the room at the different projections, he couldn't help but pity those dragons being carried to their internment, to live out the remainder of their days in that horrifying environment, so totally alien to any and all dragons. Even worse, to know that you would end up dying there as well, with absolutely no chance of ever successfully mating or reproducing at all. A wave of sorrow washed over him and once again he thought of Troydenn and wondered exactly how things had gone so horribly wrong.

Everybody's focus was with the here and now, given that the group were on their approach to what was effectively their jail for the rest of their natural lives. As minutes passed, the images on the walls started to deteriorate... becoming blurred, or cutting out altogether. Unbelievably, Axus became even more frantic, something that had to be seen to be believed.

"What seems to be the problem Axus?" asked the king, calmly.

"It's the telepathic booster Majesty. We've increased the power output to beyond maximum, but the range is just too great. It might be that the cold is having an effect as well. I'm afraid the images will continue to break down. There's nothing more that can be done."

"How long before the convoy reaches the cavern?" enquired the king.

Striding over to a great map on the desk at the very front of the room, Axus began to study it carefully, just as the projections on the walls began to flicker more frequently. Turning from the king, the touch of a grin beamed past his scraggy beard.

"They're only a few minutes from the entrance, Majesty," he sighed, sounding relieved.

As the king nodded, everyone went back to work, focusing their efforts on getting everything they could from the projections.

Although George could see the left and right side projections out of the corner of his eyes, his concentration remained on the back wall and the view from the dragon flying far behind. It seemed there was less interference with this projection, maybe because it wasn't quite as far up the trench as the others. As far as he was concerned, it was also easier to make out exactly what was going on.

All of a sudden Axus pointed at the front projection and excitedly cried,

"There it is, the entrance to the cavern!"

Everyone in the room, even George, turned to face the projection on the front wall. Through the distortion and interference they could just make out the gaping entrance to the containment facility, backlit by the artificial lights that Axus and the other engineers had installed for the prisoners' benefit.

At that exact moment... ALL HELL BROKE LOOSE!!!!!

It was difficult to tell where, or how, it all started because of the poor quality of the images, but one thing was for sure... the supposedly sedated prisoners were all transforming from their human guises back into their natural dragon forms. Everybody in the room looked slack-jawed and stunned at this shocking revelation, everybody but the king, and Osvaldo Rosebloom.

Some of the prisoners had broken free of their restraints and had changed back into dragons while dropping towards the ground at perilous speeds. Heading towards the ground as tiny black dots on the projections, arms waving precariously on either side, they dropped like a stone, only to blur and transform before hitting the bottom, swooping back up as a dragon, fully ready to join the fight against their captors. Other were changing while still attached to the guards that were carrying them, some bursting free, taking their subjugators by surprise, others spiralling out of control towards the ground, their new found bulk too much to maintain steady flight. Mundane had turned to chaos in the blink of an eye, as magic ricocheted around the cavern.

Every projection in the control room was the same: dragon fighting dragon. Flame spewed from the mouths of different beasts, talons raked, heads butted, tails thumped, with putrid green blood splashing everywhere. It was difficult to make out from the black and white images exactly who had the advantage, as wings were punctured, sending guards corkscrewing down to their deaths, momentum used to skewer the enemy onto stalactites and stalagmites indiscriminately, and razor-sharp teeth slashing mighty chunks of scale and flesh throughout the aerial battle. Deep in the middle of the skirmish was the terror-inducing sight that they all feared... the huge matt black dragon that was Troydenn, going on an absolute rampage.

Back in the control room, the king, not taking his eyes off the scene of carnage and mayhem before them all, asked what they were all thinking.

"Where are the closest reinforcements Axus?"

"Not close enough I'm afraid, Majesty. The prisoners would easily be able to get back to the Falkland Islands and escape in plenty of time before we could gather even a meagre force together," he replied, shaking his head gloomily.

With his attention, like everyone else's, firmly focused on Axus, George caught a glimpse of something odd out the corner of his left eye. Totally the opposite of all the other onlookers, who were unanimously shocked and horrified by the surprising turn of events, leaning against one of the elongated desks off to one side, Osvaldo just looked... SMUG!

Abruptly the projection on the left wall cut out totally. The dragon operator on that wall dropped to the floor, howling in pain, hands wrapped around the shiny metal helmet with wires in it that sat firmly fixed on his head, trying with all his might to remove it, without any luck, which might have had something to do with the smoke and acrid smell that it was giving off. From out of nowhere, two medics arrived and started treating the stricken dragon, but not before he'd let out a blood-curdling scream and lost consciousness. Every being there could see what had happened from the images on the back wall. There, through a crowd of wrangling dragons all fighting for their lives, smack bang in the middle of the cavern's entrance was a pale dragon with bright flecks up its back and tail. One of the dragons that had been specifically selected to telepathically send back the black and white images, its long slender neck was now being crushed by the giant vice-like jaws of... Troydenn. Both dragons hovered in mid-air as the chaos ensued all around them, long after the life had left the innocent pale projectionist. Drawing a short, sharp gasp of horror from every being in the control room, Troydenn's gigantic jaws finally clasped together, totally severing the poor dragon's neck, letting the two pieces of the decapitated body tumble uncontrollably towards the bottom of the cavern. The dragon sending images back who was furthest away from the action, focused in on the crazed figure of Troydenn. Flapping his massive matt black wings furiously, head shaking violently from side to side, his angled face turned in the exact same direction from which he was being pictured, almost as if he knew that the king and councillors were watching, something that just couldn't be possible. Could it? More than a hint of insanity clouding his eyes, the charismatic leader's face broke into the biggest, scariest grin in the world. In that moment, in everyone's minds, things changed forever.

The atmosphere in the monitoring room at that very moment could be cut with a knife. Enveloped in stony silence, everyone there looked towards the king for an answer. Suddenly he stood, and in a move so quick nobody could have seen it coming, he smashed a vacant stool halfway across the room with his left forearm.

"ENOUGH!" bellowed the king. "Blow the explosive charges... NOW!"

Shaking somewhat, Axus turned towards the king.

"But Majesty, what about the guards? They'll be trapped along with all the prisoners."

With a look of absolute fury on his face, the king roared,

"DO YOU THINK I DON'T KNOW THAT? TRAPPED AND LOST FOREVER. DO YOU THINK THAT'S WHAT I WANT FOR THEM? THINK HOW MANY HUMANS AND DRAGONS ALIKE WILL BE KILLED IF TROYDENN AND HIS FOLLOWERS ARE ALLOWED TO LEAVE THAT PLACE. THE WHOLE WORLD WILL BE THROWN INTO PERIL, AND I WON'T ALLOW THAT. I COMMAND YOU TO BLOW ALL OF THE CHARGES AT ONCE. NOWWWW!!!!"

Despite the fact that all the blood had totally drained from his face, ever the professional, Axus turned and walked over to the table with the giant map on it. Pulling open a drawer, he withdrew a small box and flipped open the lid. Closing his eyes, and with a small shake of the head, he depressed the red button inside, knowing that there really was no other choice.

Bright explosions blossomed simultaneously across all three of the remaining projections. Dragons from both sides were pulverised by superheated exploding rock and ice. The detonation encompassed everything in sight, causing two of the remaining images to cease almost instantly, signalling the deaths of two more of the projectionist dragons. Back in the dragon domain, the control room darkened considerably with only the back wall now showing anything at all from the outlandish events in Antarctica.

George felt helpless as the incident on the other side of the planet spiralled out of control. Despite his feelings, and so desperately wanting to, he couldn't look away from the images that started to turn his green blood cold.

Turning away from the cavern entrance, the lone surviving projectionist was now heading at breakneck speed along the trench, back towards the Falkland Islands. Swerving erratically to avoid enormous stalactites and stalagmites, the dragon appeared to be flying as fast as was dragonly possible in the comparative darkness, clearly aware of the fate of those behind him. While still flying ahead in the trench, briefly he glanced over his shoulder, projecting the image back to the others. Fleeing dragons being dashed by rock and ice, all following hot on his tail, as well as a cascading barrage of explosions bursting up from the trench floor, shone onto the taut canvass as everyone looked on, speechless. Incredibly, the fleeing projectionist seemed to have found a little more speed from somewhere, offering up just a smidgen of hope to those in the darkness. Silently they willed him on, willed him to live.

Soaring incredibly fast now, it seemed the only possible outcome was for the dragon they all now had so much invested in, to outrun the wave of death behind him and cheat his certain demise. Until, that is, an explosion detonated about ten metres in front of him. The last thing those in the room saw before the wall went dark, was a torrent of rock, ice and fire closing in on all sides of the brave dragon. Plunged fully into darkness, the control room was as silent as a crypt in the dead of night.

"Lights," commanded Axus.

Immediately they came on. Glancing around, George had never seen members of his own race look so sombre.

The shock and horror at what they'd witnessed here today would stay with them forever.

"REPORT!" commanded the king.

Axus studied the information on the map table before turning around and addressing the monarch.

"All the charges detonated successfully Majesty. Anyone still alive will remain encased in that icy hell hole for the rest of their lives."

Emotional turmoil threatened to drop George to his knees. The trial of Troydenn himself was bad enough but this... this was beyond belief. Guilt, sadness, remorse, relief... was it even possible to feel all of these things at once, he asked himself. On reflection, he knew his emotions would always overwhelm him when he thought of the events that surrounded the last week or so of his life. But today the greatest threat his race had ever faced had been thwarted for good, finally. And that in itself must be the most important thing. At least that's what he continued to tell himself.

*   *   *

"And so students, for those of you who didn't already know it, that is the true story of George and the Dragon. Nothing like, you may note, the dismal and dreary tales you will hear on the surface from the misinformed humans, if and when you finally make it up there. That will be all for today. Don't forget this week's homework. Lessons will resume in the morning. Do not be late!" said the *tor.*

Young dragons from across the marble covered courtyard eagerly leapt to their feet, pushing and shoving each other out of the way, to see just who would be the first to leave the classroom.

2 A TAIL OF HUMILITY

Peter leapt down from the thick rock wall that surrounded the nursery ring, instantly missing the comforting heat, provided by the tiny lines of lava, that it had provided over the hour or so that he'd been sitting there. Heading east on one of the wide paved walkways that littered the underground domain of the dragons, he pondered much of what he'd just heard.

It had been three years since he'd left his nursery ring (this one in fact); however, something always seemed to draw him back. On feeling the urge to return, he'd always try to do so late in the afternoon, knowing full well that the young dragonlings could choose the subject matter at that particular time of day, something he remembered fondly. Dragon lore was always a popular choice, along with magic and myths. He'd lost count of the number of times he'd heard the legendary tale of George and the Dragon, probably at least fifty by now. Even so, he still ended up being spell-bound, with goose pimples running the length and breadth of his body, almost certainly just like the pupils in the class. Strolling purposefully towards the monorail station, instinctively jumping across the much bigger gaps in the floor in which rivers of dazzling orange and red lava flowed, helping to keep the entire area heated, he made sure not to let even a drop touch his brand new trainers.

Dragon families and relationships, unlike those of humans, appear to have no rhyme or reason. Some parents visit their children in the nursery ring every day, others just deposit the newly formed egg there, never to return. Some dragons are maternal, others not at all. Peter had never met his parents. In fact, as hard as he'd tried, he hadn't been able to find out a single thing about them. In the end, he'd given up trying, putting it down to them being that way genetically inclined, but on doing so he'd sworn to himself that if he were to ever meet the right dragon and be in the position of becoming a father, things would be very different, and he'd move heaven and earth to make sure that was the case. Like thousands of others, his earliest memories after hatching from his egg were those of the *praeceptors* or *tors* as the students liked to refer to them. The *praeceptors* act as tutors and mentors to the young dragons, only in a much more holistic way than up above on the surface. Their guidance not only covers the academic studies that dragonlings will learn during a fifty year compulsory attendance period, but also much more personal skills that include learning to fly, changing and maintaining shape, grooming, diet, family history, economics, relationships and social skills (both dragon and human). Given the complexity and sensitive nature of all of this, it's no surprise that most dragons tend to form really strong bonds with their *tors*, particularly if they have no recollection of their real parents. Quite often the youngsters come to think of their tutors as a parent or guardian figure.

A dragon's growth rate far exceeds that of a normal human being. Physically a dragon can reach full grown maturity by the time he or she reaches the ripe old age of ten years, with most two year olds having a far greater intellect than the average human adult. Peter reached his tenth year maturity celebration in the nursery ring without any fuss. He hadn't particularly excelled at any one thing, unlike most of the others in his class; he didn't really know what he was going to do when he left the nursery rings (not that many dragons do at that age, particularly given that they have another forty years of study ahead of them), and although he admired and respected his *tor*, he hadn't built up the kind of relationship with him that others in the class had. There were, however, two things that tended to stand out in his mind from that time in his life. The first was the friendship he had formed with two of his classmates, a friendship that was as strong today as it had been back then, some fifty two years ago.

Richie Rump was a beautiful, slim, sleek dragon. She'd hatched just a few months after Peter, and after only a matter of weeks they seemed to have formed an incredible bond of friendship. As dragons go, Richie was a real eye-catcher. While Peter was more short and round with a longer than average neck, small jaw and great big floppy undragon-like ears, more suited to a rabbit than a dragon, Richie was petite, shapely, perfectly formed with a gorgeous sparkling emerald green hue, except on her tummy, where the green gently blended into a lovely soft shade of yellow. What she lacked in stature, she more than made up for in grace, speed, determination and just outright effort. From an early age, Richie had always out-performed the rest of her class at anything physical. She was the first in the ring to master flying (although she had a sneaking suspicion that one of her best friends had been holding back on that front) and even now can out-fly dragons twice her size, matching them easily for speed and aerobatics. No slouch on the academic front either, most of the young dragons knew better than to challenge Richie to anything either physical or mental, because it was almost certain to end in humiliation, for the challenger anyway.

Peter's other friend was called Tank. Although relatively naive (just like most of the dragons in the nursery ring) Peter thought Tank was the most caring, thoughtful and considerate dragon in the whole world. A huge mountain of a dragon, Tank's huge bulk could easily fit Peter's squat little frame underneath one of his giant wings. Had he more speed and dexterity he might have been groomed to be a professional laminium ball player, he was certainly the right shape and size for it, but whenever the subject was brought up, Tank always managed to wriggle out of talking about it. What his friend did have though, was a great affinity for nature, always knowing even more than the *tors* seemed to about anything related to plants or animals, much to their utter amazement. Always the first

49

to jump in and stand up for his friends, Tank never ran from an argument or confrontation, not that Richie ever found herself in a position to need his help. Peter though, well that was a different matter altogether. Teasing and taunting were commonplace for him, some of which would end up going too far, but Tank was always ready to step in and help his friend. It always seemed to be the same culprits but the *tors* preferred to step back and let the young dragons deal with it themselves, classing it as part of their development process. This protection was just one of the reasons Peter supposed that the bond between himself and Tank had grown as strong as the one between him and Richie. The three of them were inseparable in much the same way then as they are now.

The second thing Peter remembered vividly from that period in his life was the dragon in human guise that often came along to watch lessons (much as he himself had done today) and see how the dragons were getting on. Even though Peter had no family to speak of, he always thought fondly of that particular dragon, and although they had only ever exchanged a few polite words, he always got the impression that the dragon was keeping an eye out for him in some way, shape or form. He always appeared in the human guise of an old man with long, straggly, grey hair flowing down past his shoulders, a captivating walking stick made of light coloured oak, and an air of importance. Whenever Peter thought back, the walking stick always stood out. If you had a million walking sticks to choose from, and had to go through them all, this was the one you would have. It seemed somehow... special.

Never sticking to a routine, the old man would show up at the nursery ring, much as Peter had just done, but would also turn up at Lava Falls and watch the young dragons practice their aerial manoeuvres and impromptu laminium ball matches.

The last time Peter had set eyes on him was on the day the whole class graduated. Traditions vary from nursery ring to nursery ring across the entire planet, but they all have them. Peter's nursery ring at Purbeck Peninsula was no different, with the entire class of young dragons finding themselves atop the highest cliff at Lava Falls on this very special day. Watched by the entire staff, the youngsters gathered in their human forms, just over a mile above the roiling lake of super-heated lava, bubbling ferociously away beneath them. Peter could vividly recall trying not to choke on the acrid fumes as the heat and steam buffeted his face, even at that distance. He could also recollect glancing over his shoulder at the staff from the nursery ring and, just out of the corner of one eye, catching sight of the old man, who, when their eyes met, gave Peter a wink and a smile. With little chance to dwell on it at the time, he was suddenly caught up in a mad rush of graduating dragons running at full speed off the cliffs in their human forms. Pulled over the edge clumsily, he ended up diving head first off the cliff, a very scary feeling in his human form, even though it was comparatively tame compared with the kind of flying that most dragons were used to.

The idea behind this particular tradition was that the youngsters would leap off the cliff in their human guises, and on the drop down would transform back into their natural dragon selves, flying up into the air to celebrate. Changing shape halfway through a drop like this would be taxing for an experienced adult dragon. Thus, there was a definite element of danger to the whole thing. Peter remembered the effort he had to put in to effect the change to his dragon form. The sheer exhilaration that he'd experienced once he'd completed the change and zoomed up into the air, after being only metres away from the vicious looking boiling lava, was unlike anything he'd ever felt, up to and including this very day.

After a few minutes of flying around to celebrate, the whole class had flown down to meet the staff for a final meal that had been prepared and laid out on the cliff top.

As they did so, Peter sought out the old dragon, hoping to have a friendly chat, but much to his surprise and disappointment, he was nowhere to be seen. That was the last time he'd seen the old man. He often found himself wondering what the old dragon was doing now, and if like Peter he still visited the nursery ring from time to time. Looking back, Peter assumed the old man/dragon must have been taught at the Purbeck Peninsula nursery ring, and that's why he liked to return, much like himself. What other reason could there possibly be?

From his tenth year onwards, lessons at the nursery ring, as far as Peter was concerned, became vastly more interesting. Up until then, their education had consisted of the kind of things humans would learn: maths, languages, history, science, economics, geography and a broad range of religious and human studies (everything about the human world that had not already been covered). They had also covered dragon basics, such as flying, grooming, mating, diet, dragon beliefs and the founding principles. But things were about to get more interesting, in the shape of dragon lore, self defence, moral standing, spatial awareness and mantras in all their shapes and forms.

Mantras were the one subject guaranteed to put a glint into a young dragon's eye. All had heard what they could achieve, but only a few had ever seen examples in real life. None had ever cast a mantra themselves because they were too young, although Tank might have a few secrets in that department. Mantras could do pretty much anything from healing humans, dragons, animals and plants, to repairing machinery of any kind. Common everyday uses for mantras included being used to effect a dragon's change from its natural form *(solitus)* to the surface disguise of a human *(mutatio)*. That particular mantra takes years to perfect and it requires the utmost concentration to hold that form for a sustained period of time. This was basically what the next forty years in the nursery ring would hold, learning to swap forms and more importantly maintain the unfamiliar human guise indefinitely, without any flaws or imperfections. Once the young dragons had mastered that, they would learn how to make subtle changes to their guises, which would let them blend in on the surface, in whatever role would be assigned to them. Of course they would be taught other mantras and magical abilities along the way, but transforming into a human shape would almost certainly be the most important.

Recalling his very first mantra lesson with great clarity, the thought of sitting on that cold marble floor in the courtyard caused him to shiver uncontrollably. The *tor* had demonstrated how to use the mantra properly, with the students standing around, expected to repeat the process. Their class was never a particularly quiet place even when it was supposed to be, but on that day, in that class, you could hear the sizzling of flames dribbling from nervous nostrils across the room, as the dragonlings all watched each other to see just who would be brave enough to go first.

A small dragon by the name of Tempest was the first to try. Usually shy and retiring, it was something of a surprise that she'd plucked up the courage to have a go. Sitting in the middle of the courtyard she took a deep breath, unrolled her parchment and, closing her eyes in concentration, recited the mantra. Even though they were all supposed to be getting on with the exact same thing, the other students couldn't take their eyes off the young, female dragon.

The single most important aspect of casting a mantra successfully is channelling the concentration and belief behind the words. This will nearly always determine whether or not a mantra will succeed or fail. It also determines just how effective a mantra will be. For example, a healing mantra being used on a deep, open wound, if used by an experienced healer, will heal the wound, destroy any infection, and remove any scar tissue. The exact same mantra used by someone less experienced, and not directing the same sort of concentration or belief into it, may not have the same effect. It may fail to close the wound properly, leave an infection, or it may heal it all up, but leave a massive scar. The difference between total and faltering concentration and belief is staggering; the results can lead to the mantra not working at all, working less effectively, or sometimes producing unpredictable side effects.

All the dragon students had been taught this, many times over, but most had not really paid attention; they were too excited about the prospect of performing their first mantra. That was why the *tor* had chosen this particular one and why, if the students had looked closely at their tutor, they would have noticed the beginnings of a smile forming at the bottom of his huge, prehistoric jaw, something that this most serious of dragons rarely allowed to happen.

Tempest, although she tried, clearly hadn't put enough belief and concentration into her mantra, and was just starting to learn the true meaning of unpredictable side effects.

Demonstrating the mantra some five minutes earlier, the *tor's* tail had, starting at its tip, shrunk until it was no longer visible. This was the mantra's purpose and what should have happened if used properly. Known only to the *tor* was the fact that this particular mantra was unbelievably specific and amazingly sensitive to incorrect pronunciation or not enough channelled belief. A look of utter horror and humiliation was etched across Tempest's face at the moment, as not only had her tail begun to grow bigger, but it had also split into three parts, each of which were now growing and snaking across the airy courtyard of their own accord. Students occupying the area directly behind the stricken student were dumbstruck momentarily. That soon changed as they were forced to dive and roll out of the way of the ever expanding tails and flee back into the adjacent indoor teaching area, or try and make a dash to get round the front of the horror stricken Tempest.

Looking back on the whole thing, Peter thought it absolutely hilarious, but at the time it seemed anything but. Eventually Tempest's tails stopped growing, but not before each had split into three again, leaving the poor dragonling rooted to the spot in the middle of the courtyard with nine tails embedded firmly in the broken marble floor.

The lesson for the classmates had ended there that day, with them being dismissed and sent off to Lava Falls to practice their aerial combat techniques. Everyone, with the exception of one or two of the bullies that occasionally picked on Peter, was aghast at what had befallen Tempest, with very little flying taking place, most preferring to sit on the cliff side and speculate on the aforementioned events. That night Tempest was missing from her dormitory, with nobody in authority having the faintest idea of her whereabouts or wellbeing. The next morning, all of the students except Tempest sat waiting nervously for the *tor* to arrive for that day's lessons. To their surprise, in he walked with a big beaming smile broadcast across his face, followed closely by a very healthy and happy looking Tempest.

Missing pieces of the puzzle soon began to fall into place. The *tor* had undone all of the tail trouble in only a matter of moments after the students had left the previous day. Proceeding to repair all the walls and the marble flooring in the courtyard, he then treated Tempest to a slap up meal, persuading her to stay in alternative accommodation that night, just to make the students sweat that little bit more. The entire scenario had been designed to show the students what could potentially happen if mantras were not used with enough conviction and belief. You might have the world's supply of mana (the magical supply of an individual's natural energy) to power the mantras, and you might be able to pronounce the text faultlessly, but without the right conviction and belief behind them, they could be almost worthless. Peter was certain that none of the students that witnessed the events of that afternoon would ever forget the lesson it was designed to teach them.

Reality flooded back as the walkway he was on started to widen and fill up with dragons of all shapes and sizes. Focused firmly on not bumping into any of them, he marvelled at the surrounding area, wondering just what the humans on the surface would make of the secret world just beneath their feet.

Purbeck Peninsula was one of the oldest dragon enclaves in Britain, second only to London itself. Based beneath the south of England in a region that covers the area from the east of Bournemouth through to the west of Swanage, as far south as the most southerly point of the Isle of Wight, and as far north as Wimborne Minster, Purbeck Peninsula dates back over three thousand years. It draws its name from the fact that its centre is located directly beneath the beautiful Isle of Purbeck, and because the underground area on which the community is built is surrounded by unusual layers of molten lava, making it almost inaccessible from other dragon communities.

It was originally built with only one point of access underground, from the north, which is remarkable in itself as most dragon towns or cities across the world have at least five or six main entry points, because despite their knowledge and power, dragons still acknowledge that they are susceptible to natural disasters and unforeseen circumstances. Although there is only one underground point of access to Purbeck Peninsula, like all dragon-inhabited areas there are hundreds, if not thousands, of secluded entrances to the surface. Most of these are tiny, located in either shops or private residences, with slightly larger ones existing in more out of the way spots on the surface, so that unsuspecting humans don't stumble across them accidentally. Those around Purbeck include caves, abandoned mines, secretly activated entrances in various ruins, two or three rather creative underwater access ways, and some very interesting ones based around a series of puzzles.

With only one main underground route into Purbeck Peninsula it was no surprise that the monorail station was a terminus. However it wasn't just any terminus: the place was huge, even by dragon standards. No mean feat.

Cresting the brow of the hill, the winding path that Peter was on dipped sharply, allowing him to take in the sight of the busy, bustling terminus from above.

Directly opposite, across from where he stood, embedded into the rock face of the hill on the other side of the monorail station and overlooking the whole complex, was the main office that controlled the monorail carriages as they pulled into and departed from Purbeck, making sure everything ran to schedule and that each car alighted onto the right platform after coming down the single line and out of the gargantuan tunnel that fed the station. The individual carriages glided to a halt at the exact individual berth, or platform depending on how you looked at it, on one of the eighteen branch lines that spread out to form the station proper. Passengers disembarked from one side of the car before arrivals filed on from the other side, to depart. Monorail carriages would only be at a rest for a matter of moments, before powering silently back towards the gaping tunnel in the direction that they'd only just arrived from. It was a magnificent achievement, not just here, but across the entire globe: the perfect exercise in dragon management and individual movement, allowing things to run almost to the second.

As Peter ambled casually down the slope of the path overlooking the station, he was struck by the speed with which the blurring silver monorail carriages moved so elegantly. Outside the station, the cars themselves could move in excess of six hundred miles an hour, while obviously going much slower than that while in the station. Even so, it was still all pretty much a blur... that's how fast things were flowing. If any human had been standing there watching, heaven forbid, their limited senses, compared with those of a dragon, would barely have been able to comprehend exactly what they were seeing. Huge LCD screens were displayed across the entire complex, updating nearly every second, the words and numbers on their screens distorted beyond belief by the speed. Dragon passengers in all their forms, big, small, dragon and human shaped, all managed to digest the information and make their way on time to where they had to be. It wasn't the biggest monorail station in the world, but one of the most standout in terms of natural beauty, creativity with what was already there, and sheer efficiency in terms of getting beings where they were supposed to go at the right time. It was absolutely outstanding.

Unlike most dragons, Peter couldn't remember a time when the monorail hadn't been around. Having been up and running for over sixty years now, it connected every dragon community on the planet via a series of subterranean tunnels, some of which had previously been used to allow dragons to fly between said communities, though most were newly carved, especially for this modern miracle of transport. Throughout his time studying in the nursery ring, the *tors* and other accompanying adult dragons had taken them on class field trips, using the relatively new form of transport to show the young dragons faraway places, enhancing their understanding of different cultures, both above and below ground. They would also, on the journeys to and from these faraway places, learn a little about dragon history in the form of a series of facts about the monorail itself, such as how it had taken over two hundred years to complete, about the state of the art techniques used to develop it and keep it operational and about the geothermal power across the planet that it harnessed to keep it running. During those particular lessons, it was inevitable that at least one of the *tors* would drone on about how in his or her day, they had to fly everywhere and not be pandered to by some fancy new transport system. It made him smile just thinking about it.

Getting closer to the station, Peter spotted a speeding silver carriage zip out of the tunnel and crisscross the different lines, heading for the platform that his transport was due to depart from. Breaking into a jog, much to the disdain of the other dragons around him, he arrived at the platform just as the silver monorail car he'd picked out docked. Electric doors opened with a WHOOOSH! Passengers exited from the opposite side to Peter, while the doors on his side remained closed for a couple of seconds longer. Without warning, and with the same accompanying WHOOOSH, the doors slid back inside the carriage, allowing all the passengers to board.

'Nice and orderly, or dragon-like,' thought Peter. 'Absolutely nothing like the chaos on the surface,' he laughed to himself.

Once inside, he plonked down on one of the long, garishly red, sofa-like seats that ran the length of the carriage on either side, and waited for the monorail to leave the station. The seating had been designed to accommodate dragons in both their human and natural forms, easily accomplished in carriages that were thirty feet tall and nearly four hundred feet long. Most dragons boarded in their human guises, but for those that stuck with their natural forms, nearly every other seat in the carriage had a rather large, adaptable hole in the back, for their tails to fit through. Occasionally, exclusive, first class carriages could be spotted on different lines, provided for privileged, private parties willing to part with a lot of money, rumoured to be staffed by dragons that would cater for your every whim. These exceptional carriages were easily spotted at a station or junction because, instead of sporting the usual bright shiny silver, they were instead decorated entirely in black, making them appear sought after, rare and unusual. Thirty seconds or so after boarding, the doors to Peter's carriage slid closed, allowing the monorail car to negotiate the intricate series of points, before accelerating into the gaping mouth of the dark tunnel on its way out of Purbeck Peninsula.

Through the windows of the carriage, Peter could see the dark rock face whiz by at speed on one side, while on the other, dragons of all shapes and sizes walked side by side along the trail that had been the main entrance to the Peninsula for hundreds of years. The pathway ran parallel to the monorail for some fifteen miles or so, before splitting up and winding off in several different directions. Dragons came from across the domain just to walk that path and witness the sheer beauty of staggering underground formations of rock, crystal and lava, as well as learn about its intriguing history. The path itself had been the base of the tunnel that dragons used to fly along, long before the monorail itself had been constructed.

From easily identifiable to a messy blur, in the blink of an eye, that's what had happened to the shapes of the landscape outside the window as the monorail had increased speed even more. Try as he might with his heightened senses, every time he came this way, he still couldn't make out any of the details. Eventually he gave up, just as the winding path branched off in a different direction.

Peter's destination was the beautiful city of Salisbridge, some fifty miles or so away in southern Wiltshire, England. Having worked and lived there since leaving the nursery ring and integrating fully into the human society he had sworn to help guide and protect, Peter couldn't think of a more beautiful place to call home. Had he been travelling between the two destinations above ground in a car, the journey would have taken well over an hour. On the monorail, it would take a little under eight minutes.

Only the occasional vein of molten lava illuminated the inside of the carriage now that they were away from the pedestrian walkways. The monorail designers had wasted little time in deciding that only the bigger underground caverns or areas would be illuminated, leaving the vast majority of travel through the solid rock cuttings in near total darkness, punctuated by the odd monorail car heading in the opposite direction, something even a dragon could miss if they blinked or sneezed at the wrong time. Peter let his head fall back onto the comforting fabric of the seat, and wondered just what it would be like for an ordinary human to experience a monorail journey. It could of course never happen; aside from the security implications, the incredibly high G forces would all but destroy their weakened charges from the surface. Dragons were built to withstand all but the highest G forces, experiencing them over and over again when flying, hence their ability to perform amazing aerial feats such as tight turns at speed, pulling out of death-defying drops, barrel rolls and just flying at around five hundred miles an hour. But he guessed that if a human were with him now, able to withstand the forces, it would feel as though they were riding the biggest and scariest rollercoaster, only with sooooo much more ooomph.

Dragons' physical characteristics were taken very much into account during the monorail's construction, meaning that routes through the rock strata could take the most direct route nearly all of the time, only changing direction for insurmountable obstacles like gigantic lava flows, large veins of problem metals or potentially explosive pockets of dangerous gas, thus meaning that the monorail would travel in a straight line for much of a journey, before suddenly veering off on all sorts of random twists and turns, drops and ascents, just to avoid a potentially problematic area. For the most part, dragon passengers barely noticed. Humans would never have been able to survive it intact.

Slowly the monorail car started to decelerate, Peter's cue that they were approaching Salisbridge station. Abruptly the dark tunnels were replaced by the soft orange glow of the platforms. As smooth as always, the carriage pulled up perfectly, just above the platform, and the doors whispered their usual whoosh, opening to allow departing passengers off. Making his way along the platform, and up some very worn marble stairs, the soft sound of the monorail departing whispered to him before he'd even reached the top.

In front of him, the station opened out into a vast courtyard, with various distinct walkways heading off in a dozen different directions. Although small compared with the likes of London, Glasgow and Purbeck stations, the painstaking detail with which the Salisbridge station had been decorated put all the others to shame. Surrounding the courtyard, twelve soaring, black and white marble pillars, matching the dazzling floor, supported the cavernous ceiling above. Carved intricately into each pillar was a legendary figure from history, with their natural dragon form on one side and their human guise on the other. A sparkling golden fleck, almost as if gold leaf had been mixed with the marble, allowed the characters to shine like stars in a black and white night. Eye-catching didn't begin to cover it. Each time Peter travelled through here, a sense of history and a thrill of excitement ran through him, almost as if he himself were a part of it. Stupid really. You couldn't get much further away from that, than him.

On reaching the top of these particular stairs, Peter always came face to face with a pillar on which a very familiar hero was etched... George, from the George and the Dragon tale that he'd once again heard recounted, less than an hour ago. Stopping for a few seconds to take in the magnificence of the carving, the same sense of familiarity that he always got washed over him, before he decided it was time to move on. As in previous times, he wondered if somehow he weren't linked to the story in some way, as at times, it appeared to be all around him. Ludicrous really, he knew. Dragons didn't believe in fate or destiny. They were a much more practical race, dealing with the present as it unfolded before them, much less concerned with the past or future.

Peter's fanciful thoughts seemed to be blown away as his highly attuned senses started to come under attack in a variety of different ways. The sickly scent emanating from some of the Mediterranean plants dotted around the courtyard made his nose tingle and itch. Most underground areas used plants from warmer climates, which he supposed were better suited to the humid conditions. A loud WHIRRING noise from one of the five or six vendors that plied their wares around the edge of the courtyard, nearly day and night, caused Peter to jump slightly. Peeking to his right, he could see that the vendor in question had just primed his machine to start making fresh charcoal doughnuts, in time to attract the attention of the passengers just reaching the top of the staircase. As the dough whizzed around and around in the noisy mixer, Peter watched mesmerised as different coloured tiny chunks of charcoal dripped from above into the gooey mixture, before it slinked its way into a funnel, and then plopped out into the hot fat as a doughnut shape at the other end. It continued to wind its way through the river of bubbling, hot fat, until it was suddenly flipped over, allowing the other side to cook, while Peter's mouth watered in anticipation. All the time the dragon vendor eyed him with a knowing gleam in his eye that almost said, "Gotcha!"

Concentrating so hard on the doughnut, Peter had only just begun to realise that the sickly sweet scent of pollen had all but been replaced by a much more pleasant smell. His highly sensitive nose had detected the delightful aroma of lemon, cinnamon and slightly burnt charcoal. Leaving the doughnut maker, much to his disappointment, Peter inquisitively headed over to the next vendor, just in time to see a spindly-framed dragon toss a giant pancake into the air, before expertly bringing it down on to the sizzling hot plate in front of him, all with more than a hint of showmanship.

His nostrils now felt overwhelmed as the courtyard filled up with passengers, and every vendor did their very best to entice them into buying some of their wares. Gorgeous aromas wafted over from the vendors cooking on the other side of the courtyard. Through the crowd, Peter could just make out magnificent multicoloured bread coming out of an oven, which he assumed was the fresh candy floss and toffee apple smell he was currently inhaling. Spying the adjacent vendor frying mouth-watering strips of dark brown meat in a skillet with all sorts of wonderful fruit and vegetables, creating a silky sweet, barbecue smell, made his stomach rumble loudly, having not eaten all day. Taking an age to try and choose between the tasty treats, he finally settled on the pancake over everything else. Once the experienced vendor had cooked him a fresh one, and with it firmly wrapped in a cardboard cone, ignoring all the delicious foodie smells he cut his way through the throng of passengers to the narrowest of the walkways and started following its incline. After two or three minutes of swift walking, he found himself in near total darkness, the path's twists and turns cancelling out any of the remaining light from the station. Not bothered in the slightest by all of this, because of his superb dragon vision that he could change at will, enhancing it to see in the dark as clearly as if it were a sunny day, Peter arrived at the secret underground entrance to the house he owned. Sliding through a small gap in a wall, while wolfing down the last remnants of his pancake, he made his way up a set of very narrow, stone steps. Having done this journey many thousands of times in his relatively short life, he slipped through an even narrower gap at the top of the stairs, glad that he didn't have to do this in his dragon form. Not even his tiny dragon frame would have been able to negotiate this.

Facing a solid block of impenetrable stone, in total

darkness, he raised his left hand up along the wall beside him. With his thumb and forefinger he found two indentations, and at exactly the same time, he forced his digits into both, squeezing down as he did so. A soft 'click', only noticeable because of his enhanced senses, followed by the turning of tiny gears further back down the passage, echoed in the darkness. As if by magic, but more likely awesome engineering, a huge chunk of the wall silently slid upwards and out of sight. Ducking his head ever so slightly, Peter moved on through into a dusty old cellar, where cobwebs hung down from wooden beams crisscrossing the ceiling, while clouds of fluff adorned light coloured dust sheets littering the room, underneath which all sorts of different shaped belongings sat. Off in the far corner, a black, ornate, metal staircase, wound tightly up to the ceiling, where it just... STOPPED! The ceiling itself was totally intact, and if anyone had bothered to climb the Victorian staircase, they would have had nowhere to go. It didn't perturb Peter though. He dodged past all the dusty objects and squeezed onto the first rung of the staircase, just as the solid, outside rock wall slipped back into place. Circling around three times on the staircase, he stopped just before his head touched the ceiling. Reaching down to a rust-covered black flower that was part of the intricate Victorian design, he twisted the petals anti-clockwise, before craning his neck up to look at the ceiling. He was rewarded with a small hole getting gradually bigger from above. Poking his head through, he climbed the remainder of the rungs, emerging into a very ordinary, very small, modern day sitting room. Stepping out from the corner of the room, he skirted around the light brown piano, before reaching past its keys, and yanking hard on a tall glass Galileo thermometer that sat atop it. The brightly coloured glass balls inside crashed violently together as the thermometer went from vertical to horizontal in an instant, the result of which would surely see them break. Surprisingly, they didn't. As the glass vessel sprang back to an upright position, the whole piano slid around ninety degrees on the wooden floor, to sit snugly in the corner of the room on top of the concealed opening. Anyone entering the room the conventional way would be none the wiser.

Peter's small terraced house comprised a sitting room, a small kitchen, a bathroom on the ground floor, a sixty foot long, narrow garden, and three bedrooms, one of which was a study (up in the roof). A former railway cottage built around the early nineteen hundreds, it was situated close to the modern day station, and was only a ten minute walk from the centre of town. It had always been owned by one dragon or another, hence the concealed passage to the secret world below. As long as intelligent humans have roamed the earth, dragons have sought to live side by side with them, blending in with them in an effort to help fulfil their sworn pledge to guide and protect them. Throughout history, homes bought by dragons have often had access to the domain below, nearly always hidden, more often than not in a completely obscure fashion that nobody would ever stumble across by accident: from revolving wardrobes, to hollow bottomed washing machines, fridges to climb inside, to showers that drop you into a slide so sheer, you wouldn't stop screaming for days, to clandestine garden entrances guarded by all manner of unusual animals.

With their natural affinity for all things mechanical and armed with a variety of mantras, virtually nothing is beyond a dragon when they set their mind to it. Putting an updated spin on things has become the main challenge over the years, so that things blend into their contemporary surroundings. The piano, for example, had been in Peter's house for many decades, not really unusual at all, whereas the lever that had originally started off atop it had been an old fashioned candelabrum, that most certainly would have looked out of place now, so replacing it with something more modern (the Galileo thermometer) allowed it to blend in and go virtually unnoticed should any unexpected visitors decide to take a closer look. Specially crafted by an expert in modern mantra mechanics, based in Purbeck Peninsula, it was fitted by one of the designers that routinely update dragon abodes across the country.

Glancing at the rocket shaped clock on the opposite wall, it told him he was close to running late.

'Hmmmmm,' he thought. 'Better get a move on or I'm gonna be late for training.' With that in mind, he raced up the stairs to his bedroom and quickly changed into his hockey kit.

A keen hockey player and a member of the local club, he was a stickler for attending training on a Tuesday evening at seven o'clock. Having thrown on his shirt, shorts, socks and loosely laced up his Astro trainers, he grabbed his shin pads off the side, picked up his stick bag from behind the bedroom door, and just before heading downstairs, caught the faintest hint of his reflection in the full length mirror. Pausing briefly to admire the complex mantras that held his false human form in place, he couldn't decide what he was most proud of. The long wavy black hair that adorned his head, straight out of the eighties, that over the course of time he'd have to use another mantra to add just a touch of grey to? The light line of stubble around his chin that he liked so much, the 'run of the mill' face with no really distinctive features, it was all rather difficult to choose. Of medium height, not at all skinny, but certainly not overweight, he decided he looked good in his hockey kit... it suited him, and felt like a second skin... well, third actually. Nodding his head at his reflection, he bounded down the stairs two at a time and headed for his car. Five minutes later he pulled into the car park of the sports club, situated just outside the city limits away from any residential areas, at this very moment standing out like a lighthouse in a storm, with its brilliant bright floodlights blazing across the countryside for all to see. Consisting of a large two storey pavilion overlooking an Astroturf hockey pitch and grass rugby and lacrosse pitches. Picking a space in the large tarmac car park that serviced the pavilion he grabbed his gear and headed towards the changing rooms and sports pitches which were located on the opposite side of the building. Inside, the pavilion consisted of one long bar and dining area on the ground floor that looked out onto all three sports pitches, with a members only lounge, a committee room, the chairman's office, a storage area and a small bar with a balcony used only for private parties, all upstairs on the first floor. Walking past the dark reflective windows, part of him couldn't wait for the training to be over, so that he could wander into the bar in the hope of finding his two best friends. Not only was Tuesday the night for hockey training, but for lacrosse and rugby training as well, which meant that Richie would be here playing lacrosse, and Tank would be taking on all challengers at rugby. Things really didn't get any better than this.

Training went reasonably well, with Peter larking about some of the time with different members of the second XI (his team), before heading to the bar afterwards and spending over an hour catching up with his two best friends. By the time he got home it was late, leaving him with barely enough time to shower before sliding into bed and drifting off to sleep. His final thoughts before he dropped off had him wondering just what the following day at work had in store for him.

3 A MAJOR DISAPPOINTMENT

Woken abruptly by the piercing sound of his alarm clock, Peter rubbed the sleep from his eyes and, almost on autopilot, wandered downstairs to the bathroom and began cleaning his teeth. Aware that most humans have their breakfast first and then clean their teeth, this wasn't really an issue for him, given that everything about his body was a lie. He did however try and get into a routine of doing all the right things to blend in, exactly as he'd been taught during his years of training. So he stood, tried to smile, although the early hour did little to help with that, finished his teeth, smeared a blue globule of gel into his hair, smoothing it back with his fingers before rinsing them off, and then headed back to the bedroom to get dressed. Grabbing a tie off the rack in the wardrobe and slapping the 'off' button on his clock radio on his way out of the room, he leapt down the stairs and into the kitchen, feeling much better than he had ten minutes earlier.

Pouring himself a bowl of cornflakes, he grabbed the milk and a strawberry yoghurt from the fridge and sat down at the small pine dining table, smack bang in the middle of the kitchen. He drizzled milk over his cornflakes and munched his way through the whole bowl, before quickly wolfing down the yoghurt.

Earlier than he'd planned on being, he decided to quickly catch up with events in the dragon world. Sitting back in the chair, a contented feeling of a full stomach washing over him, he closed his eyes and began to concentrate. It felt like flying. That was the only way he could think of to describe it. Reaching out with his mind, he searched for the nearest crystal booster, which not only had the power to amplify the telepathic information sent out, but was also able to store that self same information for dragons to access at will. Sitting at the table with his eyes closed, all the time maintaining his focus, small beads of sweat started to form on his forehead as his consciousness soared up and away over the rooftops of the adjacent houses, momentarily hovering uncertainly before suddenly shooting off in a south westerly direction. Even though it was only his mind racing through the cold, morning air, he was sure he could feel a chilly breeze brushing the hairs on his arms, making them all stand to attention. Thirty seconds or so later, he finally caught sight of his target. On the outskirts of the city, beautiful, famed gardens wandered along one of the main rivers, revealing amazing views of the fantastic cathedral and the picturesque water meadows. Twisting paths lined with flowers, punctuated by the occasional bench and a popular playground for young children, stood out for all to see.

Opposite the children's play area, in the middle of the duck laden, lazy river, sat a small island with a huge oak tree growing out of it. Close enough to the bank for older children to jump over to, it stood out as a marked attraction. Swooping down and across the park, strangely, the oak was Peter's destination. His consciousness headed at speed towards a particular branch that instead of tapering off to a point, had a small dark hole in the end of it, through which Peter's wayward mind now dived. The pitch black interior came as something of a shock after the bright, gaudy colours of the playground. Nevertheless, he pressed on, his sense of speed gradually fading. Knowing what to expect because he'd done this hundreds of times before, a sudden encompassing bright light offered up a sense of familiarity. In a virtual room that disappeared off as far as he could see, glancing down row after row of huge wooden filing cabinets, he scanned the italic writing on the front of each for what he was looking for. *Sol (April-May), Speculum (March-April-May), Liber (April-May)* and *Stella (April-May)*.

Seconds later, he had it... *The Daily Telepath (April-May)*. Using only the will of his mind, he pulled open the drawer, swooped up and dived in head first (well, since his head was back in his kitchen, that wasn't really possible... but you know what I mean), rifling through the thick wad of pages. To him it felt as though he was swimming through a book just as someone was flicking through all the pages. Odd and yet strangely compelling, particularly the smell, which for some reason reminded him of old books. He was so immersed in everything that he nearly missed last month's copies whizzing past him, but not quite. He knew he was close. Grinding gradually to a halt, he found himself right in front of today's copy, grasped it with his mind, and leapt right on out of the cabinet. Immediately an explosion of information wrapped itself around his conscious will and followed it back, exactly the same way it had come, until it plunged back down into his house and forced its way back into his head. With the information downloaded, it was no trouble now to access it inside his head, pretty much, in fact, like turning the pages of a real, tactile newspaper. The front page of today's Daily Telepath looked like this:

Claw Sharpening Mantra Free in Tomorrow's Paper

The Daily Telepath

Britain's Oldest Telepathic Newspaper   Issue No 252171

New Theme Park Opens in Hawaii

By Rainbow Swan

Yesterday saw the opening of the fabulous new lava theme park Mauna Loa Falls underneath the Island of Hawaii. It features raging lava rapids, forty super size lava plunge pools, three lava cleansing steam caverns, lava geyser challenge flying course and the amazing star attraction 'Molten Meltdown'.

The spa has its own eight crescent spa pool. Treatments include full body scale polishing, stomach descaling, tail sharpening and nostril enhancement therapy. Visitors are advised to book early to avoid disappointment. The main park entrance is only a short flight from the Honolulu monorail station.

Monorail Preliminary Test

By Tawny Clockface

Three new test bore holes have been drilled, two in Europe, one in Australia. The idea of having a monorail link that goes straight from Europe,

through the Earth's crust, narrowly missing the core and heading directly to Australasia took another step forward yesterday. Four sites in Europe have been determined as having the potential for the proposed cross planet link, with the engineers involved having already solved the problems caused by stress tolerances, seismic pressure and power requirements. It only remains for the team to find a route for the proposed monorail that satisfies safety and stability requirements. A spokesdragon for the engineers involved said that "the project was progressing at a satisfactory rate and that the real possibility of a direct transplanet monorail could only actually be a decade or so away." Apple Pink, speaking on behalf of the dragons against technology movement, was quoted as saying "of all the disastrous ideas, this seems to be the most ridiculous. The current monorail infrastucture is already damaging the planet's core. This potentially threatens the safety of the whole planet and every dragon should wake up and realise this. We will not sit by while the King and his Council jeapardise every living organism on the planet, just so that dragons can travel from A to B just that bit quicker." More test bores are planned for central Australia next month.

New Rule Change?

By Rushton Boat

The world Laminium Ball Association (WLBA) is understood to be considering changing one of the main rules to our beloved sport. At the moment the goals each end of the giant cavern are formed by six huge stalactites and stalagmites, meeting up to form six columns of rock, with each team aiming to use the laminium ball to destroy as many columns as possible. The WLBA is thinking of extending the six columns to eight. Outrage surrounds the plan as six columns have been the standard since Roman times. Watch this space for regular updates on this most important matter.

Council to Discuss South Pole Warning

By Chief Political Correspondant Briony Ingham

The next monthly meeting of the King's Council will raise the issue of global warming at the South Pole. Ever increasing angst amongst human scientists over the issue has seen

Councillor D'Zone table the issue for the next meeting. Top level dragon specialists will be consulted on how best to proceed, with some already calling for a fact finding mission. At this moment in time the council seems split on whether already overstretched dragon resources can cope with what would be a long and potentially waste of time and invaluable equipment. For the first time in a while, it may be that the King has the final say in the matter with his casting vote.

Envoy to the Nagas

By Pliers Appleworth

The King's special diplomatic envoy has been dispatched to the Southern Hemisphere to try and re-establish diplomatic relations with the notoriously nomadic Naga community. The Nagas were last seen over two hundred years ago in the vicinity of Isla de los Estodos, off the Eastern coast of Argentina. The council are keen to offer out an 'olive branch' in the hope of forming a friendly, diplomatic relationship.

Play Fantasy Laminium Ball in Sunday's Paper

After a quick flick through the headlines, he decided to store the rest of the paper to peruse later. Concentrating hard in his mind, mentally he screwed up the paper into a ball, and threw it into a huge green bucket marked LATER on the front. Twice the size of the green one, a red bucket marked RUBBISH looked full to the hilt, on the edge of darkness, deep inside his mind.

Leaving the table, he grabbed his sandwiches from the fridge, sports jacket from the coat stand and keys from the bowl on the table by the front door, before jumping into his car, which, much to his surprise, started first time. He then headed off to work.

His dragon cover involved him working for the biggest employer in Salisbridge, Cropptech: a highly specialised and world renowned supplier of precious metals and valuable stones. Located on the western outskirts of the city, the main facility comprised a large office block, a small industrial area and a warehouse and logistics setup. The office complex housed the company's marketing, accounts, payroll, sales, administration, technical support, training and web management departments. The industrial aspect of the site dealt with the polishing and cutting of gems, refining and experimenting with rare and unstable metals. Responsibility for both the distribution of the newly cut gems and the safe delivery of the raw materials required, fell on the shoulders of the warehouse and logistics department.

Cropptech's interests didn't just extend to the site here. They had numerous mines, small specialist production facilities, experimental bore holes, as well as tiny satellite offices dotted all around the globe, making them one of the leading experts in their field. Set up some one hundred and twenty years ago, it has been a family run business ever since. Currently in charge was the last living descendant of that family, a confirmed bachelor in his late forties by the name of Al Garrett. Plain enough that he wouldn't stand out in a crowd, his lean frame and shiny bald head with just a few etchings of grey hair around his temples were neatly complemented by a ferocious looking, matching grey moustache. Known affectionately by his staff as the 'bald eagle', he never seemed to miss anything that was going on inside his company. On inheriting the firm twenty five years ago, it didn't take long for Garrett to figure out that it was on the verge of bankruptcy, with very

73

little in the way of future prospects. He was, however, a driven man and the thought of letting down the significant number of workers that he now employed, spurred him on to single-handedly turn the company's fortunes around, making it now one of the most financially prosperous corporations in Britain. As well as having brilliant business acumen and acquiring a substantial personal fortune (most of which he donated to charity), Garrett had become renowned for his generosity and the favourable way in which he treated his staff. Everyone who worked for him always thought of him as approachable and caring, with a wicked sense of humour that was almost legendary.

Richie and Peter both worked for Cropptech and had started there, straight out of the nursery ring, some three years ago. Working in the training department, Richie regularly ran courses on anything from the latest payroll software to new health and safety requirements. Positively thriving in that environment, she'd been promoted twice in her short tenure. Starting off as a guard on the nightshift in the security department, Peter's dedication and enthusiasm for the job had seen him promoted to Assistant Security Co-ordinator, working mainly days, with the odd night shift when holiday cover required it. He had his own tiny, ground floor office in the main block, just across the road from the main security gate outpost. A desk with a workstation, an array of grey metal filing cabinets, a bank of security monitors and a great view represented everything that kept him company while he was tucked away.

Peter's promotion into his new role thrust an enormous amount of responsibility onto his very young and inexperienced shoulders. Just as well he was a dragon, with a bucket load of training behind him. All that stood between him and Garrett in the chain of authority was the chief security co-ordinator, who had been off sick with a mysterious virus for a matter of weeks now, resulting in Peter reporting directly to the head honcho himself.

Dealing with Garrett on a daily basis had led Peter to re-evaluate his opinion of his boss. He'd thought the rumours of his generosity and kindness were all exaggerated, only to find out now that they were indeed all true, having witnessed some firsthand, as well as finding himself unexpectedly on the end of some of it. He now felt as though he had a rapport with Garrett, especially when the man himself constantly berated him for not using the term 'bald eagle', something Peter just couldn't get used to.

With everything going swimmingly at work, Peter couldn't wait to get to get in every day.

Parking his car, he walked briskly across the car park in the biting wind towards the security lodge at the main gate. Although no real need presented itself for him to go to the lodge, it was something of a habit he'd gotten into, to check that everything had gone smoothly the night before and that there were no outstanding issues. Smiling, he was reluctant to even admit to himself the other reason, which was the cheeky banter the staff threw his way, first thing in the morning. Having learned not only to take it, but to dish it out as well, it had become one of the highlights of his day, and his own personal mark that he'd put on the department in light of his direct superior's absence.

'Just as well they're excellent at their jobs,' he thought, twisting the handle of the white, double glazed door to the lodge. Squeezing through, out of the wind, he strode up the short corridor, past the water cooler, toilets and photocopier and rounded the corner, drawing to a halt at the open plan area.

"Good morning slaves," he announced sarcastically, ready for any and all x-rated replies. All he got instead, was a mumbled, "Morning."

Turning to Jessica Freeman, currently in charge, but also the closest, he leaned in towards her and whispered,

"What's going on?"

Jessica replied in a low voice,

"Not sure, but Mr Garrett wants to see you in his

office, ASAP."

"Mr Garrett?" replied Peter.

"Hmmmm... that's right," whispered Jessica, looking straight at Peter and rolling her eyes.

"Okay, ahhh, thanks, I think. I'll catch up with you a little later," said Peter, heading back the way he'd come in.

'Odd,' he thought as he crossed the road that separated the security lodge from the complex that housed his office. Sensing that something was out of the ordinary, he paused briefly in his office to hang up his jacket and put his lunch in the top drawer of his desk, before heading for the lift that would take him up to the fourth floor and Al Garrett's plush set of offices. On the way up in the lift, Peter caught his reflection in the mirrored walls and straightened his tie, determined to look professional as he strode down the long, oak panelled corridor, past Garrett's personal secretary whom he smiled at, all the while his feet sinking into the plush, expensive carpet. Stopping outside the oak door with a brass plaque on it that read 'Al Garrett Chief Executive', he took a deep breath and knocked twice. A growl of "ENTER," reverberated through the door from deep within. Letting out his breath, he turned the handle and went in.

Overpowering darkness was the first thing that struck Peter as strange, particularly given it was after nine am, and a beautifully sunny day outside. The second was not only the large, stocky figure peering through the drawn blinds of the window, behind Garrett's desk, with only his back on show, but the peculiar aroma that hung in the air throughout the room. All sorts of possibilities ran through his head, without much success. It was then that the seated Garrett peered up from behind his reading glasses.

"I've implemented some changes, effective immediately, that you need to know about Mr Bentwhistle," Garrett declared, very much out of character.

"Until further notice, every department head, yourself included, will report directly to Major Manson."

The man stood at the window turned round to face Peter, a charmless grin smothered across his face.

"Major Manson is from Darktech Technologies," continued Garrett, "a leading security consultancy. He will be carrying out a review of our security and operational procedures. I expect nothing but full co-operation from you and your staff. Do I make myself clear?"

"Absolutely Al," answered Peter, smiling.

"That's 'Mister Garrett' to you," announced a haughty voice from behind Garrett, dripping with condescension.

"He's right," added Garrett.

Looking straight into the unnaturally dark eyes of Major Manson, Peter needed all of his self control to keep his temper in check. Difficult to see in the lightless environment, he quickly applied his enhanced dragon senses to get a clearer picture of this uppity newcomer. Manson appeared stocky, but was about the same height as Peter. He had straight brown hair, or 'used to', Peter thought with a smirk. The left and the right side were now clearly having a race to see which could get to the back of his head first, that's how badly receding it was. Clean shaven with a square jaw, Peter hadn't been mistaken about his eyes. There was something just... wrong.

Garrett cleared his throat, jolting Peter from his train of thought.

"Sorry, MISTER Garrett, "Peter said with just a tinge of sarcasm.

"That will be all. You're dismissed," announced the Chief Executive, not even bothering to look up from the paperwork on his desk.

Frustrated, Peter wheeled round and headed out of the door without giving the other two a second glance. Barely managing not to slam the door on the way out, he returned to the lift, his head awash with thoughts, the first of which was, 'What the hell is going on?' Eccentric didn't even begin to cover it. The lighting, the bizarre smell, the whole, 'call me Al' one day, and then 'Mr Garrett' the next, and that's without even mentioning the elephant in the room. That made him smile, because of the very nearly direct comparison. Who was this security consultant, and why all of a sudden did the company need him? When Peter had used his senses to study the Major, he was half expecting to sense some sort of evil dragon. He hadn't of course, try as he might. There was nothing out of the ordinary about him. Nevertheless, something about the whole situation sat uneasily at the back of his mind. He vowed to keep a close eye on things, as he stepped out of the elevator.

Peter spent the next few hours skulking in his office, making sure everything was up together should the worst happen, like getting an inspection from his newly appointed, interim boss. On three occasions he spotted the man, once going into the security lodge, once on the way to the distribution depot, and then again getting a big black box out of a shiny new Mercedes in the car park. What stood out on each of these occasions was that Major Manson walked with a limp, and was aided by a stick, made from rich, dark wood with an ornate silver ornament on top. He couldn't tell exactly what it was from so far away, even using the security camera's zoom function.

After lunch, he paid another visit to the security lodge. Back in the familiar office, the unusual atmosphere stuck out like a sore thumb, with everyone there keeping their heads down and getting on with their work, in pretty much total silence. The atmosphere was most out of place for the normally jovial, well run, efficient department.

Having sorted out his paperwork and spoken to the members of his team, he walked down the corridor towards the exit. Weaving his way past the large photocopier, he felt like banging his head against the wall in frustration. Things had been working so well, everybody had seemed so happy... and now this. The atmosphere was terrible wherever he'd been today, and he was sure the staff... his friends, hated what had happened, but were too afraid to speak out. He couldn't really blame them. With a view to getting some perspective, he resolved to speak to Richie that night.

The end of the working day arrived, with Peter doing his normal trick of staying on just that bit later to avoid the worst of the traffic, in particular the queues out of the massive car parks from within Cropptech. Spending this last hour or so looking out of his office window and using the security cameras to try and gauge the mood of the workers all heading for their cars, he was puzzled to find only a few glum faces amongst the majority, who, on inspection, looked like their normal, happy selves. He wasn't sure if that bothered him more or not, after the kind of day he'd been through.

At precisely a quarter to six he grabbed his jacket and lunch box and, with his phone in his hand, raced across to his car which looked rather lonely in the depleted car park. Texting his friend on the way, he marvelled at how difficult it was for him to type and walk at the same time. Sending his message off into the ether, he jumped into his car and started it up. As he made a sharp turn, heading towards the exit, his headlights lit up the shiny black Mercedes that belonged to Major Manson. Shaking his head and uttering a very bad word under his breath, he made for home.

Richie's reply to his text startled him in the middle of cooking tea, and a small smile at her willingness to meet him later in the bar of the sports club peeked through his gruff demeanour, caused by his worst working day ever. Food eaten, household jobs done, he walked out of the front door with a spring in his step.

Pushing through the giant double glass doors, he skipped past the notice boards, deserted reception area/shop and turned the corner into the bar proper, only to be greeted by a riot of noise and colour. A raucous game of pool was taking place, in between some drinking. An even noisier battle was taking place between two stocky chaps on the arcade 'shoot-em-up' game off to one side. On top of all of that, drunken men enthusiastically playing a fruit machine and a dozen or so track suited males flipping a matchbox furiously, amid drinking their beer as fast as was humanly possible, all added to the atmosphere, if indeed that's how it could be described.

Closing his eyes and shaking his head, he had but one thought.

'PANTS... it's Wednesday!' A rugby coaching course had been going on all day, which went some way to explaining the ensuing chaos and high jinks. Weaving in and out the chairs and tables, narrowly missing the game of pool that looked as though it was about to turn into a contact sport, he reached the bar and ordered his usual: large diet Pepsi, lots of ice. Scanning the room for Richie, it didn't take long to spot her tucked away in the far corner, nursing her drink, on a table next to two young rugby players arm wrestling each other. Even from this distance she looked stunning. Long, dark brown, curly hair flowed down the back of her neck, framing her ever so cute face, completed by a freckly complexion and a petite body that perfectly mirrored her dragon form. For a few seconds he stood captivated by her beauty and thoughts of something he could never have, before realising that he probably looked a bit odd, which was enough in itself to get him scuttling on over in her direction. The closer he got to her table, the more apparent it was that the arm wrestling rugby players were trying to impress her with their macho deeds. Ignoring their scowls, he pulled up a chair and sat down opposite her. As he did so, one of the tough guys piped up,

"Look, it's one of the juniors from the hockey club."

His friend joined in the fun,

"You'd have thought it would have been well past his bedtime."

They both seemed to think this was hilarious, as they sat waiting for Peter to react. Richie leant in close to Peter, nodded her head in the direction of the two idiots and said,

"Aren't you going to say something?"

"It's not worth it," he whispered back, hoping the whole thing would just go away.

But Richie had other ideas. With the two drunken rugby players laughing louder than ever now, bringing their antics to the attention of the rest of the clubhouse, a mischievous glint flickered briefly in Richie's eyes. Before he could stop her, she stood and addressed the two rugby players, in a very loud and very confident voice.

"You two so-called real men think you're tough eh? I'll arm wrestle you both at the same time and still win. How about that?"

Everyone had now focused their attention on what was happening, including all the staff. If nothing else, the challenge had momentarily wiped the smile from the two drunken rugby players' faces because they, like most there, were well aware of Richie's reputation, not only as a supreme athlete, but as someone capable of 'pulling a rabbit out of a hat' anytime she liked, so to speak. Deep down they knew her to be formidable and not someone to be trifled with, but as they looked her up and down, taking in her diminutive frame and her skinny little biceps, the alcohol kicked in.

"No problem luv," said one, as they simultaneously slammed their fists down on the table.

Almost as one, the rest of the room shook their head, rubbed their eyes, and then SMILED! As everyone slowly gathered round to watch, the two rugby players took a seat next to each other.

"You sure you wanna do us both at the same time?" one tittered.

Again the crowd shook their heads, all speculating inside their minds about the amount of humiliation that was about to be dished out.

"We'll try not to hurt you luv," slurred the slightly less drunk of the two.

This was going to be BAD!

Richie sat relaxed in her chair, smiling confidently at the two fools, as she put both her elbows on the table and offered out her petite hands. Having a pretty good idea of just how this was going to go, Peter couldn't watch. Once each of the rugby players had taken a hand, someone in the crowd started to count down.

"5... 4..."

The rugby players' biceps positively bulged as their arms tensed.

"3... 2..."

The smile still on her face, Richie closed her eyes and...

"1!"

SMASH!!!!!!!! The two rugby players yelped with pain as their bruised hands bounced back up from the undamaged table.

"Thanks guys," Richie scoffed, as she got up and performed a mock bow for the crowd, who all, right on cue, erupted with applause and laughter.

Heading off through the crowd towards the bar, the two rugby players were mocked and ridiculed relentlessly.

Dropping back into her seat opposite Peter, with everyone having dispersed, Richie took a big swig of her drink, before looking at Peter and saying,

"That's how you handle them."

"That's not really how we're supposed to do things... is it?" replied Peter, rolling his eyes for effect.

"Yeah, yeah, yeah."

"It's not exactly BLENDING in, is it?" he whispered, sternly. "If the Council heard about all this, you'd be in so much trouble."

"You don't get it Pete. I don't care. Some of these humans desperately need some lessons in manners."

"I can't say I disagree with you. But it's not your job to teach them."

"Isn't it?!" declared Richie. "I don't stop being who or WHAT I am as soon as the clock strikes five and I head for home every day. And you can't tell me you don't either. So why shouldn't our mandate extend a little further? If you ask me, our roles do extend outside our jobs, and this is exactly the kind of thing we should be doing."

Abruptly the two friends brought their conversation to a halt, realising that someone was approaching the table. Richie's beautiful face cracked a grin as one of the shamed, arm wrestling rugby players approached carrying fresh drinks for them both.

"We're both very sorry... and... um... have both learned a valuable lesson today," he managed to stutter, looking as though he'd sobered up considerably over the course of the last few minutes.

"Good," quipped Richie, raising the fresh glass in his direction, the natural balance of things restored, with her looking cooler than a polar bear in the Arctic, eating an ice cream, sponsored by Ferrari.

With the ambient noise having dropped to its lowest since he'd arrived, Peter figured now was his chance to talk to his friend about work.

"So, how's your day been Rich?" he asked.

Still smirking from her easily won victory, she pondered the question for a few seconds before replying.

"Pretty quiet really. Health and safety training this morning, which was all over by lunch time, so quite an easy afternoon."

"You haven't heard then, about a new consultant guy that Garrett's brought in?"

"Oh you mean Major Manson."

"That's the one," muttered Peter, frowning.

"What a charming man. We were all introduced to him this afternoon when Al showed him around our offices. I'd say he'll fit in nicely around here."

"WHAT!!!" fumed Peter, nearly knocking over his drink. "You've got to be kidding me!"

A worried look on her face, Richie leaned across the table and took hold of Peter's hand.

"What is it? What's the matter?"

He snatched his hand away from Richie's grasp, shaking ever so slightly. Richie decided she'd wait for him to explain what the problem was. Letting his anger drift away, after a short while he took a sip of his drink, looked his friend in the face, and continued.

"Could you not see how he was manipulating Garrett?"

"What on earth do you mean?" she responded, puzzled.

Trying his best to keep calm, he said,

"Major Manson, the guy from Darktech, has got some sort of hold on Garrett... I'm sure of it."

"What makes you say that?"

Over the next fifteen minutes, Peter explained what had happened that day, particularly the encounter with Manson in Garrett's office, the darkness, the smell, the odd behaviour... all of it. Richie listened intently, not interrupting once. After having finished, he waited patiently for her take in his views, giving her the time and space she'd afforded him earlier. Not knowing quite what to make of Peter's account, she dived in head first, explaining how they'd been introduced that afternoon by Garrett, and how after the guided tour, all of her colleagues had gone on and on about just how considerate, witty and charming the new man had seemed. Almost the perfect gentleman you could say. Needless to say, Richie's experience was almost a polar opposite to his encounter, and was about as far removed as it was possible to be. Richie rounded off her tale by saying that Al Garrett had dropped by much later on, to ask the staff's opinion of Manson. Everyone had told him what they thought, with nearly all agreeing that they'd be happy to report to him regularly. For his part, Garrett went on to explain the reason for Manson being there was to gain fresh perspective and insight into the way the company operates, and to take a little bit of the responsibility and pressure away from himself, which everyone agreed, after he'd left, could only be a good thing.

After Richie had finished recounting her story, the two friends sat in silence for a good few minutes, both gazing into the bottom of their almost drained glasses. By this time the clubhouse was nearly empty, but that didn't stop Peter from looking around conspiratorially, making sure no one was listening in.

"Listen Rich, I know from everything you've said, that you can't see anything untoward in what's going on, but I swear to you on our friendship that there's something very wrong with this Manson guy."

There was a long pause as Peter considered his next words carefully.

"It's almost like he's... one of us."

"Are you INSANE?" countered Richie, lowering her voice immediately. "We'd know if he was a dragon; we'd sense him, and he just isn't."

"I know he doesn't feel like a dragon," retorted Peter, "but... there's something else that just makes him feel really, really wrong to everyone of my senses."

"Have you considered the possibility that your dislike for him stems from the fact that he's just waltzed into Cropptech, and you've gotten off on the wrong foot? Or that you don't like the thought of having to report to someone new, someone who's been here less time than you have?"

"I know it sounds a bit like that Rich, but there's more to it than that, I'm sure. You have to believe me... please. I've never been so sure about anything in my entire life," Peter pleaded.

"Enough with the begging, alright. I'll do what I can to keep an eye on him, as should you. With both of us working together, nothing suspicious or out of the ordinary will go unnoticed. Deal?"

"Deal," agreed Peter cheerfully.

With proceedings concluded, and both of them stifling yawns, the friends deposited their empty glasses on the bar, and after a quick goodnight embrace in the car park, went their separate ways.

Driving home, Peter wasn't sure what to make of their conversation. Glad that Richie had agreed to keep a watchful eye on Manson, but concerned that the entire office staff thought him to be a decent chap. As he slipped into bed, he hoped things would look better after a full night's sleep.

Following his normal routine, right down to the letter, the next morning. It was only when he'd closed the front door and headed down the path to his car that he realised the difference between this day and all the rest. For the first time ever, he wasn't looking forward to going into work. Quite the opposite in fact.

Thursday and Friday passed without incident at work. Atmosphere wise, in the security department, it was pretty much as it had been, an overwhelming cauldron of negativity, leaving the staff there with little choice but to knuckle down and get on with their work, with not a hint of the little jokes or quirky humour that Peter so loved.

For him, Friday was spent touring the whole site, checking security standards and protocol, making sure that as a company they were being extra vigilant, not wishing to give Manson any cause to pick fault with his work, but also it was an excuse to gauge the mood of a larger cross section of Cropptech employees, and get some sort of insight into just how they were feeling.

For the most part, the workers across the rest of the facility appeared happy and productive. Not sure what to make of all of this, he replayed that day over and over in his mind, wondering if, as Richie had suggested, he'd made a mistake, or jumped to a rash conclusion. Could it all be completely innocent, with him being the one to blow everything out of proportion with his vivid imagination? Despite going over it dozens of times, he still didn't think he was wrong. Something else he found suspicious was that Al Garrett had stayed in his office throughout normal working hours all day on Thursday, something that was practically unheard of. He'd checked.

'Very unusual,' he thought as he wandered the entire site, whilst also trying to keep an eye out for Major Manson, without much success. From reviewing the recordings in his office, he could see that the Major returned to his parked car every three to four hours, sitting in it for approximately five minutes, before heading back up to Garrett's office. It was impossible to see what exactly he was doing, due to the heavily darkened windows across the whole car, but he pondered all of this right up to the point that he left for home, his head buzzing with everything that had gone on that week. The only thing he knew at the moment was that he was glad it was the weekend.

4 A TICKET TO THE BALL? LAMINIUM BALL

Walking from the car to the front door cleared his head of all the doubt and confusion he had about work. Turning the key in the lock felt like a breath of fresh air. Cogs in the machine all suddenly lining up, he realised that it being Friday night could only mean one thing... laminium ball!

With a renewed energy he sprinted upstairs, swapping his suit for jeans and a T-shirt. Buoyed by knowing that his rumbling stomach, instead of being quelled by a ready meal from the fridge, would have an assortment of delicious treats from the food stalls at the stadium to choose from, he descended the stairs in two giant leaps.

Pulling shut the curtains in every room of the house before picking up his wallet, keys and phone, he raced into the sitting room and pulled hard on the Galileo thermometer atop the piano. Silently, the light coloured instrument swung out from the corner of the room, revealing a gaping hole through which the top of the Victorian spiral staircase was just visible. Tugging the thermometer again as he sprinted past, winding his way down into the darkness, he'd just reached the floor as the hole in the ceiling closed fully, encasing him in the total pitch black. Needing no help in the dark, he snaked in and around all the obstacles, before reaching up with his left hand, standing in front of what he knew to be the secret exit. Running his hand along the uneven wall, he finally found an innocuous, finger sized hole next to a beam. Thrusting his finger in as far as it would go, the welcoming sound of tiny cogs and gears moving into place, which he always associated with a pleasurable return to the underground world of the dragons... his home, tickled his sensitive ear lobes.

Sprinting down the stone steps and vaulting the wall at

the bottom to land perfectly on the walkway that led to the monorail station, he knew there was no time to lose, so broke into a jog, his keys jangling in the pocket of his light blue jeans as he did so. Moments later he slid to a halt on the shiny marble floor, ignoring the incredible sensation from the aromas of all the delectable food, carried on the breeze throughout the station plaza, despite the protests from his stomach. Getting busier with every second that passed, nervously he scanned the concourse for his friend who'd procured the tickets for the game. Startled as a large hand dropped onto his shoulder, he whirled around, only to end up staring right into his friend's battered, bruised and smiling face.

"Crikey, you're a bit jumpy aren't you?" teased Tank.

"Sorry," replied Peter, patting his friend on the back. "Rough week at work. Must be getting to me."

"It's great to see you, but we need to hurry if we're going to get there in time for me to grab some food before the match starts."

Tank let out a raucous laugh, alarming more than a few passing passengers.

"That's what I love about you Peter. For someone so small, you're always thinking about your belly."

'It's true,' thought Peter. 'I am nearly always thinking about my stomach. Must be the dragon in me.'

Tank, like Richie, very much mirrored his natural form with his human guise. He was huge, a mountain of a man. Well over six feet tall, with a body packed full of muscle, rugby had certainly been the right choice for him. He had sparkling blue eyes, and what would have been a wild array of floppy blonde hair had it not been cut so short, primarily for the sport he loved. Always clean shaven, his face looked like a cross between Desperate Dan and Action Man, apart from his nose, which looked as though it had taken one too many punches on the rugby pitch, either that, or he'd taken up chasing parked cars.

The two friends hastily boarded the Burton-upon-Trent

bound monorail carriage, where tonight's match was taking place. Nearly two hundred miles away, and at least three hours in a car, the journey below ground was expected to take about twenty five minutes. Taking place beneath England's beautiful Peak District in a huge, purpose built cavern, they both had tickets for the Burton side of the stadium, which would tonight be acting as the home side. Agreeing not at all on the predicted outcome of the match, they argued, much to the other passengers' amusement, all the way there.

"Steel will be man of the match, and we'll get through to the Global Cup 4-2," announced Peter excitedly, all the time clutching the shiny silver ticket that his friend had given him.

"Steel's good, I'll give you that, but I'm pretty sure it'll be Silverbonce that will be man of the match. He's as good as a couple of goals saved, even before they start. We'll win 6-2, mark my words."

"Six!" exclaimed Peter. "You think we'll get six? Have you been eating butterflies again? How many laminium ball matches have you ever seen where a team scores six? You must be mad."

"At least we both agree the Warriors will win, and get through to the Global Cup," uttered Tank.

Peter nodded his agreement as the sleek, silver carriage whizzed them towards their destination, and a night of full on team sport.

That was how it progressed all the way to the Burton monorail station, lots of friendly banter about the game, all thoughts of anything else forgotten.

For those of you that don't know what laminium ball is, perhaps I should explain. Since before records began, dragons have been playing this as a sport and sooooo much more.

Laminium ball is almost the equivalent of football. Groomed for decades, after which only the best are selected and thrust into the limelight of the biggest full on sporting battle on the planet, the players can look forward to league and cup matches coming thick and fast throughout the season, pitching dragon against dragon in unmatched, adrenaline fuelled, jaw dropping action. Constant jeopardy, gut wrenching challenges from fully committed players on both sides, all at eye wateringly high speeds, put the sport on a pedestal like no other to dragons as a whole. If a human somehow managed to watch one of these matches, they'd need to find a whole new definition of the word sport.

Played in specially designed caverns located across the world, the playing zone in each is two miles long, a quarter of a mile wide and half a mile high, with a river of burning lava running beneath. Embedded in the cavern's walls, about half way up at each end of the two mile long stretch of playing area, are two 'mouths'. In the middle of each 'mouth' sit six stalagmites and six stalactites, joined in the middle, known as the 'teeth'. The game itself can last for up to two hours, unless all six of the 'teeth' are knocked down before then. The winner is declared to be the side that has knocked out the most 'teeth' during the two hour time span. It is incredibly rare for any team to knock all six 'teeth' out, happening on average every decade or so.

Dragon teams competing against each other consist of four outfielders and one 'mouth guard'. Outfielders are allowed to control the laminium ball with any part of their body, with most preferring, and trained, to use their tail, and are able to dribble, slap, roll, slam, tackle, intercept as well as perform tricks with the ball.

Once any of the outfielders think they are in range, they can attempt to shoot at the 'mouth'. The 'mouth guard' can stop the ball hitting the 'teeth' with any part of his body, from the tip of his tail, to the end of his nose.

As the name suggests, the ball itself is made of laminium, covered in a coat of ionised platinum, making it all but unbreakable and even able to withstand a substantial amount of time submerged beneath the lava foundation. Teams make good use of this by performing dangerous 'flying dives' that start high up in the arena and end up with the player diving into the lava, popping up somewhere near the opposition's 'mouth', making it so outrageously difficult for the 'mouth guard' to defend against. Encased at the centre of the ball, the metal after which the game is named, laminium, is incredibly precious and rare, and is highly valued by dragons because of the magical way it can enhance a dragon's own natural abilities. Boosting their telepathic talents, enhancing their strength, stamina and reaction times, as well as adding power to any mantra cast, these are just a few of the long list of wicked side effects that close proximity to the hard to extract metal, can have. Only found in exceedingly small quantities, usually deep underground in remote and inaccessible areas, it is one of the more valuable things that Cropptech specialise in, hence the reason for dragon infiltration of the company at all levels. Guarding the prized metal, for fear of it being stolen and falling into the wrong hands, has long since been a dragon concern, and to this very day, remains a very high priority for the Council and the king himself. Down to the tiniest amount, dragons have records that span back centuries, covering any laminium mined, traded, or experimented on. Using a whole host of different shell companies, the dragon world, through one channel or another, receives every ounce of laminium that is discovered in the world. A considerable amount is used in their favourite sport, with most of the rest stored safely away. Far in the past, the cherished metal was used to make everyday items, worn to show one's status and power ranking. Jewellery was popular... necklaces, earrings, rings, brooches, all of that, allowing the wearer to not only show off their wealth and any sway they might have, but also magically enhancing their powers, there and then. A double whammy so to speak. Rumours have abounded over the centuries of much bigger and more powerful pieces. Individual items of armour, embossed tome covers, timepieces and even weapons were all reported, at different times, to have been crafted, before being stolen, and then of course lost. Occasionally the odd item or trinket has surfaced, causing a stir in the papers and a frantic bidding war, but these are usually only tiny items of jewellery. With these minuscule mites of metal being coveted so, it's easy to see how the much larger sphere of the precious metal, hidden beneath layers of platinum, would attract so much interest, and heighten the powers of the player on the ball. It can also make it mighty hard for the opposition to wrestle the ball away from the player who has it, making possession key for every team that plays.

For each team to be easily recognised by the spectators during the match, the players from the two teams are allocated different coloured auras, dished out in the form of a mantra, before the game by the referee. Normally the opposing teams have red and blue mantras, with the referee enveloped in an all green one.

More than just sport, laminium ball has become a way of life for many dragons, following their heroes in the papers, as well as attending home matches, travelling across the globe in some cases for away games, buying all the merchandise, and emulating the players in everything they do. With so much coverage given over to the teams and matches in the telepathic press, the players themselves are treated very much like gods, or rock stars. Once selected and part of a team, nothing other than a career crushing injury or retirement can remove that dragon from that team's squad. That's why getting selected is so important, it's like tenure... there for life. Only a small percentage of hopefuls are chosen to compete in this male only sport. To be a celebrated laminium ball player sounds perfect, and most would agree that it was, with but one exception, the one sacrifice those players had to make. Under no circumstance were they ever allowed on the surface. So highly valued were they that no risk, however insignificant, could be taken with their safety. Nearly all of them were okay with that; why wouldn't they be? So the decades in which normal adolescent dragons were taught how to transform and maintain human guises, were instead used to learn about flight, fight, character, and teamwork. It was by no means easy, but for those who reached the top, it was a magnificent achievement and the fulfilment of dragonling dreams.

On their way to Burton to watch the match between the Indigo Warriors (Southern England) and the Crimson Crusaders (Northern England), the two friends were mad keen on laminium ball and huge supporters of the Warriors, having both been brought up in Southern England.

Each laminium ball player is easily as famous as any sporting figure from the human world above. All receive an amazing amount of daily fan mail, with offers of mating or bonding, endorsement opportunities, or dragons just wanting to be their friends and hang out. Each and every player features heavily in all the telepathic papers: their black and white pictures blazed all across the back pages, everyday, accompanied by rumours and gossip of new mates, new scale colouring, a new home or some exotic new training regime that would change the team's fortune, and the Indigo Warriors were no exception. Legends to their fans, even though they'd won nothing for the past fifty years, underachieving with their current squad for the last ten, the one thing you could be assured of was that there was always HOPE! Each time they played, they always gave everything they'd got. They might lack the talent of the other teams in places, but nearly always made up for it with blood, guts and thunder. Their fans could ask for nothing more.

The Warriors team consisted of Steel (Captain), Flamer, Cheese, Barf, Silverbonce (Mouth Guard) and Zip (Substitute). Their names were with them forever now, but that hadn't always been the case. Laminium ball players are given new names on turning professional and being picked to represent a team. Chosen by a panel of experienced judges, any number of reasons can be taken into account for a new name, once that player has reached the required standard. The judges will have watched the young players all trying to make the grade, so will be familiar with their personalities, traits and quirks. Once chosen by the judges, that name can never be taken back. Scary for some, a celebration for most, as it represents the culmination of many decades of work.

Both friends could recite every detail of the Indigo Warriors squad. Steel was aptly named because he had nerves of steel and had proved so many times, never ducking a challenge or tackle, sometimes winding up with the most horrendous injury because of it. Flamer was so called because of his highly powered breath which produced the most extraordinary amount of heat and flame extension... something many of his opponents could attest to. Cheese only ever seemed to eat cheese, and had often claimed that his diet was what gave him the incredible turn of speed whenever he needed it, although some fans of other teams claim he'd been named that because he smelt of cheese. Quirkily, he never seemed to appear in a photograph without a piece of cheese, unless it was during a laminium ball match. The ever so slightly eccentric one of the team, he was incredibly popular with the fans.

Barf had been named because of his sheer resilience. During the final match to choose which dragons were going to make it as professionals he'd become seriously ill, something incredibly rare for a dragon. A medical opinion suggested he shouldn't have even been at the game, let alone been playing. Against the expert's better judgement, they let him play. Performing poorly by his own high standards for most of the game, he could feel his chances of selection slipping away with every passing second. Determined to give it his all for the remaining few minutes, he produced the tackle of the game, which unfortunately for him took place during a steep power dive towards the lava. Approaching his opponent, the speed and angle of the descent caused his poorly stomach to react violently. Even though he was throwing up with the kind of power not even seen in most human babies, he carried on and made the incredible tackle, moving the ball onto one of his teammates, who went on to score. His team won the match, and he became a professional player. Hence the name... Barf.

Silverbonce, the Warriors oldest, and most famous player, and their 'mouth guard', had gained his name because of the colouring of his scales. Common for dragons to be named in this way, after either a specialised colouring or a particular pattern, in this case the silver that encircled his skull before flowing halfway down his back, merging seamlessly with the rest of his rather pale green body, was the reason for his given moniker. Having constantly seen off competition for his place, and more recently, calls for his retirement, more often than not he'd saved the team by pulling something from his substantial bag of tricks, gained from the years of experience that made him not only the oldest on the team, but the oldest professional Laminium ball player EVER! If fans of opposing teams across the world had to name and favour one Indigo Warrior, it most certainly would have been him, not just because of how long he'd been going, but because almost certainly he was the most cunning and craftiest dragon ever to have played the game.

Last but by no means least, was Zip, the squad substitute, whose name stemmed from the mottled cream and gold colouring that traversed the length of his belly, so much so that when he was flying, his underneath looked as though it were held together with a giant zip.

Having suffered a disastrous league season by their standards, the Global Cup represented the only chance for the Warriors to win a trophy. Qualifying would be an achievement of some sort, as they had not done so in their history, having never before reached this far (one round, one match away). They would not, however, underestimate their opponents, the Crimson Crusaders, who would be anything but a pushover, particularly given that they sat second in the league's top tier, and whose form would suggest they were on fire, sometimes quite literally. For the Warriors to get this far and fail to go through would be devastating, not only for Peter and Tank, but the rest of their devoted fans who'd turned out in their tens of thousands to offer their support.

Exiting the monorail at Burton, the two friends followed the crowd along the walkways that led to the underground stadium. All but carried along in the midst of a throng of other dragons, most of whom displayed something to show off their allegiance to one team or the other, Peter and Tank were bowled over by just how many spectators had turned up to take in the match.

Rounding a sharp bend, the merging paths began a shallow descent, eventually opening up into a colossal mall, leaving everything that little bit less packed. On either side of the mall, wide burrows had been excavated out of the rock faces, making space for traders to set up their shops, plying their stunning selection of goods to all plodding past. Originally opening up into more space, the further into the mall they got, the more crowded it seemed to get. Yes, there were thousands of dragons, many in their natural form, all heading in the same direction, but there didn't seem more than there had before. And then suddenly the friends spotted the reason why. Smack back down the middle of the mall, a long line of market stalls had been erected to provide even more vendors the opportunity to promote their material. That, combined with all the dragons slowing down on the outside to look at each of the merchant's products, had created a dam in the almost unstoppable river of dragons that wove its way forward towards the many different gates of the stadium.

Staying close together and working on the theory that if you can't beat them, join them, the two friends started browsing some of the shops and stalls, ignoring all of those selling Crimson Crusader memorabilia.

Bustling their way to the front of the crowd, the first stall they came to appeared to be selling mantras. Dodging left and right, desperately trying to look over the shoulder of the gentleman shaped dragon in front of him, hoping to glance the demonstration that was going on, all Peter could really see was the vendor reading something aloud. Wondering just what all the fuss was about, a brilliant bright explosion followed by an ear splitting WHOOSH, abruptly caused him to jump, as a firework shaped like a dragon flew straight up into the air, before exploding with a loud BANG. Bits of bright, fiery exploding dragon rained down and then, completely unexpectedly, formed the words STEEL IS THE BEST in brilliant blue writing, hanging there for a few moments before burning itself out, from one end to the other.

"Available for every member of the Indigo Warriors team, including Zip!" shouted the owner of the shop, out across the heads of the crowd, no mean feat in the case of some of the dragons. A mad scramble ensued as everyone tried to get to the front to purchase the particularly worded mantra they wanted. Three minutes later, the crowd thinning out, both Peter and Tank emerged relatively happy, having got a mantra each; Peter had the last one for Steel, while Tank had gone for one with Silverbonce's name on it.

Continuing to browse the stalls and shops at a leisurely pace, on reaching the end they both looked like an advertiser's dream. As well as the mantras, they both sported mammoth floppy blue hats that had 'INDIGOS RULE' written on them, had matching blue rosettes and scarves, as well as a bin sized bucket of multicoloured, flavoured charcoal sticks each.

A huge food court connected the end of the mail with

the multiple entrances of the stadium, where massive queues of dragons tailed back from each tiny ticket booth. Once again Peter's sensitive nostrils were tickled by the overpowering aroma of the sensational food on offer, so much so that the grumbling from his stomach got him looks from other dragons over twenty feet away. He cast his eye about like a predatory eagle looking for that solitary fish.

"Don't tell me you're hungry..." Tank quipped, catching sight of his friend's eye-popping gaze at all the food on offer.

"Sorry, I didn't have time for something earlier."

"Gosh, I'm shocked," replied Tank shaking his head. "Well, I'm going to the seats. I don't want to miss the start."

"I'll be really quick. Can I get you anything?"

"No, I'm fine thanks," answered Tank, before turning away and heading towards ticket booth number three.

After a quick scout around, Peter decided to join the queue for the delicious smelling charcoal and bacon omelettes. Tenth in line, he waited patiently as a booming voice announced over the PA system that the match would start in ten minutes. All of a sudden, out of nowhere, a foot kicked him just behind his left knee, causing him to drop to the polished floor. Ignoring the pain, he leapt to his feet, coming face to face with three chuckling youths, all sporting the colours of the Crusaders.

"Ah, look who it is guys. It's Bentwhistle!" one sneered, as the others burst into laughter.

"Where are your two girlfriends then... Richie and Twonk?" All three doubled over at this, all clutching their stomachs with mirth.

Peter closed his eyes, wishing that he was anywhere else but here. The three dragons in front of him were former nursery ring classmates of his and had picked on him throughout his whole time there, when Tank and Richie hadn't been around. He hadn't seen Theobald, Fisher and

Casey since graduating, and by the look of things not one of them had matured at all since leaving. The same sense of dread and foreboding rushed through his body, just as it had all those years ago when he was being bullied.

"So Benty, what have you been up to over the years?" snarled Casey.

"Sewer cleaner probably," chipped in Fisher.

"Probably had to work his way up to that," blurted Theobald, punching Peter in the shoulder.

Peter fought back a grimace, knowing from firsthand experience that he shouldn't show any pain. Although the punch had deliberately looked playful to those all around, Theobald had clearly added more than a little dragon power to it, intending to inflict as much pain as possible in the sneakiest kind of way, in this very public place.

Forcing a smile to his lips, Peter announced proudly,

"I'm head of security at Cropptech, actually."

"The rest of the employees must be monkeys then if that's the case," Casey growled.

"Perhaps we should see how tough the head of security really is?" suggested Theobald, a menacing look in his eyes.

Abruptly, Theobald was hoisted three feet into the air by the scruff of his neck. Swiftly turning around, Theobald raised his fists ready to strike until, that is, he was met by the large steely eyes of... Tank.

"Is there a problem, Tiny?" asked Tank softly.

Theobald looked to his friends for support but they, like the cowards they naturally were, had backed off some way and were looking distinctly uninterested in getting involved now that Tank had shown up.

"Umm... errr... I... no problem. Just catching up on old times. Isn't that right Bent... I mean, Peter?"

Theobald hung in the air like meat on a butcher's hook, gazing submissively across at Peter. The scuffle had, by now, attracted the attention of lots of onlookers, all wondering what was going on and if they needed to intervene.

In his mind, Peter imagined Tank using his big fists to punch Theobald halfway across the food court, sending him smashing into one of the ticket booths. He knew it was the wrong thing to think, but it did at least give him a momentary sense of satisfaction.

"It's okay Tank. We were just... catching up," stated Peter, almost reluctantly, secretly wanting the bully to hang there indefinitely.

"Ah... well if that's the case..." Tank said, lowering Theobald gently to the ground.

Once his feet were firmly on the ground and he was out of Tank's reach, Theobald's expression turned to one of rage, his face turning a fetching shade of scarlet.

"Nice seeing you both again," he blustered sarcastically, before mouthing the words "I'll get you for this," to Peter, making sure he turned away so that Tank couldn't see. Like a lost dog looking for its owner, he quickly shot off into the crowd in search of his friends, who had mysteriously developed an acute case of spine-turning-to-jelly and had legged it.

Turning to Peter, Tank asked,

"You okay?"

"I'm fine thanks," replied Peter, a little downcast.

"You know you should stand up to them," Tank whispered, as the two of them shuffled forward in the food queue. "It's all bluster and bravado, as you've just seen. Underneath, they're as scared of you, as you are of them."

"I know, I know," said Peter. "It's just not that easy. As soon as I saw them my legs turned to jelly and my stomach started doing somersaults, the exact same feelings I used to get when they bullied me in the nursery ring.

Gently, Tank placed his hand on his friend's shoulder and said,

"I know it's not easy, I do. But I also know that you have it in you to stand and be counted."

"Thanks, that means a lot coming from you," Peter

replied, sheepishly. "Just out of interest, how did you know I was in trouble?"

Tank burst into a great big belly laugh and looked down at Peter, a huge grin chiselled into his face.

"I didn't know. I just changed my mind about wanting something to eat."

The two friends chuckled all the way to the front of the queue.

Having bought an omelette each, the two of them made their way past the ticket booth and then into their seats with mere moments to spare. Tiny crystals in the roof of the stadium dimmed, leaving only the fiery hot, bubbling lava, for illumination. A trumpeted fanfare echoed around the giant cavern, signalling the build-up to the players' arrival.

Suddenly, five red blurs and five blue blurs, on exactly the opposite sides of the stadium appeared. The blurs performed a circuit of the lava at speed, flying only a couple of metres above the roiling magma, much to the crowd's delight. The match hadn't even started yet and the crowd were going wild, stomping their feet, clapping their hands, shouting, cheering, blowing rip roaring streams of flame from their mouths, with a few even letting mantas off, just like the ones Peter and Tank had purchased. It was chaos. It was also... intoxicating. The noise, the smell, the atmosphere, all sent shivers up the dragons' spines. All thoughts of their everyday life forgotten, nothing now existed apart from those dragons about to do battle with each other, all for the chance to go through to the Global Cup proper. Let the action begin.

As suddenly as they had appeared, the teams stopped and flew up to the middle of the purpose built cavern, hovering there for all to see. Announcing to the crowd that the Crimson Crusaders would be playing in the red aura and the Indigo Warriors in the blue, the commentator wished both teams luck, before signing off.

A countdown of ten red crystals above each 'mouth' at

both ends of the stadium, started to glow, and then individually wink out. As it did so, the crowd began to chant.

"9... 8... 7... 6... 5... 4... 3..."

The noise was almost unbearable.

"2... 1..."

Abruptly the crystals in the ceiling burst back on, illuminating the whole cavern. Out of a hole in the roof shot a glowing silver ball, about the size of a football. Quick as a flash, the dragons were on to it, batting it with their tails, moving faster than the eye could see, the human eye that is. With their enhanced senses, the dragon audience registered every millisecond of action. As the outfielders fought doggedly for possession of the laminium ball, tackling, blocking and dodging as if their lives depended on it, the 'mouth guards' from both teams beat hasty retreats back towards the areas they were tasked to defend.

The game itself was a scrappy affair; to say it was by no means a classic, was something of an understatement. But the fans loved every second of it, and were constantly on the edge of their seats, given exactly what was at stake. At one point, Barf made an awesome interception from one of the opposition's outfielders, speeding off towards the 'mouth' the Warriors were attacking, rounding their 'mouth guard', and having a shot at an open 'mouth'. As he did so, Tank and Peter, along with nearly every other Indigo Warrior fan there, stood and willed him to score. Unbelievably, he missed, by some margin. Tank raised his hands to his head in dismay, but as he did so, realised just a little too late that he'd let go of the rest of his omelette. He spent the next few minutes apologising profusely to the nice family sitting in front of him, much to Peter's amusement.

Silverbonce made some absolutely stunning saves throughout the match, with nearly everybody agreeing, whether at the match, or in the newspapers the next day, that the Warriors would have been heavily defeated without him.

In the end, the game, scrappy as it was, was decided by one moment of brilliance. Silverbonce slapped the ball out to Steel who was high up, right at the top of the cavern. Bringing the ball beautifully under control, Steel tucked the ball under one arm and dropped down into a steep dive towards the lava, catching everyone, even his own teammates, by surprise, as he was still in his defensive half of the cavern, and way too far out to perform a 'flying dive'. With nobody in range to tackle him, Steel had a free run at the lava, and by the time he hit the surface, he was travelling at an alarming speed. Nobody could believe what they were seeing, all sure that it was some kind of bluff. As the seconds drained away, with Steel still missing, the Crimson Crusaders 'mouth guard' looked at first perplexed, and then worried. Fearing something dreadful had happened beneath the lava, the 'mouth guard' lost his concentration momentarily. In a fiery haze of smoking hot magma, up popped Steel behind the 'mouth guard', letting fly with the ball in one swift move. Striking one of the middle teeth true, the Warriors went in front.

Supporters from every corner of the stadium went absolutely mad, even most of the Crusader followers. Quick thinking on Peter's part led him to let off his STEEL IS THE BEST mantra, swiftly followed by everyone else that had splashed out on one. The glowing blue words lit up most of the cavern. Nobody had ever seen a goal like it. All of the Crimson Crusaders were dumbstruck. After that, they tried to get back into the match, but unsurprisingly, their confidence was shot, ending up lucky to lose by such a close margin.

As the final horn trumpeted, Warriors fans celebrated like never before, barely able to believe their team had made it through to the Global Cup for the first time in their history, with a shot at becoming the best on the planet.

Partying well into the night, most fans chose to celebrate at the stadium's food court and mall. The friends were both glad it was Saturday tomorrow, with both intent on having a lie-in before turning out for their respective hockey and rugby teams in the afternoon.

Much later, well into the early hours of the following day, Peter and Tank sat giddy with joy on the monorail, heading back to Salisbridge. Surrounded by a mixture of fans coming back from the match and everyday dragons going about their business, they were not only ecstatic at the result, but almost hoarse from all the screaming they'd done.

"I'll try and get tickets for the first round of the Global Cup," rasped Tank over the noise of the continuing festivities in the carriage.

"That would be great, but it could be absolutely anywhere on the planet, as not all the qualifiers have been played yet," responded Peter, as the words 'SILVERBONCE FOR KING' came whizzing down the carriage, narrowly missing his floppy hat, casting an eerie blue reflection in the darkened windows of the monorail car. Clearly not all the mantras had been used at the match.

Pulling into Salisbridge station at exactly 4.12am, Peter came to the conclusion that even with his supposed lie-in, he still wouldn't get very much sleep. Parting, sleepy eyed, the two went their separate ways, each knowing they would see the other later on in the day at the sports club. Ten minutes later, Peter was tucked up in bed, dreaming of Steel's audacious move and wishing that he could perform something amazing like that on the hockey pitch, later on that day.

5 SMOKIN'

Blaring into life at precisely twelve-thirty, the alarm shattered Peter's deep slumber, with the light from around the ill-fitting curtains in his bedroom preventing him from going back to sleep, despite burying his head firmly beneath his pillows for some time. Even though he felt exhausted, he grudgingly admitted defeat and threw back the duvet, planting his feet firmly on the floor. Slipping straight into his hockey kit, he stopped only to grab a bite to eat, his sticks and change of clothes already in the car. Fifteen minutes after waking up, he pulled into the overflowing car park of the sports club.

Walking to the changing rooms, he bumped into a few of his new found human teammates, who gave him a ribbing for looking rougher than a sandblasted tramp.

'If only they knew what I'd really been up to,' he thought. 'Their minds would be totally blown away.'

Ten minutes in the changing room came and went, as he put on his shin guards and fiddled with his stick, all the time listening to the captain talk about the tactical side of today's match.

Stripping off to reveal their matching orange tops and white shorts, they all marched purposefully outside to the Astroturf pitch to begin their warm up exercises, focused fully on what was to come, much of the clowning about forgotten. Usually the pitch was fully booked up on a Saturday, from around nine-thirty in the morning through to nearly six at night, with the use of the towering floodlights that encircled it. Today was no different, and as they all walked out, Peter noticed the men's first team were already playing in a match that looked as though it would end shortly. Heading to a small area of Astroturf reserved for warming up, behind one of the goals, separated by a metal fence, his opponents already there, knocking hockey balls to and fro, Peter started to go through his usual pre-game series of stretches. Five minutes later, with the action-packed match still going on in the background, he swapped the stretches for his stick, and started hitting a ball back and forth with one of his teammates, the rest of the squad doing likewise. With it nearly being time to start, Peter gathered in with the rest of his team, halfway through a conversation as to the identity of a new first team player nobody seemed to recognise. Peter listened as he continued to stretch.

"Well, I've never seen him at training," said one.

"There's a surprise," added another, cynically.

"You should know by now that not all first teamers are required to attend training," piped up another.

Finally, the cheekiest of the lot quipped,

"Perhaps he's the captain's new boyfriend."

With this the rest of the group shook their heads and wandered away a little.

"Whaaaaat?" said the cheeky one, practically standing on his own now. "You were all thinking it."

Having not been paying much attention, instead concentrating on his warm up, Peter decided to take a look at the newcomer. Glancing over to the very far 'D', he could barely believe what he was seeing. There, rushing about in full first team kit, was Major Manson. His heart sank. What the hell was he doing here? A sudden tap on the shoulder made him turn around with a start.

"Are you okay Peter?" asked Andy, the captain of the second team. "You look like you've seen a ghost."

"Ahh... I'm fine. Must have been that dodgy kebab last night," he lied, still reeling from seeing Manson on the pitch.

"Okay," replied Andy, giving Peter a sneaky wink.

Taking a large swig from his water bottle, trying to compose himself, the full time whistle from the first team's game rang in Peter's ears. Joining his teammates to head out onto the pitch proper, he hung about the entrance, pretending to fiddle with his shin pads. Eventually the first team players trudged off the pitch, nearly all carrying grazes or burns on their knees, legs and arms. Watching as Manson picked up his kit and walked around the pitch towards him, Peter made sure he stood in the way of the narrow gated entrance as his nemesis reached it. Chatting to one of his new teammates, Manson approached the entrance to the pitch, only to find Peter in his way, making himself as big as possible. With no choice but to wait, Manson stared directly at Peter, a scowl of epic proportions stamped on his face. For his part, Peter looked straight ahead, noticing that Manson made no effort to acknowledge him, as he headed to the halfway line to join the rest of his team. Sneaking a quick peek over his shoulder, he noticed that Manson didn't even look back at him, and had gone straight off to the changing rooms. That was when it hit him. There was no sign of a limp, or even his walking stick. How odd!

"Come on Peter, let's go. It's time to start," called Andy, the captain. Slipping his fingers into his hand guard, he jogged off into his position, thoroughly fed up and distracted.

The match did not go well. Not only were the opposition very good, but Peter found himself distracted by everything he'd seen before the game. Distracted didn't begin to cover it. So after the worst possible preparation for a game ever, Peter played like a drain. Within ten minutes they'd found themselves 3-0 down, and by half time it was 4-1. Andy the captain made the decision to substitute Peter at halftime, and although staying in his kit, ready to return to the action (rolling substitutes are used in hockey, meaning a player can come off and go back on as many times as he or she likes), he knew full well that because of the way he'd played, he would not get called back on.

Fighting hard in the second half without him, the team gave a good account of themselves in eventually losing 5-4. Those early goals that Peter had played a part in had gone on to cost them dearly, something he, and everyone else in the team realised. Normally full of laughter and high jinks, the changing room was as flat and subdued as it had ever been.

Once showered and changed, Peter thought about driving straight home, that's how bad his mood was, but even through the dark mist enveloping his mind, he knew that it would be perceived as unsportsmanlike if he disappeared now, without even talking to their opponents for ten minutes. Batting his worry about running into Manson to one side, he strolled into the bar, bought himself a drink and started chatting to the opposing team. Minutes drifted away, as he unintentionally started to have a good time, the fact that Manson was nowhere to be seen contributing greatly to this. After an hour or so, the opposing team left to return home. It was only then that Peter realised that he'd forgotten about all his worries. Thinking about going home for something to eat, abruptly he received a well timed pat on the back.

"Nice job Peter," announced Andy, noticing the puzzled expression on Peter's face.

Peter stood perplexed.

"Socialising with our opponents."

"Ahhh," muttered Peter.

"Now about the game today," continued Andy, putting his arm around Peter's shoulder and slurring his words slightly. "You came in afterwards and behaved really well, which as far as I'm concerned, was the best thing you could have done. Everyone has a bad game from time to time. The secret's forgetting all about it, moving on and playing your best in the next match. I'll tell you a little secret," uttered Andy, getting right in Peter's face, and touching his nose for emphasis. "Some of the team thought you were going to drive off after the game in a huff. I told them you wouldn't."

Peter smirked a little at that, knowing full well that he nearly had.

"But you didn't," continued Andy. "It's good to have you in the team Peter. I'll see you at training on Tuesday. Now you'll have to excuse me, but there's a rather attractive lacrosse player that needs me to entertain her," he said winking, before staggering off into what had now become a rather crowded bar.

Finding himself smiling, Peter was glad he'd stayed, and stood for a moment just taking in the atmosphere of the packed clubhouse.

Filled with people, practically all the chairs in the place were taken, with most watching the sports news on the massive flat screen telly at the far end, waiting not so patiently for the football results. Arcade machines boomed every now and then, while the 'ching, ching, ching' of money crashing out of the fruit machines provided occasional interruption. Add the thud of pool balls crashing together with the sound of friendly rivalry, it all made for a very eclectic and very intoxicating mix.

He found the whole thing very special and felt privileged to be a part of it. There was nothing quite like this in the dragon world he'd been brought up in. As he took in the rowdy atmosphere, he found himself thinking of the one thing he really didn't miss. Going back a couple of years, the atmosphere probably would have been about the same, only a huge blanket of cigarette smoke would have hung in the air throughout the room, infecting everyone's clothes, hair and skin with its disgusting aroma. Not to mention the unseen damage it was doing to people's lungs and other internal organs. Thankfully the government had chosen to implement a ban in public places, with the sports club only reluctantly complying right at the very last minute, unlike many of the other establishments in the area who had gone smoke-free long before the deadline had come into force. Credit to them though, they had swapped out all the soft furnishings, including the carpet, making the place a much brighter and fresher place to hang out. Of course there was always the spilt alcohol, something he had no doubt was going on around him right now, given how busy it was, and how drunk many of the patrons were. In places, the carpets were stickier than a gecko's tongue, however, he didn't mind that too much. What did bother him was having to walk through the constant cloud of smoke from all of the barred smokers who lurked outside the main doors, come rain, sunshine or snow, with little regard for anyone but themselves. Sometimes he thought that smokers were the most selfish people on the entire planet.

The humans' constant propensity to harm themselves never ceased to amaze the dragon community. Generally not a week went by without some new story or other appearing in one of the telepathic papers, showing how the humans had discovered some other way to do themselves considerable harm: if not smoking then drinking, drugs, chemical additives in food or unhealthy diets. Over the years dragons have tried to intervene, trying desperately to guide the humans in different directions to their so-called vices, but it seems the will of the people and the money behind it all are very hard to stamp out once and for all. In recent years the dragons have had more luck in reducing the impact of tobacco, through encouraging awareness campaigns, restrictions on sales, government taxes and the kind of blanket ban in entertainment establishments that currently exists in England and other countries around the world. Peter could of course see the irony in the fact that dragons have tried so hard to stop people smoking, when they themselves can produce flames from a single breath and enjoy nothing more than chomping on a whole load of burnt charcoal. The difference, most dragons will tell you, is that dragons' flaming breath is essentially pure, although it causes damaging smoke, depending on what it is burning. However, the modern day cigarette is filled to the brim with a cocktail of chemicals including nicotine, carbon monoxide, tar, acetone, ammonia, arsenic, benzene, cadmium and formaldehyde, all of which are pretty harmful on their own, let alone when put together.

What fewer dragons, and virtually no people at all realise, is that the introduction of tobacco to the civilised world was an accident. Columbus thought that he and his crew had stumbled across it in 1492 when they first set foot onto the New World. Sir Francis Drake brought tobacco back from the Americas in 1573, before introducing Sir Walter Raleigh to it in 1585. The faction that had thrust tobacco at both Sir Francis Drake and Sir Walter Raleigh, were actually a band of rogue dragons known as the *obscures* (which means 'darkling'). Their plan was to take over large parts of the human world by tobacco addiction, with them controlling the supply of it. Fortunately the dragon Council got word of what was happening, and managed to head it off, with the dark dragons responsible being rounded up and captured, but not before tobacco had been introduced virtually worldwide, and compromised a large percentage of the population.

The *obscures* actually invented tobacco for the sole purpose of corrupting human society, and by and large did quite a good job, only being stopped right at the last. Ever since, the dragon Council and its kind have been trying to rid the world of it, without much success. These facts have only come to light quite recently in dragon society (mainly due to the much more open regime of the current king) and the revelation of documents discovered in a deserted part of Rome's Grand Library. The story of the introduction of tobacco is now told in every nursery ring so that young dragons can hopefully learn from it, and prevent the same mistakes being made in the future, as have already been made in the past. Peter only learned about this in his last years at Purbeck Peninsula, right after the information was made public.

A sharp pain in his posterior jolted Peter back to reality, causing him to drop his half empty pint glass. Watching in slow motion, the glass and its contents headed comically towards the beer stained carpet, knowing that an almighty roar from the patrons all around would be soon forthcoming. To his utter amazement, out shot a slim, graceful hand and caught the glass mid-flight, without spilling a single drop of its contents. Smiling, Richie handed him back the glass, before smacking him on the same area she'd just pinched.

"Nice bum Peter," she ventured, raising her eyebrows at him.

Shaking his head, while trying not to blush, he replied,

"Crikey Rich, you frightened the hell out of me."

"Lighten up Pete. It's only a bit of fun."

"Yeah, I know," replied Peter, taking a breath. "How did you get on today? Did you win?"

"Of course we did dopey. 9-4! Guess who scored the winning goal and a hat trick?" Richie bragged, raising her glass in his direction.

"Hmmm... let me see. Was it that beautiful redhead Charlotte by any chance?" Peter said, wincing, knowing what was coming next.

STAMP!!!!

"Ouch!" yelped Peter, hopping about madly, after Richie's nearly playful stomp.

"You know full well it was me," added the lacrosse star. "And I won player of the match."

"Nice," said Peter, nursing his sore foot.

"How did you get on?" asked Richie, turning things around whilst taking a huge gulp of her drink.

"Don't ask," was all that he could mumble in reply.

"No go on. Tell me."

Knowing that he'd get no rest until he did, Peter reluctantly spilled the beans.

"We lost 5-4."

"That doesn't sound too bad," replied Richie.

"I was subbed at halftime. Not brought back on either."

"Oh," said Richie, beginning to understand. "Ah well.

Everyone has bad games Pete. Well... nearly everyone," she said, winking and smiling, all the time referring to herself.

He wondered just where she got her self assured cockiness from.

"Do you want to know why I played so badly and got taken off?"

"Of course," she replied.

"When I got to the pitch, who should be playing in the game before for the first team...? MANSON," he whispered, for fearing of being overheard.

"Hmmm... so?"

"What the hell is he doing here? Don't you find it just a bit odd?" he pleaded.

Richie shrugged.

"Not really. I did mention it to him on one of his first tours of the offices."

"WHAT!!!" exploded Peter, turning a furious shade of scarlet.

"It's not a big deal," replied Richie calmly. "He mentioned he was a keen hockey player and how he'd played at quite a high level, so I told him about the sports club and the setup here. Apparently he talked to the first team captain and told him about his playing history, and that was enough to get him in the side. I'm not sure what all the fuss is about."

Face pumped far too much full of blood, Peter pulled in and let out a couple of long, ragged breaths as he tried to contain the anger welling up inside him.

"You've got to be kidding me Rich. Do you have any idea of the misery he's caused at work for me since he's arrived? And now the one place on the surface I go to enjoy myself, and he's here, playing for the flippin' first team."

"Peter... calm down. It's not a problem. So he's here. It's not the end of world."

That's not how it felt to Peter, standing in the middle of the crowded bar, staring at his feet in much the same way a petulant child would. His thoughts in utter turmoil, he looked as though he might cry. Not any part of his decades of training had prepared him for this. Reining in his emotions, he lifted his head and looked Richie straight in the eyes.

"I thought you understood Rich. Something's happening here, something big. I can't put my finger on it, but this is something that affects us all. I'm sure of it."

"You can't fathom that just because you don't get on with the guy, Pete," whispered Richie, leaning in closer. "He's not a dragon. He's just an ordinary bloke, doing his job. This is the first time since you've left the nursery ring that anyone has challenged you about anything. And you don't like it! You need to remember what we were taught. Blend in and act like normal humans. Don't upset the status quo."

With so much fury returning to his face, he looked like he was about to explode, he hit back at his best friend.

"ME! Remember what we were taught! That's a laugh! You constantly abuse your powers, in front of the whole world. Arm wrestling rugby players and goodness knows what else! If the dragon Council found out about half the stuff you get up to, you'd be for it. Anyway, what about being vigilant and looking out for anything unusual? We all had that drummed into us. That's pretty much the point of us all being here. And that's what's happening with Manson, but of course you wouldn't see that. You're too busy being caught up playing the 'beautiful kick ass heroine', that you're blinded to the reality of what's really going on," Peter raged.

This was the first time ever that he and Richie had exchanged cross words. Normally he wouldn't say 'boo' to a goose.

As he turned to leave, Richie reached out and grabbed his arm in an attempt to stop him, but he shrugged her off. He had to leave, so he did. As he weaved in and out of the revelling patrons, a hulking great figure stepped out into his path.

"Hey Pete," cried Tank, looking like he'd been at the epicentre of a bomb blast. Sporting a black eye, bruised lip and a bandage across his hand, it was hard to believe the happy go lucky smile that adorned his face.

With Tank in his way, you might have thought Peter would have stopped and spoken with his friend. But he didn't. Swerving at the last second, he quickly threaded his way through the throng of people between him and the exit, before jumping into his car and racing home. Tired, hungry and emotional, he decided to skip having a meal, instead choosing to go straight to bed, wishing he lived and worked somewhere far away from Salisbridge.

Unusually, Peter woke up really early and despite trying, couldn't go back to sleep, and so after a big breakfast, he headed out for a walk around the city. It being early on a Sunday, there were not many people about. He took a leisurely wander along the old path that crossed the water meadows, taking in the stunning views of the cathedral in the crisp morning air, dressed only in his favourite grey shorts and hockey tracksuit top. Strange for any dragon to do, given their extreme dislike of the cold, and he assumed from the looks he was getting from what few passersby there were, that he currently stood out as a human. Still, mentally he chastised himself for not doing this more often, and taking the extraordinary beauty all around him for granted. As he exhaled and his breath froze in an almost perfect cone, it reminded him of his other guise, the one that would have produced a cone of fire instead of cold.

Following the winding path until it reached the point where the river gushed white water out in the form of a little waterfall beneath the historic hotel, he flopped down on a bench in the park opposite, watching the ducks and their newly hatched chicks flit about in the clear, shallow water right in front of him, his mind awash with confusion.

Sitting in this idyllic scene, he felt like part of a Constable painting. Time slipped away as he sat there and let the world pass him by. Eventually it got busier with dog walkers, parents taking their children for a walk, and even the odd tourist snapping away with their fancy cameras. Behind him, teenagers began a game of football, using their jumpers as goalposts. He thought of all the wondrous scenes he'd witnessed throughout the dragon domain. Some breathtaking, others rivalling the seven wonders of the world, all skilfully concealed from these fragile human beings. Briefly he wondered what the humans would make of it all. He had to confess to himself though, as he sat and basked in the lukewarm rays of the April sun, that very little came close to the natural beauty of what he was witnessing here today.

The bells of an ice cream van resounding to the theme of a children's rhyme pulled him out of his daydream, with him only then realising it was early afternoon and that he'd sat there for well over four hours. Shaking the pins and needles out of his arms and thighs as he stood up, he started to head home, grabbing an ice cream from the van on his way past.

Ambling back, all the time continuing to wrap his tongue around the ever decreasing scoop of mint choc chip ice cream, he was amazed at how much busier things had become. Walkers and cyclists of every age careened around one another on the nearly full to bursting path. Cameras and camcorders were commonplace now, out to capture the magnificent sights that lay before them. As he passed groups of tourists from America, Europe and Japan, it suddenly struck him. He too was a tourist, only from the humid depths of the planet. That made him chuckle as the final pieces of the now soggy ice cream cone slipped down his throat.

On getting home, the first thing he noticed was the flashing red light on the answer machine, indicating that someone had left a message. It must be Richie he thought, wanting to apologise. This brought him swiftly back to reality, after a rather surreal start to the day, reminding him of work, his friends and of course... Manson!

Pressing the green button, he waited patiently as the electronic voice said,

"You have one new message."

He was surprised, when the voice turned out to be that of Tank, and not Richie.

"Hi Peter, just phoning to see if you're okay. You seemed a bit fed up last night. Rich told me what happened, and I just wanted to let you know that I'm here for you, if you wanted to talk. I'm in all morning, but have some rugby coaching this afternoon that might go on into the evening. Give me a call when you finally fall out of bed you lazy git," Tank finished, mischievously.

Smiling at that last comment, Peter deleted the message.

'Lazy git indeed,' he thought to himself. Pleased that his friend had phoned, he convinced himself that he couldn't have cared less that he hadn't heard from Richie. Knowing that it was unlikely he'd catch up with Tank today, he considered finishing work early tomorrow with a view to seeking his friend out for a much needed chat.

6 A SIGN OF THE TIMES

After an uneventful day at work, Peter used his flexitime to leave at half past two and headed home. Once there, and without bothering to change, he made his way through the concealed entrance to the monorail station and boarded the first carriage that arrived, on his way to London. Just over three minutes later, he arrived at Fleet Street station, where he alighted and headed for Tank's workplace.

Trotting off into one of the darkened alleyways that littered the edge of the station, hoping that it was indeed the right one, he marvelled at how space was at such a premium, with shops, small and large, lining either side of his route, and not a bare rock wall to be found. Nearly all the dragons here had preferred to appear in their natural form, making for lots of stops and starts, whilst letting dragons through on these narrow little walkways. Still in his human form, Peter stuck out like a Wookie at a hair loss convention. Shops and tiny houses started to appear higher up, jutting out from walls hundreds of feet above Peter's head, serviced by tiny little walkways and bridges that from this distance looked way too narrow to support most dragons. Shocking red and orange lava sizzled its way down what little space was free on the walls, sometimes splitting off into two or three houses at a time to keep them toasty warm, while at other times dribbling down over the roof itself. Spectacular, and almost as different from dragon domain places like Purbeck and Salisbridge as it was from the stunning water meadows of the day before. Diversity in all its forms, that's how Peter liked to think of it.

In places such as Purbeck and Salisbridge, the unwritten rule is that human form is fine to travel about in. This generally applies throughout the world. Not so in the capital cities and their surrounding areas though. Nobody knew why, and to be honest, nobody really cared. Those that lived there had gotten used to it long ago, and were almost too stubborn to change anyway. He'd always thought of this as stupid, particularly given the distinct lack of space. Think how much easier it would be to traverse all of these walkways in a taut little human guise, instead of a giant, ungainly dragon form, who either has to stop, or fly up into the air to let someone coming the other way, go round. It made no sense.

As he travelled deeper into the suburbs he became more self conscious, aware that almost everyone was scowling. They knew him to be a dragon... they could tell. Their resentment almost certainly derived from the fact that most dragons despised any sort of clothing that restricted their movement, and although a lot of them would have to wear a suit in their human guise, they always slipped free of it as soon as they returned to the dragon domain. Often tales would be told in the nursery rings of dragons who live on the surface, but on coming back to their human houses immediately strip off, spending their remaining hours until they have to leave the house again totally and utterly naked. Bizarre!

Feeling ever so slightly claustrophobic as the buildings loomed larger, some hanging out precariously over the walkway he was on, seemingly unbalanced and unsupported, he began to wish he was wearing something more comfortable as the temperature and humidity continued to increase.

'Most dragons like it hot,' he thought to himself, 'but this is getting beyond a joke,' his shirt and tie dripping with sweat, like a bully's victim. Rounding a corner and continuing under a small arched stone bridge, he turned immediately left into Camelot Arcade, following it down until a sign in the distance read 'Gee Tee's Mantra Emporium'. Strolling up to the door, he turned the squeaky metal handle, to be greeted by a rush of cool air as he entered. In stark contrast to the shadow filled, narrow walkways outside, he found himself in a very well lit, high ceilinged, open, shop floor, surrounded by ancient wooden bookcases fifty feet high, covered with dust and cobwebs, filled from floor to ceiling with old books, tomes and parchments, separated by super wide walkways. In human terms, it could only have been described as a warehouse or industrial hangar. The place was HUGE!

Having never been to his friend's place of work before, he had however heard all the rather interesting and as far as he was concerned, exaggerated stories. Here and now, he started to wonder if they were actually that exaggerated.

Through the maze of bookshelves, which not only dwarfed him, but would probably have seemed tall to almost any dragon, he could just make out the abandoned looking counter, with just a solitary pile of dusty books resting there. Thinking that was a good place to start, he headed off down a wide aisle in that direction, not before noticing that most of the cobwebs which hung throughout the shop hosted at least one spider, none of which were particularly small. On approaching the counter, it was then that he spotted something which made his false heart almost leap out of his fictitious mouth. In a web some twenty feet wide, up high behind the shop counter, sat a rather large tarantula. Knowing his fear was irrational was one thing; accepting it was something else altogether. Skirting that part of the deserted counter, he moved along its edge, never taking his eyes off the giant spider, all the time wondering if he could get away with leaving. It would be a shame to get this far and not see his friend, but things were getting just a little too strange for his liking, so it might be time to call it quits, even though he'd always wanted to see the renowned emporium where his friend worked.

'Legendary... just like its owner,' he thought, wondering if any of the stories about the old master mantra maker were true. You'd think not, given the nature of them, but Tank always swore they were, and Peter had never met a more trustworthy dragon than his friend. Gee Tee, the mantra emporium's owner and proprietor, was renowned throughout the dragon domain for his knowledge of all things mantra and magical. That was pretty much a fact... you could ask any dragon across the world. One of the many rumours that surrounded the master mantra maker was that he had lived for over six centuries, something Peter found hard to accept. He'd tried to quiz Tank on the subject, but all he would say was that Gee Tee was a great employer, though rather misunderstood, due in part to his eccentricities and idiosyncrasies, and could come across as rather menacing, if you didn't know him. Not something Peter really wanted to focus on at the moment, wandering around all alone in the old dragon's store.

Reaching the end of the counter, he decided enough was enough. It was time to leave, and catch up with Tank later on in the week. Nothing was worth all of this, especially since he was sure the huge blessed tarantula was watching his every move. Turning around and taking no more than two steps in the direction of the exit, he was suddenly startled by someone clearing their throat.

"Hhhuuurrrgh... hhhuuurrrmm."

Peter searched, wide-eyed, for the source.

An enormous dragon head with long wavy grey hair, wearing a pair of large, square spectacles, peered around the dusty pile of books on the counter. Relieved at finally finding someone, Peter turned instantly around.

"Before you take another step, child, you can take that damn thing off," boomed the dragon, pointing directly at Peter. "We do not tolerate those in this shop, EVER!"

Peter stood, transfixed, lost for words. The dragon continued with whatever he was doing, beneath the counter, it might have been reading or writing, he was too far away to tell. Quickly considering his options, he realised the only real choice he had was to take off his clothes, if they were that offensive. Wishing beyond belief that he'd stayed at work, reluctantly he undid his tie, slipped off his jacket and neatly slipped them onto an empty shelf on the bookcase he was stood next to. Nervously unbuttoning his shirt, he glanced around uncomfortably. Unbelievably, the huge spider dangling from the web behind the counter winked at him. He couldn't believe it. Shaking his head to free whatever madness it contained, his shirt hanging open, he did a double take, only to find the spider facing away from him, spinning a thin line of silky web. He didn't consider himself easily spooked, but now he was tempted to just leave the rest of his clothes and run away. Deciding against it, but only just, he removed his shirt and flipped off both shoes, not bothering to untie the laces, all the time trying to ignore the very bad feeling that was running through each and every one of his bogus bones. Wanting nothing more than to get it all over with, in one swift move he took off his belt, trousers and socks, stuffing them onto the shelf, on top of the rest of his neatly layered clothes. Standing all alone in his white briefs, he had no idea what to do next. Seconds seemed like days as he waited for the shopkeeper to look up. You'd have thought he'd have been a bit cooler having stripped off, but not so. Quite the opposite in fact. He felt like a volcano heating up, ready to explode. Why oh why had he done this? Thinking about whistling or clearing his throat, eventually he managed to squeak a meek, "Is that better?" in the direction of the counter. Simultaneously the shopkeeper and the spider above him looked up from what they were doing. The spider once again winked at him, a gaping grin revealed its teeth as it did so. The shopkeeper looked aghast.

"What on earth do you think you're doing, CHILD?" he yelled.

"Ummm... just what you told me to," Peter quivered.

Standing up straight, taking his huge square spectacles off, the dragon addressed Peter with thunder in his voice.

"I told you to take off THAT!" fumed the dragon, pointing at Peter's naked chest.

"I don't understand," insisted Peter, his comfort zone

now measured in terms of millimetres.

The shopkeeper's arm swung round until it pointed towards the entrance.

"Look at the sign above the door child," he said, exasperated.

The sign (which Peter had not seen as he'd entered) read 'ONLY THOSE IN SOLITUS FORM ARE WELCOME HERE'.

Immediately Peter understood. It wasn't his clothes he was expected to get rid of, it was his human form. Only dragons in their natural state were allowed in the shop, which seemed ironic given that Tank nearly always maintained human form, and more than a little... judgmental. Both shopkeeper and spider glared at him, now that the penny had dropped. Closing his eyes, and more self conscious than ever, he focused on unlocking the dozen or so bonds within his DNA that regulated his human appearance. Recently he'd got into the habit of sticking with his human guise, even when visiting the dragon domain, so he didn't do this very often, but he was always flabbergasted at the ease with which it happened, when he did. Three seconds, that was how long the complete transformation took. Staggering really. It started with a warm tingling feeling all over, that swiftly progressed to a kind of citrusy flavour within, ending with the swirling noise of what felt like a hurricane rushing through his ears. Looking down, the first thing he noticed were his ripped briefs lying on the floor.

'Oops!' he thought. 'Looks like I'm going home commando tonight.'

"That's better, child," commented the shopkeeper. "Come closer so that I can have a better look at you."

Stepping over his shredded underwear, Peter plodded over to the counter, his comparatively small body and wingspan making him almost look like a dragonling, in the huge space of his surroundings. It was only now that he realised why there was so much space throughout the store. It made perfect sense if only dragons in their natural form were allowed in. Briefly he wondered why his friend had never mentioned all this, and just exactly where he was.

Slipping his square spectacles back on, the shopkeeper made his way around to the shop floor and gave Peter the once over.

"Hmmmm... nothing special," he said, lifting up Peter's wing. Peter tried to pull away, but the old dragon had a grip of steel and would not let him go.

"Ahhh... what's this then?" he remarked, mainly to himself, looking below Peter's left wing at the markings on his belly. Peter's belly was predominantly brown, although on the left hand side there was a strange pattern, made up of matt green scales, that had helped give him his name. It was not unusual to be named after a pattern or bodily marking, and Peter had just come to accept it, as had most dragons, unless of course you had a very rude or stupid characteristic, which sometimes happened, and presented the *tors* in charge of choosing a young dragon's name with a very difficult set of circumstances. In Peter's case, the matt green scales stood out, looking like a whistle. A whistle where the part that you blow into was crooked or bent. Hence Peter's dragon name was Bentwhistle.

Continuing to poke at Peter's matt green scales that formed the whistle, the old shopkeeper frowned, before going on.

"I know this from somewhere. But I don't seem to know you. Have we met? I don't remember if we have. Hang on a second, it's all coming back to me now. You're Tank's friend. He's told me all about you, you know."

Peter smiled. Finally a mention of his friend.

"Has he really? All good I hope."

"Of course, of course," replied the old dragon.

"Is he about at all? It's just that I wanted a quick chat with him if it's possible."

Stepping out from underneath Peter's wing, the

125

shopkeeper urged Peter to follow him, adding,

"He's been here all the time, right in plain sight," chuckled the old dragon, wandering back behind the counter and doing the very last thing Peter expected.

He reached up into the big silver web, and retrieved the gargantuan tarantula. At this point, Peter's eyes nearly popped out. What on earth was going on?

Holding his hand out flat, allowing the spider to get comfortable, the shopkeeper then proceeded to rifle through a dusty red book from the pile on the counter, looking for... something.

It didn't take long to find, and so with the book open in one hand, and the spider held steady in the other, the age old dragon closed his eyes. It was then that he noticed.

'It can't be... it just can't,' thought Peter, having spotted the same inane grin on the spider that normally occupied his friend's battered and bruised face.

Muttering a language Peter couldn't recognise, abruptly the old shopkeeper tossed the spider high up into the air, taking a step back as he did so. As the spider reached the highest point of its trajectory, tumbling head over legs, it started to spin uncontrollably, as if caught in a vortex. Peter watched, astonished, barely able to focus in on the spider, it was moving so fast. But he could at least tell something... it was getting bigger, and even changing colour. Still muttering undecipherable tones, the shopkeeper looked up from the book, pushing his glasses as far up his nose as they would go, before finishing the mantra with one word.

CRASH!!! Tank was thrown out of the mini tornado at full speed, rocketing into the nearest bookcase. A hail of books toppled down onto his head as he tried to sit up against its base. None of this prevented him from having his usual stupid inane grin.

"Excellent, excellent!" cried the shopkeeper, appearing in front of Tank. "A morphic mantra from Roman Times," he said to Tank, as he picked himself up from the pile of books.

"Quite a find, even if I do say so myself. You can tidy the books up later. Take your friend into the workshop and have your chat now. Don't be too long though, we have that Aztec flying mantra to test out later," pointed out the old dragon, disappearing off into the depths of the store.

"That was just unbelievable," exclaimed Peter, as Tank came over.

"Just run of the mill here I'm afraid, Pete."

"Really?" asked Peter in total disbelief.

Tank escorted him to the workshop that sat back behind the counter, barely visible from the shop floor. Four dragon sized desks were cluttered up with piles of books, bunches of scrolls, oversized dragon pens, mantra ink, brushes and flimsy rolls of paper. A special dragon sized chair accompanied each desk, and like the monorail, there were holes at the back of each, so that a dragon could slip his or her tail through. Comfy!

Unable to contain his curiosity, Peter blurted,

"What happens here?"

"This is where we repair broken mantras, and sometimes try to create new ones. It's our workshop."

Peter gazed in wonder.

"I didn't even know it was possible to repair a broken mantra."

"Most dragons don't," replied Tank, matter-of-factly. "It's not something needed very much anymore. A lot of mantras nowadays can be memorised, or can be stored on mobile phones, laptops or tablets. All relatively recent developments, before which mantras would need to be repaired, especially mantras that only had a one-off use. This was where most dragons would have had it done."

"You sound as though they don't come here any more."

"Oh the odd dragon wanders in to have a really rare or old mantra fixed, valued or researched, but sometimes we don't see a customer for weeks on end."

"That's really sad," replied Peter, concerned.

"It's just a change in times, or so Gee Tee says," commented Tank, quietly. "These new dial-a-mantra services haven't helped very much either."

"Uhhh?"

"Trust you," said Tank to his friend. "You must have seen all the adverts in the telepathic papers."

"Nope," replied Peter, shaking his head.

"Well, anyway, it's very much like the dial and download a ringtone the humans use for their mobile phones, you get the mantra of your choice, sent directly to your phone, as either a text message or email, ready and waiting for whenever you need to use it," Tank uttered, disappointingly.

"So it's affecting business then?" queried Peter.

"Yeah, I've never known it so quiet. Gee Tee's already laid off two of his staff. It's only him and me left now."

Peter paused for a moment, before saying,

"I'm really sorry Tank. I had no idea. You should have said."

"It's not something I like to talk about. Besides, it's not like he can get rid of me. He needs my help, as you've already seen," Tank stated, grinning.

"That must have been some special mantra to change you into something that small," ventured Peter, changing the subject.

"Apparently, the Roman dragons had a special knack of doing it, almost famed for it you could say. But like so much information in our world, it's been lost over a period of time. As a race we're not renowned for storing information, or even looking back into our history and valuing it for what it was. It's such a shame we can't do that. We've lost so much already that's so valuable. And what's most ironic is that our charges, the humans with whom you and I mix on a daily basis, they can do all of that. But we can't. What on earth does that say about us as dragons?"

Peter admired the way Tank got passionate about all sorts of different subjects. The depth of his feelings always shone through.

"Anyway," he perked up, "if I feel miserable about our lack of customers, I can always visualise you standing in the front of the shop in just your briefs."

As Tank fought back tears of laughter, Peter held his head in his hands, blushing with embarrassment,

"Yeah, thanks for that. I'm sure it will always help me to think of you as a spider."

"Anyhow, what brings you to our famed establishment on this bright, sunny day, Pete?" said Tank, spreading his wings wide and turning around.

"I wanted to talk to you about my work, and... Richie."

"Ah... I thought it might have something to do with that. She told me on Saturday night that you'd argued, and why," Tank said, sitting back in one of the oversized chairs, his tail hitting the floor with a THUMP.

Peter slouched in the opposite chair, letting his wings flop over the sides until the tips touched the floor. The two friends started chatting, with Peter explaining to Tank all about Manson and how he seemed to be manipulating Al Garrett. He also tried to convey his belief that Manson was dangerous, as well as his regret for falling out with Richie. For his part, Tank listened patiently for over forty minutes, considering carefully everything that he'd heard before he spoke.

"I think the first thing I should say, Pete, is that Richie feels the same way about your argument. She told me exactly that, and wants to go straight back to being best friends again. So stop worrying about that."

This brought a toothy dragon smile to his face, accompanied by two tiny dribbles of smoky flame from his nostrils. The realisation that he'd been worrying about nothing dawned on him, making him recognise quite how stupid he'd been.

"As for Manson," Tank continued, "You must understand, Pete, that it's very hard for me to gauge exactly what kind of person he is without having met him, and although some of the things you've described are a bit odd, perhaps Richie's right and you've just gotten off on the wrong foot."

Peter sat silently and nodded. Having learnt his lesson with one friend, he had no intention of falling out with the other.

"Or maybe you're right. Maybe Manson is a conman or a criminal and is planning some kind of crime. Either way, it's not as bad as you think. If that's the case, you should have no problem apprehending him at the appropriate time. After all, your superior dragon intellect should give you a huge advantage against even the cleverest human. Remember, no dragon in our history has ever been bested by a human. You're not about to become the first. This guy, if he's up to no good, stands absolutely no chance. And it's not like he's anything other than a human... right? You and Richie would both have noticed that."

Peter let out a long sigh.

"He's not a dragon. It's just that... that... that... well, he's different, almost... evil. I can't really explain it, but that's the only way to describe it."

"As long as he's not a dragon, you've got nothing to worry about," added Tank reassuringly.

A harsh coughing noise from just inside the door surprised the pair. Both turned to find the master mantra maker standing there, a stern look on his face, his square spectacles dangling from the end of his nose.

"I sometimes wonder if you're worthy of being my apprentice," he announced, his velvety smooth voice unable to hide the real edge his words carried.

Tank was used to the old dragon's eccentricities and sometimes mischievousness, but here and now he knew his employer had something more on his mind.

"If it's what I said about knowing my job's safe, I...

apologise," said Tank, nervously.

A small frown, practically unnoticeable, developed behind his spectacles.

"No it's not. But I'll bear that in mind," growled the old dragon.

"Why don't you tell your friend about the mantra you found last month? You know, the one that produced the purple emperor butterfly, or as you like to call it *apatura iris*."

Peter smiled as he recognised the tone in Gee Tee's voice which implied Tank had been showing off with the butterfly's Latin name. Having spent decades alongside Tank in the nursery ring, nobody knew better than Peter did just how annoying it could be to spend ages learning about a plant or an animal, just to have Tank pop up out of nowhere, knowing everything about it, including its correct name. Clearly whatever had happened with the mantra, Gee Tee had taken offence at Tank's special talent.

"Would you perhaps prefer it if I told him?" Gee Tee asked Tank, in a tone that was more an order than a request. Tank sat dead still and nodded his head.

"Well, young Bentwhistle, one day my apprentice here was going through an assortment of Egyptian mantras, out on the shop floor. I was away at the time, trying to procure some high quality ink, which with every passing year gets harder and harder to find. So anyway, spotting one that he recognised, or so he thought, my clever apprentice decided to use the mantra to bring forth the aforementioned emperor butterfly. Reciting the mantra correctly, for it was nearly all in ancient Egyptian, and adding all his belief, he managed to produce a stunning emperor butterfly that duly followed him around the shop as he worked."

From the way in which Tank was squirming with discomfort, Peter had absolutely no idea where this was going at all.

"Now I'm sure I don't have to tell you about my apprentice's love of everything living," the old shopkeeper declared, looking directly into Peter's eyes. Peter nodded.

"When I returned to the store later that morning, I could scarcely believe my eyes. Flying freely around the shop was an Egyptian morphbeetle, one of the most dangerous beings the world has ever seen. And to make matters worse, there was my clever little apprentice, petting it at every opportunity. Needless to say we had to call in the King's Guards to get rid of it, what with it being a class nine mantra and all. We're not nearly well enough equipped to do it ourselves. Eventually they managed to facilitate its capture and subsequent termination, but in doing so, delighted in wrecking half my shop. I thought, at the very least, that episode would have provided a valuable lesson to my ever so clever apprentice, but from having overheard part of your conversation, it would appear I'm very much mistaken.

Tank, sitting up much straighter, tried to put the pieces of the puzzle together, the lesson, and the relevance to the conversation. Try as he might, with his employer bearing over him, his mind just went blank.

"For Bentwhistle's sake I shall put you out of your misery. The valuable lesson you should have learned, was that evil comes in many guises, not always visible to everyone. For you, the butterfly was as real as it gets, and you couldn't see beyond that, but as soon as I came through the door I recognised it for what it truly was," Gee Tee sighed as he finished.

Peter thought he knew what the old dragon meant.

"So what you're saying is that I could be right about Manson and that he could be immensely evil and dangerous, even though nobody else can see it."

"That's one way to put it I suppose," offered up the old dragon. "But perhaps you should expand your narrow way of thinking somewhat. Tank thought the butterfly was real, but it wasn't. What if this 'Manson' is not all that he appears to be? What if, like the butterfly, something much more sinister lies beneath?"

"Are you saying he could be a dragon?" asked Peter, wide-eyed.

Tank quickly butted in and said,

"But that's just not possible. They would both sense it if he were a dragon."

"Would they indeed...?" answered Gee Tee, with just the tiniest glint in his eyes. "If history teaches us anything, it's that you can always expect the unexpected, my naive apprentice. Dragons throughout the ages have hidden themselves before, and I don't doubt at some point they will do it again."

"Really?" gasped Peter, fascinated.

"Of course," added the shopkeeper. "It can be done. It's very difficult, but it can be done. Anyway, I'm sorry to cut this meeting short, but I need Tank, I'm afraid. We have many more tomes to sort out, starting with the 'Mechanical Repairs' section, after you have shown your friend out," Gee Tee told Tank, before turning to face Peter.

"It's been a pleasure meeting you, child. Consider yourself welcome any time. It's not like we're busy here or anything. I hope you sort out your little problem at work," he added, before bowing and heading back off into the twisted maze of dusty old bookcases.

Peter rose from his chair, having to wiggle about a bit to get his tail out of the hole, and followed his friend back through the shop, remembering to collect the remains of his human clothes. The two friends bade each other farewell, with Tank returning to work and Peter heading off to the monorail station, more suitably attired this time.

That night Peter sat in front of the television, trying to unwind. His visit to the Mantra Emporium had been absolutely fascinating in so many different ways. A tiny part of him envied Tank for working there, but not the bit about being transformed into a spider. Never that. Learning from Gee Tee that it was possible, however hard, for a dragon to conceal their dragon-ness was just breathtaking, and something that had never been mentioned at the nursery ring. Eventually heading upstairs just after ten, his head spinning every which way with thoughts from his astounding afternoon, before he nodded off, he vowed to himself to keep an open mind about... everything.

7 SECURITY SWEEP (SOOTY OR SUE?)

Peter went through his normal routine the next morning, deciding to send his consciousness off to get a copy of the Daily Telepath. He didn't get it every day, purely because he was too lazy, but today was important because the details of the Indigo Warriors' first Global Cup match should have been announced. Sending his mind off in a kind of autopilot way, it wasn't long before it had retrieved the paper and he was able to access it. The first page looked like this:

PAUL CUDE

The Daily Telepath

Britain's Oldest Telepathic Newspaper   Issue No 252231

Are Teaching Standards in our Nursery Rings Declining?

By Mike Frame

More young dragons leaving the nursery rings are being turned down for top jobs because they just don't make the grade. A report commissioned by the SDC (Scientific Development Centre) states that the quality of applicants for entry level jobs has dropped by nearly ten percent in the last five years. The number of applicants failing to get posts attached to the King's Council has also risen by fifteen percent. Nursery ring development coordinator Leyla Buttercup said, "the nursery rings strive to move with the times and constantly aim to provide young dragons with the best education possible."

Charcoal Targets Announced

By Pedro Rodrigez

Councillor for 'above ground resources' Professor Enzo Thorndagger has announced new targets for the effective management of dragon charcoal consumption. The guidelines refer to coppicing. This had been regarded for several hundred years as the best way to sustain and manage the woodland required to supply charcoal to dragons throughout the world. While coppicing has been used by most suppliers, one or two have recently been found to be taking wood for charcoal production from non-sustainable resources, something which the dragon council finds wholly disturbing. With charcoal consumption reaching an all time high last year, the council feels that it is high time to increase the previous ninety percent coppicing target to ninety eight percent. Despite opponents insisting the target should be raised to one hundred percent, the council feels this would be unrealistic and that the targets should be reviewed on a yearly basis. For great new and innovative charcoal recipes, see our twenty eight page Sunday supplement.

Latest Success- The Giant Lau Lau

By Holly Origin

European Ped Labs claim to have followed the success of growing the star fruit underground by announcing successful trials of sustained growth of one of the dragon community's most desirable delicacies - the giant lau lau. The subtle sweet taste of the large, crunchy, well flavoured fruit has long been one of the most sought after foods of the dragon domain. Demand has long since outstripped supply for this brightly coloured fruit, which up until now has only been found to grow in Papua New Guinea and some of the other pacific islands. Although still in its early stages, Ped Labs claim to have used one of their underground greenhouses to grow the equivalent of one year's worth all in one go, despite a few problems still surrounding the seeds, some of which can lose their viability quite rapidly. A spokesdragon claimed, "the research is progressing on schedule, with giant lau lau supplies set to treble in the next four years." Ped Labs, made famous by their amazing fruit embued charcoal, the recipes of which are still a secret to this very day, are always way ahead of any competitors in their field. When ruthlessly questioned on what their next project might be the comunications dragon declined to comment but gave a very knowing smile when the phrase 'melt in the mouth chocolate flavoured charcoal' was mentioned. Don't forget folks........you heard it here first.

South Pole Timetable

By Chief Political Correspondant Briany Ingham

The King's Council met over the weekend, with one of the subjects on the agenda being global warming and in particular the South Pole. The Council all agreed that the issue needed further study and Councillor D'Zone was appointed the task of putting together a group of dragons to form the expedition by the time of the next meeting. The Council's overwhelming agreement on this issue has come as a surprise to most but has been welcomed in practically every quarter. Further news on the make up of the experdition when we get it.

New Plant Opens

By April Brown

Yesterday a new geothermal power plant opened beneath Mount Fuji, just west of Tokyo. The turbine used is the biggest on Earth, making this new plant the second most productive in the world.The plant will provide energy for the entire Southern Hemisphere's monorail.

Enter our competition and win a trip to a dragon spa   Free dial-a-mantras inside p8

'Wow,' Peter thought, after studying the Global Cup section. 'The Warriors are playing the Coral Rock'ards.' It would be a tough game, but as a one-off contest, he was sure they could win and progress to the semi final.

'I wonder if Tank's tried to get any tickets yet?' Arriving at work, he buried his head in some timesheets, finding himself missing the old atmosphere that used to prevail before Manson had arrived. Only a relatively short time ago, he'd have known where to go for a joke and a laugh, but at the moment you couldn't even buy a smile from any of his staff, let alone a comic moment.

An hour or so later, his phone rang. He promptly picked it up to find that it was Dr Island, head of the scientists on the Cropptech industrial site. Peter prided himself on the fact that he got on pretty well with the heads of department, or had done up until the arrival of Manson.

"Hi Peter, it's Sheridan Island here from industrial," came the polite voice down the phone.

"Good morning Dr Island," replied Peter. "What can I do for you today?"

"Could you come on over please? We seem to be having a bit of a problem with some of the guards."

"What sort of problem?" demanded Peter, keen to get to the bottom of things.

"They seem to be conducting some sort of security sweep, and it's interfering with our work rather a lot."

"I don't understand," muttered Peter. "I've authorised no such thing."

"Uhhhh... I don't think it's you," said Dr Island. "According to the guards, the delightful Major Manson is behind it all," she added, dripping with sarcasm.

Letting out a long sigh that clearly wasn't missed by Dr Island, he told her he was on his way, before hanging up, grabbing his coat and heading out of the door, covering the five minute walk in just over two, keen to sort out the problem. On his way, he wondered just what the hell Manson was up to. Did he not realise these scientists were a special breed of people? Brilliant in their respective fields, they carried out some of the most critical work on the site, and Peter had long since learned from experience, and those around him, that it was best to try and let them get on with their painstaking and exacting work with as little fuss as possible.

Getting thoroughly drenched, despite his coat, Peter arrived at the industrial unit and made his way into the interior. His senses always seemed to go a little wayward whenever he was here. On one hand the environment was very clinical and sterile. On the other, massive machines zipped and turned, spraying hot metal and a bonfire night's worth of giant, molten sparks all over the place. Was it a laboratory? Was it a factory? Somewhere in between, his brain reluctantly told him.

Amongst all the machinery, scientists in gleaming white lab coats stood around in disbelief, looking on as a dozen guards wandered in and out of all the heavy equipment. Peter walked over to Dr Island and put a gentle hand on her shoulder.

"I'll try and sort this out straight away."

She nodded and tried to force a smile, but given that she looked like she was about to pull all her hair out, it came out as more of a grimace.

Striding over to the guard who looked reluctantly in charge, someone Peter knew as a hardworking and decent man, Peter reluctantly asked,

"What's going on, Phillips?"

"Just following orders, boss," Phillips replied anxiously.

"We can't just come in here and interrupt their work whenever we like," Peter whispered, knowing how far the sound travelled in this environment.

"But that's exactly what we CAN do," boomed a snarling voice from the opposite corner of the industrial unit, over sixty feet away. Everyone looked around as the voice reverberated throughout the equipment. Out from behind some of the larger machinery, stepped Manson, menacingly, tapping his walking stick on the polished white floor as he did so.

"Did you not understand when Mr Garrett put me in charge, Bentwhistle? I am in charge of security now, and I can perform a security sweep of any part of the complex whenever I like. Do you understand, Bentwhistle?"

Manson used Peter's surname as if it were some kind of embarrassing fungal disease you might have in your unmentionables.

"Yes sir, I understand," ventured Peter, humiliated, with the dozen or so guards and ten or so scientists looking on.

"You had better," added Manson, steel in his voice, "or you'll be looking for a new job. Now, what I've seen today is nothing short of disgraceful. The security here is woefully inadequate, laughable in fact. Any of these workers," he said, pointing at the group of scientists, "could smuggle equipment or valuables out of here at practically any time."

"Now you listen here..." started Dr Island, looking as though she was about to erupt. "How dare you accuse any of my staff of impropriety? Every last item is always accounted for, and my staff are all as honest as the day is long."

"Have you quite finished, WOMAN?" Manson sneered with contempt.

Peter and everyone else couldn't believe what they were hearing. In all the time Peter had worked there, he'd never heard anyone speak with such rudeness, and by the look on the faces of those around him, they hadn't either.

"I'm not standing for this a second longer!" raved Dr Island, furious. "Nobody speaks to my staff that way, especially not some jumped up, snotty nosed ex-officer. I'll have you know that I've worked here for over thirty years and I've never been treated like this. Al Garrett is going to hear about this, straight away," and with that she stomped off out of the building.

Manson just stood there, twisting his finger in the air.

"One down, several hundred to go," he said grinning from ear to ear. "You can all get back to work," he said to the remaining scientists. "I will be introducing my own specialised guards for duty here, so you had all better watch yourselves."

The scientists, clearly distressed, made it look as though they were going about their jobs, but were more likely waiting for Dr Island to come back from speaking to Al Garrett.

"You can all resume your normal duties," Manson told the guards, who all dispersed in the blink of an eye. He really couldn't blame them. Turning, Manson looked Peter straight in the eye.

"I wouldn't bank on the good doctor having too much success if I were you."

As Manson left, Peter hoped with all his heart that Dr Island's explanation of events would be enough to see Manson on his way.

How wrong he was.

Returning to his office, eating his lunch and non-stop into the afternoon he wondered just how Dr Island had gotten on. He didn't have to wait very long. Noticing a new email had just arrived in his in box, he opened it, anticipating news of Manson's sudden departure.

One click of his mouse had him aghast. Al Garrett's email to all department heads read that Dr Island had been fired this morning for a severe breach of discipline and that without a natural successor, that department would be run in the interim by Major Manson.

Peter had assumed his day just couldn't get any worse. It turned out that he was wrong. A phone call later that afternoon informed him that Chief Security Co-ordinator, Mark Hiscock, another dragon and his direct superior whose shoes he'd filled, being off long term sick, had died last night. Shocked to his core, Peter had no idea what to do. It's rare that dragons die. Really rare. He'd never known anyone, human or dragon, who'd passed away. He remained in his office for the rest of the afternoon, overcome with grief.

8 THE FAINT WHIFF OF... OCTOPUS

Unable to concentrate on anything at all, Peter felt like he was in a constant daze. The first thing he'd done the following day was check the telepathic papers for details of Mark Hiscock's demise. Sure enough, in two of the more reputable editions he'd found obituaries for his deceased colleague. Holding with dragon custom, the funeral would take place exactly ten days after his death. Undoubtedly, dragons who'd known him would attend, probably from all across the globe. Peter would most certainly be going to not only that, but the human service as well.

Staff at Cropptech found it difficult to come to terms with Mark's death. Every time Peter ventured out to a different part of the site, he caught someone weeping or trying to conceal their puffy eyes from having just done so. It was a testament to just how popular a figure Mark had been in his role as Chief Security Co-ordinator. Over and over, Peter chastised himself for not realising just how ill his manager had been, and for not having visited him. He should have known something was up. It was rare that dragons get ill, even more so for it to be anything serious. He'd naturally assumed he was being treated by dragon physicians below ground, but hadn't actually checked to see if that was the case. Perhaps he should have. It had never actually occurred to him at the time to do so. Even more surprising was the fact that in dragon terms, Mark was relatively young, only 120 years old.

Peter's sour mood wasn't helped by having no outlet to let off steam. The hockey season had just finished, with very little else for the second team players planned until pre-season training, which was months away.

With the above ground funeral scheduled for Friday, many at Cropptech had contributed towards a fitting wreath, with the vast majority of the staff that had known him personally planning to attend. On his travels across the site, Peter had taken to eavesdropping with his dragon abilities. Possibly frowned upon by his dragon superiors, he justified it by telling himself that it was all about the security of the company, which was indeed why he was there in the first place.

Wandering around the day before the funeral, he started to notice a definite theme as he picked up on conversations between people: anger and confusion at just why Al Garrett hadn't appeared at this time of need. He'd always done so in the past, taking the initiative, offering the family any assistance they needed and always reassuring the staff in whatever way possible. But here and now, just when they needed him the most, he was nowhere to be seen. Worse still were the whispers centred around whether or not Garrett would attend the funeral. It was unthinkable really that this should be in doubt, given his kind and caring nature, but with his current odd behaviour, nobody was sure just what would happen.

Friday arrived, and after having crossed the crisp fresh grass from the car park to the chapel, Peter chose a seat in the very back pew, nodding at the staff he recognised as they came in. He tried to look unaware of what was going on, but even without his dragon senses, it was obvious everyone was looking to see if Garrett was there.

With the chapel full to bursting and Garrett nowhere to be seen, the vicar checked his watch, before reluctantly starting. Peter sat and listened to the kind words, all the time looking around at the others there, all in various states of emotional distress. There and then it brought home to him just how much deception was involved in a dragon's life. People here were genuinely upset at the death of a man they probably, in reality, never really knew, because at the end of the day he was a dragon. That in itself would have meant keeping numerous secrets as well as not revealing very much about his personality. And yet, with proof sitting all around Peter, he'd still made friends, lots of them, all sitting there grieving for him. Sitting there amongst them he felt confused, especially at the realisation that Mark's body wasn't actually here. His true body was being prepared for the underground service, many miles away. Clearly the dragon Council had more than a hand in this cunning deception. Yet more dragon lies. Where would it all end?

Following the queue of mourners outside, Peter found himself making small talk with those staff that he vaguely knew, aware the mood had turned from sadness to quiet contemplation. Staring out at the well maintained grounds, a tap on his shoulder surprised him. He turned to face a well dressed, middle aged gentleman whom he didn't recognise.

"Excuse me, but are you Peter Bentwhistle?" the gentleman asked.

Suspicious of everything at the moment, and always more pessimistic than not, Peter suddenly became alert and aware of everything around him.

"I am," he replied cautiously.

The man offered out his hand.

"Good morning. I'm Oliver Burns, of Burns and Haybell solicitors."

Shaking the outstretched hand, Peter looked bemused.

"Nice to meet you."

"You don't know why I'm here?" asked Mr Burns.

"Sorry, no," replied Peter.

"We're handling Mr Hiscock's will."

"What has that got to do with me?"

"Mr Hiscock made you the sole executor of his will. You didn't know?"

"I had no idea," announced Peter, shocked.

"Well it's a little unusual," said Mr Burns, "but never mind. Basically Mr Hiscock left his whole estate to charity. There's some paperwork to do, and then you need to arrange for his possessions to go to the charity in question."

"Can I ask what the charity is?" Peter enquired.

"The children's hospital over on the other side of town."

Peter nodded thoughtfully.

"I wonder why he chose me?" he mused, out loud.

Mr Burns flipped open his paperwork and began to scan through it.

"Ahh... it says here, that as well as working for Cropptech, you are both of the same descent."

It was all Peter could do not to choke, as panic raced through every fibre of his body. He wanted to snatch the papers and destroy them, but instead stood very still, with everybody all around, watching.

Mr Burns studied the document in closer detail, before looking up. Peter's heart was in his mouth.

"Ah yes. Here it is. It says that you are both originally of Irish descent."

Relief, as well as steam, poured off Peter.

"That's right," confirmed Peter, "I'd forgotten I'd even told him about that."

"Well, that's cleared up why he selected you," said Mr Burns happily.

Before leaving the crematorium, Peter signed Mr Burns' paperwork, and told him that he would go round to Mark's house and sort out his belongings. Mr Burns told Peter to make an appointment to see him once he was ready, and handed him Mark's house keys.

Having left the crematorium, Peter really couldn't face going back into work as he'd planned, so phoned and told them he'd be back on Tuesday, having already booked Monday off to attend the dragon funeral for Mark.

With the hockey having finished, the weekend passed really slowly, with odd jobs around the house that had been put off for months, the name of the game. Having ticked off nearly all the jobs from the list stored in his eidetic dragon memory, pleased with his day's work, he vowed that Sunday would be all about Mark's house.

After something of a Sunday morning lie in, Peter

crawled out of bed, downcast at the thought of having to go to Mark's house to sort out all his belongings. It wasn't something he was looking forward to doing, and was compounded by the guilt that he felt for not having even thought about going to visit the sick dragon. If he could turn back time he'd have made much more of an effort, something of course we all wish we could do.

Making sure he had the keys to Mark's house, he drove with care through the quiet, suburban streets of Salisbridge. Turning into Romany Road, he tootled along with all the speed of a pensioner at the wheel, all the time keeping an eye out for number seventy-two. That was more difficult than it seemed because of wayward hedges, and the fact that some of the houses had names instead of numbers, so it was only when he reached number ninety that he realised he'd gone too far. Opting to park in a free space there rather than turn back around, knowing that he was only really going to be checking what was there rather than anything else, he headed back off down the street, looking for number seventy-two. Abruptly, the butterfly feeling he'd always associated with being bullied in the nursery ring, hit him like a sucker punch from a boxer. Scanning the immediate area, there was no sign of the nursery ring bullies.

It was then that he stopped dead in his tracks, the uneasy feeling in his stomach trebled. There, parked right outside number seventy-two, was the black Mercedes that Manson drove. He didn't even have to double check it. He was good with cars anyway, maybe because he had a fascination with them. That, combined with his eidetic memory, sent his stomach into a series of somersaults. Sweat starting to sting his eyes, and the thought of sticking out like a sore thumb in this quiet, leafy, suburban street, prompted him into action. Opening the gate and stepping onto the crazy paving path, Tank's words came bubbling back to him.

"I know you have it in you to stand up and be counted."

'Well,' he thought, taking the house key out of his pocket and lining it up with the lock on the door, 'I'm not at work at the moment, and I have every right to be here. So I WILL stand up for myself.'

Clutching the key tightly, he took a deep breath, and on deciding it was best to make as much noise as possible, he turned the key sharply in the lock and pushed open the door. Stepping over the threshold, he gazed down the long hallway, just making out the kitchen at the end. Out of the blue, a door halfway down the left hand side as Peter looked at it, snapped open, followed by the familiar sight of Manson, slapping his walking stick on the bare wooden floorboards as he moved. Framed by the open front door behind him, Peter stood still and waited for Manson's next move.

"What the hell are you doing here?" Manson sneered, his top lip wriggling like a caterpillar at a disco.

Using all his courage to compose himself, Peter replied,

"I might ask you the same question."

Manson appeared to consider his response carefully, something that set alarm bells ringing deep inside Peter's head.

"Mr Hiscock and I were friends," Manson said, changing his tone from disdain to blasé. "He even gave me a key," he added, holding one up that was identical to Peter's in every way.

"Still doesn't explain what you're doing here."

Manson's tone turned back to one of contempt, screwing up his face as he replied.

"I lent Hiscock a book and wanted to retrieve it before it was thrown out. It's very important and has been in my family for generations."

"Where is it then?" asked Peter, trying desperately to sound confident, even though that's not at all how he felt.

"It doesn't appear to be here," Manson said with murder in his eyes. "You still haven't told me what you're doing here."

"I'm the executor of Mark's will. I'm here to sort out his things," replied Peter smugly.

A tense silence enveloped the hallway. Manson appeared to be weighing up his options. Seconds passed as both stood in silence, glaring at one another. Finally a look of resignation crossed Manson's face.

"I'll be going now. If you find my book, give it away with the rest of the stuff," he quipped, barging past Peter on his way out.

Peter stood in the entrance, watching him go. As Manson reached the pavement, he turned and shouted back to Peter, a mean expression imprinted on his face.

"I expect I'll see you at work."

Standing stock still, Peter watched as the black Mercedes tore off down the street, narrowly missing a cyclist.

Shutting the front door and making sure it was locked from the inside, Peter wandered back down the hall and into the room that Manson had just come out of. Unmistakeably it was the living room, but it looked as though a hurricane had cut a path through it. Books were strewn across the floor, DVD's littered the sofa, some open, all mixed up. The cupboard doors on the dresser were open, with the entire contents emptied out onto the carpet in front of it. A very odd and powerful smell seemed to be ingrained in just about everything.

'What the hell has Manson been doing?' Peter thought to himself. There was definitely something very... how would the humans put it? Something very... crabby? No... eely? No... Ah yes! Something fishy was going on.

Touring the rest of the house, he found that every other room was in the same state. He started to tidy, not really knowing where to start. But as the time ticked by, he couldn't help being concerned about Manson's actions. After about an hour of thankless tidying, worry prompted him into action. He phoned a twenty-four hour locksmith, and got them to change all the locks on the house. Now he was the only one with a set of keys.

With about half the house having been tidied to some degree or another, he eventually left at about nine-thirty, eager to get home for something to eat and a shower before bed. It was only on the short journey home that it occurred to him that the smell permeating Mark's house, was the exact same one that he'd noticed in Garrett's office. Confused and tired, he drifted off to sleep, trying to put the pieces of the puzzle together in his mind as he did so, the spectacle of the dragon funeral the following day barely entering his thoughts.

He awoke the next morning from the worst night's sleep of his entire life. Not so much sleep, as a series of twenty minute naps with an hour of being awake in between. Tired and emotional at the thought of the funeral, he dipped into the secret cubby hole at the back of his wardrobe and found the brightest cloak he owned, and in nothing but his birthday suit, made his way through the concealed entrance and out into the steamy dragon domain. Concealed by the darkness, he changed into his dragon persona as soon as he hit the public walkway, having dropped the garish cloak on the cool stone floor. Change complete, he strapped the cloak around his neck, and headed off into the humid tunnels in the direction of the monorail station, the cloak billowing out behind him as he walked. His destination was the Dragon Bereavement Grotto at Honister Pass Boulders in Cumbria, over three hundred miles away.

Every dragon community in the world has its own bereavement grotto. Some, such as the United States, Russia and China, have more than just one. The grottos are the final resting places of dragons who have passed away. The word grotto implies something small and cosy, which in some cases is true. Take for example Liechtenstein. The grotto there is only fifty metres long and thirty metres wide, adjacent to an underground lake that has a stunning waterfall that trickles down a rock face imbued with marble and gold, occasionally spilling over into the lava, throwing up huge plumes of steam that carry nearly two miles overhead, eventually breaking the surface. Accessible only from under water, those that pay their respects must all swim the length of an underground river, maintaining their human forms at all times. It is most unusual. That said, there are few more enchanting sights throughout the dragon domain than a bereavement ceremony in the country of Liechtenstein, although no dragon has died there in over a hundred years. Taking this to the other extreme, some grottos can be the size of a laminium ball stadium.

No matter what their size, all of these grottos have several things in common. First is the fact that somewhere inside them there is always an area of lava large enough to submerge a fully grown dragon. Secondly, the grotto must be able to accommodate one dragon scale from any corpse that is submerged there. Normally incorporated into the cavern's ceiling, occasionally something different is done, with walls, murals, and even self sustaining floating islands, being just some of the ways that the dragons who've passed away can be remembered. Last, but by no means least, the grotto must be looked after and guarded so that it is only used for these ceremonies, being such a sacred place. Throughout dragon history, there is no record of such a place ever being violated, despite a whole host of disagreements and wars.

Striding onto the correct platform, feeling a little self conscious about his cloak, Peter waited patiently, knowing that his whole journey would take about fifty five minutes, but only because he'd have to change three times, first at Birmingham, then Manchester, and finally Windermere; from there the monorail would travel straight into the reception area of the grotto.

Tail slumped comfortably through the hole in his seat, watching the darkened rock faces whizz by, he tried to relax, thinking of everything going on around him. While he'd been the only one wearing a cloak at Salisbridge station, he found he wasn't alone after changing at Birmingham, with many other dragons sporting similar bright, gaudy attire. By the time he alighted at the grotto there were literally hundreds of dragons, all wearing brightly coloured cloaks. Having never been to anything like this before, Peter found himself following the crowd, something easily done, all the time hoping the overwhelming colours of the cloaks didn't provoke some kind of adverse reaction. Thankfully it proved the right decision as they all moved from the reception area through a single tunnel and into the grotto itself. As the throng of dragons came out the other side, a very tall, serious looking, female dragon, dressed in long shimmering purple robes, handed everyone a silver horn from a large wooden table that was stacked high with them.

Peter accepted his when it was offered to him and nodded a thank you to the serious dragon. Moving deeper into the grotto, he suddenly became more aware of just how beautiful this place was, as an usher led him towards the next available free seat on a rock ledge overlooking the swirling mass of bright orange lava that continually twisted and writhed, forming eddies and whirlpools every now and then. Bright light from the lava's intense orange glow reflected off the high grotto ceiling, making it look like the surface of a strange and distant world, set amongst a celestial backdrop. It was mesmerising. He knew that what appeared to be stars high above him, were actually scales from dragons long since passed. Each dragon has a scale removed from his or her body when they go through the funeral rite and that scale becomes part of the ever changing starscape that visitors to the grotto will always remember.

The steady trickle of dragons entering the grotto died away to nothing, the silence only interrupted by the occasional bursting bubble of steaming hot molten lava wriggling about below them. Sitting back, he took in the whole ceiling of star-like scales. It was such a peaceful moment, unlike anything he'd ever experienced before. Taking a sneaky look at those around him, he noticed they were all doing the same thing. Some were even whispering a silent prayer, although who to, it was difficult to tell. He now understood just why the grottos were so sacred, and why working in them was such a sought after and highly valued occupation.

Startled out of his musings by the sound of rock grating on rock, he looked over to his right and could just make out a huge disc of rock rolling along the wall, revealing a dark passage behind it. At first, his highly advanced dragon senses could only detect movement. Rapidly, a line of dragons flew out of the darkness, eight in all, with the last two clutching the wings of the perfectly preserved corpse of Mark Hiscock in his natural dragon form. Something akin to an aerial display, the troupe flew in formation in and around the grotto for over five minutes, swooping low, and close to the audience at times, affording everyone a good view of the deceased. As one, the flight stopped and hovered in the exact centre of the grotto, above the roiling lava. Glancing left and right, Peter watched all the other dragons bow their heads in respect. Immediately he followed suit, adding a silent farewell as he did so. From out of nowhere, the master of the bereavement grotto flew silently up to Mark's dragon body, and using a sacred set of ceremonial clippers, that looked more like bolt cutters, clipped a single scale from his tail, which she then slotted elegantly into a prearranged space in the ceiling. Mark was now at home with the rest of his brethren, watching over them all.

The all encompassing silence was broken by the ting of a triangle echoing gently around the grotto. As one, every dragon instantly placed the silver horn to their lips. Peter did the same, a split second behind everyone else. As the last note of the triangle faded to nothing, all of the dragons blew into their horns simultaneously.

At that exact same moment the two dragons holding Mark's corpse released it, letting it tumble down into the lava below. The giant dragon body hit the molten liquid with a mighty splash, floating on the surface for a few seconds before slowly sinking, and with one final gurgle, disappeared beneath the lava forever.

As the horns stopped playing, the formation of flying dragons did one more lap before disappearing back down the dark tunnel, which was in turn covered back up by the moving disc of rock.

As the rock crunched back into place, the grotto became a whole lot lighter, dragons filed back out towards the reception area, handing back their horns as they went. Peter followed, handing his back to the serious looking female dragon, who now just looked relieved, more than anything. Heading back through the tunnel, he patiently waited his turn as hundreds of dragons boarded the silver monorail carriages, all shooting off in different directions. Standing, head bowed, on the shiny stone floor of the platform, he felt empty. He'd thought the service would give him closure of some sort, but it hadn't. If anything, it had sent his thoughts racing, about Mark, the events leading up to his death and about what part, if any, Manson had played in it. The whole house thing was odd. Very odd. With nearly all the dragons having departed, Peter reluctantly boarded the last carriage bound for Manchester.

Hurtling along at nearly five hundred miles an hour, dragons all around him chatting, laughing, joking and just generally getting on with things, he felt miserable. Before he knew it, the monorail had pulled onto the Manchester concourse. Stepping off, he looked around for the next carriage to Birmingham. As he did so, a London bound carriage glided effortlessly into the adjacent platform. The word 'London' conjured up only one image in his head. Tank! Wishing for nothing more than to see his friend, he jumped through the whooshing doors, just before they closed, and took a seat.

Less than forty minutes later, he found himself walking through the narrow, shadow filled streets that led to Gee Tee's Mantra Emporium. Buoyed by the thought of seeing his friend, he quickened his step, smiling as he realised that he was even in the right form to enter the shop without getting an ear bashing from the owner, unlike last time. Trying desperately to clamp down on what he knew to be his scarlet cheeks (he was still full of shame and embarrassment at the whole 'underpants issue' and just recalling it was enough to turn him a totally different shade), he turned into Camelot Arcade, making his way along until he reached the old wooden door with the squeaky handle.

Stepping inside, the shop looked exactly like it had last time, right down to the last cobweb. The obsessive compulsive in him wanted a vacuum cleaner here and now, although given his last spider encounter, the rest of him wasn't so sure. Making his way straight to the front of the shop, all the while keeping an eye out for anything exotic and unusual, he tried to make it obvious he was there, without being obvious about it. As you can imagine, it didn't go well. He looked like an uncoordinated, drunken dinosaur that had been out in the sun for far too long. All he could think of once he'd reached the shop counter, was,

'Why don't they get a bell on the front door? At least that way they'd know when a customer came in.'

Flapping his wings while blowing hoops of crackling yellow flame in the hope of attracting some attention, he failed to spot the ancient figure looming out from one side of a bookcase that he'd already passed.

"Hello child," ventured a velvety smooth voice.

Peter nearly choked on his own flames at the sight of Gee Tee emerging from behind the bookcase.

"Uhh... hi there Mr... Tee," uttered Peter nervously.

"Hello again, child. What can we do for you today?"

"I was hoping to speak to Tank," stuttered Peter, totally

PAUL CUDE

flummoxed.

"I'm afraid he's not here at the moment... child."

"Oh... okay. Can you just tell him I'll catch up with him later?" said Peter, disappointed.

"Certainly," replied Gee Tee, sensing Peter's disappointment. "Is there anything I can help you with?"

"No I don't think... well, actually, maybe... yes," answered Peter.

"Is it regarding the man you work with that we discussed last time?" remarked the old shopkeeper, peering over the top of his precariously placed square plastic glasses.

"Yes it is," replied Peter, keen as mustard.

"Right, I'll tell you what. You help me put some books back on the shelves, and I'll listen to what you have to tell me. Deal?"

"You're not going to turn me into a spider are you?" added Peter, only half joking.

"That rather depends on how well you put the books back," cautioned the master mantra maker, the tiniest of grins etched across his face.

What remained of Peter's nerves, tried to make a break for the door. Today was not going well.

"I'm kidding of course," said the old shopkeeper smiling. "I mean how hard can it be? You can't be any worse than that best friend of yours."

Peter followed the old dragon back through the maze of bookcases, wondering exactly what he'd let himself in for. Pulling up in front of one that said 'Mantra Additions For The Human Form' on the top, it was only then that he noticed the dusty pile of tomes that rose up past his waist on the floor beside it. It looked like he was very much going to fulfil his need to clean something. Gee Tee explained that the books needed to be cleaned and then returned in alphabetical order, from the top of the pile. Taking the strange feather duster offered to him by the old shopkeeper, one that looked as though a chicken had been

154

involved in a very violent and bloody confrontation with a rainbow, he picked up the top book entitled 'Abdominal Flab And How To Coax The Beer Belly Out Of You', and gave it a quick clean.

"So child, why don't you tell me what troubles you?" spluttered Gee Tee, blowing a whole load of dust from the front cover of a book called 'Nose Hair - Amazon Rainforest, Or Well Manicured Garden'.

"Well, it's like this..." Peter began, updating the shopkeeper on his encounter with Manson at the industrial unit, telling him about Dr Island's shock dismissal, and about discovering Manson at Mark's house. All the time the two of them continued to put books back on the shelf after having cleaned them, with the latest clutched in Peter's hands, being called 'Double Chins - The Best A Man Can Get'.

After having listened intently to everything Peter had to say, Gee Tee put down the next book he was holding, took off his glasses and scratched his nose vigorously.

"Well child, it does all sound very suspicious. Can you describe in detail the aroma from Garrett's office and Mark's house? Were they identical?"

"It's difficult to put into words. Really bitter and overpowering, with just a hint of... something... citrusy, I think."

"Have you ever had any problems with your sense of smell?" asked the old shopkeeper, curiously.

"No," replied Peter. "Never. I passed all the senses tests in the nursery ring with flying colours. Not quite top of the class, but nearly."

"The young female, the third of your little trio, I would guess."

Peter nodded.

"That's right. She was top for most things."

"So I gather, so I gather," Gee Tee chuckled softly to himself, all the time pondering everything he'd been told. "It's most odd that you struggle to identify this mysterious smell, but then again, perhaps not. After all, most poisons are designed to be hard to identify, particularly slow acting ones, so maybe we shouldn't be surprised."

"You think Mark was poisoned?" declared Peter, taken aback.

"It does at least seem to be a possibility."

Peter let his big dragon bum slide down the wall beside the bookcase, until he slumped to the floor with a 'THUMP', and just sat there dejectedly. With his tail curled up and his wings folded over his head, he looked a forlorn sight.

"I can't believe all of this is happening to me," he announced from beneath his wings. "What am I supposed to do? I'm pretty sure there were no lessons that covered this in the nursery ring. Who do I trust? Who will believe me?" he said, holding back the tears.

Gee Tee let out a little snigger. Peter looked out beneath both wings, rage building up on his face.

"It's all right child. I'm not laughing at you... honest! It's just this whole situation reminds me of something I've been involved with before. The other person I helped was a lot like you."

"Does that mean you're going to help me?" Peter queried hopefully.

"Ummmmm... I suppose so... yes," replied the old shopkeeper smiling, "but I'm not exactly sure how much help I'll be, as I've never taken human form, let alone met a real one in person, or even been to the surface. I've only ever read about their customs and beliefs, so I have no real firsthand experience of what you're talking about."

"Who cares?" raved Peter, grinning from ear to ear. "Someone who believes in me, how fantastic is that?"

"Well, you can blame Tank partly for that," replied the old dragon, getting back to business. "You see, although I may think you're okay, the fact that Tank thinks of you as his best friend, counts for a great deal. In all the time I've worked with the young fellow, the only time I've known his judgement to be suspect was the incident with the Egyptian morphbeetle that I told you about. I would suggest he has a better understanding of dragons, humans, plants and animals than any other being I've ever encountered. On that, I trust him totally. So if I can't help out his best friend, what would the world be coming to?"

Gee Tee proffered an outstretched hand, and pulled Peter up off the floor.

"Perhaps we'd better devote our time to something more productive than cleaning books," the shop owner said, as he led the young dragon back through the maze, towards the shop counter.

"It's such a shame dragons don't do autopsies. In that we could take a lesson from our charges on the surface."

Peter looked on astonished.

"Close your mouth child, before something unpleasant takes up residence in there."

Peter did as he was told.

"I might not have been to the surface, or have ever met a real human, but I've studied them inside and out. A very contradictory species if you ask me. Full of real promise, but with an innate desire to self destruct, particularly when things seem to be going so well. Like Indian food and steam trains, two things I'd very much like to try, this autopsy thing of theirs seems a well thought out idea. If one had been done on Mark's dragon body, then just maybe we would have found something of the poison's identity, which would have been a start. Without that though, things are going to be tough. Never mind. We'll just have to find another way."

Slumping down in one of the oversized dragon chairs in the workshop, the old shopkeeper let out a giant sigh, while indicating to Peter that he should sit in the chair opposite. He duly complied.

"Now tell me child, do you have to go back to Mark's house again?"

"Yes," replied Peter. "I have to finish sorting out all of

his stuff and make sure it gets to the children's hospital as per his wishes."

"Well," said Gee Tee, rummaging through the bottom of a stack of books, "I'm not sure being exposed to whatever is in that house for a prolonged period is a very good idea."

"But... but..." Peter started to protest.

"Yes I know. You have to go back and sort it out. Ahhhh... here it is. Just what we need. Now let's have a look and see if this will do," mused the old shopkeeper enthusiastically, sweeping books, papers, pens and bottles of ink off the desk he was sitting at and onto the floor with a flick from one of his giant wings. Opening up a rolled up sheet of parchment, he began to study it intently.

Waiting in silence, Peter tried to glimpse over Gee Tee's shoulder, hoping to get some idea of just what he was so engrossed in. After a few minutes of muttering and mumbling under his breath, the old dragon turned round to face Peter.

"It's not quite what I had in mind, but I think it will do."

This was the first time in both visits that Peter had seen the master mantra maker smile, and looking at the parchment on the desk had clearly put a spring in the old dragon's step. It was more than a little disconcerting.

Gee Tee ushered Peter to the centre of the room with one large wing, before asking him to stand still. Returning to the table, he stretched out the parchment once again, holding it in place with two bottles of rainbow dazzling mantra ink. Turning back towards Peter, he said,

"Although not specifically designed to protect against poison, I do think it will be strong enough to grant you temporary immunity to whatever evil lurks in that house. I strongly suggest you try your best to keep everyone out of the house in general until we can come up with a way to neutralise whatever it was that was being used."

Poking his glasses high up his nose, he turned to look

at the parchment on the table, all the time addressing the young dragon.

"Stand perfectly still; this will only take a few seconds."

Closing his eyes, the old shopkeeper began muttering words in a language Peter couldn't understand, made all the more remarkable because all dragons are masters of languages, encouraged to learn at least twenty different tongues in the nursery ring, with most going on to learn a lot more.

Concentrating on standing perfectly still, Peter chose to focus on Gee Tee's square plastic spectacles. On doing so, he could just make out small beads of sweat, from the effort, wriggling down the old dragon's nose.

'These words seem to be taking a lot out of him,' he thought, just as Gee Tee finished. Staggering over to where he'd left the chair, the master mantra maker collapsed bum first into it, the wheels beneath the legs squeaking as he did so. Peter, who was by now tingling all over, hurried over and knelt beside the chair.

"Are you okay?" he asked, concerned.

Struggling to catch his breath, Gee Tee replied,

"I will be in a few minutes child. Reciting ancient Polynesian mantras takes a lot of energy, and I'm not as young as I once was."

Unexpectedly, a voice from the doorway behind them, interrupted.

"What on Earth is going on here?" demanded Tank, rushing in and barging Peter out of the way so that he could get to his employer's side.

"It's alright, my young apprentice," murmured Gee Tee, still wheezing, "I was just showing your friend here a mantra or two."

"You know you're not supposed to cast powerful, high draining mantras, when there's nobody else present," chided Tank in his best school master voice, while glaring daggers at Peter.

Gee Tee smiled.

"There was somebody about," he said, pointing at Peter, who was now really confused as to exactly what was going on.

"You know what I mean," Tank added with scorn on his face.

"I know, I know," ventured Gee Tee remorsefully. "Why don't you take your young friend here and make us all some steaming hot charcoal?"

Tank knew better than to argue when he heard that tone of voice.

"Come on Peter," Tank said, motioning to the door with one of his wings.

Peter followed Tank out onto the shop floor, when suddenly the master mantra maker's words came booming out from behind them.

"Marshmallows!"

"He'll be lucky," whispered Tank quietly, leading the way towards the deepest, darkest part of the shop. In between two of the dustiest bookcases Peter had seen so far was a dark red wooden door. Peter followed his friend inside, to be greeted by a very small ramshackle room, used as a makeshift kitchen. Flicking the gas on the hob on, Tank lit it with a flimsy streak of flame from between his jaws, before putting a gigantic copper coloured kettle, filled with water, on to boil.

"What went on while I was away Peter?"

"Well I came to see you and you weren't here so Gee Tee and I talked and I told him what was happening with Manson and then he agreed to help me, and then he cast a mantra on me to protect me from the poison and..."

"Whoa, whoa. Poison? What poison?" Tank asked, worriedly.

While the steaming kettle whistled quietly, Peter explained what had been happening regarding the funeral and being the executor of Mark's will, as Tank carefully sorted heaped spoonfuls of dark black charcoal into three oversized, ultra thick mugs, with huge handles that only a dragon could grip. Peter smiled at Gee Tee's mug that had a script he didn't recognise going all the way around it, while Tank's had a tiger morphing into a butterfly on it. The remaining mug which he assumed was for him, was just plain purple and had obviously seen better days.

As Tank poured the steaming hot water onto the contents of each mug, he turned to Peter and said,

"There's something you need to understand. Gee Tee won't reveal his true age to anyone, but it's thought that he's over six hundred years old."

Peter nearly dropped the mug that Tank had just handed to him.

"Over six hundred years old! I think someone's been pulling your leg. No dragon can live that long."

Tank just stood with a sombre expression.

"Just between us, it's true Peter. He is over six centuries old. He's also very frail and gets tired incredibly quickly. When I told you the other day that I wouldn't lose my job, it wasn't only because of the work that I do here. It's because I help look after him as well. The doctor visits once a week and he's on all sorts of medication. He may act all tough and arrogant, but he's really not like that at all. He shouldn't be wearing himself out performing crazy protective mantras when they're not required."

"I didn't make him do it... honest Tank," Peter pleaded.

"I'm sure you didn't Pete. But it makes no difference. By spinning him your tale, he thinks he can help you and turn things around. He's not willing to admit to himself just how unwell and fragile he really is."

Peter glugged down a huge mouthful of the eye wateringly hot drink, before looking up at his friend.

"I'm sorry Tank. I had no idea."

"I know you didn't. Hardly anyone does. All I'm asking is that you try not to get him too excited and involved in stuff. I know how his twisted mind works. Conspiracies and underhanded schemes all too often feature. He claims to have thwarted many in the past, some singlehandedly, others by just providing his valuable knowledge. Whether it's true or not, I don't really know. All I do know is that he's attracted by the idea, something I believe will do him no good at all in his current state. By all means talk to him and pick his brain, but try not to wear him out, and quit if he starts to look too tired."

"Sure thing," Peter agreed as the two friends headed back across the shop floor with their hot drinks. Tank smiled at his friend.

"So a protection mantra, eh? Just one more thing you should be aware of Pete. Gee Tee is probably the world's foremost expert on everything and anything to do with mantras. Those in this shop are unlike any others found on this planet. Some of them date back thousands of years and he is the only one that can make head or tail of them. That said, even the great dragon himself can make mistakes from time to time, especially when he's tired and hasn't taken his medication."

"What are you saying?" asked Peter anxiously.

Tank smiled in a way that made Peter feel very nervous.

"Be thankful that you didn't end up in the body of a spider."

Most of the time Peter could tell when his friend was being serious or whether he was joking, but at this exact moment, he really didn't have a clue. Returning to the workshop, they found that Gee Tee had recovered from his exertions and was gathering up everything he'd previously strewn across the floor. The three of them each took a chair and sat sipping their drinks in comparative silence. That is, until the old shopkeeper piped up.

"I knew there was a reason I continue to employ you," he said smiling and licking his great big jaw. "In all my years I've never come across anyone that can make steaming hot charcoal like you can."

Tank's moody expression seemed to soften just slightly, particularly when his employer let out a resounding 'BURRRRRRRP'.

162

Looking directly at Tank, Gee Tee pushed his glasses as far up his nose as he could, and said,

"I know you only have my best interests at heart apprentice, something I really do appreciate, and show far less frequently than I should. But I'm not quite as frail or infirm as you would believe."

Tank's softened expression turned back to one of moodiness, and Peter could see that his friend was just about to lecture the old dragon again, when the shopkeeper held up his wing to stop his young apprentice.

"I've lived for a very long time and have a great many experiences to call upon, all of which currently tell me two things. One is that your friend, Peter, has got himself tangled up in something very unusual indeed and needs OUR help. And two, despite my vast years, I'm still a very long way off joining the great river of lava."

At this last comment, Tank broke into a real smile, the first time Peter had seen him do so today.

"So," continued Gee Tee, "we will continue our research here and try to find a mantra that will totally neutralise what we believe to be poison in Mark's house on the surface. While you, young Peter, must practice caution. If indeed Manson is not as he appears to be, then he could potentially be very dangerous. If I were you, I would continue to gather more information and avoid any unnecessary confrontation with him."

Peter nodded his agreement and left the Mantra Emporium feeling genuinely happy for the first time in as long as he could remember. He would continue to watch Manson and with the help of his friends, old and new, he was sure he could thwart whatever evil the crafty Major had in mind.

9 HERE TODAY, GUN TOMORROW

On arriving at work the following day, the first thing Peter did was to email Richie, to ask if she would meet him for lunch in the staff restaurant. She replied almost instantaneously, agreeing to meet, much to his relief. He spent the rest of the morning doing staff appraisals in his office, whilst worrying about what he was going to say to his friend at lunch. Occasionally he would check the security monitors to see if he could pick up any sign of the elusive Manson, but the smug ex-officer remained absent all morning, despite the fact that his car was parked in its normal spot.

At five to twelve, Peter logged off his computer and took off through the building towards the restaurant. Normally preferring to bring in sandwiches for lunch, not because of the cost (as the restaurant was heavily subsidised) but mainly so that he could eat his lunch and work at the same time.

Rounding the corner, he caught sight of Richie standing outside the restaurant entrance, people pouring in on either side of her. Noticing his approach, she flashed him one of her classic grins. It was then that he knew everything was going to be okay. Greeting each other with a hug, unusually Peter gave Richie a kiss on the cheek, which managed to pleasantly surprise her, something she commented on as the pair of them took a tray each from the pile and joined the end of the queue. Shuffling forward as one, the two friends eyed up the menu for today.

Richie opted for lasagne, while Peter thought he would make the most of not having to cook a hot meal today and went for the roast of the day, which turned out to be his favourite, roast beef. Both added a soft drink to their tray, and, upon reaching the checkout, Peter offered to pay for both his and Richie's meals, thinking it might go some way to make amends for falling out. Richie didn't put up a fight, which Peter thought strange, right up until a very pleasant lady on the till announced that the grand total for the two meals was a hefty £3.45. Blushing upon realising his mistake, he quickly made his way to one of the few remaining free tables, with Richie following. As they both sat, Peter said,

"I didn't really think that through did I?"

Spooning a large chunk of lasagne into her mouth, Richie smiled and waited until she'd finished her mouthful.

"What a friend. Treating me to a slap up meal at one of the best restaurants in town," she said sarcastically.

"How about I promise to take you out somewhere really nice? You choose. Whenever you're next free in the evening," Peter said, taking a huge bite of his wall clock sized Yorkshire pudding.

"You don't have to do that Pete."

"I know I don't have to. But I really want to, to... make up for the way I acted," he pleaded awkwardly.

"A meal with my best friend would always be welcome. Anyway, we were both at fault for what happened. Let's just put it behind us and move on. Our behaviour is always put to shame by Tank. Good job we've got him to look after us and show us our flaws."

Peter nodded his agreement, as a huge slab of roast beef lathered in gravy slipped between his teeth.

"Yeah, he does always seem to know what to say. I bet his pet plants don't give him nearly as much trouble as we do, though."

Richie laughed and replied,

"They know not to give him any trouble, because if they do he'll just spend more time talking to them, and they can't run away. He puts Prince Charles to shame on that front."

"That sounds about right," agreed Peter, mopping up the last of the gravy on his plate with his Yorkshire.

Unexpectedly a figured loomed over their table.

"Sorry to disturb you Mr Bentwhistle, but could I have

a quick word?"

Peter looked up into the face of one of the scientists from the industrial area, and try as he might, he just couldn't remember the man's name.

"Of course you can, um..."

"It's Jake. Jake Brown," said the scientist.

"Sorry Jake. What can I do for you?" Peter replied, wearing his best smile.

"Well it's uhhh... the new guards. We're all finding it quite hard to concentrate with... you know."

Looking as puzzled as ever, Peter replied,

"You're going to have to be a little more specific, Jake, I'm afraid."

"The new guards and their... equipment. It's making everybody over in industrial very... nervous, you might say," Jake said, looking up at the ceiling.

"I'm really sorry Jake, but I don't have the faintest idea of what you're talking about. What exactly is making everyone so nervous?"

The scientist leaned in close and looked around to make sure nobody was listening in.

"The guards, they've all got... well, see for yourself," observed Jake, standing up and pointing in the direction of the restaurant's entrance.

All around the restaurant heads turned and conversations suddenly dried up, as everybody started to notice the pair of guards that stood at the back of the queue. Dressed from head to toe in a light blue uniform, the guards certainly stood out from the mixture of smart casual that most of the other employees wore. That, however, was not the main talking point. Strapped around each of the guards' waists was a shiny black belt that held a holster on one side. Poking out from the holster, the dark metallic grip of a gun was just visible. As if to make matters worse, dangling from the back of each belt was a serious looking baton, a handheld radio, and a silver pair of handcuffs. Peter was visibly taken aback, along with half the restaurant by the look of things.

"What the hell...?" he muttered to nobody in particular. Shaking his head and giving Richie a kind of 'I told you so' look, he got up, mumbling,

"This just can't be happening..."

With the restaurant reaching perhaps its busiest time, nearly two hundred employees watched, fascinated, by what Peter's next action would be. Taking a deep breath, he made his way through the mass of tables, winding like a snake as he headed for the two guards towards the end of the line, all eyes watching him like a reality TV freak show. Eventually reaching the guards, his mood had darkened no end by now, which was highlighted by the scowl on his normally friendly face. Peter leaned in close and whispered,

"Can you please tell me what the hell is going on?"

"Step back please, sir," commanded the taller of the two guards.

Feeling unbelievably lonely and realising that not a single sound could now be heard in the entire restaurant, Peter began to get just a little hot under the collar. The situation rested on a knife edge and was rapidly becoming as tense as walking into the shower and catching your granny in nothing but her beard.

Poking his finger into the guard's chest, Peter fumed,

"Listen sonny, don't you know who I am?" for all to hear.

The other guard began to fumble with the cover of his holster nervously, not sure quite what to do with the furious man close to abusing his partner. Peter spotted the second guard's hand straying towards his gun and something inside him snapped. Feeling like a volcano about to erupt, he sought to convert all of his built up rage into dragon power and knock the two idiots fully across the room. The guards looked panic stricken and confused as Peter finally seemed like he was about to lose the plot.

Out of nowhere, a slender, freckled arm weaved its way around Peter's waist and pulled him gently away from the guards and towards the exit.

"You'll have to excuse my friend," prompted Richie, leaning away from Peter towards the two guards. "I think some of his roast beef went down the wrong way, and with him not having taken his medication today, he can sometimes get a little... cranky. He's a little... SPECIAL," she said, giving them a wink and a smile, like butter wouldn't melt in her mouth, as she whisked Peter out through the double doors and into the corridor. Her vice-like grip didn't diminish even though they were now out of the restaurant. Maintaining her hold, she guided Peter subtly along until they reached an innocuous looking glass door, leading out to a very small, secluded courtyard, right in the middle of the building. About half the size of a tennis court, the space was awash with many varieties of ferns and other large plants, which all provided shade and a certain degree of privacy. A small rectangular pond, packed to the brim with koi carp of every different colour stood, raised above the ground, in one corner, camouflaged by the giant green plants that towered above it.

Richie led Peter out into the courtyard, steering him through the fern leaves, round a raised flower bed and onto a small wooden bench that looked as though it could do with a fresh coat of varnish. Looking up, Peter could just make out a couple of white fluffy clouds through the tangled mess of leaves and branches. It took a few seconds for it to dawn on him, but then he realised he was right, smack bang in the middle of the office complex. Looking more than a little perplexed, he also realised that he previously had no idea this place even existed. Richie, having taken a seat on the bench, looked at him in a very peculiar manner.

"This is a turn up for the books," she scoffed, a big smile blossoming onto her face. "ME, having to take you away before you do something you'll regret for a very long time to come."

The surprise at having found this place, coupled with

the relaxing sound of the tiny movements of water in the pond, drained Peter of all his pent up aggression and anger. As quickly as his rage had appeared, it was now nowhere to be seen, and the normally quiet and reserved, awkward youth was back to his shy self.

Rolling his eyes and pointing discreetly with his finger in an upwards direction, he said,

"Uh... Rich, we're surrounded by three storeys of windows on all sides. I'm sure everyone at their desks doesn't want to listen to our conversation."

Richie just sat there and smiled at him.

"Not only are all the windows double glazed, but none of them actually open up. We're perfectly secluded here. I can't believe you didn't know about this place. Some security co-ordinator you are," she mocked.

He looked up at all the windows looming over the courtyard, trying to confirm what his friend had just said.

"Of course I knew about this place."

"Oh please, don't try and hide it from me. I could feel your shock the moment I opened the door to come out here. You had absolutely no idea it even existed, did you?"

Peter just nodded his head. He knew it was impossible to hide anything from his friend.

"I can't believe it. It's like a little oasis of calm tucked away where no one can find it."

"So anyway, back to what happened in the restaurant," challenged Richie, knocking Peter out of his daydream.

"Yeah... sorry about that," he replied, not able to look his friend in the eye. "And thanks for pulling me out of there before I lost my temper and did something really stupid."

Richie shook her head and laughed.

"I just kept looking at your aura with my dragon abilities," she whispered. "It looked like you were going to explode at one point. I thought it best to get you out of there... although I have to admit a big part of me was desperate to see the dashing Peter Bentwhistle, head of

Cropptech security, in handcuffs," she confessed, a big toothy grin on her face.

"Wasn't gonna happen, trust me."

Winking, Richie said,

"You should give it go. You don't know what you're missing."

Shaking his head and starting to blush, Peter replied,

"You know my feelings about that Rich. One day, you're going to get into so much trouble with your... your... human dalliances."

"Not gonna happen, trust me," Richie said, imitating her friend. "Seriously though, Pete, what happened? I've never seen you lose your temper at all. Yet if I'm not mistaken, you were ready to finish those guards off."

Sitting on the old bench, head in his hands, he let out a long breath, before looking up at the huge fern leaf that was currently providing him with shade. Watching intently as a brightly coloured ladybird crawled across the leaf's arched centre, his emotions barely in check as his mind struggled to answer Richie's question.

"It just seemed like the straw that broke the camel's back. Head of security? My arse! Oh I might sign off the timesheets and do the appraisals, but obviously I'm no longer in charge here."

Richie sat and listened, fully aware that her lunch hour had long since passed, but not really caring very much.

Riveted by the ladybird's delicate actions, he watched as it unfolded its precise, flimsy looking wings, seeming as though it was about to take flight.

"Guns, armed guards... What the hell is this place coming to? The security provisions that were already in place were more than adequate for the site we have here. In its entire history, Cropptech has never been the victim of a major theft or incident of any kind."

In the meantime, the ladybird had decided not to fly away, instead just fluttering its wings for no apparent reason.

"I know you might have disagreed with me before about Manson's motives Rich, but can you not see now what's going on? Something here is very, very wrong. I just can't seem to work out exactly what it is, and it's driving me crazy. It's as if, as if... the answer is right in front of my face, but for the life of me I just can't seem to see it. It's so frustrating."

Richie studied her friend, while he in turn continued to study the ladybird. They had been friends for such a long time, and she had never seen him so... out of sorts. Not wanting to upset him and fall out again, she considered her words carefully.

"I know it seems strange Pete, but perhaps Manson is just doing his job. Maybe armed guards are a little over the top, but the Cropptech industrial unit does house a variety of valuable metal and gems. Not to mention the reason you and I are here... the laminium! We both know how valuable that is," she added, raising her eyebrows.

"It's much more than that, it really is," Peter pleaded with his friend. "Don't ask me how I know, I just do."

Not wishing to press the point any further, whilst also recognising that Peter seemed to have reached the end of his tether, Richie leaned over and kissed her friend smack in the middle of his forehead.

"Well if there's anything I can do to help, don't hesitate to let me know. I've got to get back to work. Think you can find your way out?"

Waving his mobile phone in the air, he replied,

"I'll call you if I get lost."

The two friends waved goodbye to each other, with Peter remaining in the courtyard a little longer, trying to decide on a course of action. What could he do? Ranting and raving at Manson would clearly get him nowhere, and it might even get him fired like Dr Island. Al Garrett was about as visible as a needle in a haystack at the moment, so it wasn't as if he could just bump into him somewhere and raise the issue. What he needed was an excuse, an excuse to go and see Garrett and then tackle him about these armed guards and Manson in general.

Peter racked his brains trying desperately to find the answers that he needed, but after a few minutes he gave up. Nothing he could think of would be important enough to get him a one to one with the boss and still be credible enough to fool Manson, or at least not give Manson a reason to have him fired.

Sitting in the shade watching the fish glide gracefully through the water, Peter started to think about all the other things he had to do outside work. Top of his mental list was to go back to Mark's house and finish the packing, after which he had to go and visit the solicitors. Before he did that though, he was waiting on Gee Tee and Tank to see if they'd made any progress in finding a mantra to rid the house of whatever evil loitered inside.

Out of nowhere it came to him.

'That's it!' he thought. 'Mark.' Why hadn't it occurred to him before? The perfect excuse that he needed to visit Al Garrett was right in front of him: a memorial in Mark's memory. It had been done before, plenty of times in fact. Cropptech's grounds were littered with beautiful wooden benches, many dedicated to former employees who had passed away. Better still was the thought that Manson wouldn't even object to the idea, as he'd already claimed to be Mark's friend when Peter had caught him at the house.

'Perfect,' he thought, 'absolutely perfect.' So perfect in fact, that he was going to march up to Al Garrett's office right now. Ducking in between the giant green leaves, he made his way back to the glass door. Instead of turning left and heading back towards the restaurant and his office, he turned right and headed for the nearest staircase. Once there, he climbed to the top floor, made his way through the open plan offices of the accounts department, and into the executive part of the building.

A rueful smile crossed his face as he exchanged the world of notice boards and narrow corridors filled with photocopiers and printers, for a world of lush carpets, hi tech coffee machines, oak panelled walls and polished brass fittings. Turning the corner, he spotted the shiny lift doors that he normally used. Swaggering confidently down the corridor towards Al Garrett's office, he knew that whoever was in there would already know he was on his way. He'd already noticed a couple of the security cameras tracking his every move. Rapping on the door, he forced himself to stand up straight. A husky voice resounded from inside.

"Come."

Taking a deep breath and forcing a smile onto his face, he turned the handle and entered. Just as last time, it was dark, only tiny slivers of light finding their way through the blinds on the full length window. Peter was struck dumb by the overpowering stench that pervaded the room. If he hadn't been totally convinced before that it was the same smell as in Mark's house, he was nothing short of one hundred percent sure now.

Stepping through the gloom, he stopped in front of Garrett's desk, staring intently at the old man slouched in the chair behind it. Although it hadn't been long since he'd last seen the 'bald eagle', the physical change in the man seemed quite remarkable. Previously, Peter would have regarded Garrett as being in pretty good shape for someone of his age, but now... he looked positively ancient. His skin seemed pale, clammy and gaunt. The trademark moustache and the small amount of hair on his head looked slick with grease, as if he hadn't washed in weeks. A closer inspection suggested Garrett's eyes were overly bloodshot and that the smell of severe body odour was so bad, it could nearly walk out of the room on its own accord.

Standing up tall and straight, he waited patiently for either the seated Garrett, or Manson who was standing by the window at the back of the room, to address him.

"It's... it's... Bent-thistle isn't it?" Garrett babbled,

leaning across the desk to try and get a better view.

"Bentwhistle sir," replied Peter loudly.

"Ahhhh... Bentwhistle," said Garrett, as if trying to remember something important.

"What is it you want, Bentwhistle?" Manson demanded, facing away, looking out of the window.

Addressing Garrett, Peter said,

"It's about Mark, sir. Some of us in the security department wondered if you'd made any plans for a memorial of some kind?"

Garrett looked bewildered.

"Mark. Who's Mark?" he asked, puzzled.

"Mark Hiscock sir," replied Peter. "You know, the ex head of security, who died about two weeks ago."

"Died! Why wasn't I informed?" snapped Garrett angrily.

Peter took a step back, shocked and outraged.

'How could he not know?' he thought.

Manson moved away from the window, wisp-like. Putting a hand on Garrett's shoulder, he whispered,

"It's alright Al. You've had a lot on your plate. We did tell you, but you've been so busy that it must have slipped your mind."

With Manson so close by, Garrett's mind seemed to be struggling to cope with the situation.

"Yessss... slipped my... mind," uttered Garrett, groggily.

"I'll personally make sure he gets the memorial he deserves," assured Manson, his hand still firmly connected to Garrett's shoulder.

"Was there anything else, Bentwhistle?"

Peter knew there was no point in bringing up the business with the armed guards, here and now. From the look of it, Garrett looked as though he was struggling to stay awake, let alone hold a meaningful conversation. Peter looked Manson directly in the eye, and said,

"No, I think that was everything."

"You'll have to excuse us then, Bentwhistle. We have a

lot more work to be getting on with," stated Manson, waving his hand as if to dismiss Peter from the room.

Turning around, Peter headed straight for the door, determined not to show the worry that he felt for Garrett's safety on his face. Grasping the handle, Manson called out from behind him.

"I do hope you like my new guards, Bentwhistle."

He always managed to make the word 'Bentwhistle' sound like something you'd scrape off your shoe after a walk in the park. Turning the handle without looking back, he contemplated everything that had happened on the walk back to his office. Things seemed so wrong. He felt so helpless. And worst of all, he had no idea just how to put things right.

Filled with concern, later that evening Peter decided he was going to keep a diary of all the things that happened at work, relating to Manson and Garrett. Despite not needing to because of his eidetic memory, he thought it wise to have a back up and have something to show others if necessary. Finding a nice notebook that he'd won in a raffle, he opened up the front cover and began jotting down all of the details of today's encounter. Just as he'd finished writing up the day's occurrences, his phone chirped to indicate an incoming text message. It was from Tank. With a mixture of relief and disappointment flooding through him, Peter read that his friend would be coming round later to drop something off, and that he'd had no luck in procuring tickets to the much anticipated match that they'd both hoped to see.

Deleting the message, he decided to unwind by playing one of his favourite computer games, an MMORPG (Massively Multiplayer Online Role Playing Game). He'd tried out a few different games before settling on this particular one, which he really liked. What they all seemed to have in common though, which amused him no end, was the fact that at some point in each and every one of these games, you would wander across a dragon and no doubt have to slay it.

'If only they knew the truth,' he thought, as the start screen flickered into life.

At twenty to nine there was a loud knock at the front of the house. Peter pulled open the front door to reveal a very out of breath Tank in a garishly red tracksuit, all sweaty and dishevelled. Briefly, the man mountain of a rugby player explained that he had run over from his house, in preparation for rugby training which started in less than two weeks time. Peter rolled his eyes and gave his friend a 'you really don't need to be doing that' look, but it just went straight over Tank's head.

With his breathing slowly recovering, Tank handed Peter a wooden prism, or as Peter liked to think of it, a Toblerone-shaped box. Tank explained that his boss had gone to great lengths to obtain both the box and its contents. He added that the items were very old and possibly unstable, and that the fine powder needed to be used in conjunction with the first item, but both should be fit for purpose. Ever so grateful, Peter thanked his friend and asked him to pass on his regards to his boss. With a wave and a nod, Tank headed off into the night, on the return leg of his run home. After watching his friend's giant frame disappear off into the distance, Peter returned to his gaming, not the least bit tired.

10 AN UNUSUAL REQUEST

Eight hours later, Peter sat in his kitchen devouring his breakfast, tired from the hours of gaming. Although weary, he was happy that Tank had come round and dropped off a mantra for him to try at Mark's house.

Gee Tee had said that the mantra, if used properly, should get rid of any toxins throughout the house and the surrounding area. He'd also passed on a second mantra that would confirm everything was totally safe and free from any contaminants. Peter was eager to try it, and had planned to take the afternoon off from work this coming Friday, to finish off clearing the house and try out his friend's hard work. Not only would it be a job out the way, but any time away from Cropptech at the moment seemed like a complete bonus as far as he was concerned.

Chomping on another mouthful of cereal, he decided he'd grab a copy of the Daily Telepath and put it away to read later. Closing his eyes, he used all his will and concentration to send off his mind on its usual route to find the newspaper. Doing it on autopilot so to speak, meant that he was free to finish off his breakfast. Halfway through another giant mouthful, he realised something was dreadfully wrong with the download. Squeezing his eyes together tight, his conscious mind managed to catch up with the part of him that was off in the ether, desperate to see what the problem was. Problems like this were fairly commonplace, generally tending to be difficulties at the other end, complications due to weather conditions or the individual newspapers themselves trying out something new to improve their services. When he'd encountered these problems in the past and caught up with his outstretched mind, he'd always found giant worded messages floating around the filing cabinet area, informing everyone of the problem and announcing when a fix would be in place. Although this produced the same feeling in him, it did feel slightly more... urgent!

Linked fully with his mind once more, he expected to see the giant messages flying around in the air. But this was not the case. Instead, he found a huge blinking red arrow pointing only him in the direction of an old wooden filing cabinet that looked as though it had seen better days. With an air of caution, he guided his mind over and very carefully opened it up.

Instinctively he pulled back a little, expecting an array of information to come screaming out over the top of the drawer at him. But not so. Out flew a little paper plane, dancing and swirling in the air, doing loop the loops, shaped like the iconic Concorde itself, right down to the very last detail. He could have sworn there was even a cabin crew inside the cockpit. Without warning, the plane bucked, headed straight upwards, inverted on itself and, putting on a spurt of speed, flew directly into Peter's consciousness. Overwhelmed and surprised at first, it took him a few seconds to realise that he had to unfold the plane to read the message within. On doing so, he was surprised to see a very unexpected invitation.

YOU ARE SUMMONED TO A MEETING WITH COUNCILLOR HITCH ROSEBLOOM OF THE DRAGON COUNCIL ON SATURDAY AT 5.30PM ROOM 54367 OF THE COUNCIL BUILDING. PUNCTUALITY IS EXPECTED.

After recovering from the initial shock, Peter filed the message away in his subconscious and whizzed off to retrieve the newspaper he'd been looking for in the first place. On his return he finished his breakfast, all the time wondering why he'd been asked to meet the councillor. The rest of the week passed without event and although Peter had tried extremely hard to keep tabs on the ever elusive Manson, it had proved all but impossible, with just the occasional glimpse of him coming and going in and out of Garrett's office. Friday afternoon came along and after changing into some casual clothing, he drove straight from work to Mark's house.

After a couple of hours, Peter had logged and neatly packed the remainder of Mark's belongings (at least those that would fit) and put them safely in his car. He had searched the house as thoroughly as possible and had not come across Manson's lost book, or anything else that would have interested him. The only thing he'd really discovered was that the foul smelling toxin was absolutely everywhere, even in the dank, dark old loft and the tiny cupboard under the stairs that contained only the gas meter and the vacuum cleaner.

With the house all but empty, apart from the larger furniture which he'd arranged to be picked up at a later date, he opened up the wooden prism that Tank had given him, in the middle of the living room. As he did so, Tank's words about Gee Tee being incredibly old and more than a little forgetful rang in his ears. Combined with the worry that he might not be up to the task (after all he was still in his infancy in dragon terms) he could positively feel the butterflies fluttering around inside his stomach. Pulling out a small packet of powder that was wrapped in a flimsy sheet of parchment, he unfolded it, noticing that Gee Tee had written on it to make sure that all the windows and doors within the house were open. Making sure they were, Peter opened the packet and poured the powder into the palm of his hand, having already memorised the mantra from his brief glimpse of it. By the look of things, the master mantra maker had not only translated the mantra into English, but had also made it rhyme to add more power to it. No wonder it had taken the old dragon a little while. Translating was one thing, translating and rhyming, that was something altogether more complicated.

'No surprise he's the best in the business then,' thought Peter. Changing his focus from the old shopkeeper to the matter quite literally at hand, he closed his eyes and started to recite the words of the mantra.

Powder of bat, essence of lynx,

Do your job and be rid of this jinx.
Seek it all out and blow it away,
Once gone for good, away it will stay.

Feeling the cool rush of air on his skin, Peter opened his eyes to see several cyclones whirling around the room, causing the cushions on the sofa to fly and the old wooden legs on the dining table to creak in despair. After three circuits of the living room, the cyclones shot out of the door and scattered in different directions. Retrieving the cushions, he sprawled out on the sofa, waiting until he could no longer hear the flapping of curtains or the rustling of blinds. It didn't take long. A quick tour of the house revealed everything was back to normal, with absolutely no sign at all of any horrible smell. Opening up the prism once more, he removed the second mantra, the one that would check just how safe the house and surrounding area were. Reciting the words, he chuckled to himself on noticing the old shopkeeper had done the same with this one as he had with the last.

Oh wonder of wonders, check all of this dirt,
And see that there's nothing to cause any hurt.
Check everything here is protected and clean,
A message from you we will wait to be seen.

As the last word rolled off his tongue, a small ball of intensely bright light appeared in the centre of the room. Abruptly, two dozen fluorescent blue dragonflies emerged from it, swiftly zooming off in every different direction. Again, Peter chose to wait in the living room, hoping that whatever sign would appear, he would be able to spot it when it happened. Some of these mantras were renowned for being unreliable, or for having a message that lasted half a second. Even as a dragon, it was easy to blink and miss it. He was determined that this was not going to happen. A few minutes after having left, the dragonflies, one by one, all started to return.

As the last dragonfly entered the brilliant ball of supernatural power, it began to spin violently. Beams of light started to erupt from it, causing Peter to have to shield his eyes. Suddenly a loud 'POP' shattered the silence, revealing a giant worded message that ran mid-air around the room, again and again and again. In the same colour as the dragonflies, the words 'ALL CLEAR, ALL CLEAR' soared through the air, weaving in and out of lampshades, lifting the curtains almost clear of their rails, and once again bringing a whole new meaning to the words 'scatter cushions'. After a minute or so the letters started to fade, with the words eventually fizzling out about half a minute later. Standing in the middle of the room, Peter breathed a sigh of relief. The house had been made safe, and could now be sold without endangering any innocent bystanders, the clearance men could now safely collect all the furniture to be sold, and the monies from all of that could be transferred to the children's hospital as per Mark's wishes.

Pulling out his phone, Peter flipped it open and looked up the number for Burns and Haybell solicitors which he'd already pre-programmed in. Eventually he got through to Mr Burns, informing him that the house had been emptied apart from all the large furniture which would be gone within a day. The solicitor told Peter that he would have to come into the office to complete some forms and arrange for the funds from the sale of Mark's effects to go to the hospital, which would all but complete the entire process. Peter agreed to go in just before five o'clock that afternoon.

Entering the offices of Burns and Haybell at exactly ten to five, Mr Burns met him and escorted him through to his office. Peter handed over two newly cut sets of keys and all the relevant paper work that he had. Mr Burns checked that everything was in order and asked for a couple of signatures from Peter, to which he duly obliged. Once it was completed he got up to leave, but Mr Burns ushered him back into his chair.

"There's one last thing that I have to do," said the

solicitor, walking over to a large, dark coloured wooden cabinet in the corner of the room. Much to Peter's surprise, it turned out to be a safe, and once sure that he'd obscured Peter's view, Mr Burns entered the digital pass code, before the tiniest of 'clicks' opened the door. Pulling out a small package, Mr Burns closed the safe door, before returning to his seat opposite Peter.

On the table he carefully placed a small wooden jewellery box. Peter wondered what was going on. The solicitor looked across the desk at Peter and said,

"The last request in Mr Hiscock's will was that you should take possession of this item after completing all the deeds as executor." With that, he pushed the small wooden box across the shiny surface of the table towards Peter. As Peter picked up the box, Mr Burns stood up and offered out his hand.

"Our business here is complete, Mr Bentwhistle. Do have a lovely weekend."

After shaking Mr Burns' hand, Peter left the offices and walked back to where he had parked his car, more than a little intrigued as to what Mark had left him. On getting into the car, he slid the key effortlessly into the ignition before hesitating. With an unbridled curiosity burning inside him, he was unable to resist any longer. Making sure nobody could see, he opened up the wooden box in his lap. His eyes grew wide with surprise. Inside was an intricate silver chain with a tiny, sparkling trident hanging from it.

He stared in wonder as he held the trident up in the palm of his hand. Although it was made of some kind of metal, the colour it gave off was purple. Not only that, but it kind of... pulsated. He'd never seen or heard of anything quite like it.

After a few more minutes of gazing longingly at it, he drove home, where he spent the rest of the evening thinking about the necklace. A quick search of the internet came up blank. It was a mystery, and one that intrigued him like nothing had for some time. In fact he was so taken with the necklace that by the end of the evening he'd decided to wear it, even though he'd never before felt the need for jewellery of any sort. To be honest, as a dragon, it was all a bit of a burden, because necklaces and rings would either drop off or be destroyed during the change from human to dragon and vice versa. There was something about this necklace though. He felt he should be wearing it and could almost feel the power radiating from it. With it fast approaching midnight, and his newly gained trinket firmly around his neck, he sloped off to bed hoping to get as much sleep as possible in preparation for his meeting with Councillor Rosebloom the very next day.

Rising much later than usual, Peter spent most of the day doing household chores that he'd put off during the week, a sense of nervousness steadily building as the day moved on. It was unusual to be summoned to see any of the councillors and he had to wonder why his presence had been requested. Eventually it was time to leave and so he did, allowing more than enough time to reach London, and the council building.

As usual, the monorail was its efficient self, departing exactly on time. Instead of alighting at the normal stop to go and see Tank at the Mantra Emporium, he continued on to Buckingham station. As the name implies, the station itself is located almost directly beneath Buckingham Palace. He'd never been to this part of London before and was surprised at the difference in architecture between here and the area in which Tank and Gee Tee worked. Here the buildings all seemed relatively new, as well as spacious and... decadent. In contrast, the area where the Mantra Emporium was located was a spider's web of cramped passageways and narrow bridges, with the buildings all being single or double storey at most, and at best being described as run down, unlike the wide, clean polished streets that Peter now found himself walking down in the direction of the council building.

Turning a corner between two rather tall structures, he let out a gasp at what lay before him. He'd thought that the other buildings were new, outrageously large and self-indulgent, but what stood before him now was something else altogether. Of course he'd seen it on the front of the telepathic papers a few times, but in all honesty had paid it scant attention, what with it seeming so far away from everything else in his life. But here and now, it oozed magnificence in a way that just didn't come across in the pictures from the papers. At least thirty storeys high, it might have even been more, given that for the first time he couldn't see where the roof of the cavern started.

'Remarkable,' he thought. The height, however, was not the most amazing aspect of the building. Dragon buildings (whether homes or workplaces) are generally made out of stone, carved into rock, or very occasionally made from the remains of spectacular lava formations. He knew from the papers that this building was special, but this was not what he'd expected at all. As well as being tall, the building was a litany of curves, with not a right angle in sight, the construction seamless. No join, no gaps, nothing. He couldn't even take a guess at the material used in its construction. He'd never seen anything like it. Part of him wanted to call it metal, as it had that underlying look, but he knew it couldn't possibly be, with its incredible reflective properties gleaming with an ever changing oil slick of colours. If you continued to look for too long, it almost looked as though it was moving. Unreal.

Stomping his tail on the path in admiration, he continued on the walkway towards the main entrance. Just when he thought it couldn't get anymore surreal, he stumbled across two gurgling pools of lava on either side of the main steps that led to the official entrance. Both pools were made from the same material as the building, and most dragons either slowed or stopped when passing the pools, gazing contently in quiet contemplation into the steaming, writhing, hot mass.

Ignoring his body's need to stop at the lava pools, he passed through the giant arch denoting the entrance to the building, noticing two hulking great dragon guards stationed off to either side, hidden from sight by a row of gigantic pillars. His body's need to stop at the pools had now been replaced by the irrepressible urge to run. Run as far and as fast he could, just to get away from those guards. They were the most ferocious and frightening dragons he'd ever seen, and from the colours adorning the shining pikes that they carried, he knew they were part of the King's Guard. He stumbled on, unable to look directly at the dragons, feeling more than a bit guilty, although why, even he didn't know, much in the same way totally innocent humans feel guilty around a policeman in uniform.

Weirdly, the lobby of the council building was much the same inside as it was outside. Every part of the building had that metallic sheen to it, emphasised to a point by the highly polished floors. It felt very space age, and almost a bit too much for Peter who was much more comfortable in traditional dragon surroundings.

Or so he thought. It struck him that he thought Gee Tee was stuck in his ways for only letting dragons in their *solitus* form enter his shop, when here he was himself wishing that the very modern building he was standing in was much more low tech. Smiling to himself, he realised that he had much more in common with the master mantra maker than he cared to admit, although he certainly wouldn't be telling the old dragon as much.

Tearing himself away from thoughts of his friends, he turned his attention to the row upon row of touch screen LCDs that occupied the lobby. Wandering up to the nearest, he scrolled through the display, brought up a map of the building and found that the office he was looking for was about as far away as you could get from where he now stood, the furthest corner of the twenty ninth floor to be precise.

Instantly his eidetic memory remembered the route. It was then that he noticed a button at the bottom of the screen marked 'route planner'. Pressing the button, the screen asked him for the office number, which he duly entered. Suddenly a huge green illuminated arrow appeared on the floor in front of him. Bemused, he took a step forward onto the arrow. Another arrow appeared in front of him again. Shaking his head, he took another step forward. Again another arrow, and again, and again. He followed them all the way to his destination, taking a very different route to the one his eidetic memory would have guided him along. Arriving outside Hitch Rosebloom's office, he took a seat in one of the silver, oversized dragon chairs that adorned the corridor.

'Not as comfy as the ones in Gee Tee's workshop,' he told himself, wondering just how long he'd have to wait to be seen.

Unlike the waiting area in, say, a dentist's or doctor's surgery on the surface, there were no books or magazines to peruse because nearly all dragons had access to papers and other reading materials via their telepathic abilities. Peter thought about accessing the latest edition of the Daily Telepath, but with the clock on the wall reading 5.22pm he decided against it, especially as his nerves had started showing over the last few minutes. All sorts of thoughts were currently running through his head as to why he'd been summoned here, and none of them were good. Was it because he was spending too much time in his human form? He knew they kept an eye on that, for fear of young dragons getting addicted to it. Rumours around the nursery ring would have young dragons believe it can go so badly wrong that those in question are unable to use their powers to revert back to their dragon forms, with a Council based specialist unit on standby at all times, ready to forcibly change dragons back using unique and varied mantras. Much time had passed since anyone was reported to have needed these services, or so rumour had it, mainly due nowadays to the Council's diligence in that particular area.

He shuddered at the very thought of that. More likely it was some of Richie's antics that had been stumbled upon and he would be grilled about her arm wrestling rugby players, or the incident with the gang of youths who tried to relieve her of her phone one dark night in the car park of the sports club, who all coincidentally ended up in hospital with multiple broken bones each, or heaven forbid the day she took on three of the biggest, most obnoxious rugby players in the world at 'tug of war' and singlehandedly, in front of a huge crowd, beat them hands down. Or, of course, the dreaded dalliances. On no, not that. Anything but that.

'Please don't let me be quizzed about Richie's actions,' he thought, trying hard to focus on something else, without much success. Without knowing it, he began to finger the mysterious trident that hung around his neck. On transforming earlier, he'd forgotten he'd had it on in his human guise. It was only once he'd changed that he'd realised. Unbelievably, to him anyway, was the fact that the trident had changed with his bodily shape, now hanging around his prehistoric neck that was ten times the size of his usual human guise. Impressed and amazed didn't really cover it. Although he didn't know anything about the trinket, it was already as magical an item as it could be to him.

Wishing it to be 5.30 just so that the ordeal could be over, the clock on the wall told him he had a few minutes left to wait. Not helping was the fact that he was letting off a lot of steam, so much so that he wouldn't have been out of place at a redeveloped railway or a kettle testing facility, and was a sure giveaway of the nerves that he felt. It was everywhere, and try as he might to regulate his temperature, it did little to affect the plumes spewing out of his nose and the top of his head. He was getting very strange looks from passersby. It was then that another thought occurred to him.

'Please tell me they haven't found out about the incident with the neighbour's cat,' he thought, dejectedly. About a month ago he'd been out in his garden, just tidying up, you know... cutting the grass, a little bit of planting, that sort of thing, when he'd discovered a large area of lawn right at the back was covered in massive amounts of cat poo. Not a particularly keen gardener, he did however like to keep the house and garden looking neat and tidy. So he was quite appalled to see the mess all over his lawn, and even more disappointed to have to move it all so that he could mow the grass. Over the next few days he had kept a close eye on the state of the lawn and discovered that the cat belonging to the people two doors away was coming into his garden, doing its business, and then returning home. This was happening at all times of the day and night, and it made no apparent difference when Peter ran out into the garden to shoo the cat away. In the end, he went round to the house the cat belonged to and explained the situation to the people there, expecting them to be sympathetic to his cause. But they just laughed and said cats will be cats, before slamming the door shut in his face. Not much made him angry, but as he walked away from there, he was absolutely fuming, and had decided, very un-Peter-like, that he would do something about it. Later that night, after dark, he crept silently out into the garden. Adjacent to the lawn was a small wooden construct that held all the different recycling boxes, until every couple of weeks it was time to put them out for the refuse people to collect. The recycling, as it happened, had been collected that morning, freeing up about enough space for someone to hide inside. So, cloaked in stealth, he slid inside, left the wooden door slightly ajar, and switched on what can only be described as his dragon night vision. He didn't have to wait long. Slinking its way through a small gap in the fence at the bottom of his garden, the cat sauntered its way across the path and onto the lawn, not six feet from where he was hiding. The cat was facing the opposite direction, as it started to do its business.

'Perfect,' he thought. Silently moving the door open to create a slightly bigger gap, Peter drew in a deep breath, and concentrated with all of his dragon ability. Now it's not impossible for a dragon to breathe fire whilst in human form, but it's very, very difficult. It's also frowned upon by most other dragons, and in particular, the dragon Council. At the nursery ring, the young dragons were taught it was never appropriate to do such a thing because it was deemed there would never be a situation where a dragon would need to do it. Even so, the youngsters practised it anyway. As the pleasurable sensation of the warmth tickled its way up his throat, he'd long since decided he couldn't give a stuff about being frowned upon. Opening his mouth and tilting his head slightly to get the right angle around the door, he focused with all his will and let rip with a searing stream of crackling fire that caught the cat right on its tail. Although relatively narrow, the stream of flame was unbelievably hot, with the cat's tail disintegrating at the point of contact. So accurate was the flame, that it didn't even singe a single blade of the freshly mown grass. The piercing howl of terror from the cocky cat was something that to this day, still brought a smile to Peter's face even though he knew it shouldn't. On the plus side, his garden had been poo-free since that very day, and the cat now gets mistaken for a Manx cat, much to the disappointment of its owners, so he'd heard.

'Oh God, please don't let that be the reason I'm here,' he thought, folding his wings over his steaming head in shame. As the clock struck the half hour, he unfolded his wings and sat up straight. Right on cue the door to Rosebloom's office opened, with a booming voice inside announcing,

"Please come in Bentwhistle."

He stood up and, after a deep breath, walked on through into the office. The councillor offered a chair, which Peter duly sat down in. Instead of getting straight down to it, Rosebloom continued rifling through a pile of papers on his desk, adding to Peter's already nervous state. The young dragon tried to distract himself by concentrating on something else. It was then that he took a good look at the councillor for the very first time. Surprisingly small by dragon standards, his colouring was nothing special - light green all over, except for a big white mark that resembled a blooming rose across his stomach.

'Ah... must be where he got his name from,' he thought, his nerves having fully retreated to the back of his mind. The councillor's head though, was something to behold. A huge long swathe of black hair flowed down past his neck, the pony tail it was tied into zigzagging throughout the protruding scales on his back. Peter had never seen anything like it. As if that wasn't strange enough, glittering red jewel piercings ran in two lines up either side of his nose, until they met a pair of darkened, space age, wrap around glasses. It looked for all intents and purposes like he was trying to emulate all of the famous laminium ball players, all at once. It was most disconcerting, and just looked... WRONG! Caught up in the moment, Peter could feel his body temperature start to rise, just when he'd thought he'd got it under control, as he realised the self styled, hip and trendy councillor was glaring over the top of his glasses in his direction.

"Everything alright Bentwhistle?" the councillor enquired.

"Ummm... sure... yep... everything's fine."

"You do know why you're here, don't you... Bentwhistle?" asked Rosebloom, scratching his scaly jaw line.

"Well," replied Peter nervously, "...not exactly."

The councillor slammed down the papers he'd been sifting through, and stared intently at Peter.

"I would have thought it was obvious... youngster."

Peter sat there under the intense scrutiny of the

councillor, imagining that a giant crevice had opened up and swallowed him whole, and that he was now tumbling off into oblivion. It almost seemed a kinder fate. Unfortunately he was still glued to the chair, with Rosebloom sitting opposite, waiting for some kind of response.

Peter could feel his temperature rising as though it was about to shoot through the roof, and had decided to just admit that he had no idea why he'd been summoned. Before he could do that though, the councillor began to speak.

"You have been summoned here today due to the untimely death of Mark Hiscock. My understanding is that you now hold the highest position of any dragon throughout the Cropptech company. Is that correct?"

Peter was so relieved to hear that this was all about his job, and not any of the crazy ideas that had been going through his head beforehand, that he managed in one go to bring his body temperature right down, looking both calm and composed at the same time.

"That's correct," he agreed, nodding his head.

"Well, as I'm sure you're aware, we take a great deal of interest in what goes on there, mainly due to it being the leader in the field of extracting and processing laminium. Our domain would be in grave trouble if something untoward should happen to Cropptech. It's vital that every precaution is taken to safeguard its wellbeing."

Peter nodded his head in agreement with everything the councillor said, wondering where on Earth all of this was going.

"Mark Hiscock was always the Council's point of contact within Cropptech. That responsibility has now fallen to you. So you might find from time to time you get asked to speak to Mr Garrett about specific arrangements that have been made, sometimes about deliveries, often about newly found deposits in out of the way places. You can liaise with this office any time you like, and if there are any problems or anything you're worried about regarding your work, please don't hesitate to bring them to me directly. I will give you my card on the way out."

Sitting in the huge oversized chair, his tail dangling through the hole in the back, its tip flicking against the floor every now and then, Peter felt a great weight had been lifted off him.

'At last,' he thought, 'somebody I can turn to and trust about all the odd things that have been happening at work. Somebody that will know the right thing to do.'

Rosebloom leaned across the desk and said,

"Anything you're unsure of or want to ask?"

"There is something actually," he replied, relieved to be passing the burden of Manson and his antics on to somebody else. Over the next ten minutes, he sat and outlined what had been going on at Cropptech, particularly the effect he seemed to be having on Al Garrett and the ever changing state of power. Much to Peter's delight, the councillor sat and listened very carefully to every word that he'd said, even at one point jotting down notes on a pad, despite his perfect recall.

"So you see, after the funeral I spoke at length with Gee Tee and he suggested we use a mantra to cancel out the toxic effects in Mark's house and..."

"Hold on a minute Bentwhistle," ordered Rosebloom. "Gee Tee?"

"Yes that's right. My best friend Tank works at his Mantra Emporium in London and that's how I got to know him and he suggested..."

"ENOUGH!" roared the councillor, slamming his wings onto the table, causing all his papers to fly off in different directions.

Shocked by the outburst he'd just provoked, Peter remained seated and wide-eyed as Rosebloom leaned across the counter, so close that Peter could almost taste the acrid stench of his smoky breath.

"That old dragon is nothing more than a meddling

idiot, with barely any idea about mantras or any other dragon lore that he claims to understand," the councillor admonished.

Not quite sure what kind of reaction was expected of him, Peter sat stock still and remained silent. The councillor pulled himself back to his side of the desk and bent down to retrieve some of the things that had flown onto the floor in his fit of rage that now seemed to be over. After a few minutes passed in total silence, and Rosebloom had finally returned everything to its rightful place on the desk, he turned once again to face a very intimidated Peter.

"Listen very carefully... Bentwhistle," Rosebloom ventured, with an edge to his voice, "as I'm only going to tell you this once. I don't want any more of this Gee Tee nonsense. Do you understand?"

Peter started to open his mouth to protest, but read the glint in Rosebloom's eyes and decided against it, realising he was only going to make his predicament worse.

"That dragon," continued the councillor, "is nothing but trouble, and if I find out that he is in any way involved in events taking place at Cropptech, then there will be serious repercussions for you... Bentwhistle. Do I make myself clear?"

Peter slumped in the chair and nodded obediently.

"Now... get out of my office," instructed the councillor, gesturing towards the door. "And I would suggest you use your initiative to take care of that Manson fellow. After all he is only human, and shouldn't present too much of a challenge even for you."

Closing the door gently on the way out, Peter breathed a sigh of relief, wanting to sit down and sort out his thoughts, but desperate to leave the building and be as far away as possible from the irritable councillor. Hurriedly, he followed the same route out as he'd come in, not once appreciating the majestic surroundings he found himself caught up in. On reaching the exit, he bounded down the outside steps two at a time, getting disapproving looks from the dragons that had stopped to gaze into the bubbling lava pools. He didn't care. But once out of sight of the council building, he had no idea what to do next. His head was buzzing from all the things going on inside it. Continuing to walk, all he could think was that he needed somebody to talk to. But who? Tank, Richie, Gee Tee... oh, he just couldn't decide. Looking up, he found that his prehistoric body had taken him back to the monorail station of all places. Instead of boarding the waiting carriage that would have taken him home in the blink of an eye, he opted to sit down in one of the very few seats on the platform, watching the steady stream of dragon passengers coming and going. He had never really thought about it before, but he supposed the reason there weren't many seats at monorail stations in general, unlike the railway stations above, was that nobody ever had to wait more than a couple of minutes for the monorail to arrive. Yet another contrast between the two worlds he loved.

Frustrated, and not for the first time today, he buried his head in between his wings, confused and unable to come up with a course of action. He was so consumed with his own predicament that he failed to notice somebody slide into the oversized chair next to him. After a few more minutes of self pity, he decided that he would be better off at home. Unfurling his wings, he noticed for the first time the occupant of the next chair. It was the old man, the same one who used to come and watch him in the nursery ring. What a coincidence! Unusually in human form... well, for anyone around here, he looked much the same as Peter remembered him, but with slightly longer grey hair and a face that looked just a little more weary and tired, despite the fact that it was currently flashing him, a great big smile.

"Peter, isn't it?"

"That's right," he replied. "Long time no see. Fancy

meeting you here," he said noticing that the old man was staring intently at the trident hanging around his neck.

The old man managed to tear his gaze away from the trident long enough to look Peter in the eye.

"I have an office close by and was just on my way to catch the monorail when I thought I recognised those markings," he said, motioning towards the bent whistle markings on Peter's body.

Peter nodded his head, and asked,

"Have you been back to the nursery ring recently? I go when I can but it's not as often as I'd like."

The dragon in his old man guise smiled, a faraway expression etched into his face.

"I've not been back for quite some time. Like you, finding the time becomes increasingly difficult."

Peter nodded in agreement.

"So anyway young Peter, you look... troubled."

"More than you could ever know," Peter uttered in reply.

Stroking his grey stubbly chin, the old man considered Peter's words carefully.

"Perhaps it would help to talk about it. I'm a very competent listener you know."

Shaking his head, Peter stressed,

"I've already told too many people about it as it is, but thanks anyway."

"No problem," said the old man, getting out of his chair to continue his journey. But before he did so, he turned to Peter and added,

"This may not be much help, and I don't know the details of your dilemma, but having witnessed some of your time in the nursery ring, I have little doubt that you will make the right decision in whatever it is that you have to do. I've always found that trusting my gut instinct has served me well, whatever the situation. Go with your gut feeling and trust your friends. It will all work out for the best, of that I'm totally convinced."

As the old man staggered off down the platform, Peter was left speechless at what he'd said. Bounding up from his seat, he raced after the old man, finally catching up with him just as the next carriage arrived.

"Who are you?" Peter asked. "I don't even know your name."

"Trust me, it's much better that way," the old man replied, and with that he squeezed his way through the closing doors of the carriage.

As the monorail pulled away, Peter locked eyes with the old man through the window of the double doors and sensed there was much more to him than there seemed. With the glistening silver carriages having disappeared into the dark circumference of the tunnel, Peter stood stock still on the platform for a few minutes, pondering the encounter that made him feel more than a little... uncomfortable. But the more he thought about it, the more the words the old man had uttered made sense. He regarded himself as a great judge of character (don't we all), and thought that he had the best friends on the planet. All of which led him to believe that he should go and see Gee Tee, no matter what that... berk of a councillor... thought.

With a course of action decided upon, Peter startled himself out of his daze and looked around the platform to see where the cross-London monorail would depart from. He garnered the required information from the nearest LCD screen and noticed just how busy it had become since he'd arrived. Carriages were turning up full to the brim with dragons decadently dressed, brightly coloured cloaks, hats and even tights seemed to be the order of the evening, the kind of wear generally reserved for some sort of ball or formal dinner.

Instead of using the bridge provided, Peter flapped his wings twice and delicately looped over to the opposite platform. He could of course have taken a flying jump, but that in itself presented an ever present danger. Although there wasn't one due any time soon, it wasn't a given that a monorail wouldn't come charging through the station at top speed. Occasionally heavy test rigs filled with equipment ran the line, and were to say the least, unpredictable. If anyone were hit by one of these, then all of their dragon abilities, along with the services of the nearest dragon medical facility, would be required to keep them firmly in the land of the living. So although it was okay for passengers to cross the tracks themselves, the unwritten rule was that they should allow enough height not to get hit by an onrushing carriage, something that seemed prudent to say the least, and was in the most part obeyed.

As he stood waiting for his ride to arrive, it suddenly occurred to him that it being Saturday evening, the Mantra Emporium would be well and truly shut, and he had no idea whether Gee Tee lived at that address or not. He could have phoned Tank to ask him, but he hadn't brought his phone with him. There had seemed no point. Much as it was a handy piece of technology, for the most part they didn't work underground. The domain was catching onto the fact that they needed to address the issue, what with so many of their kind working and supposedly living amongst the humans. To be out of touch when they returned to their true home for any period of time had started to become more than just an inconvenience. There were a few places that had transmitters which acted as boosters to the very different phone networks, but not nearly enough. It was something the Council had agreed was a very high priority to sort out. He supposed here in London was no doubt one of those places that he could have gotten a signal, had he thought to bring his phone with him.

'Oh well', he thought to no one but himself.

As the lights of the carriage he was expecting appeared in the darkness of the very narrow tunnel, he decided he would go to the Emporium anyway and see if the old shopkeeper was there. It wasn't as though he had anything better to do. Squeezing past more partygoers alighting, he boarded the monorail for the three and a half minute journey, including stops.

Disembarking, he made his way towards the Emporium feeling almost claustrophobic in the confined narrow streets and alleys after the openness and freedom surrounding the council building from where he'd just come.

Hardly anybody appeared to be about away from the monorail station, which he thought odd, as the only other times he'd been this way there had always been plenty of dragons around. But not now, it seemed. Finally reaching the door of the Mantra Emporium, he knocked and waited. After two minutes of no response, he knocked and waited again. Still no reply. Peter took a few paces back and looked up at the front of the building. A dim light shone out of a small, grubby, first floor window. Peter gave it one more go, knocking as hard as he dared on the wooden front door. Waiting another three minutes without any response, he decided to leave. Just as he did, a noise from above caught his attention. The small grubby window creaked open slightly and Gee Tee's nose poked out.

"Hello. Who's there?" remarked the old shopkeeper from above.

"It's me... Peter. Peter Bentwhistle. Tank's friend," said Peter, trying unsuccessfully to whisper.

Gee Tee's head disappeared, and then, after some fumbling, reappeared with his glasses firmly attached to his nose. As the old dragon looked down from the window at him, Peter found himself suppressing a laugh, due to the fact that the master mantra maker was wearing a red and white stripy night cap, and looked like something from a Victorian story.

"Ah... youngster," chided Gee Tee. "Don't you know what time it is?"

"It's five past seven," replied Peter hesitantly. "I'm

sorry if I've woken you."

"Five past seven? Really? In the evening?" queried the old shopkeeper.

"Yes," replied Peter, nodding vigorously.

"Hey ho," laughed Gee Tee, throwing something in Peter's direction.

Stretching out, Peter caught the object, which turned out to be a brass key, much to his surprise.

"Let yourself in and lock the door behind you," ordered the shopkeeper. "I'll be down shortly."

Peter slid the key into the lock and after about thirty seconds managed to jiggle it so that the door opened. Entering the shop, which was now in total darkness, he proceeded to try and lock the door back up, which to his amazement took longer than it had to open it. Eventually he managed it, by which time a light had appeared at the back of the shop, in an area that Peter had never seen before. He could just make out Gee Tee making his way down a steep set of stairs, painfully slowly. Weaving his way in and out of the bookcases, Peter skilfully avoided piles and piles of disregarded books, which by now would have tripped up almost any human, on his way to meet his host at the bottom of the stairs.

It was only when he reached the base of the stairs, that it dawned on him exactly how old and frail the elderly dragon really was. He suddenly felt racked with guilt about involving the old shopkeeper in any of this. What had he done? Why couldn't he handle things on his own, as Rosebloom had suggested? These thoughts ran through his mind as he watched Gee Tee negotiate the last two steps. Poking his glasses as far up his nose as they would go, the master mantra maker leant forward so that Peter could feel the old dragon's breath on his face. The old shopkeeper looked right into his eyes and just stared for what seemed like an eternity. Peter felt like he was back at the nursery ring, under the scrutiny of one of the stricter *tors*.

"I'm sorry you have to see me like this child,"

whispered Gee Tee, "but I don't need your sympathy or pity."

Peter was shocked. Was the shop owner reading his mind, he wondered? Before he had a chance to ask, Gee Tee continued.

"Your expression says it all child. When you've lived as long as I have, you tend to pick up a thing or two."

Peter felt relieved that the old dragon hadn't been reading his mind, but was still concerned that he'd got him involved and had woken him up.

"Do you know why I don't need your pity, child?"

Peter shook his head and stared at the wooden floor.

"I don't need it because I've lived longer already than any other dragon in history my young fellow," said Gee Tee cheerfully. "And I don't intend on getting deep fried in lava just yet, thank you very much."

Peter felt the tip of Gee Tee's wing under his chin, pulling his face up from the floor.

"I've had a wonderful life, child. The most amazing adventures. I wouldn't change a single thing. How many dragons can say that? Eh? And most importantly, if I want to help someone, like I've helped others many times before, then I think that should be my choice. Don't you?"

Peter looked up at the old dragon, lost for words. There was such passion in his face. His eyes seemed full of... adventure and mystery. He just nodded his head in acknowledgment. As he did so, Gee Tee caught sight of the trident which hung from the chain around Peter's neck. Leaning in close, the old shopkeeper put the tip of one wing under the chain, pulling it taut.

"Just when I think I've seen everything, something jumps up and bites me on the bum, as if to prove me wrong," pondered the master mantra maker, shaking his head.

Without another word, the old dragon relinquished his grip on the chain and turned away, walking over to the counter. Leaning over it he flicked a switch, and the room suddenly becoming bathed in light. Hobbling off towards the workshop, the old shopkeeper turned towards Peter.

"Let's see if we can't find something to drink and then you can tell me what brings you here at this... early hour," he muttered with laughter in his voice.

"Do you want me to boil the kettle?" Peter offered, pointing off towards the small kitchen.

"No, no, no child. We can do much better than that."

Peter followed Gee Tee into the workshop and took a seat in the chair he was guided to. Pulling out a small stool, the old shopkeeper moved it in front of a very tall bookcase that contained many varieties of parchment and ink. The master mantra maker climbed awkwardly onto the stool and started hunting around on top of the bookcase. After much rummaging around, he finally retrieved what he was looking for.

"Ah, here it is. Just right for special occasions and times of need," said the shopkeeper, stifling a laugh. "And right now I feel the need."

As Gee Tee turned around to step down from the stool, Peter finally caught a glimpse of what he had been searching for: a tall metallic flask, covered in dust, through which Peter could just make out some writing that said "12th Century Peruvian Ink (only to be used with 12th century Peruvian parchment)".

Peter wondered what on earth was going on.

Gee Tee held the flask up to examine it, a playful glint in his eye. Blowing some of the dust off it, the old shopkeeper twisted off the cap, as Peter sat, intrigued. Holding the flask up to his nostrils, the old dragon inhaled deeply, clearly liking what he smelt. Just as Peter thought it couldn't get any weirder, Gee Tee did the last thing that he would have expected. He took a swig from the flask. Peter sat gobsmacked in the oversized chair, watching as Gee Tee swilled some of the flask's contents around in his mouth. Suddenly the old shopkeeper turned sharply and blew out an almighty stream of searing blue flame across

PAUL CUDE

the room, hitting the wall on the other side, leaving the mother of all scorch marks.

"Your friend will have a hissy fit when he comes back into work on Monday and sees that on the wall," joked the old dragon, licking his lips.

"What on Earth is that stuff?" asked Peter, warily.

Gee Tee gave a huge guffaw and held out the flask.

"Well... it's not Peruvian ink, that's for sure."

Both dragons spontaneously burst into laughter, which lasted for what seemed like an age. When Gee Tee finally finished laughing, he held out the flask and offered it to Peter. Unsure of what to do, the young dragon reluctantly took it from the shopkeeper, holding it up in the air as if it were a ticking time bomb.

"That, my young friend, is the finest, most potent and most enjoyable drink you will ever try."

"Why does it say Peruvian ink on the side?" asked Peter, more than a little confused.

Gee Tee chuckled and smiled at the young dragon.

"If your best friend found out what it really is, you can bet that would be the last I would see of it. Much as I appreciate his constant fussing over the state of my health, I do like a little treat every now and then. And it says 'to be used only with Peruvian parchment' simply because there's no such thing, reducing the chances of anyone opening it by mistake."

"Sneaky," declared Peter, proudly.

"I sometimes feel that's what I should have been named," bragged the old dragon, smiling.

Shaking his head, Peter held the flask under his nose.

"Smells like petrol."

"Petrol?" enquired the old dragon, confused.

It suddenly dawned on Peter that Gee Tee, having never been on the surface, would have absolutely no idea what that was.

"Ah... it's the fuel that the humans use to power their vehicles."

202

"Oh... I see. Well, anyway, this is, as I was saying, simply... magnificent. It was a gift to me from the king," stated the old shopkeeper proudly.

"The king!" exclaimed Peter.

"Oh, not the current king, child, although I'm pretty sure he owes me more than a favour or two. If he ever remembers, that is."

"If it's not from the current king, how old is this stuff?" queried the young dragon nervously.

Gee Tee casually shrugged his giant scaly shoulders.

"Nearly three hundred years if memory serves me correctly. Go ahead child... try it!"

"I... I... I couldn't," refused Peter, offering the flask back to the master mantra maker.

"I wouldn't offer it if I didn't want you to have any, child. You really should give it a go. That might be the only one of its kind left on the planet. My understanding is that it was a gift to the king of the time, from the nagas in the frozen north. A peace offering I believe. When else would you get an opportunity like this?"

"Sounds important," ventured Peter. "Why did the king give it to you, if you don't mind me asking."

Gee Tee turned and gave the young dragon a knowing look.

"You wouldn't be the first dragon that I've helped. Not by a long way. And some of the things I've been privileged to be involved in, well let's just say that not only have I experienced a great deal of history, being as old as I am, but I've helped shape a fair bit of it as well."

Peter looked at the old shopkeeper, jaw wide open, in a completely new light.

"Now stop gawping and start drinking," ordered the old dragon, indicating the flask. "Just a small mouthful, savour the taste. You'll know when it's time for the flame."

Holding the silver flask up to his mouth, he swigged as much as he dared. Rolling effortlessly over his huge tongue, the thick gooey liquid left a gorgeous sweet, fizzy, tangy aftertaste as it slid slowly down his throat. The flavour seemed to penetrate not only his nose, but his throat and the top of his stomach as well. It was bliss as he stood in the middle of the workshop, all thoughts of everything else forgotten, the sensation of the drink all encompassing. Never before had he experienced such wonder, not even the first time he'd taken to the air. Through the haze and the ecstasy, he began to wonder why he'd never heard of such a drink and why it was not available to dragons everywhere. At the exact same moment of these thoughts, a fuzzy, tingling feeling erupted in his mouth. Opening his eyes for the first time in what felt like a year, Gee Tee stood directly in front of him, grinning from ear to ear. In the split second it had taken him to open his eyes, the tingling had turned to... BURNING! But not just any burning: ice cold burning that made every one of his sharp teeth feel as though they were being hit individually with a hammer. Briefly this masked the uproar in the back of his throat and stomach that was starting to come to the fore. It felt as though flesh was being stripped. Panic started to consume him. Looking back at the shopkeeper, he was surprised to see tears of laughter racing down the old dragon's face, sizzling as they came into contact with the heat from his nostrils. Fear and anger threatened momentarily to consume Peter, when all of a sudden he felt his stomach make a giant... bubble.

'Oh my God,' he thought, 'I'm going to explode.'

Spinning around in blind panic, the bubble that had started in his stomach had gathered momentum and was now making a mad dash for freedom up his throat. Clenching his jaw, Peter was determined not to let it out, but that was not quite what the bubble had in mind. Nothing was going to get in its way. Abruptly Peter's jaws shot open as wide as they possibly could. A resounding 'BUUUUUUUURRRRRRRRPPPPPPPPP' emanated from his mouth, followed closely by a huge blue fireball that crossed the room in blaze of light, hitting a grey metal filing cabinet, instantly reducing it to a steaming mass of burning slag. Spent, he slumped down into the oversized chair, relieved that the bubble no longer resided within him. Wiping away the tears of laughter, Gee Tee wandered over to the blackened remains of the filing cabinet.

"I'm not nearly so concerned about the scorch mark on the wall now," he professed, teeming with sarcasm. "You're supposed to produce a concentrated stream of fire, not deliver a ball of absolute devastation."

"Sorry," Peter burped, feeling a little light headed.

The old shopkeeper shook his head.

"It's not your fault child. I should have explained a bit more. Anyway, what do you think? Awesome eh?"

Letting out a long breath, Peter could still taste the after effects of the drink inside him.

"Oh yeah... awesome."

"That's the spirit," stressed Gee Tee, slapping Peter firmly on the back, causing him to splutter uncontrollably for a few seconds.

Peter surveyed the mess they'd made of the workshop.

"How are you going to explain all of this to Tank?"

The master mantra maker pondered the question a few seconds before replying.

"I'll just tell him I was rooting about and found an unfamiliar mantra which I couldn't resist trying. If he asks where I found it, I'll just point to that," Gee Tee laughed, pointing directly at the steaming mass of molten mess that only a few moments ago had been a filing cabinet. "Like I said before... sneaky."

Peter chuckled under his breath and thought,

'What a way to spend a Saturday night.' It was only then that he realised he didn't mean it sarcastically, and in actual fact had been having a really great time just talking and mucking about with the old shopkeeper.

"Anyhow, I haven't asked you what you're doing here tonight. Much as I enjoy your company, it's an odd time for a social call."

Recalling the events of today that had led him here, Peter once more felt the weight of the world on his shoulders. He began to tell Gee Tee about his trip to the council chambers, but only got as far as mentioning Hitch Rosebloom's name, before the master mantra maker interrupted.

"Bloody Hitch Rosebloom, the bane of my life," fumed the old dragon, clearly annoyed. "Let me guess. You started telling him about the events at Cropptech and then unwittingly dropped my name into the conversation after which he probably went off on one. Would that be about right?"

"Pretty much," confirmed Peter, surprised.

"That dragon should be frozen in ice and left there to rot for a thousand years," proposed Gee Tee, venom lacing his raised voice. "I'm sorry child," he added, noticing the worried look on Peter's face. "It's just, as you might have already guessed, we have a little bit of... history."

Peter nodded, waiting to see if the old shopkeeper would expand on what he'd just said.

Pacing up and down the workshop, visibly upset and agitated, wings swishing, totally oblivious to the still smoking molten scrap heap behind him, Gee Tee began.

"Of all the councillors that could have responsibility for Cropptech, it would have to be him, wouldn't it," he said shaking his gigantic prehistoric head from side to side, looking for something to kick. Abruptly, there was a change of direction, with the old dragon deciding to sit down in the chair opposite Peter.

"I'm sorry if you've got it in the scales from him, but I'm glad you came and sought me out, particularly after the, no doubt, bad things that he's filled your mind with about me," added the smiling shopkeeper.

Smiling back, Peter was pretty sure his gut feeling about Gee Tee was right, despite what that crazy councillor had tried to peddle.

"It all started a very long time ago. Long before you were hatched. Although it doesn't look like it now, this shop used to be incredibly busy and successful. At our peak, nobody else in the world could match us for mantras, whether it was new or everyday mantras. We were renowned for creating and selling the best. Our healing mantras on average were between fifteen and twenty percent more effective than anyone else's, purely because of the quality material we used to craft them. Dragons everywhere knew that if they came to Gee Tee's Mantra Emporium, they were getting top quality merchandise. We even had the King's Council's Seal Of Approval.

All in all, business was booming. The shop itself already had a staff of ten, not including the five dragons employed in the workshop, tasked with repairs, research and development, which incidentally is where I spent a great deal of my time. Even with that level of staffing, things were spiralling out of control and I decided that I really needed someone else to help on the research and development side of things, almost a right hand dragon, you could say. So I advertised for one in the Daily Telepath. Combined with the prestige of the company and the fact that the position would have been working right alongside me, well let's just say things went berserk. If memory serves me correctly, we had nearly five thousand applicants."

"Five thousand!" exclaimed Peter.

"That's right. And just like you, I was gobsmacked. It never occurred to me that it would be such a sought after post, but that's indeed what it was. I spent weeks whittling down the candidates, which of course meant the shop was getting busier, and I was even more behind with my work. After a month or so of working day and night, I managed to get it down to a manageable twenty dragons, which was no mean feat, I assure you."

Peter nodded, riveted by the thought of the deserted old shop that he was sitting in, having been so successful and busy.

"Anyway, I proceeded to interview each of the applicants and finally cull it down to four outstanding dragons, all of whom were nearly straight out of their respective nursery rings. One of the four was a particularly arrogant young dragon called... yes, you've guessed it, Hitch Rosebloom."

Peter was starting to see what the old shopkeeper meant when he said that he and Rosebloom had history.

"Well, I agonized long and hard about the four prospective candidates. It was, to this day, one of the hardest decisions I've ever had to make. Needless to say, the very pleasant Hitch Rosebloom wasn't the applicant that I chose. At the time I didn't think very much of it. The job went to an outstanding, clever and shy young dragon called... CAT! Ahh... Cat. She was wonderful in every sense. Oh in case you're wondering, Cat was short for Catfish, as that was what the prominent marking sprayed across the back of her neck resembled."

Peter's mind drifted far into the past at the mere mention of that. Although eidetic, his memory was sometimes slow, and a little hazy. Somewhere inside there, he recalled a visit from a dragon who certainly fitted that description. Could it be the same one?

"Anyhow, she came to work for me and I let all the other dragons that I'd interviewed know that they hadn't been successful, and thought nothing more of it. Apparently the boy Rosebloom and his family were more than a little offended that he hadn't got the job. Not only that, but his family were ever so well connected, if you know what I mean. I had one or two visits from associates of his family, trying to persuade me to relent and give Rosebloom the job. In the meantime, however, Cat had excelled in the few weeks that she'd been with me. Never having given in to bullies before, I wasn't about to now and so I told those associates in biologically specific terms exactly what they could go and do."

At the mere mention of bullies, Peter's stomach clenched and all he could think of was Fisher, Casey and Theobald. A shudder ran the entire length of his body at the thought of the three of them. Concentrating hard, he turned his attention back to Gee Tee, who momentarily looked lost in thought.

"At the time it seemed like the right thing to do and with hindsight, it probably still was. But what I didn't realise was the extent of the power Rosebloom's family actually had, and quite how vindictive they would be. To cut a long story short, through manipulation and their contacts, they managed to get the King's Council's Seal Of Approval revoked from the shop for some trumped up reason and things went rapidly downhill from there. The family's influence persuaded important customers to go elsewhere and so I ended up laying off most of my staff, including the delightful Cat I'm afraid to say. My fortunes went from bad to worse, unlike those of that weasel Rosebloom, who through his family connections managed not only to get voted in as a councillor, but the youngest one in dragon history. Unbelievable!"

Gee Tee got up and paced about a bit more, shaking his head, looking thoroughly angry. Peter was amazed to think that any one dragon could be so vindictive and petty as to totally destroy something just because he didn't get selected for a job.

"If anyone tells you that dragons are not like humans at all child, or that dragons are somehow better than humans, think again. This story, along with others just like it, should always remind you how much we have in common with our so-called 'barbaric' charges on the surface.

Where was I? Oh yes, the delightful Rosebloom. You might have thought that ruining my business and becoming the youngest councillor ever would be enough for the delightful young dragon because I clearly did. But not so.

About a year after he became a councillor, I had a visit

from a troop of the King's Guard, supposedly looking for illegal mantras and stolen artefacts. When I questioned the commander, he stated that the search had arisen from a tip-off received from a highly placed source. Of course they didn't find anything, but they did manage to trash the place in the process. To this day, I still get a visit from the King's Guard every six months or so, looking for the same thing. Luckily for me, I've helped their new commander out on a number of occasions, so whenever the order comes down from above, he brings a few trusted troops and I feed them hot charcoal and regale them with tales from the past. Once done, they report that a thorough search of the premises was carried out. A win for everyone, except that deceitful councillor.

Peter felt numb at the thought of one dragon doing all that to another.

'Surely all of that resentment would fade over time?' he thought to himself.

"So there you have it child, the reason why the beloved councillor and I don't quite see eye to eye."

"That's something of an understatement isn't it?"

"Now," announced Gee Tee much more calmly, "why don't you tell me about that interesting trinket around your neck, child?"

"It was left to me by Mark Hiscock, in his will," replied Peter, twirling the trident around on the end of its chain.

"Really," said the old shopkeeper, poking his large spectacles as far up his nose as they would go. "Do you know what you have there, child?"

He smiled and looked up from the trident.

"A cool piece of bling, as they would say on the surface." (Although trying to inject a little humour, whilst being a little bit hip at the same time, Peter failed spectacularly. It was much like a parent talking up the music their teenage son or daughter liked to listen to. Off the scale uncool!)

The old shopkeeper looked completely confused at

Peter's description.

"Never mind," ventured the young dragon. "I don't really know what it means either, and I'm supposed to be young and trendy. By the interest you're showing in it though, I'm assuming it's more than just a stunning piece of jewellery."

"Very much so, if I'm not mistaken. And I rarely am," replied the master mantra maker, a sparkle in his eye. "Would you take it off so that I can have a better look?"

"Sure," said Peter, unhooking the clasp of the chain and handing it all over to the old dragon.

Shoving a few books aside on the bench that he was sitting at, Gee Tee switched on the overhead light to get a better view. The two of them hunched over the desk, studying the trident.

"I've never seen one quite like this," muttered Gee Tee with just a hint of awe in his voice.

"One what?" enquired Peter, gazing down at it.

"What you have here child, is known as an *'alea'*, which roughly translated means 'gamble' or 'last chance'."

Peter looked at the shopkeeper with a blank expression, still not knowing what it was.

"It's a mantra child, and not just any mantra, either. An extremely powerful one, only to be used as directed, as a... last chance, a final roll of the dice."

"I'm sorry I still don't understand," confessed Peter, feeling more than a little stupid.

"Let me try and explain from the beginning," offered the master mantra maker. "My understanding is that the Aztec dragons were the first to try and develop *aleas*. If I remember correctly, a group of dark dragons tried to take over a large part of South America, and as a result the Aztec dragons had little choice but to try and bring them back into the light. That didn't happen, and a small and very bloody war erupted. Dragons on each side became proficient at killing each other, in the most brutal ways possible. The dragon in charge of the light warriors... his name eludes me at the moment... fed up with losing so many dragons, ordered his mantra specialists to come up with something that would turn the tide of this small, but very nasty historic episode.

I believe he was hoping for something on a bit of a larger scale, but this is what his specialists came up with, the *alea*. Of course at the time, the *aleas* were a lot cruder than what you have here, but the principle was very much the same: a piece of jewellery that had a mantra embedded within it.

Now the only problem with doing this, as the Aztecs were the first to find out, is that when you try and imbue something that has physical form with any kind of mantra, the physical element more often than not alters the very nature of the mantra. Bits and pieces that I've read on the subject start to get a bit vague at this point, but it seems that the very first *aleas* had shield mantras imbued into them. They were supposed to, at the very last minute, provide a powerful shield that would allow the user to fend off multiple attacks and make a successful escape, when said user used the mantra and broke the particular piece of jewellery. Perfect if you've just been caught in an ambush. You live to run away and fight another day."

"The first couple of times they were used they worked as intended. A shield sprang up around the dragon and enabled it to escape and report back that the *alea* worked perfectly. Not so, however. The more the war raged on, the more desperate encounters there were. Dragons with *aleas* were found dead in extraordinary circumstances when they should have escaped, some even taking whole groups of enemies with them. Others reported that instead of a shield appearing when used, the *alea* produced powerful streams of lightning that struck all of those around them, killing them instantly, no mean feat where dragons are involved."

"The Aztec specialists tried and tried to work out what was going wrong, but to no avail. Eventually the light side won the war, bringing the dark dragons back under control, but only after substantial losses to dragons and humans alike. The *aleas* proved something of an enigma to all concerned. After that, the Aztecs gave up totally on the concept, believing them too unstable and dangerous.

That, however, is not where things ended. Different dragon factions throughout history have sought to emulate the *aleas*, all having about as much success as the Aztecs did. Oh, they all claimed to have solved the stability problem, but alas nobody to my knowledge ever came close to producing a stable and reliable *alea* that worked as it should, all the time."

Peter sat in the chair, hooked on every word the shopkeeper was saying.

"You should come and teach at my old nursery ring. That was absolutely fascinating," praised the young dragon. "Nothing like that was ever covered in my education. Why don't they tell all young dragons?"

"Ah, that, child, is a very good question. Why do YOU think they don't teach it?"

Peter scratched his chin, pondering the question.

"I suppose they don't want dragons tinkering, trying to create their own *aleas*, what with the instability issues and everything."

Gee Tee nodded in agreement and said,

"That, and the fact that it might encourage some sort of rogue movement, like the dark dragons of the Aztec period. Things like that have started over a lot less in the past."

"Really," exclaimed Peter.

"Of course," replied the master mantra maker. "It might sound unlikely, but I assure you it's a possibility. Evil is always around. You may not see it, but it lurks, waiting for an opportunity in the shadows of the tiny little cracks of reality just outside our souls, waiting for an opportunity to corrupt or exert itself. The king and the Council are fully aware of all of this, and that would be my guess as to why the curriculum is so carefully monitored and set in stone across all nursery rings."

Peter felt as though his head were about to explode with all the new information he'd gleaned today. Briefly, he felt a small pang of envy that his friend was working here full time, day in, day out with Gee Tee.

'What must that be like?' he wondered. The two of them continued to sit in silence for some time, both lost in their thoughts, staring in wonderment at the *alea* hanging off the chain on the workshop bench. Finally, Peter broke the silence.

"Can I ask how you use it?" he asked, cautiously.

"You really want to know after everything I've told you?" cautioned Gee Tee suspiciously, peering intently over his huge square glasses.

"I'm not going to use it," stammered Peter, unconvincingly.

"You'd have to be either incredibly brave or unbelievably stupid to do so. Makes no difference to me whether you are or not." Picking up the tiny trident, the old dragon waved it around in the air, the purple glow leaving a dissipating trail that took a few seconds to disappear completely.

"If you look past the purple glow child, you should be able to make out a series of words, running down the length of the main shaft and also on each part of the fork."

Leaning in close, Peter squinted intensely, trying his hardest to see the writing that was microscopic at best.

"Come on child, if an old dragon of over six hundred years like me can see it, surely you must be able to make it out."

Peter used all his magical abilities to flick through the range of dragon visions available to him. Finding one that worked, he concentrated on the shaft and prongs. After a few seconds, the letters of the words swam into view and he could just make out the words beneath the purple glow.

"Amplificare... Magicus... Nunc," he said, finally.

"That's right," coaxed Gee Tee. "And that means...?"

He knew what was coming and silently cursed the fact that Latin was easily his worst language. He thought hard and tried to imagine his language *tor* standing in front of him with the answer. Eventually it came to him, but by now he was feeling unusually hot and more than a little stressed, particularly as the old shopkeeper had been staring at him all this time.

"Amplify Magic Now," he blurted, mentally exhausted.

"Nursery rings seemed to have lowered their standards no end since my day. Anyway, we got there in the end. Amplify Magic Now. It's a bit vague isn't it? It could mean absolutely anything. Anyhow, you wanted to know how to use it."

Peter nodded, not quite sure what he was letting himself in for.

"As with any normal mantra, you can either say the words out loud, or project them in your head, but the difference here is that at the same time, you must use all your strength to snap the trident in half."

"Break it?"

"Of course," stated the master mantra maker. "How else do you think you would release the power that has been imbued in it? Well, as I said before, brave or stupid. I really wouldn't recommend it, so... think very carefully before using it."

"I really have no intention of using it... honest," stressed Peter.

"Whatever you say child, but don't say you haven't been warned," lectured the old dragon. "If you end up with five ears, no nose and a tongue long enough to lick your own tail, you can be sure I'll be the first to say... I told you so."

"I know, and thank you for your advice. It's much appreciated," replied Peter, smiling at the thought of licking his own tail.

"So, is there anything else that an old dragon can help

you with? I confess to feeling somewhat tired now, but don't fret child, I've had a very enjoyable evening," said the old shopkeeper, more than a little drained.

A wave of guilt rolled over Peter at having worn the old dragon out again. Tank's words came flooding back. Nevertheless, he decided to press on, knowing that he really needed some guidance on what his next steps should be.

"I don't know what to do about the situation at Cropptech. Rosebloom was no help whatsoever and... I just don't know what to do next."

Gee Tee fiddled with his glasses, thinking about what to tell his young friend.

"It's clear from what you've said that the mantra used at Mark's house was successful, which leads me to conclude that it might rid Garrett's office of whatever evil lurks there, in much the same way. The problem there though, is that even if you got into Garrett's office to use it, there's nothing stopping Manson coming back and starting all over again, because I very much doubt Garrett would be cured instantly; it would only be the first step on his road to recovery."

Peter nodded in agreement.

"That makes sense," he said.

"So, with that out of the question, the only thing I think you can do, is bide your time and try and find some evidence against Manson or something that indicates what his eventual goal is, be that taking over the company, stealing something, or whatever else."

Peter could see now the toll the night's events had taken on the master mantra maker. He looked worn out, and kept yawning between each sentence.

"That's good advice, thanks. I think I'll do just that. Thank you for an unforgettable evening. I won't keep you any longer," declared Peter, meaning every word.

"You are of course, very welcome child," yawned Gee Tee, showing Peter out of the workshop and back to the front door. "Go careful now child, and don't forget you're welcome anytime, but daylight hours are always best."

Peter strolled out into the street, waving the old shopkeeper goodbye, waiting to make sure he could hear the key turn in the lock. Once sure it had been properly secured, he made his way back through the deserted streets and alleys towards the monorail station, feeling happier than he had in some time.

11 HOLLY JOCKEY STICKS

Peter woke full of energy. Normally on a Sunday he was bleary eyed and not at all keen on getting up, but the previous night's events had him feeling hugely optimistic about everything in his life. He could still taste the Peruvian Mantra Ink though, almost as if it had merged with the cells in his throat, despite the fact that he'd changed forms since drinking it.

'Hopefully it will dissipate over time,' he thought. Checking his phone once downstairs, he found a text message reminding him that hockey training started the following Tuesday, signalling the start of the season, something he found he'd been missing like crazy all summer.

It was, of course, Richie that had got him into playing hockey after he'd been complaining about a lack of interest in his life, apart from his work, which of course he took very seriously. She'd taken up playing lacrosse some time ago, something most dragons not only frowned upon, but couldn't really see the point of. Yes, dragons had begun to infiltrate most of the popular sports at all levels, mainly professional sport, particularly because the power and adoration that most of them commanded enabled them to influence all levels of society and guide the humans in the right direction. To assume human form and participate in their sport just for fun, without using your dragon abilities seemed... unthinkable to any and all dragons. There had even been stories written in the dragon press about Richie playing lacrosse purely for pleasure, none of which cast her in a very good light, with most questioning, at the very least, her sanity. But as far as Peter could see, it was lava off a dragon's tail to her.

So, after hearing him complain about lacking something in his life, Richie dragged him down to the sports club in Salisbridge one busy Saturday afternoon. He spent all afternoon wandering around the ground, marvelling at the sheer enjoyment all the humans seemed to be getting from being part of a team sport. He'd never really paid any attention to it before, either on the television or anywhere else, and like most dragons, couldn't really see the point, but to see the games up close and personal was just... unbelievable. The passion with which the players pursued their sport, the bonding that seemed to go on in each side, the ferocity and commitment of the challenges being made against the opposition... it was all truly a wonder to behold.

That very afternoon Peter watched Richie play a whole game of lacrosse for the first time and was absolutely agog. Most of the comments in the dragon press referring to Richie almost always maintained that it was impossible for her to play without using her dragon abilities, thereby cheating. This seemed to be the most contentious part of the complaints levelled against her, with most dragons unable to comprehend why she would bother in the first place. But as Peter sat in a cold, wet dugout adjacent to the pitch and watched Richie play, he got a glimpse of something very special. Not only could he tell that Richie didn't use her abilities throughout the whole of the match (something that even he had had reservations about secretly, even though Richie had given her word on more than one occasion that she didn't use her magical abilities) but also it was blatantly obvious to Peter, who had known her nearly her whole life, that she was happier playing lacrosse than Peter had possibly ever seen her. And that includes the moments she would dazzle everyone with her amazing aerial acrobatics, something every dragon loved more than just about anything else.

'How can this running around with sticks, chasing a silly little ball produce so much pleasure?' he wondered for days afterwards. Talking to Tank didn't help either. In fact Tank was so taken aback at what Peter had said, that he had to see for himself the pleasure Richie was obviously getting out of playing in a team alongside humans. Over the coming months, the two friends attended every one of Richie's home games, hoping to find the secret to her happiness, but to no avail. However hard they tried, they just couldn't seem to hit the nail on the head as to what was so captivating about playing in a team. After a few months, Peter and Tank sat down with Richie and asked her to explain it to them. After laughing at the pair of them for what seemed like an age, and then playfully banging their heads together, she told them the only way to find out what they were missing out on, was to try it.

More than a little unsure, Peter and Tank didn't want to let their friend down, and so both agreed to go and train for a few weeks at different sports. Peter chose hockey and Tank rugby. His bigger, stronger build was ideally suited to that particular sport, even though both had really wanted to try lacrosse. Richie insisted that they try something different and said that they could always swap sports further down the line.

Peter could vividly remember turning up to his first hockey training session on a cold, wet Tuesday night. Richie came along and introduced him to the coach and then turned around and left him there... on his own, well... not exactly on his own as there were thirty other players there, but that's how it felt. The previous night Richie had shown him how to hold a stick and how to strike the ball, in his back garden.

Joining in with the other players as they did a gentle warm up in the cold November weather, he noticed even though there was no game going on, they weren't even holding their hockey sticks for goodness sake, there was still an incredible amount of... banter! Everyone from the smallest to the biggest, oldest to the youngest were all chatting, making jokes and just... bonding. Previously he'd thought the bonding thing must have just been during the matches, but on that cold wet windy night, suddenly he wasn't so sure.

Brief warm up finished, the players started to partake in exercises with a stick and ball. He joined in and although he wasn't anywhere near the best, strangely, even without all his magical abilities, he wasn't quite the worst either. Marvelling at the continued banter throughout all the exercises, something he'd wondered if the coach would stop, he was still no nearer to discovering the secret of Richie's happiness. The exercises with a stick and ball were okay, but they sure didn't set Peter's world alight. As the night progressed it got colder and wetter, which strangely, he thought, nobody seemed to mind. Just when he considered calling it a night, the coach blew his whistle (which wasn't bent... get it?) and called everyone in. Divided into two, and given blue and red bibs respectively, the group started a game.

While Richie had been showing him how to hold a stick, she also took to explaining the rules to him, something he had brushed up on much later that evening, via YouTube. It had all kind of gone in, but it was difficult to understand without experiencing it first hand, something he was now doing, and wishing with all his might that things would slow down a bit. The ball was almost a blur. Tackles were being made left, right and centre. Players were shouting for passes and screaming for their teammates to close down the opponent with the ball. He could feel his heart pounding and his temperature rising, no mean feat in the cold and the rain. Rushing about like a headless chicken, he tried desperately to get in the right place to receive a pass from one of his own side. Unfortunately one of his opponents had picked him out and decided to mark him rather tightly, making any pass seem more and more unlikely. He continued to run, trying to lose his marker, but to no avail. Just when he'd thought his chance at getting in on the action had passed, the guy who'd been marking him received the ball from one of his teammates and looked to dribble straight past him, down the wing.

By now he was fully engrossed in all the excitement and adrenaline of the match. More than a little disappointed that he hadn't seen the ball yet, he was determined to take it from the opponent now heading straight for him at quite a speed. Having watched some of the better players tackle throughout the evening, he knew just what to do. He waited until the onrushing player was nearly on top of him, and moved his stick to the open side, leaving an inviting hole to his left hand side, knowing full well his opponent would perform a dummy and take it down his so-called weaker side. The player took the bait and the dummy came. At the very last moment, Peter flipped his stick over and laid it flat on the Astroturf, as strong as he could with his one handed grip, taking the ball off the opponent with an amazing reverse stick tackle that anyone there would have been proud of.

Having made the tackle, he could feel the excitement running through his veins (although technically not his) but was determined not to get carried away and fought the impulse to try and do anything else clever, but instead played a simple pass to one of his teammates on the other side of the pitch. Within seconds, words of encouragement from all around bombarded him, with even the odd pat on the back being thrown in for luck. That feeling was like nothing else he'd ever experienced. It was amazing. It was then that he realised. THIS WAS IT! Richie's secret. He knew that the current smile on his face would easily match any of Richie's from her lacrosse matches.

'It was so simple,' he thought. 'I just had to join in.'

The training match continued a little longer, during which time he made another couple of tackles and a few more passes. As the session came to an end, he received more pats on the back, whilst at the same time getting on the end of some of the banter. One of the captains came to take Peter's contact details on his way out and the rest, as they say, is history. He was well and truly hooked.

It was pretty much the same scenario for Tank, except

that he didn't get the same lightning bolt of excitement until he played in his first game proper on a Saturday. After that, he too was hooked in very much the same way as Peter and Richie. For the three friends, the thought of not joining the humans to participate in team sport was now unfathomable, something alas most dragons could not comprehend, more's the pity.

Really excited at the thought of going training on Tuesday, Peter wondered if he'd be selected for one of the two sides to play the following Saturday. With it being September, there were usually two or three friendly or interclub games before the league season started, normally in the first week of October. Peter's thoughts turned to Tank, who had resumed training many weeks ago and would be participating in his first league game this coming Saturday.

'Perhaps I'll go and watch some of his game and get to play hockey as well. Things are looking up,' thought Peter.

With a spring in his step, he wolfed down his breakfast, breezed through the housework and settled down in front of his computer. Much as he fancied gaming for a few hours, he needed to sort some things out beforehand. Determined to design a spreadsheet that could be easily filled in with all the information he was gathering on Manson, he cleared his mind and concentrated on the task at hand. He'd thought that by putting it all in spreadsheet form, in a clear and concise manner, he might be better able to see where all of it was leading, if indeed that was at all possible. Also, a plan had been brewing deep in the back of his mind, to design a computer programme that would collect all the data from Manson's computer at Cropptech, if, that is, he could find some way of downloading it onto the former Major's computer in the first place. His software and programming skills were nowhere near what they should have been, having not been his strong suit in the nursery ring, but he did have a strong grasp of the basics, which in time should allow him to carry out his plan.

It didn't take long to create the spreadsheet, but it was time consuming adding all the data he'd already collected. He struggled to read his own writing when looking at the notes he'd already jotted down.

'Clearly,' he thought, 'I'm qualified to be a doctor or maybe even a teacher, going by this. On second thoughts, even my writing's not illegible enough to be a teacher's and I'll be damned if I'm wearing one of those crazy jackets with the patches on the elbows,' he thought with a smile on his face. 'Human teachers seem to have the worst fashion sense on the whole planet. Fact!'

After a couple more hours he'd finished transferring all of his previously collected data. He sat staring at it for an hour more, without gaining true insight or finding any significant pattern. It was then that he gave up.

Grabbing himself some lunch, he returned to his desk, determined to make a start on producing a programme that he could upload to Manson's computer. This proved harder than even he would have thought, having not been under any illusions in the first place. During his search of the internet, he'd had to be very careful. It wouldn't be prudent to type into the search engine: 'Wanted - computer spy programme, Trojan or virus', particularly if he didn't want anyone to know what he was up to. Peter's head felt like the hard drive of his computer sounded... in need of a rest. So far today he'd spent over five hours sitting at his pc, and it was only mid-afternoon.

Closing down the computer to give the whirring components a break, he slumped down on the sofa and decided to catch up with all the news from the Daily Telepath. Closing his eyes, he dispatched his consciousness, just giving it a little prod now and then to guide it in the right direction. It returned in no time at all with that day's edition. Remarkably, it contained the scores from last night's Global Cup Quarter final games. He was astonished. He'd been so caught up in the events of yesterday, that he'd totally forgotten that the Indigo Warriors were playing one of the most important matches in recent history. Speed reading the back page, his heart racing, he noted with relief that the Warriors had won and made it through to the semi finals. He continued to the in depth match report that was further inside.

Sometime later he opened his eyes and stretched his entire body, almost off the end of the sofa.

'That was pure bliss,' he thought. 'Well, nearly anyway. The only thing better would have been to be at the match itself. Pity Tank couldn't get any tickets, nevertheless, being through to the semi finals... FANTASTIC!'

Sitting up sharply, he got a bit of a head rush for his troubles, having been lying down for so long. Jumping to his feet, he proceeded to search the house for his mobile phone. Not for the first time, he couldn't remember where he'd left it. Where was that eidetic memory now? Eventually finding it in his bedroom, he fired off a text to Tank, asking if he knew any teams good enough to get to the semi finals, including a plea for the possibility of any tickets to the match. Tank replied only moments later saying that he was off coaching rugby and that he would check out the ticket situation later that evening. Peter rubbed his hands together and did a little jig on seeing Tank's reply. The Warriors reaching the semi final of the Global Cup was beyond his wildest dreams.

Returning to work the next day, he was exhausted from everything that had happened at the weekend. Although tired, he was still on a high from hearing about the Indigo Warriors and couldn't help but check his phone regularly in the hope of a text from his best friend. He had no idea how Tank managed to get hold of good laminium ball match tickets, particularly since demand always considerably outstripped supply, but he knew the contacts Tank used usually dealt in days rather than hours. Still, he could hope, couldn't he?

After clearing a little of his backlog, he focused all his

attention on trying to account for all of Manson's movements, seeing if he could determine some kind of goal that his nemesis might be working towards. With access to all the security systems (CCTV, web cams, computer access and one or two trusted allies) you would think that tracking Manson's whereabouts at any one time wouldn't be too much of a challenge, but things were quite the opposite in reality. All too often he managed to slip out of the upper building undetected and then turn up in some far flung part of the complex completely by surprise. All routes in and out of Garrett's office were covered by the security cameras, and there were no blind spots: he'd checked. That said, Manson seemed to have a knack of somehow getting out of Garrett's office without being seen. The more Peter tried to work out what was going on, the more puzzled he became. Eventually he decided to get the maintenance crew to strip down all the cameras in the main building and give them a thorough overhaul, on the grounds of routine maintenance. Crews were also ordered to look out for anything suspicious and report directly back to him. Twenty four hours later, the crew chief made his way to Peter's office to report his findings.

A tall, pale skinned, gangly man named Alastair, who Peter had dealt with many times before and found very competent and extremely knowledgeable on any technical subject, knocked and entered Peter's office. The two sat either side of the paper strewn desk.

"Hi Alistair, how's it going?"

"Good thanks Peter. We've finished the maintenance you requested," affirmed Alistair, sliding a huge pile of paper across the desk. "There were no problems to report. One or two of the cameras in the stairwells had got a significant amount of dust in them, which if left much longer may have caused an issue, but other than that, nothing untoward."

Peter nodded as he picked up the top piece of paper from the pile to study.

"So does that mean it would be prudent to decrease the maintenance intervals of all the cameras in stairwells across the entire complex?"

"Already done Peter," remarked Alistair, sitting back in his chair proudly. "We've adjusted the schedule on the computer system to flag the stairwell cameras every nine months instead of every eighteen, as it was previously."

Peter leaned across the desk to shake Alistair's hand.

"Great work as always. Thanks for fitting us in at such short notice."

"Anytime, for you Peter. We value the security of this place almost as much as you do, so adjusting our schedule isn't that much of a problem. I have to ask though... it sounded when we first spoke as though you were looking for something specific. Clearly we didn't find anything. Is it something that I should be concerned about?"

For a split second Peter's brow creased as he thought about sharing his burden with Alistair. He was sure he could trust the man and didn't doubt for second that he was sincere in valuing the security of the complex, but he just couldn't bring himself to do it.

"No, it's nothing to be concerned about. I just... well... I've just been working hard and have had a few late nights. I must have imagined the odd glitch on one of the monitors and wanted to be safe rather than sorry," Peter lied.

"Well, I know the feeling about working too hard. Try and catch up on your sleep. You're no good if you're nodding off in front of the monitors. And don't worry, your secret's safe with me. We've all done it at some point." With that the two shook hands and Alistair turned and headed towards the door. Before he left, Peter called out,

"Don't forget to thank your team for me, for doing such a great job."

"Of course," replied Alistair, disappearing off down the corridor.

Peter sat back in his chair, more puzzled and frustrated than ever, now that each and every camera had been checked. He felt guilty about lying to Alistair about the reason he wanted the cameras checked in the first place, but deep down he knew it was probably best not to get anyone else involved, especially as he didn't know exactly what he was dealing with.

The day dragged on, with Peter mainly staying in his office fielding phone calls, catching up on emails, all the while keeping a close eye on the security monitors. The thought of hockey training that evening was the only thing keeping him going.

With only an hour of the working day left, a high pitched warble from his phone disrupted his chain of thought. Retrieving it from his jacket, which was hanging up on the back of his office door, his heart nearly skipped a beat when the phone's display showed there was a text from Tank.

'He's got the tickets... YIPPEE!' thought Peter, opening up the message. Peter's joy soon turned to sadness. The message read:

'Sorry couldn't get tickets to the game. However, may still be able to watch it. Will be in touch soon. Regards.' Peter let out a long sigh, disappointed at the lack of tickets.

'The biggest match of my life and I don't get to go,' he thought. 'I wonder what he meant by "may still be able to watch it"?'

Saving the email he was working on, he shut down his computer and grabbed his jacket before leaving, slightly earlier than normal. He'd had enough for today, and was once again taking advantage of his accrued flexi-time. About to get into his car, he suddenly noticed that Manson's Mercedes wasn't parked anywhere. He'd spent all afternoon keeping a close eye on the car parks, or so he thought, and Manson had still managed to slip out, in his car this time. He felt like banging his head against the roof of his car in frustration, but didn't, mainly due to the number of other workers leaving all around him.

'How does he do it?' he thought as he started up the engine and clicked his seatbelt into place, before driving home.

On getting home he made himself a light snack, and continued for an hour or so with the programme he was trying to develop on his computer. Although nothing special so far, he was quite pleased with his progress, given his limited skill set in this particular field. Zooming upstairs, he slipped effortlessly into his freshly ironed hockey kit, grabbed his water bottle, stick bag and trainers (which smelled as though they could have walked to the sports club on their own) and just about remembering to grab his phone and keys, he headed out to his car and off to the sports club.

Surprised by the sheer number of cars on arrival, it took him nearly five minutes to find a parking space. The place was nearly full, and that hardly ever happened on a busy Saturday, let alone in the week. What was going on? On his way to the pitch, he noted that not only was it hockey training, but the men's and ladies' lacrosse teams seemed to be here as well as the entire rugby club by the look of things. As he watched the rugby players trot out of their dedicated dressing room, he spotted Tank jogging out onto the pitch. His friend must have sensed this, as he turned his head and gave Peter a little nod, which Peter duly returned. As well as all the sports, there seemed to be some sort of function going on in the clubhouse, with lots of well-dressed people going in carrying gifts and flowers.

'No wonder it's so busy,' he thought. As he got closer to the Astroturf, he had to join a queue to get in.

'Wow, I've never had to queue to get into training before. Lots of new faces as well as old ones. Everyone seems to be here, they must have missed it as much as I have over the summer.'

At precisely seven o'clock, the two groups of footballers that were using the pitch finished and the queuing hockey players streamed out onto it. As Peter made his way through the crowd, he nodded and exchanged a few friendly words with teammates. All in all it was a staggering number of people for just training, especially considering all of the first team squad was missing as their training session was separate and didn't start until eight thirty, directly after this session finished.

Being back on a hockey pitch with all these people was nothing short of awesome for Peter, with it only now dawning on him just how much he'd missed playing, and how much it meant to him. Starting with some light fitness work, the session then split the ladies from the men to work on basic stick skills. As the evening wore on, the exercises became more intense and complicated, eventually leading to a series of mini games for everyone. Eight thirty came around, with the coaches wrapping things up, allowing the first team men and ladies respectively on to the pitch.

Exhausted and baked in sweat, Peter trudged over to the sideline to find his stick bag and, more importantly, a drink. As the cold water trickled down his throat he noticed a familiar, smug face looking with contempt at those already leaving the pitch... MANSON!

'Why on earth would anyone look down on others representing the same club as you?' he thought, wiping the sweat from his forehead and neck with the bottom of his tee shirt. 'It makes no sense.'

Slinging his stick bag over his shoulder, he made sure to keep his back to the first team players, for fear of being confronted by Manson. After grabbing his wallet from the car, he headed for the bar in the hope that Richie and Tank would be there, given that the lacrosse and rugby had finished at exactly the same time as his session.

Slipping quietly into the clubhouse, he was pleasantly surprised to find the bar wasn't nearly as busy as he'd thought it would be. The private function was being held in the room upstairs that had its own bar, keeping the large main bar free downstairs for all of those club members who had just finished outside. Peter waited his turn; even though it wasn't that busy downstairs clearly some of the bar staff were serving upstairs.

Eventually getting served, he scanned the room for his friends. Richie was ensconced at the far end with a gaggle of lacrosse girls all chatting and making far too much noise for his liking. Glancing through the mass of rugby players, he could just make out Tank having a very animated discussion with two other players about tactics or a game or something, waving his hands all over the place to emphasise a point. Rather than interrupt Tank's heated conversation, he chose to prop up the bar instead, way too intimidated by all the gorgeous lacrosse girls to even think about approaching Richie. Shuffling along the bar, he turned his attention to a rather competitive doubles pool match that was taking place in the far corner between four of the rugby boys. Abruptly a hand landed on his shoulder. He turned ready to confront Manson... only to find it was the second team captain, Andy, who was clearly disturbed by the look on Peter's face.

"Sorry Andy, I thought you were someone else," Peter quipped, breaking into a big toothy smile.

"That's quite alright Peter. Good to see you at training. How was your summer?"

"Quite lazy really. Didn't do too much. Missed playing hockey like crazy though."

"Good to hear," replied Andy, producing a notebook and pen. "Are you available for Saturday?"

"Sure am. In fact, barring injury, I'm available every weekend throughout the season."

"Good man," maintained Andy, slapping Peter playfully on the back. "Well, I've got some friendly games lined up over the next few weeks and then the league starts. Hopefully we can kick on from last year's mid table position and aim to finish in the top two and gain promotion. A few new faces out there tonight that might

231

bolster the squad from last year, especially since Ben and Matt will be missing, having both gone off to university. Anyhow Pete, I've got to catch up with some of the others before they slope off, so I'll see you on Saturday, two o'clock for a two thirty start. Okay?"

"Sure thing Andy, see you Saturday," answered Peter, raising his pint glass as Andy disappeared into a mass of hockey players.

'Fantastic, I'm in the side,' he thought, as he spotted Tank making his way towards him through a dwindling number of rugby players.

"Good training?" asked Tank, leaning over the bar, trying to attract some service.

"Yeah, it was great to be back playing again. Why are you training twice a week now?"

"Well," said Tank, "we do light work and tactics on a Tuesday, and the more physical work on a Wednesday."

"How was it?" enquired Peter.

"It was okay, but as you probably know we had our first game on Saturday and got our arses handed to us on a plate," observed Tank, shaking his head.

Peter had seen the result and match report online only that morning and was surprised that Tank hadn't mentioned it. Not that Peter would have been too much help. He didn't fully understand the rules of rugby, so anything more complicated such as tactics and formations would go straight over his head.

"Any reason why you lost?"

"Hmmm... lots. Let's just say the coach and I have differing opinions on that."

"That explains the rather frantic debate I could see you having a while ago, you know... with all the arm waving. I thought you were going to take off at one point," mocked Peter, trying to lighten the tone.

"Very good," sneered Tank sarcastically. "I don't think it was quite that bad. Anyway, how would you feel if your hockey team was going to hell and you knew how to put some of the bad things right, but the so-called important people refused to listen to what you had to say? Wouldn't be so funny then, would it?"

For the first time in what felt like forever, Peter could see his friend in real distress.

'It means so much to him, just like the hockey does to me,' he thought, slurping what was left of his drink.

"I'm sorry Tank. I understand how important it is to you, I really do. Perhaps you need to change the way you approach the problem. You've completed all the coaching courses, and teach the youngsters on a Sunday. Is there nothing there that can help you?"

Deep furrows appeared across Tank's forehead as he considered what Peter had said.

"Well, maybe I could... yeah, that just might work."

Peter stared at him blankly.

"I could simplify some of the tactics and get the kids to use them on a Sunday. The result should be about the same, maybe not quite as dynamic and full on, but just maybe those narrow minded idiots might get the idea if they see the kids using it to great effect. Thanks Pete. That might just be a great help."

"You are, of course, very welcome. On an entirely different subject though... your message mentioned something about watching the game even though you couldn't get tickets. What's that all about?"

That got Tank's full attention.

"You see, I've been working on something in my spare time. Something that should allow us..." Tank looked around to make sure no one was listening in, and then leant in close to Peter, "should allow us to watch the match through a television."

Peter was gobsmacked. He'd never heard anything that ridiculous.

"Through a television? Are you mad? How the hell do you think you can do that?"

Tank put one of his gigantic arms around his friend to

calm him down and try to limit the amount of attention he seemed to be attracting with his little outburst.

"It's not as hard as you think... Pete. Would you like me to explain the details to you?"

Peter thought for a moment, slightly unsure, because Tank had that 'be careful what you wish for' look in his eyes. After a few moments had passed, still unsure, Peter decided he did want to know a little more about it.

"Go on then."

"Well, you know how you access the ... papers?"

"Yes," replied Peter carefully, fully understanding Tank's meaning.

"It's kind of like that. You see, what happens is that the match is transmitted out to the papers so that they can do match reports and snatch pictures for publication from it. The whole game remains in a giant buffer for a few more days until it is no longer required, when it's just deleted to free up space for the next one. The reason they don't transmit the whole game to every dragon out there, is that most dragons wouldn't be able to process that level of information. Also there aren't enough broadcasting nodes to transmit something of that magnitude to everyone. It's broadcast to the papers and that's it. I've developed a crystal node that can access the information at the papers' headquarters via the local node and then display it in digital form, hopefully on a television.

"Hopefully?"

"Well... it's not fully functional yet, but it will be by the day of the game. I just need to buy a new television to test it on, that's all."

"What happened to that nice big fifty inch flat screen that you had?"

"I... um... hooked up the crystal to it and... umm... didn't regulate the power properly and it... um... kind of... exploded... umm... a bit anyway."

"IT EXPLODED!!!!!!" exclaimed Peter. "How can it explode a bit?"

"It exploded a bit," insisted Tank, "because some of the screen was still left intact, alright."

"Right," said Peter, nodding his head.

"I don't suppose..." Tank started.

"NO!" countered Peter. "Not going to happen."

"It's just that it would speed things up while I wait for a new television to be delivered."

"I like my television just how it is... thanks."

From out of nowhere, a very loud 'BOO' echoed out from behind them. Peter's glass tumbled into the air as it jumped out of his hand. Time slowed as the spinning glass headed swiftly towards the floor, and a shattering conclusion... before being expertly caught once again by... Richie.

"Crikey, you guys are jumpy," joked Richie, offering the glass back to Peter.

For his part, Peter gave Richie one of his best 'I'm more mature than you' looks, taking the glass from her before returning it to the bar.

"What's going on guys?" she demanded.

"I was just explaining to Peter how we might all watch the Indigo Warriors in the Global Cup together," whispered Tank.

"You've got tickets... fantastic!"

"Not exactly," uttered Tank, bursting Richie's rather premature bubble.

"Oh, how are we going to watch it then?"

"On a television," chipped in Peter, rolling his eyes. "It's something Tank's been working on."

"For a second there, I thought we might actually get to see the game," Richie said to Peter, knowing all about Tank's little projects.

"Hey, that's not fair. I know I've had a bit of bad luck in the past, but this stands a real chance of working. I just need Peter to let me use his television to test the thing on. Please Peter, I know I can get this to work... honest. And once I do, we can all sit down and watch the match together, doesn't that sound great?"

It did sound great, both Richie and Peter had to admit that, but it also sounded a mite farfetched. Also, Tank's track record on succeeding in these little projects was practically zero. Still, he did find it hard to turn down his friend, particularly when he thought about all that Tank had done for him in the past.

"Okaayyyy... what do you need?" asked Peter reluctantly.

Tank lurched forward and gave his friend a huge hug.

"You won't regret it, I promise."

Peter looked over Tank's shoulder at a grinning Richie and rolled his eyes again.

"I just need to come round and use your television a couple of times between now and the match, " said Tank innocently. "That's all. Nothing will go wrong... honest."

"Sure Tank. Come round whenever you like."

And that was that. The friends chatted for a few more minutes, catching up on their respective sports and training routines. Just as Peter thought it was time for him to think about leaving, the main doors to the bar opened, and the men's first team hockey players started to file in.

'Oh crap,' was Peter's first thought. He'd hoped to leave before Manson had finished training, to avoid bumping into him. Richie caught Peter looking nervously towards the entrance.

"It's alright Pete, he's just here playing hockey. Just ignore him," remarked Richie confidently.

"The slimy rat I've been hearing about is here, is he?" I was just about to leave anyway Pete. Why don't we all go out together?" Tank gestured at Richie.

"Good Idea," added Richie, starting to lead the way.

They made their way through the very quiet bar area, returning their empty glasses en route. There couldn't have been more than twenty people left in the whole place, a dozen or so of whom were the men's first hockey team, who had just come in as a group from the Astroturf. Peter strode down the length of the bar, flanked on either side by Tank and Richie. He stared at the floor, not wanting to make eye contact with Manson, hoping he could leave without being noticed. No such luck. About eight feet from the end of the massive bar, just as Peter had thought he'd made it out without being spotted, a body moved out in front of the three of them.

"Ahhhh... if it isn't my little underling. I didn't realise you had any friends. How unlikely."

He looked up into Manson's smug, round face and noticed for the first time a bottomless blackness at the centre of his eyes. He fought back his bubbling temper, knowing that whatever happened, his friends would have his back, but he realised that if something happened here, Manson would no doubt exact some sort of retribution back at Cropptech. So in a split second, he decided he would take a leaf out of Richie's book and be diplomatic and polite.

"Good evening Mr Manson. Did you have a good training session?" he said with just the slightest hint of sarcasm.

"Yes... I certainly did. It was very physical and tactically demanding. I would explain it but someone from the lower echelons of hockey like yourself would of course be hard pushed to understand it," boasted Manson, trying to provoke Peter.

Every atom in Peter's body wanted to jump up and spank Manson. Peter used all his self control and just smiled.

"See you back at work," he said, sidestepping Manson and heading towards the door. With his friends at his side, Peter had got no further than a few paces before he heard Manson's twisted voice.

"Good work checking out the security cameras. Find anything useful?"

He turned around to see Manson, hands on hips, smug as ever. As he looked deep into Manson's eyes from six feet away, everything suddenly became crystal clear. Manson knew that he'd tried unsuccessfully to track him with the security cameras. In that moment, the entire situation had changed. Manson wasn't just your run of the mill criminal trying to make some material gain. He was far more than that. Far more than a human being, Peter suspected, even though there were no obvious signs, not even to a dragon.

Breaking eye contact, the young hockey playing dragon turned slowly, and strode purposefully out the main entrance, Tank and Richie hot on his heels. The slightly chilly night air washed over him, cooling down his overly warm body and bringing his temper back into line, both at the same time. His friends walked next to him in silence as he made his way across the near deserted car park to his car, even though theirs were in a totally different place to his.

As they all reached his car, Peter turned and faced his friends.

"Well?" he all but demanded, expecting them to have had the same kind of epiphany about Manson that he'd had.

"Well what?" replied Richie.

"Well, did you not see what just happened?" snapped Peter sharply.

"Yes, the nasty man tried to get a rise out of you," Richie sneered sarcastically.

Peter's temperature rocketed, so much so that boiling steam rolled off him in waves in the chilly evening air.

"The whole thing, Rich, not just him provoking me."

"Yes, I can see now that he's a bit of a git, something I hadn't noticed before, for which I'm sorry, but that's all. Get over it," stormed Richie, marching off towards her car.

Peter took a step forward to follow her and continue the argument, but a huge arm came out to block his way.

"I don't think that's very wise, do you?" asked Tank

quietly.

Peter took a deep breath and ran his hands through his slick hair.

"Did you notice anything?" he asked Tank hopefully, not really wanting to hear the response. Tank considered his friend's question carefully.

"As Richie said, he certainly is a first class git."

Peter's head dropped, knowing his friend was once again going to side with Richie. Tank continued.

"I tried using all my dragon senses on him as he stood there, but sensed... nothing. Just a plain old human being, albeit a git, but a human git."

'There it is,' thought Peter. 'Again he's sided with Richie. Why can't they see what's happening?'

"Despite sensing nothing other than human, there was something else," Tank said, screwing up his face in concentration. "A feeling of... it's so difficult to explain. Like the whitest cold it's possible to have. Pure, calculated malevolence. It didn't really come from him, it was just out there. On top of that, the human felt... too good to be true. Almost too human. That's the only way I can describe it."

Peter knew exactly what Tank was talking about, but was surprised to hear that he hadn't felt it radiating off Manson, as he had. It was, however, Peter thought, a start.

The two friends said their goodbyes, with Tank adding that he would be in touch about coming round to use the television. Whilst they were chatting, Richie's car sped out of the car park, something akin to a Formula One driver.

12 A MEMBER OF THE MAGIC CIRCLE?

September seemed to positively fly by from Peter's perspective. Having returned to the hockey, he was happier than ever, despite the obvious ongoing tensions at work with Manson and the fact that Richie hadn't spoken to him since their argument after the first night's hockey training. She had been avoiding him ever since.

Hockey though, was great. He'd been to two more training sessions, comfortably getting his eye in, and had played in two matches. With the league starting in two weeks time, the games at the moment were all friendlies, all of which had been won by his second team, the last one by eight goals to nil. Finding their form early on, and gelling as a team, the side were playing much better than last season, with the new additions only strengthening things further. As standards go, they weren't that far off the first team.

During his evenings, Peter had spent the vast majority of time trying to develop the spyware program that he hoped to upload at Cropptech with a view to finding out just what Manson was up to. He knew, of course, that even if he managed to perfect his program and get it past the company's mainframe, there was still no guarantee that anything would come of it.

Tonight was going to be another night in front of the computer, trying to put the finishing touches to his rather pieced together program, before testing it with the aim of uploading it sometime next week. Having just finished his rather bland tea, he headed for the living room, plopping down in his big black swivel chair that was parked in front of his computer. As he did so, the doorbell rang.

'Let me guess,' he thought, 'someone wanting me to change my energy supplier, no doubt. Only been three of those already this month.'

Strolling down the hallway, he could just make out the

silhouette of someone tall through the semicircle of triangular windows at the top of the wooden door. He psyched himself up to be brutally rude to whatever sort of salesman it was, knowing full well that he was normally a soft touch when it came to this sort of thing. Putting on a steely face, he opened the door sharply to find... Tank, grinning inanely at him.

"Wotcha guv'nor, I've come to fix your telly," Tank said in a comedy voice, as he squeezed by into the narrow hallway, carrying a huge tool case.

"Come in, why don't you," Peter put in, to Tank's wide back, which was quickly vanishing up the hallway.

Turning into the living room, Tank opened his toolbox on the floor, and proceeded to pull Peter's television out from the wall, so that he could get to the back of it, all the time ignoring his friend hovering over him.

"So... heard from Richie?" Tank enquired, as he unscrewed the back cover from the TV.

"Nope... you?"

"Well, I tried ringing her mobile, but there was no answer and it didn't even go to answer phone so that I could leave a message. I guess she just wants a little space. Nothing unusual there I suppose," said Tank, sliding a long, thin flat-bladed screwdriver behind the back panel, trying to lever it out.

Peter stood wincing, waiting for the television to shatter into a million pieces. He could see in all their detail, Tank's huge arm muscles straining with the effort he was putting in to trying to lever out the panel, and with the television looking so delicate, he just knew a busted set was only moments away.

Suddenly there was a tiny little 'pop' and the panel came away from one side in Tank's enormous hands. The strapping rugby playing dragon repeated the feat on the other side of the panel and, much to Peter's amazement, the whole thing came away in one piece, exposing the inner workings of the television. As Tank propped the panel against the wall, out of the way, he turned to Peter.

"Surprised?"

"Not at all," Peter lied. "Just curious, that's all."

"You're such a terrible liar Pete. I could see your reflection in the blade of my screwdriver. You looked like a little toddler needing to use the potty. You were just waiting for something awful to happen."

"Yes, yes I know, I'll leave you alone to get on with it. Can I get you a drink or anything?"

"No, I'm fine thanks," replied Tank, his head once again buried in the back of the television.

Slumping back down in his computer chair on the opposite side of the room, Peter started to test his program, occasionally glancing over to see how his friend was progressing.

As the evening wore on, the two friends working in silence were polar opposites. Frustration threatened to overwhelm Peter, with his program doing nothing that it was supposed to. Tank, on the other hand, was getting on much better. Well, I say much better... the television was now in fifty different parts, but... they all seemed to be laid out on the living room floor in a clear and logical manner, all undamaged. Seemingly satisfied with his progress, Tank got up from the floor and made his way out to his car. Engrossed in what he was doing, Peter didn't even realise his friend was missing. When Tank came back in a few minutes later, Peter was swearing and cursing like a Premiership footballer, most unusual for him.

"What's the matter, bud?" enquired Tank.

Peter explained what he was trying to do and why, also adding the fact that he couldn't make the program work as it was supposed to, despite his best efforts. Tank agreed to take a look at it when he'd finished with the television, telling Peter to take a break for a while. Peter did as his friend suggested, taking a seat on the sofa, secretly relieved that his friend was going to bring his superior programming skills to the party. Tank was way better with computers than he would ever be.

In the middle of the living room floor, Tank unwrapped a large object shaped like a pyramid from a flowery old tea towel that he'd brought in from his car. Peter sat transfixed as a bright and sparkling translucent crystal pyramid, a cable running out of its base, was revealed.

Tank held up the crystal for Peter to see.

"This, my friend, is the clever bit."

"What does it do?"

"This is what allows us to pick up the feed, whilst at the same time converting it into a digital format that the television can display... hopefully."

Tank ran the cable from the crystal carefully to the back of the television, and after plugging it in, started to put the components so carefully laid out on the floor, back into place. Peter remained totally silent, knowing just how much his friend was having to concentrate. After about fifteen minutes, Tank let out a visible sigh of relief and looked over towards his friend.

"Want to give it a try?" asked Tank, a manic grin scrawled across his face.

"What can we expect to see?" replied Peter nervously.

"Dunno. Depends on what's in the buffer at the other end. Whatever it is will be in tomorrow's newspapers, that's for sure."

Sceptical as he was, he knew he had no chance of getting out of what was to come, so Peter put on a little smile for his friend and said,

"Sure, let's do it."

Tank plugged in the mains lead and switched the set on, causing the pyramid to glow ever so slightly. Peter was sure something bad was about to happen. Holding the remote, Tank started the manual tuning sequence, not entirely sure what he was looking for as he scrolled through the static-filled screens, absolute confidence about what he'd done encompassing him totally. As the static started to form a black and white picture, the two of them tried to make out what they were seeing. After a slight re-tune, both realised they were looking at a mass of sand dunes in a desert. That's all they could see... sand everywhere.

"Nice picture. Not very exciting though. Do you think the papers are running a count the sand grain competition tomorrow?"

"Give it a minute," added Tank, squinting hard at the picture.

The two friends studied the vivid, albeit black and white, picture. Peter was just impressed that his friend had managed to get the television to work with the crystal, but couldn't understand for the life of him why they were staring at sand dunes in the desert. As this crossed his mind, a small dark shape some way off, swam into view. At first, Peter thought it to be a bird swooping down low, but the more they watched, the more it became apparent it wasn't that. Whatever the shape was, it was clear it was moving at quite a speed, and was some way off, so much so that its down-draught was spraying up the sand beneath it. And that was the giveaway.

"SANDSKIMMING!" both friends cried in unison.

"That must be the new course in the Sahara," observed Tank.

"I didn't think it was supposed to be ready for at least another six months," added Peter.

"Ah... they always do that, just to create a surprise and more publicity around it all. Cool though, eh?"

"Oh God, yes."

Sandskimming was another dragon thing. Not so much a sport, or obsession like laminium ball, but more like a relaxing pastime. The idea was to fly low to the ground on a timed lap. The lap, or circuit, would be created by the first dragon, due to them flying so low the down-force would produce a pattern in the sand that looked very much like a road or route. The next competitors to go would have to follow the pattern in the sand, with the winner being the dragon whose timed lap was the fastest. Sand was the ideal game for this to be played over, with dried mud and sometimes a lake or two used in very rare circumstances.

Sandskimming had started off as a younglings game from the nursery ring, but had managed to capture the imagination of older dragons everywhere after being introduced to one particular holiday destination, and although not nearly as popular as laminium ball (what was?), every dragon knew about sandskimming and most had tried it out at some point in their life.

When young dragons were taken on field trips to different parts of the world, whenever they were somewhere exotic and out of the way, usually a desert, they would almost always resort to playing this game. However, the last fifty years or so have seen the development above ground of dragon holiday camps and it has been there that sandskimming has really taken off as a form of relaxation.

Dragon holiday camps first came about in 1956, the brainchild of a dragon called Firesworn. He was a respected scientist who'd been working on supplementing the worldwide underground monorail with solar power. Committed to his study of solar power, once his work underground had exhausted all of its theoretical possibilities, he then had to find an area on the surface to continue his experiments. Exploration and development took him to the Kalahari Desert in Southern Africa. Based there primarily because of its remoteness and the fact that human contact was unlikely at best, he also found it was possible to keep all his equipment out in the open, as well as maintain his dragon form without fear of discovery.

It didn't take long for Firesworn to realise he loved being in his natural form, soaking up the sun's rays and flying around the hot, arid desert, in between working on his solar power project.

Most dragons in Firesworn's position would have

occasionally returned underground to visit their family or friends. But he got so caught up in his work and the sheer exhilaration of living above ground that the last thing he wanted to do was to go back underground. So instead, he got his family to visit him on the surface. Reluctantly they went, and once there, were captivated by the desert and everything that involved being in their dragon forms above ground. When the time for them to return home came around, they did so grudgingly, and once back home underground, they told all their friends and neighbours about the wonderful experience that they'd had.

Soon, Firesworn was inundated with dragons wanting to visit him or help with his project. Ironic really, as before he hadn't managed to find one volunteer to accompany him. At about this time Firesworn's passion seemed to be less concerned with the solar power and more with developing a place where dragons could rest and relax on the surface, while still maintaining their privacy and keeping any knowledge of their existence a secret. Two years later, after a Herculean amount of work, not only from himself, but his family and friends, Firesworn came up with the answer... the first dragon holiday camp.

Based in the exact same place he'd been carrying out his research, an area of five hundred square miles was set aside for the camp when it was first fashioned. That sounds like a lot, but when you consider the Kalahari covers an area in excess of one hundred thousand square miles, it was really only a needle in a haystack. Basic as things went, the only feature of any real note in the camp was the stunning oasis situated almost directly in the middle. Firesworn and his friends had extended the oasis from a rather small and badly formed watering hole, into a superheated swimming pool for dragons of all sizes that was over fifty square miles in area. It was the talk of the domain.

Lookout posts with dragon guards were placed around the perimeter at ten mile intervals to make sure the visiting dragons weren't accidentally discovered. Their tasks were simple: to use their telepathic powers to persuade and encourage animals and in particular humans, to change course if they looked at all as though they might be heading in the direction of the camp, an easy feat really for a dragon with enhanced telepathic abilities.

However, at first this wasn't as straightforward as it should have been. While animals were relatively easy to dissuade, some of the human tribes in the area were rather harder to convince. The lookouts soon found the easiest way of convincing the humans to stay away, was to show them in their minds the area of the site, and just how treacherous the terrain was. That combined with the mirages the dragons created, showing watering holes and oases off in other directions, seemed to prove a huge success. This combination still works around the world today at some of the many modern day vacation camps that exist in remote areas across the planet.

Before long, Firesworn didn't know what had hit him. Dragons were coming from all over the planet to sample the delight of simply relaxing in the sun on the surface in their dragon forms. With popularity spiralling out of control, the camp was increased in size, provided with dedicated underground access and an easy link to the worldwide monorail and better facilities such as restaurants, sleeping areas and exceptional entertainment. More guards were provided as the camp expanded, and specially designated lookouts had the task of making sure the camp wasn't spotted from the air by any stray aircraft that might be passing.

Firesworn's solar power project had been totally consumed by his obsession for creating the ultimate in dragon relaxation, something he'd more than achieved. Over the coming decades that original encampment expanded even more and became the blueprint from many more camps to come. Today major dragon vacation camps can be found all around the globe, in such places as the

Great Basin in North America, the Namib in Southern Africa, the Gobi Desert in China, and the Gibson Desert and Great Victoria Desert, both in Australia.

The very latest undertaking, and the one Peter and Tank were now viewing through their television, is very special indeed. Over ten years in the making, quite a feat in a dragon timescale given what they can do with their mantras and magic, it dwarfs anything else on the planet. Sitting proudly in the middle of the Sahara Desert about one hundred and fifty miles south of Adrar in Algeria, just north of the Tropic of Cancer and just west of the Prime Meridian, its location has been subject to much planning. Apart from the fact that it needed to be remote and in a suitable climate, its current location has the added bonus in that it sits directly over the main southern monorail route out of London, which follows the Prime Meridian all the way to Accra, and then splits into two, with one heading Southwest to Rio, while the other heads Southeast towards South Africa.

Covering an area in excess of four thousand square miles, which again sounds a lot but is merely one drop in an ocean when it comes to the size of the Sahara itself, every conceivable luxury has been catered for, from lava pools with giant flumes, to a la carte charcoal dining, to death defying sandskimming courses. No expense has been spared, with everything under one roof so to speak, or not as the case may be.

Hundreds of lookouts have spent years being trained to make sure they're the best that they can be at their jobs to try and do everything to minimise the risk of discovery by the outside world. Everything that can be done has been done to make it as hard as possible to be discovered. The only eventuality that the dragons in charge seem to think presents any sort of risk, is the scenario of a passenger plane crashing down and landing smack bang in the middle of the site with lots of survivors and that, they say, is so unbelievably unlikely that the odds can't even begin to be calculated, and that's with the best dragon minds in the kingdom on the case.

So with all of that in mind, the camp was nearly ready to be opened and announced to the general dragon population for the first time. The two young prehistoric friends were currently viewing the few privileged dragon media trying out the facilities so that they could report on it for their telepathic papers the following day. Who wouldn't want to try out the most amazing getaway resort ever?

Their eyes glued to the television, Tank and Peter sat watching for the next twenty minutes or so as the images changed from different dragons flying over the sandskimming course, to views of fabulous giant lava pools, bubbling away furiously, to watching charcoal being prepared by the best dragon chefs in new and mouthwateringly exotic ways (which made both of the young friend's stomachs rumble repeatedly), all for the consumption of the expected guests.

"Well, we know it works," remarked Tank, beaming.

"I never doubted you," replied Peter, looking as though butter wouldn't melt in his mouth.

"Yeah... right," said Tank, punching Peter playfully in the arm.

"Well... maybe just a little," added Peter, rolling away and standing up.

"Anyway, it doesn't matter. We can all watch the match together... YIPPEE! Now all you have to do is tell Richie," urged Tank, uncomfortably.

"Oh good," sighed Peter, having forgotten all about their falling out.

"I'll do it if you want?" offered Tank.

"No it's all right, it should be me. I'll do it at work tomorrow."

"Want me to look at that program on the computer for you?" volunteered Tank.

"That would be great if you've got time."

"Sure... no problem."

Two hours later, having fixed his friend's computer program, Tank and his huge case made their way back through the front door and into his car. Peter walked down the garden path in the crisp night air to see his friend off.

"Thanks for the help with the program," he said, his breath starting to freeze as it came out of his mouth.

"No problem mate," replied Tank through the open driver side window, having just switched on the car's so-called heating system to clear the windscreen of condensation.

"Don't forget to talk to Richie tomorrow... tell her the good news about the game."

"Will do. Safe journey back."

And with that, Tank pulled away from Peter's house, his giant frame hunched down so low in the front seat, due to only being able to see past the condensation through a hole the size of a pea that had cleared on the windscreen. Peter smiled at his friend as he made his way back up the garden path, weaving his way in and out of the snails which were about in such great numbers that they could probably start a large scale military engagement, by the look of things.

The following day at work, Peter found himself once again scanning the bank of security monitors in his office, only this time not for the ever elusive Manson, but for his friend Richie.

'What did I do with my time before I became hooked on these?' he wondered to himself, studying row after row carefully.

Richie proved as elusive as Manson, at least until lunchtime when Peter spotted her heading for the canteen. Having waited for this chance all morning, he zipped out of his office like a bolt of lightning, slamming the door shut behind him and broke into a sprint, knowing full well that if he got a move on he could time his arrival to match that of his friend. As he rounded the last corner he slowed to a walk, all his effort rewarded by the sight of his friend right in front of him as he reached the canteen's double doors.

"Hi," he said, holding one of the doors open for her.

Standing hands on hips, she refused to go through the door that he was so gallantly holding open, to the delight of the other diners.

"Training for a marathon are we?" Richie enquired, just a little too loudly for Peter's liking.

He could feel himself start to blush. Clearly Richie had no intention of forgiving him.

'DAMN! This is going to go badly,' he thought to himself.

Suddenly Richie grabbed him by his tie and yanked him through the double doors, much to everybody else's amusement.

"Could you be any easier?"

"Probably not... no," he mumbled, not quite sure what was going on.

Joining the snaking queue, it soon became obvious to Peter that he'd been forgiven.

"How did you know I'd run all the way?"

Richie sighed and shook her head. Leaning forward so that no one else could hear, she whispered,

"You may be a prim and proper dragon, only using your senses when told it's okay to do so, but me... not so much. Heightened heart rate, perspiring badly and most obvious... your tie flying back over your shoulder," she said smiling.

"You're way too clever for me."

"I know," replied Richie, nodding her head.

The two friends went on to have an enjoyable lunch, with Richie telling Peter all the gossip from her department and Peter telling Richie about Tank and the television, and the fact that they could watch the big game together, albeit in a rather roundabout way due to the number of people close by. For once, Richie seemed genuinely surprised, something Peter could barely remember happening before. As the pair cleared their plates away, they agreed to meet in the bar of the sports club on Saturday after their respective lacrosse and hockey matches, with a view to going back to Peter's to watch the Global Cup on the rigged up television. Peter went back to work a happy man or dragon, depending on how you looked at things.

His good mood continued throughout the week, especially at the prospect of a fantastic Saturday to come, which he hoped would include a home hockey win in the last friendly before the league started, followed by a rousing night in watching the Indigo Warriors with Tank and Richie.

For the first time ever at Tuesday night's training, the entire second team squad was there, culminating in a highly charged, intense and thoroughly enjoyable session for them all. On his way home, all Peter could think about was how this season's league campaign could be their best ever, with promotion there for the taking. With just one more friendly to go this Saturday, he just knew they couldn't fail to get off to a cracking start.

Saturday morning was normally quite a relaxing time for Peter. Generally he fell out of bed quite late, had a bite to eat and then went and played hockey. Not today though. Awake at just gone six, he tried desperately to go back to sleep without any luck. Getting up, he realised just why he was too excited to sleep. The hockey... he just couldn't wait. Considering himself just like a child on Christmas Eve, he could come to just one conclusion.

'What a sad fool I am,' he laughed, whilst brushing his teeth.

With his game not starting until four, time dragged by as he tried to keep himself busy. Needless to say it didn't work. By midday he was going up the wall. All he could think about was hockey, hockey, hockey. How he would play, how the team would perform, who would be playing for the opposition, would they have their strongest team out? All these questions and more picked at his brain, like vultures on a carcass.

Eventually two fifty arrived and he could wait no more. On arrival at the sports club, he found the second team captain, Andy, waiting in the car park.

"Hi Pete," said Andy. "Looking forward to the game?"

"Can't wait," he replied, like a giddy child.

"There's been a bit of a change of plan I'm afraid," announced Andy, rummaging through his kit bag.

"Oh?" said Peter inquisitively.

Andy kept on rummaging as he talked.

"The opposition cried off late last night. Half of their team have flu. Anyway, all is not lost. The same thing seems to have happened to their first team as well, and they were due to play our first team. So, we're going to be playing our first team instead, which as it happens is not a bad warm up for our first league game next Saturday," said Andy grinning.

Peter was crestfallen.

'Oh my God,' he thought. 'I'm going to be playing against Manson!'

"You okay?"

"Ahh... yeah... fine," Peter lied.

"You just look all... pale, that's all."

"No... no... I'm fine."

"Okay, I'll see you in the changing room shortly," voiced Andy, heading off towards the entrance to the clubhouse.

Peter leant on his car, head in his hands. It felt as though his world had ended. Of all the things to happen.

'I'd rather face a team of drunken, diseased, ravaging Vikings on a hockey pitch than Manson,' he thought. Taking some deep breaths in the hope of calming himself down, he brought his head out from beneath his hands just in time to see Manson's black Mercedes pull into the car park. One word and one word only popped into his head... PANTS! Manson got out of his car and headed towards the changing rooms with some of his teammates, who had gathered in the car park. Halfway, Manson craned his neck and gave a sly glance over his shoulder in Peter's direction, making a mock salute as he did so. What was supposed to have been a brilliant afternoon had started in the worst possible way. He knew he had to get past it and focus on what a good evening he was going to have, and not worry about the hockey. That was easier said than done though.

Making his way to the changing rooms to join the rest of his team, he got halfway and then changed his mind, opting instead to head into the bar. It was still early and he couldn't face going to get ready just at the moment. Hearing that he'd be facing Manson on the hockey pitch had really knocked him for six. The bar itself was relatively empty, with only a few hockey players from earlier games gathered around the large tables at the far end. Walking the length of the deserted bar, on reaching the end he plonked his kit and stick bag down on the well worn carpet. Gazing out through the panoramic windows, lost in thought, he could see that both the rugby and lacrosse matches were in full flow. Squinting a little against the bright sun, he could just make out his friends competing in their separate sports. Richie was screaming down the wing at full pelt, her stick high above her, the ball cradled in the head, bursting through full throttle towards the opposition's goal. Tank, on the other hand, had just that second been buried beneath half a dozen hulking great rugby players. Peter watched, concerned, as play continued. His brief worry misplaced, he felt a sense of relief as only a few seconds later his giant friend stood up, covered from head to toe in mud, holding the ball aloft, players from both teams tumbling off him like rag dolls. He smiled at the thought of the exhilaration his friend must be experiencing. A light tap on his shoulder startled him back to reality. He turned to see one of the bar staff smiling at him. He struggled to remember her name, which was odd in itself given his eidetic memory. Finally it came to him.

"It's Janice isn't it?" he asked.

"That's right," replied the bubbly blonde with a beaming smile. Despite feeling thoroughly miserable, he smiled too, that's how infectious her grin had been. For an instant his mind wandered off, caught up in just how beautiful she was.

"Ummm... you couldn't do me a little favour, could you?" she asked.

"Of course. What do you need?"

"I need some more cartons of orange juice from upstairs and I can't leave the bar unattended. I wondered if you could just nip up and grab a couple of boxes for me," she continued, once again flashing her best smile.

"Sure," stammered Peter, finding it hard to concentrate, but not sure why.

"The boxes are on the right, just inside the stock cupboard door on the floor. It's unlocked, they just need bringing down."

A brief nod was followed by,

"Back in two tweaks of a dragon's nose," after which he bounded off towards the stairs right at the end of the bar, her chortling at his hopeless joke ringing in his ears. Taking the stairs two at a time, he headed towards the first floor. It wasn't just the stock cupboard that was located on the top floor, but a private function room with its own small bar, a tiny balcony overlooking the sports pitches and the chairman of the sports club's private office which was only accessible through the function room. Reaching the top of the stairs, he strolled purposefully along the corridor to the stock cupboard. Gently, he pushed open the door. Without the need to switch on the light, he could see the boxes of orange juice on the floor, just where Janice had said they were. Using one foot to prop open the door, while bending down to lift up the boxes, it was then that a bone chilling sight on the other side of the function room caught his attention. Hairs on the back of his neck stood to attention faster than Usain Bolt rushing for the last of the chicken nuggets. Outside his office, the chairman of the sports club was having a heated conversation with... Manson! A mixture of raw anger, outright bluster with just a hint of fear scored the chairman's face. He did not look happy. Knowing that he could be spotted at any moment, Peter slipped back into the dark cupboard, closing the door as much as he dared while still being able to see what was going on. Manson had his back to Peter, so it was only really the chairman's face that he had a view of. Softly whispering a very basic enhancement mantra, he was surprised when his hearing didn't pick up what the two of them were saying. Abruptly Manson turned and faced his direction, seemingly searching for something. Peter stood deathly still, the tiny slit through which he was watching concealed by shadows. Clearly on edge, Manson turned back, with the heated discussion continuing for another minute or so, the chairman becoming more and more disappointed.

It was then that the oddest thing happened. The chairman's face turned whiter than a cartoon ghost. Manson had pulled something out of a bag on the floor, and was offering it out to the chairman. For his part, the chairman didn't want to take it, seeming scared, nervous, almost petrified. Even from as far away as he was, Peter could make out the sweat pouring down the man's neck and face. Manson leaned menacingly close to the chairman and whispered something in his ear, causing him to shake uncontrollably. After ten seconds or so, he reached out and reluctantly took the object, handling it as if it were about to explode, before turning, walking into his office and putting the parcel down. After locking the office door the two men headed out of the function room, towards the corridor where the stock cupboard was. Peter gently closed the door right up and, holding his breath, stood as still as he could. Hearing the footsteps of the two men pass his hiding place he let out his breath, unable to resist one last look. Opening the door up a little, just enough for him to see out, he watched them going down the top flight of stairs, Manson clapping the chairman on the back, the chairman looking as though someone had just told him he'd got one day left to live. Leaving it for a couple of minutes, he picked up the orange juice boxes, and headed back down to the bar. A beaming Janice was there to greet him.

"I was just about to send out a search party for you," she said with that gorgeous smile.

Peter returned it with interest as he plonked the boxes down on the bar.

"The lock on the door jammed just as I was coming out. Don't worry I managed to fix it. It's fine now."

"Well, thank you very much," replied Janice, lining all the boxes up on the bar. "Perhaps I'll see you after you've finished your game. Good luck."

Peter was lost for words as he realised he should be heading for the changing rooms. Giving Janice a quick wave, he scooted out of the back entrance of the bar, and into the changing area. His team were in the changing rooms adjacent to the first team and due to the paper thin walls, could hear just how confident their opponents were. Although his team should have been on a high from all their previous results, their changing room seemed to be charged with negativity. Peter was unusually quiet, for good reason, but then he was never really the life and soul of the banter and chat anyway, so that shouldn't have made a whole lot of difference. It was almost as if a spell had been cast on them.

As the first team passed the half open door, joking around and playfully slapping each other, the atmosphere inside the Second XI's changing room resembled a morgue. Andy the captain gave his usual rousing team talk to very little effect. The passion and spirit seemed to have been sucked out of the entire squad. With time ticking away, reluctantly the players headed out to the Astroturf pitch, to do battle with the First XI.

A shrill whistle reverberated around the ground, signalling the end of the current match on the Astroturf. Both teams made their way on to the artificial pitch to complete warming up. Orange tops and white shorts were the order of the day for the first team, sporting the club's normal home strip. For the Second XI, Peter included, it was bright blue tops complemented with dark blue shorts. Knocking a ball back and forth with one of his teammates, Peter picked up on the distant cheers from the rugby and lacrosse matches. He figured they must both be coming to an end. Body on autopilot, still moving the hockey ball around, his thoughts turned to his friends, hoping they'd had an enjoyable afternoon in their respective sporting endeavours, wishing that it would suddenly be this evening and he could be with them watching the Indigo Warriors.

One of the umpires blew his whistle, indicating that it was nearly time to start. Both teams' players finished stripping off their tracksuits and assumed their corresponding positions on the pitch. After removing his top, Peter trotted from the sideline to his position as sweeper (the last line of defence except for the goalkeeper), standing just outside the twenty five, directly in the middle of the pitch. Checking to make sure Matt, his goalkeeper, was okay, he watched as Manson strolled purposefully into the opposing centre forward position. That pretty much meant that Peter would be facing him for most of the match. Taking a deep breath and rapping the bottom of his shoes with the head of his stick, something of a ritual he'd developed just as games were about to start, he focused his concentration on what was about to happen.

Both umpires checked the two goalkeepers were ready and then blew their whistles to start the match. After pushing back, the second team managed to string together seven or eight passes before being hounded off the ball by the first team. Having found possession, the first team surged forward on mass at an unbelievable pace.

'The accuracy of their passes isn't too shabby either,' thought Peter, as one of his opponents used a cunning bit of deception to slip the ball through the Second XI defence, straight to an onrushing forward.

In the blink of an eye Peter found himself faced with two opponents heading for him at full speed, the one without the ball being Manson, with only his goalkeeper behind him.

'Here we go,' he thought as instinct took over. Approaching the player with the ball, he noted Manson off to his left. Taking a deep breath, he offered his stick out to the right as if to make an open side block and then... timing it down to the very last split second, flipped his stick over and laid it down flat, reverse stick on the ground.

Much to Peter's relief, it was the perfect interception, with the player having taken the bait, trying to pass to Manson who was free, off to his right. With the ball on the end of his stick, Peter pulled it round to his open side and passed it wide to his right back, who had, along with the rest of the defence, busted a gut getting back after the defence-splitting pass had exploited their weakness. As his team went back on the offensive, Peter looked around to make sure no immediate threat presented itself. All it would take was one long ball and they could easily be undone again, something he knew only too well, given that it was his responsibility to rally his defenders and make sure they picked up their assigned players, preferably goal side.

As all of this happened, he noticed Manson growling some very harsh words at his playing partner from the previous attack, the one whose pass Peter had intercepted. Turning away from the two players, the slightest of smirks tickling his face, Peter hoped that his team could chip away at the first team's attitude throughout the match, with a view to giving them a chance at getting some kind of result.

Lightning pace would best sum up the next fifteen minutes or so, with both teams winning short corners and goal scoring opportunities but for last gasp interventions from brave defenders. One stocky first team defender blocked a rising shot right on the very goal line, tipping it around the post at chest height, while Peter made a diving reverse stick block, to a shot that Manson had seemed to spend an age teeing up. It was adrenaline pumping chaos... in a good way. But with the highly charged nature of the game and more and more reckless tackles flying in, it seemed only a matter of time until the umpire started showing his cards. As half time approached, the first team became more dominant, their superior fitness showing. However, Peter's thought about team spirit seemed to echo more and more as the match progressed. With each new onslaught the first team created, frustration seemed to stop them in their tracks, more often than not ending up in a missed chance to take the lead. Frayed tempers and verbal backlashes became the norm as one breakdown led to another, Manson generally being the main culprit. Every three or four minutes he was berating one of his own players for either a sloppy pass or just general poor play. A welcome relief to the second team players, after having been run ragged for the final ten minutes of the half, the umpires finally blew for half time, putting them out of their misery with the score remaining level at 0-0.

Plodding over to their stick and kit bags, dripping with sweat, the second team players took on some welcome water before joining their captain in the goal mouth at the opposite end of the pitch from the one they'd been defending in the first half. As the players gathered round, Peter noted how exhausted they all looked. Each and every one of them had given nothing short of one hundred percent and, although tired, most had a smile on their face. The atmosphere was electric and although the adrenaline rushing round his body was totally and utterly fake... he felt it, all of it. For him it was more real than anything he'd experienced in the dragon domain. He was where he should be, right here, right now.

Standing with the other players, he watched Andy the captain give one of his highly motivating speeches, the gist of which was that they were playing out of their skins and that realistically the first team should be beating them by a rugby score, bearing in mind the different leagues the two teams played in.

With everyone suitably pumped up, Andy asked if anyone else had anything to add. Every week it was the same, normally with one or two of the more experienced players chipping in with the odd tactical thing, or a potential weakness they'd spotted in their opponents that could be exploited. Peter had never had the courage or felt the need to speak up before now, what with his incredible shyness and the fact that he was still relatively inexperienced at the sport, compared with others. But something about this game today had... got under his skin, or scales if you like. A little reluctantly, he raised his hand, feeling his temperature rising as the whole team gazed in his direction.

"Peter," said Andy. "This is a surprise. It's not often we hear from you... go ahead."

With all eyes on him, he suddenly wished he'd kept his mouth shut. Forcing a smile onto his face and trying desperately to ignore the somersaults his stomach was doing, he forged on.

"Well... I... ah... um... totally agree with everything you've said," he stuttered. "The... um... um one thing I would add is that... well... that I think we can use their lack of team spirit and discipline against them."

A few of the team members nodded in agreement, giving the young dragon the confidence to keep going.

"The longer it stays 0-0, the more volatile they'll become. They've already lost their rag with each other a dozen times. Anything we can do to enhance that, we should. Laugh at them, mock them, ignore them - anything that gets them riled will only benefit us and, I believe, give us enough of an advantage to win."

"Who knew we had our own sports psychologist in the team?" added Andy.

Peter could feel his temperature skyrocketing, his face turning a rather dark shade of crimson.

The umpires blew their whistles to signal that half time was over. Before the players turned to walk back to their positions on the pitch, Andy said,

"You heard the man," pointing directly at Peter. "Do as he says, make them lose their tempers and we can all celebrate a stunning victory afterwards."

And with that, their captain waved them all onto the pitch, the team duly obliging, the players all taking up their first half positions. Peter felt like he'd never felt before. It couldn't be the adrenaline because, as a dragon, he had none, even though his DNA had been manipulated nearly down to the atomic level in his representation of a normal human being. The feeling was hard to describe. It felt like opening up a promotional pack of anything and winning a huge expensive prize. It felt like opening a door and finding limitless amounts of all your favourite foods, and some new ones as well.

Jolted from his reverie of foody thoughts by the umpire's whistle, he took in his surroundings, pleased to see the other defenders quickly pick up their players. Out of the corner of his eye, he spotted Tank and Richie just wandering out into the spectator area beside the pitch, both holding plastic pint glasses full of beer, which they raised on noticing they'd caught his eye.

As the match progressed, it didn't take long for him to realise that the entire nature of the game had changed quite dramatically. There was far more urgency in every aspect of their opponents' play. Their tackling, movement off the ball and passing was far superior to anything they'd done in the first half. Some of the tackles that were flying about though, were on the hospital side of dangerous. The stakes had certainly changed; clearly the first team had got a rollicking at half time from someone, and Peter was pretty sure he knew who.

Peter's team found themselves defending for their lives for the first ten minutes in the second period of the game, barely getting out of their own half and giving away numerous short corners. In his mind it seemed like only a matter of time before they would concede a goal and then the floodgates would probably open, something he was determined wouldn't happen. Bizarrely, even his idea about exploiting their indiscipline and lack of spirit seemed dead, as they were playing so well that they didn't seem to have anything to argue about.

Losing the ball once again in midfield, Peter's team looked shaky and disorganised as the first team forwards came hurtling towards him for what seemed like the thousandth time in only a few minutes. Holding his concentration and, as with the first tackle he'd made in the match, he dummied to go one way and went the other at the last second, again finding the ball on the end of his stick.

Momentarily relieved to have gained possession of the ball, he looked up to play a simple pass to one of his teammates. His first thought was that things looked pretty grim for him. Not only was there no obvious simple pass, but more worrying was the fact that three of the opposition were on their way to close him down. What to do?

From that very first training session, it had been quite apparent what type of player he was. Certainly not an attacking player, that's for sure. His dribbling skills were erratic at best and he lacked the confidence to run at people and take them on, nearly always preferring the simple pass to get himself out of trouble, knowing that the easiest way to beat a player was to... PASS, something many other players either failed to realise, or deliberately chose to ignore. If anything could be said to be Peter's best quality on a hockey pitch, then it would have to be his tackling which seemed to get better and better each time he played. It was as if he could tackle and stop a ball instinctively.

With this in mind, his current situation didn't bode well. His teammates were exhausted, he could see that in the periphery of his vision as time seemed to slow right down. His mind told him that he'd have to dribble around at least two opponents, not really a great idea, particularly at the top of his own 'D'.

All this zipped through his mind in milliseconds. Continuing to scan the field of play in front of him, he caught the movement of one of his own players through the oncoming mass of orange shirted opponents. The player in question though was at least fifty yards away, with an opposing player easily able to intercept his pass. 'Or would he?' he suddenly thought, his mind considering something of a radical alternative, picked up during the last couple of training sessions. A flick, or aerial ball, was a difficult skill to master and very rare at this level of hockey, but it was something he hadn't done too badly at during practice. Out of options (with the dribbling around two players not really being viable) his mind made up, he totally changed the shape of his body (not like his natural change!) and angled his stick under the ball. With his opponents getting nearer and nearer, he knew it would be now or never as the incoming players would soon be too close for him to safely execute what he had planned. Watching the ball intently and twisting his wrist with all his might, he pushed through and flicked the ball into the air. It was a sight to behold. Graceful, majestic, magnificent would all describe the moment perfectly, to him anyway. Having fully expected the ball to roll about two inches in front of him, he was stunned to see it cut through the air over the heads of the opposition players closing him down, continuing on towards the teammate that he'd picked out. But he was still not as stunned as the first team players, many of whom looked on in horror at the audacity of what they'd just seen carried out against them. All this happened in only a few seconds, but would be engrained into Peter's eidetic memory until the very day he died, that and the looks of the opposing players.

As the ball landed with a slight 'THUD', cushioned by the excessive sand that carpeted the pitch, his teammate steamed onto it at full pelt and after a great sequence of five passes in a row, it found its way to the second team centre forward, a nimbly built lad by the name of Malcolm. As the first team keeper sprinted off his line for all he was worth, Malcolm unleashed a vicious shot that the onrushing keeper managed to repel with the tip of his right foot. Just as the chance to go ahead looked to have been spurned, in roared the second team's left wing to stroke in the rebound, much to the disappointment of their opponents. The sound of the ball smashing against the backboard brought an almighty roar from every second team player on the pitch, along with the rest of their squad on the sidelines. 1-0 to the Second XI. Where on earth was this going?

Two or three of Peter's teammates congratulated him on the fabulous pass that had set up the goal, while their opposition seemed to be having an inquisition as to who was responsible for letting the goal in. Peter wasn't quite sure how it would play out from here on in, and in fact it took only a few moments for him to get some idea, as a sloppy bit of play from the first team allowed the seconds in on goal again, with the defender inadvertently forcing Malcolm wide, his off balance shot pinging into the side netting. If nothing else, it was a warning. In mere moments the first team's composure had been shot to ribbons, with their players openly arguing and blaming each other, left, right and centre. For the first time in the game, Peter actually started to believe that the second team could win.

With the breakdown of any and all discipline on the part of the first team, the match became more and more even, being almost wholly played in the midfield area of the pitch. Peter found he was constantly marshalling his defenders, so much so there was a real danger that he might lose his voice. Every now and then he would glance over at his friends on the sideline who, without spilling a drop of their beer, managed to offer him terrific smiles and give him a double thumbs up each.

As the midfield struggle continued, the intensity of the tackles ramped up, predictably ending with one of the umpires cautioning two of the first team, and a second team player, in the space of only a few minutes.

Foul after foul led to the game becoming very scrappy. More confident in his and the team's ability to negate any first team threat, Peter pushed further up into the midfield to support his beleaguered comrades, all the time wary of the space left behind him, as in hockey there is no offside rule (not now, anyway). With the first team's defence having done the same thing, the middle of the pitch became a frantically packed battlefield. As Peter feared the umpires might start to get fed up with the constant series of fouls and actually send someone off with a yellow card, the second team skipper, Andy, intercepted a wayward first team pass and went all out on a gung-ho run straight at the opposition's goal. Because all the defenders had pushed up, the captain found himself in acres of space after beating two flat footed opponents and used a quick burst of speed to put him through one on one with the exposed goalkeeper. For all involved, time slowed irrecoverably. As the goalie shot off his line to narrow the angle, one of the first team defenders ran his socks off to get back on the goal line and cover. By this time, Andy had reached the top of the 'D' and upon crossing the line had let rip with a fearsome shot. 'Greener', the first team goalie, had a reputation as an excellent shot stopper, which on this occasion was well deserved, as he managed to get a heavily gloved fingertip to the ball, taking all the pace off it. Spinning like an unruly planet, the ball ended up right by the penalty spot, halfway between Andy and the defender on the line. Instinctively, the pair of them raced forward with the grounded Greener unable to influence the situation in any way. Unfortunately two strides into his run, the defender slipped on the sandy surface and skidded to his knees. Andy took immediate advantage, racing onto the ball and slipping it past the flailing defender and into the back of the empty net. To everyone's amazement, the second team led 2-0.

Each individual roared as the goal went in, some raising their sticks high above their heads in celebration, much to the first team's disappointment. As the forwards made their way back to the halfway line for the restart, Andy the captain motioned with his arms for them all to calm down, knowing there was still more work to be done. While this was happening at one end, a meltdown of epic proportions was taking place at the other. Pushing, shoving, finger pointing and all sorts of recriminations were going on amongst the members of the first team. It got so bad that the umpire had to blow his whistle and tell them to calm down before the restart could take place. With everyone set to begin again, one of Peter's teammates asked the nearest umpire how long was left.

"Eleven minutes," he replied, looking up from his watch.

'All we have to do is hold on for eleven minutes,' thought Peter promisingly. 'With our opponents squabbling like toddlers, we might just be able to do it.'

As the teams lined up against one another, his attention was drawn once again to Manson, taking up his forward position after having been in the centre of the melee that had just broken up. As Peter watched his menacing adversary, he noticed that Manson was doing something very unusual with his hands. Shielding them with his body so that most of the people on or around the pitch couldn't see what he was doing, the ex-army Major started weaving intricate patterns with his fingers, while at the same time silently mouthing long and peculiar words. Peter found himself mesmerised by the patterns that seemed to almost leave a trail through the air, that is until Manson looked up... directly into his face. He froze in terror at the unadulterated look of hate aimed directly at him. Instantly his legs turned to lead, his arms to jelly. It was all he could do to stay standing up as his vision started to blur. Subconsciously he heard a noise, a sharp shrill noise. In his peripheral vision he could make out movement... shapes getting bigger and bigger. It took a few seconds for Peter's brain to register what was happening... the match had restarted and the opposition were on the attack again.

With this revelation, the fogginess clouding his brain started to part, albeit rather slowly. By the time he had any real idea as to what was going on, opponents were on either side of him, just about to enter the 'D' and have a shot at goal. Willing his lead-like legs to work, with all his might he forced the player with the ball, out wide, hoping that he'd done enough to make up for his momentary lapse in concentration. Impossibly, as far as Peter was concerned anyway, the player increased his speed, getting ever closer to the byline. Knowing he had but one chance to block the cross, Peter threw himself for everything he was worth, to make a one handed reverse stick block. It was a great attempt and nothing short of idiotically brave. It was, however, all in vain. As he followed the ball, all the time showing his reverse stick in an effort to block the shot, feeling as though he were wading through treacle, the first team forward did the unexpected and lifted it over his outstretched stick. But for that, it would have been a fantastic take. Up stepped a sneering Manson, hammering the ball into the roof of the net from only a few yards out, the second team keeper rooted to the spot. A sharp whistle and the sound of people cheering brought Peter back to earth as he brushed the sand from his bloodied arms and knees after his extravagant attempt at an intervention. The first team had scored, straight from the restart. Not only that, but most of the second team were swaying about in something of a daze. It didn't look as though anyone apart from Peter had even tried to stop them.

Just as her last sip of lager rolled pleasantly down her throat, the whistle blew to restart the match. She'd been stood talking to Tank and watching Peter now for the best part of twenty minutes, aching fervently from her agonisingly tough lacrosse match, but determined to come and show support for her friend. Moments earlier, Tank had disappeared inside to chat to one of his rugby playing mates about something. So as she pulled away the empty pint glass from her delicate lips, she was blown away by what was happening right in front of her. Nearly the entire first team surged forward as one big wave of players, passing the ball from one side of the pitch to the other, with unerring accuracy and incredible speed. That wasn't what blew her away though. They were allowed to surge forward almost unhindered. One or two second team players half heartedly waved their sticks about, but most just stood, seemingly glued to the spot, even Peter, right up until the last second anyway, by which time it was pretty much too late, despite his valiant last effort. Richie couldn't believe her eyes.

'Perhaps,' she thought, 'that's the answer.'

On taking human form, dragons generally take on a lot of their characteristics as well. A human heart with a pulse, red blood instead of the usual green, with things like fingernails, toenails and hair growing of their own accord, unlike in dragon form where once a dragon reaches maturity, nothing else will grow, no extra scales, talons stay the same length... nothing. A dragon's vision will also mimic that of a human, something that takes more than a little getting used to, because in its natural form, a dragon can see in a whole host of different ways, by, if you like, scrolling through a series of different modes. Normally, when above ground human style vision would be the default, but a dragon can also see in the infrared spectrum; it can bear witness to mantra effects and magic in general; it has a limited heat sense as well as having enhanced night vision. A dragon maintaining human form will still have access to all these talents, but it isn't easy to use them, and no dragon would go around in human form looking in anything other than the default human mode.

For whatever reason, whether instinct, suspicion or just plain curiosity, Richie closed her eyes, took one long deep breath, and let her mind slowly alter her physiology. Moments later she opened them again, taking in the sight in front of her... the hockey pitch and everyone on it with the benefit of her, if you like, mantra vision. She gasped out loud at what she saw. The scene before here bore little or no resemblance to the one she had witnessed only moments earlier with her human vision.

Every member of the second team was shrouded from head to toe in a swirling cloud of black mist, coiling around each of them like a terrifying constrictor squeezing the life out of their prey, with the exception of Peter. His cloud seemed to be slowly dissipating.

'What on Earth...?' Richie thought. Suddenly a hand touched her shoulder. Unusually for her, she jumped, startled.

"Whoa... sorry Rich," pleaded Tank, "didn't mean to startle you."

Richie pulled him closer to the small fence, from which they were watching the hockey and lowered her voice.

"Look at the pitch and tell me what you see."

Not sure what was going on, but assuming it was one of Richie's renowned practical jokes, Tank reluctantly looked out at all the players, waiting for the punch line.

"Well?" demanded Richie.

"A game of hockey?"

She leaned in close and whispered in Tank's ear.

"Now use the vision you would use if you were

experimenting with a mantra."

Tank, confused and surprised by Richie's comment, managed to stutter a loud, "What?"

"Just humour me... pleeeeeeease."

Putting his near empty glass on the ground, he closed his eyes momentarily and focused on changing his vision. It was a quick change, quicker than Richie that's for sure, as it was something he did all the time back in the workshop alongside the master mantra maker. The look of disbelief when he opened his eyes though... that was something else, and easily matched Richie's from a few moments earlier.

"Twist my tail and call me a dragon," blurted Tank loudly.

Richie clamped her hand over Tank's mouth, much to the amusement of other nearby spectators.

Quietly, Tank whispered,

"What the hell's going on Rich?"

To which she had no real answer.

Gradually, Peter came to his senses, albeit too late to prevent the first team from scoring. Smarting from the burns on his arms and knees, he felt like he'd just woken up from a sleep that would have made Sleeping Beauty's look like a mid-afternoon nap. A quick glance around told him that something very odd was going on with the rest of his team. Both umpires and the opposition seemed oblivious to this, or if they had noticed, they clearly weren't going to stop the game for it. As a matter of urgency, he needed to buy some time. Jogging over to his unsteady goalkeeper, he reached behind his right leg and in the blink of an eye undid the straps in his kicker (the protective shoe) and forced it off. Nobody spotted him doing this as everyone else was busy trying to get the woozy second team forwards to restart the game. With the keeper's kicker dangling right off his foot, Peter shouted and waved in the umpire's direction to signal that something was wrong. Raising his eyebrows, and shaking his head at yet another enforced interruption, the umpire reluctantly blew his whistle to stop time and halt the match. Jogging over to where Peter was squatting in front of a rather bewildered goalkeeper, the umpire asked,

"What's wrong?"

"Straps on the kicker are broken," replied Peter innocently, fiddling around with the kicker and its perfectly good straps. "Give me a few minutes. I think I can fix it."

"Well... try and make it snappy. We've had enough stoppages in this one game to last a whole season," said the umpire haughtily.

He knew he'd only bought himself a couple of minutes at best. He had to figure out what was wrong with everyone, and he had to do it now.

Meanwhile, Richie had just finished describing the first team's goal to Tank.

"It looks as though someone's stunned them all using some kind of mantra," uttered Tank, frowning.

"Well," whispered Richie, "you're the mantra expert... why don't you see if you can... undo everything."

"How am I supposed to do that?"

"Oh... I don't know. How about using a mantra to negate the mantra that's already been used? It's only an idea of course," remarked Richie, sarcastically.

"You know we're not supposed to use mantras out in the open, willy nilly, like that. What happens if the Council find out?"

"When has that ever bothered you before?" objected Richie, shaking her head and turning to look in the direction of the pitch, where Peter appeared to be fiddling about with part of the goalkeeper's kit. Abruptly turning on Tank, getting right up close to his face, she said,

"Whatever that is out there, it's not a natural phenomenon. You have a duty to get rid of it if you can. If that's not enough for you, you should do it for Peter. Ultimately he's the one that's being affected the most by this. Right at this very moment he's out there buying time, trying to figure out what's going on. By the time he does, it will be way too late."

Tank already knew he'd lost. When had either of them ever won against her?

'If I had access to the Mantra Emporium's vast resources, then getting rid of whatever's out there would be a piece of toasted charcoal,' he thought. Limited by the number of mantras he knew, he quickly racked his brain to find one that might help.

Peter had run out of time. Both umpires had lost their patience and had told him that unless the kicker was fixed immediately, they were going to award a win to the first team. Not knowing what else to do, and having tried everything he could to figure out what an earth was going on, he reattached the kicker and moved gingerly back in position, preparing for what he knew would be nothing short of an onslaught. Looking around, he could quite clearly see that unlike himself, none of the others had shrugged off whatever it was that was still affecting them.

Tank thought he knew what pressure was, with some of the things that Gee Tee had got him to do at work. Although he thought the world of the old dragon, at times he could be a really harsh taskmaster. That, however, paled in comparison to what he now felt with Richie standing over him, well... not exactly over him, more... staring up at him from chest height, hands on hips, and a frown on her face that was going to be mighty hard to turn... upside down.

'She could intimidate the king himself,' he thought, small beads of sweat running down his neck, which was quite something in the cool autumnal air. Then, out of nowhere... it came to him. Of course, why hadn't he thought of it sooner? The tornados. Not two weeks after joining Gee Tee at the world renowned emporium, Tank had been given the mundane task of filing away some old mantras. He'd been told one key thing: to keep his mind totally blank while doing this, because the occasional mantra will respond to the merest thought in a dragon's mind. At first, things went well, he did a sterling job, just as he'd been instructed to do, and being full of enthusiasm and endeavour, he was keen to show his new employer just how useful he could be. It was a little boring, but he seemed to be getting through it at quite a rate. However, as time progressed, he became more and more fascinated by the language and the words that made up the mantras. They were so unusual. He'd never seen anything like them, and he prided himself on his language skills. Unfortunately, being so distracted culminated in him setting one of the mantras off with a stray thought, unleashing a plague of magical, mischief making monkeys throughout the shop. They were everywhere, turning over bookcases, eating scrolls, playing chase and, the thing that the other staff members will always remember from that day... they were peeing off the rafters in the ceiling into a giant vat of freshly made mantra ink that Gee Tee had spent two weeks preparing. When he came downstairs to see what all the noise was, he went absolutely ballistic, particularly about the part with the ink. What he did do, however, was cast a brilliant mantra that Tank had never seen before, that created a series of tiny tornados that sucked in anything magically active and made short work of getting rid of the rampaging monkeys. He'd been too amazed by the mantra that the old shopkeeper had cast to be afraid of the consequences of his mistake, and had been so dumbfounded by the magic that he'd gone off and found out all about it, before committing it to memory. That was what he needed now. It should in theory get rid of everything magically wrong, but he needed to make sure it was the powerful rhyming version of the mantra that he cast. Noting that the umpires were just about to restart the game and with Richie standing next to him, glaring, he closed his eyes, combed his memory and found the words he needed. Using the full force of his mind, and with absolute belief, he whispered very carefully:

Round and round and round you go,
Tall and powerful you must grow,
Suck up magic in your path,
Don't hold back, let loose your wrath.

Opening his eyes, he stood transfixed with Richie and watched with his mantra vision as four waist height tornados zoomed through the fence in front of them, heading straight onto the Astroturf pitch. As the tornados zigzagged back and forth, he felt a little disappointed at what he'd achieved. Gee Tee had effortlessly cast the mantra back in the shop to clean up the mischievous monkeys, creating no less than eleven tornados, while his best attempt produced just four. Despite what he sometimes thought, he still had a lot to learn. Luckily he was based in just the right place, being nurtured and taught by the very best. If he took away anything from this, it would be that.

Leaves and sand scattered across the pitch didn't move an inch as the oily black vapour got sucked into each of the tornados as they tore past the players who, amazingly, suddenly started to come back to their senses, just in time for the game to restart once again. Tank turned to Richie, winked and smiled.

"Not bad, huh?"

Richie patted her friend on the back as they continued to watch the tornados, all of which had now grown as tall as Tank, finish cleansing the pitch, knowing that they were the only ones that had seen anything at all. Or were they?

Out of the corner of his eye, Peter had caught sight of his friends watching behind the tiny metal fence. He'd sorted out the kicker rather quickly after the threat from the umpires to award the match to the first team, and as he stood waiting for the inevitable assault from the opposition's forward line, willing to battle them on his own if he had to, he had the peculiar feeling that his friends were... up to something. It wasn't anything obvious, well not to anyone else anyway, it was just that they looked like they were conspiring. 'Conspiring to do what?' was the million dollar question that circled through Peter's head. Those two scheming could mean anything from the human police arriving, to an all out war to save the planet, or indeed anything in between. He didn't know what was going on, but he was sure he'd find out later.

As all this weaved through his muddied brain, his teammates for no apparent reason turned back into their normal selves from the zombie like states they'd been in for the last few minutes. To say Peter was surprised was an understatement. In each and every one of them, the swaying stopped and the blank looks were replaced by puzzled ones, just momentarily, until they realised where they were and what was going on. Peter's feeling of doom turned to elation, at the prospect of not having to face the opposition on his own. He shouted across to the nearest defender.

"We've let one back in. It's now two one. Tell everyone else!" Travelling throughout the team like wildfire, the message was reluctantly accepted by everyone, despite them having no recollection of it happening.

The game restarted with the second team pushing back; however the first team soon gained possession of the ball and began another overwhelming attack. With the rest of the second XI still shaking off their fuzzy heads and heavy legs, Peter knew the rest of the match was going to be hard fought if they were going to get anything from it. He and his team managed to weather the next three attacks, mainly due to luck rather than judgement. But as every minute passed, the second team played more like themselves, holding out hope that not only could they get something from the game, but they might just be able to hold onto their lead and win it.

More than ever now, the game was end to end, with the second team on the attack, forcing the first team players to get behind the ball. As Peter rallied his defenders, making sure they were goal side of their players for fear of the obvious counter attack, he noticed the umpires signal to each other that there were only two minutes of the game remaining. Knowing that they only had to last a couple of minutes, he became even more vocal, his croaky voice encouraging the team and urging them on to greater things. Everything looked fine until a foul by a first team player went unnoticed by both umpires, thus giving possession of the ball and a rather big advantage to the first team. They surged forward and with a couple of clinical passes, carved open the second team defence. Peter himself had been beaten by a nifty dummy and was now duly sprinting back into the 'D' to get round behind the onrushing second team keeper and provide cover on the goal line. The first team attacker with the ball reached the top of the 'D' as the second team goalie threw himself towards the ball. Peter would have bet his tail that the forward in question would have chosen to take on the keeper but, much to his utter horror, right at the last second, the player slipped the ball under his arm, straight into the path of... MANSON! And in doing so, totally took the goalkeeper out of the equation. The ex-army Major picked up the ball on his open side and stepped into the 'D'. His mad dash back to cover behind the keeper had left Peter standing squarely in the middle of the goal, two footsteps in front of the goal line. He'd never felt more alone and vulnerable than he did now. As he watched his fellow defenders give all they had left to get back and help, it was obvious no one would get anywhere near Manson before he had a chance to unleash his shot. It was now about just the two of them.

Surprisingly, as all this flicked through Peter's clumsily organised brain, rather than paralysing him with fear, he realised he was actually looking forward to the next few seconds and although it was against the odds, he felt confident he could thwart the ever nearing Manson.

Not normally having an over-abundance of confidence, he had in his short hockey playing career made some excellent goal line saves. Diving saves, one handed saves, reverse stick saves, even saves that, had he not stopped the ball it would either have taken off his head, or in one rather noticeable case, something far more precious, let's just say his... ears, for example (not really). Ears (you know what I mean) were very important to a dragon, much like other things are very important to... humans (especially male humans).

Basically, he knew what to do when it came down to goal line saves. It was almost as if it were engrained in his very DNA to do so. (Perhaps that was something he'd have to talk to Gee Tee about. Would it be possible for a mantra to make you good at one very specific part of a sport? An interesting question for another time.) In the here and now, he was going to stop Manson scoring a goal, thus levelling up the match. In a unit of time so small it would have been barely measureable, he briefly considered using the magic that was his birthright. But before the thought had even finished, the rest of his body had screamed, "CHEAT!" at him, knowing just how wrong it was, and just how disgusted his friends would have been with him for even considering it. It was fine though. With his tried and tested reflexes, he didn't need to rely on anything dragon related. He'd stop Manson in this form... a battle of equals, and one he was determined to win.

As the moment came, and with all of his senses heightened, time once again slowed. Manson was five feet into the 'D' now, his stick drawn back behind him, knees bent, eyes firmly on the ball, ready to strike. Peter tightened the grip on his stick, making sure his hands were apart on the shaft, ready to stop the ball wherever it should go, legs one in front of the other, fully balanced, his cat-like reflexes itching to be let loose. Still moving forward, Manson's stick cut through the air in a sizzling arc, about to make contact with the ball.

Focused only on the ball, Peter could just see in the periphery Manson mutter something as his stick sweetly struck the dimpled ball. A rocket powered by a god, that's how fast the ball moved, or so it seemed to Peter. Not once did he blink, or take his eye off the ball's trajectory, knowing with every molecule in his being that he was going to stop the ball going into the goal, and reward his team with a hard earned victory. Lining up his stick, he loosened his lower hand slightly, so that he would stop the ball cleanly and not let it bounce away from his stick. Inside his head, he'd already played the pass out wide to one of his defenders, who would no doubt take it up the field in time for the final whistle to be blown.

With the blur that was the white ball only a fraction of a second from the end of his stick, Peter felt all warm inside at what he knew to be HIS victory over Manson. Everything that had gone on over the previous months, all the bullying, silent threats, the mistreatment of Al Garrett, the dismissal of Dr Island... this he knew was the start of the fight back. From here on in, it changed. From here on in, he was in charge, and it would end with Manson's imprisonment and the return of a fit and healthy Al Garrett, with Cropptech back to the way it was supposed to be.

Looking down at his stick, he waited expectantly for the comforting impact of the ball, knowing that its course would put it right on the end of his stick, ready to pass it out of harm's way to one of his defenders. As he watched, filled with the thrill of the game, to his utter amazement, just as the ball was about to hit the end of his stick, it disappeared and, without warning, reappeared six inches off to one side, still travelling at the same speed. Instantly he moved his stick to try and get a touch, any touch. His reflexes were good, better than good in fact, but he never stood a chance. No one would have. It was too late. A resounding 'THUD' later as the ball smashed against the back board, he just caught sight of Manson wheeling away in celebration, a massive cheer from the first team igniting the air all around.

Rooted to the spot, Peter played out the events again in his mind. He'd watched the ball all the way. It should have arrived on the end of his stick. At the last instant it just... moved over to the right. Impossible! Absolutely impossible! But it had happened... just like that. Reluctantly striding towards the top of the 'D', passing his goalkeeper on the way, he shook his head at the injustice of it all, still convinced it had played out the exact way he'd seen it. Then it hit him. Manson had been saying something just as he was about to strike the ball. Who on earth did that? Nobody! What the hell was going on? Out of nowhere an arm appeared around his shoulder.

"It's alright Peter, it's not your fault. We should have got back quicker," put in Mark, the second team's left back.

Peter was still in a daze. He looked over at his friends on the sideline, hoping that maybe they'd seen something, but they just shrugged their shoulders in his direction.

"You must have seen what happened?" he pleaded with Mark.

"It was just a good shot mate, one of those things. Nothing you could have done. Don't beat yourself up."

"But the ball, it changed places. You must've seen it?"

"Don't worry Pete. A draw for us today is as good as a victory. Head up."

Shaking in downright frustration, he caught sight of Manson on the halfway line getting ready for the restart. The smug, arrogant sneer on his face told Peter everything he needed to know. Somehow the mysterious Major had power, magic... something. In that single moment on the goal line, everything he'd feared and suspected had been confirmed. Not only that, but Manson had risked revealing it just to take Peter down a peg or two in a hockey match.

It only then occurred to him.

'What on earth is going to happen when we get back to work?' he thought. Manson knew that Peter knew. What did it all mean?

With only a matter of seconds left in the game, the umpires blew their whistles to restart, moments later blowing them again to end the game. Each team gave the other three cheers, albeit begrudging ones on both sides, as players shook each others' hands, including the umpires. For the first time in a hockey match, he was reluctant to shake the hands of his opponents. He'd often thought the sportsmanship side of hockey had been one of the key lures for him, and before today had never had any qualms about shaking an opponent's hand, but all that seemed to have gone out the window during the ill tempered last seventy minutes. Aimlessly shaking the first team player's hands without thinking, another was thrust in his direction from off to one side. Reaching out for the hand, he looked up into the face of... MANSON! Peter's hand shot back faster than a man peeing against an electric fence. Manson walked right up to Peter and stood head to head. The two of them gazed into each other's eyes for what seemed like the lifespan of a new universe.

"Not very sporting," commented the ex-army Major.

"No... you're not," was the witty reply that Peter came back with. Manson's face was a picture... almost worth every ounce of trouble Peter was bound to get into, back at Cropptech.

As Peter continued to look into his face, unmoved by the attempt to provoke him. Manson leaned his head even closer to Peter's face, his hot breath washing over the young dragon's cheeks and nose.

"You and your kind have had your day. Looking down your superior noses at everything else, judging, manipulating. WELL NO MORE! There's a new force to be reckoned with, one that won't bend to your will as easily as everything else. Your pitiful existence will soon be put into perspective for you," derided Manson, darkly.

Peter had closed his eyes and, while trying to ignore the ever tightening knot in his stomach and the fear running down his arms and legs, had opened himself to all his dragon senses, setting them free to explore the solid pillar of hate that stood before him. With Manson's hot breath cloying at his face, he tried with everything he had to find something, anything, to explain what gave the ex-army Major his powers. But even though he stood only a few inches away from him, he could find nothing, not even a hint of magic or dragon or anything to explain what he knew in his heart of hearts. Manson came out smelling of roses and seemed to be nothing more than an ordinary human being. Opening his eyes, Peter noticed players from both sides staring at their face off, wondering what was going on. Looking into Manson's dark maelstrom eyes, Peter tried hard to think of something dramatic and frightening to say. Try as he might, nothing came to mind. Anyway, Manson had just beaten him to it.

Barely a whisper came out of Manson's mouth, designed so that Peter was the only one that could hear his words.

"Enjoy your lucky victory with all your little friends," Manson waved his arms to indicate everyone else on the pitch. "If you think you've had a tough time at work up until now, you wait until Monday. I will personally crush you like the insignificant insect that you are." With that, he dramatically turned away, head held high, waving his hockey stick above his head.

Peter turned his head as a voice from behind said,

"What was that all about?" Andy the second team captain had a worried look on his face.

Peter shrugged his shoulders.

"Dunno. Just sore about not beating us I suppose."

"Well, don't let it bother you. The whole team did really well today, and I can't believe I'm gonna say this, but the first round of drinks is on me."

And with that the two players joined the rest of the team in the showers and then headed off into the bar to celebrate their well deserved draw. Once in the bar, the celebrations began properly with Andy buying the first drinks for his team who were, for the most part, in very high spirits.

After being in the bar for about fifteen minutes, it became apparent that something odd was going on. Normally both teams who had been playing on the Astroturf got showered and then changed, before coming into the bar for a drink and some food. Peter wasn't the only one to notice that only two of their opponents had shown up. Something about it struck him as odd, just as Andy the second team captain sauntered over to the two to ask them what was going on. He couldn't quite make out what was being said, but from what he could see, Andy had clearly taken offence at what the two players had reluctantly told him. Momentarily glancing away from the disagreement, he noticed his two friends sitting at a table in the far corner. They waved him over, but he was desperate to see what was going on with the first team players, so held up five fingers to indicate he'd be over in five minutes. Richie and Tank nodded and continued their conversation. In the meantime, Andy had left the two first teamers and was headed back across the bar, a look of thunder on his face.

"What's going on?" enquired Peter as Andy rejoined the group, the highly spirited second team players having all gone quiet, eager for the response to Peter's question.

"Apparently all the first team players have gone off to one of the pubs in town to get drunk, according to those two," declared Andy, indicating the two first team players with the shrug of his head.

"Why the hell have they done that?" stated one of the players.

"Bad losers," somebody muttered, to the sound of much sniggering from the rest of the team.

"All I know," said Andy "is that they were all persuaded to go by that Manson bloke who plays up front for them. The one who went head to head with Peter here."

The whole team looked at Peter and let out a knowing,

"Ahhhh."

"Those two over there," continued Andy, "are as embarrassed and shocked about it as we are, so don't give them a hard time," he said, waving his finger in front of all the second team players gathered round.

Moments later it was forgotten, with some of the team breaking into song, while others made for the pool table and gaming machines. Due to their later start, it was now early evening, the huge bar being the quietest it had been all day, and would almost certainly have been empty if not for the match that had been played on the Astroturf. With everyone dispersing to various corners of the bar, Peter headed on over to his friends.

"Can I get you both a drink?" he asked as he approached the table.

Tank looked at his watch thoughtfully.

"Just got time for one more," he said, raising his eyebrows and winking conspiratorially.

"You've had a big day. Congratulations on the result by the way. Well done," added Richie, gulping down the last of her drink and handing the empty glass to Peter.

"Yeah, well done mate," remarked Tank. "On that subject though, we've got something we really need to talk to you about."

"TANK," declared Richie. "I thought we agreed to tell him later."

"Oh yeah... sorry Rich."

"What's going on?" asked Peter intrigued.

"Grab the drinks and we'll tell you."

Peter wandered off to the bar to get fresh drinks for his friends, carrying the empty glasses. As he approached he saw Janice slip round the front of the deserted bar from somewhere out the back. With her friendly smile beaming at him, he nearly dropped the glasses instead of putting them back on the bar itself. Only his quick dragon reflexes saved him.

"Did you win?" asked Janice in her infectious, bubbly

way.

"Ummm... it was a draw, but it certainly felt like a win," Peter managed to babble, unused to any sort of attention from someone so attractive.

"Oh look," squeaked Janice, "your friends are waving at us."

Sure enough, Peter turned to see Tank and Richie waving in their direction, having recognised a little something between the two of them, doing their utmost to try and embarrass him. Fully trained in lip reading, he was taken aback by some of the things that Richie was mouthing. They were very rude indeed. He just hoped that Janice lacked that particular skill; luckily for him, it seemed that she did. Turning back to the beautiful bar worker, all the while ignoring his friends and hoping against hope that nobody from his team cottoned on to what was happening, because if they did, Tank and Richie would be the least of his worries, he was just about to order the drinks, when he was beaten to it.

"What can I get you?" asked Janice politely.

"Can I have a pint of bitter, a diet Pepsi with some ice and... a traffic light please," ventured Peter, uncomfortable about ordering Richie her traffic light cocktail.

"Oh... who's the traffic light for?"

"It's for my friend Richie, the one who was waving and trying to whistle," cringed Peter.

"Ahhh," sighed Janice, starting to get the drinks. "Is she your girlfriend?"

He couldn't find the right word to describe it. Uncomfortable was as close as he could get, but it wasn't that. It was an odd feeling. His legs felt both light and heavy at the same time, while something strange started to happen in his stomach. Combine that with his temperature rocketing skywards, it made for a very 'out of his comfort zone' dragon. Worst of all, he didn't know why.

"No, no, nothing like that. She's one of my best friends; we've known each other since... school." Being so flustered, he'd nearly blurted out... nursery ring! That would just about have finished things off.

"Oh," countered Janice. "That's really nice. I think it shows a lot of maturity to have a member of the opposite sex as a best friend."

Peter nodded in agreement, not entirely trusting his mouth, as he handed over a ten pound note. Janice quickly returned with the change.

"Perhaps I'll see you on Tuesday after training?" she suggested, with a big smile as Peter headed off towards his friends with all the drinks. He turned over his shoulder and just managed to get out, "I hope so," before he staggered out of range. Placing the drinks on the table, he flopped down into the chair opposite his friends, waiting for the inevitable. It didn't take long.

"Wellllllllll!!!!! Look at you, you... human women attractor!" slurred Richie as she picked up her drink.

"I think you mean... magnet," added Tank, taking a big gulp from his fresh drink, trying to contain his laughter.

Peter gave both his friends the look. The one that said, "NO MORE PLEASE!" Thankfully they both seemed to take the hint, but he knew for certain he'd hear more about this from Richie at some point in the future, given her rather dubious dalliances.

"Well... ?" questioned Peter.

They both looked at him, puzzled.

"There was something you were going to tell me."

"Ahhh," they both said at once.

With nobody in eavesdropping range, Tank and Richie started to tell Peter about everything they'd spotted at the match: the swathe of strange mist that encompassed each second team player, making them unresponsive and at fault for the goal conceded, and the way Tank cast his cunning mantra to remove all trace of it. In turn, Peter told his friends about how he noticed Manson chanting something before the restart, the ball seemingly moving on the goal line, and about the threats he'd made at the end of match. Richie looked absolutely stunned, and while she didn't actually offer up an apology, he got the distinct impression that despite the alcohol taking its toll on her, she did feel very sorry for siding with that slime ball Manson. All three of them agreed to rally together and use all the resources available to them to try and find out exactly what Manson was up to, with a view to thwarting whatever dastardly plan he had in motion.

Glimpsing down at his watch, Tank was shocked at how long the three of them had been talking. Looking at his two friends, he tapped the face of his watch and mouthed the words, "laminium ball match." From the look on their faces, it was clear that they'd forgotten all about the game as well. Standing up, Peter pulled out his car keys, ready to head for home and of course the big event. Tank followed suit, leaving Richie languishing in her comfortable chair.

"C'mon Rich," ushered Peter. "Finish up your drink, it's time to go."

Richie wobbled to her feet, much to Tank's delight and Peter's frustration. Squinting and swaying just slightly, she rocked up closer to Peter and slurred,

"For now hockey player," she said poking him in the chest, "you are driving me and the big one to your... house as both me... hic... and the huge one... hic... have had waaaayyyyyy too much to drink. Onwards and upwards. My chariot awaits!"

"Yes," replied Tank flashing his best smile, "the big one has had a lot of beer but unlike the little one, has chosen not to let it affect him in any way."

"Spoilsport," slurred Richie.

All three of them made their way back through the bar towards the exit, Peter saying goodbye to the remainder of his team who were, by now, in much the same state as Richie, who was being comically guided by Tank around the maze of chairs and tables. As the cold night air hit them, Peter let go of Richie's arm, having taken it to offer up a bit of stability and support as they left the bar. Without anything to hold onto, she promptly fell flat on her face on the cold, hard concrete floor.

"Heeeeeyyyyyy!" she yelled, looking up at Peter. "That's not very friendly."

Peter leaned down very close and whispered in her ear, his breath freezing as he did so.

"You know full well Rich, that with one click of your fingers, so to speak, you could purge all the alcohol from your system. Your dragon physiology allows you not to be affected by its influence but every now and then you insist on experiencing its effects. Well, the next time you want that experience, get somebody else to carry you through the bar." With that, the hockey playing dragon turned around and stomped off towards his car, which was parked on the far side of the car park.

Rolling her eyes, Richie lay spread-eagled exactly where Peter had dropped her.

"Grumpy teetotaller!" she shouted after him. "Tank... do you mind?"

Having taken a step back, hoping not to get involved, Tank knew that it was too late now as he picked Richie up, threw her over one of his gigantic shoulders and headed off in the direction of Peter. Once at the car, he threw her into the back seat, before whispering to the sober driver.

"Just be thankful that she just gets a little silly when she's drunk. Can you imagine what would happen if she got a little bit feisty? We'd have to get the King's Guard up here to contain her."

A short, silent drive later, the three of them arrived at Peter's house. Peter and Tank got out first, while Richie lounged across both back seats. Peter stood with his hands on his hips, glaring down at her.

"All right, all right I'm doing it," she protested. And with that, she closed her eyes momentarily and... bam! Sober as a judge.

"Happy now?" she enquired, as they walked up the

garden path.

"Much better," acknowledged Peter.

"You really should try it, you old stick in the mud."

"Why on earth would I want to do that?" spat Peter. Can you remember the last time we went to the cinema? I seem to recall it was a Saturday night and the film finished at eleven. We decided to walk back to your place if memory serves me correctly."

Wishing she hadn't asked, she now had a vague idea as to just where this was going and although she was too stubborn to tell him, he did make a very good point.

"Salisbridge High Street looked like the aftermath of a war: people lying in the gutter, others throwing up, some urinating in shop doorways. And that's the best you could say about it. There were groups of girls fighting amongst themselves, three blokes having an argument with a taxi driver, passengers being thrown off buses, not to mention the two gangs of youths having a running battle at the end of the street, all watched by a van full of police, too afraid to get out and involved. And can you blame them? I mean, where on earth are they supposed to even start? That was at eleven. What's it like at two in the morning? And you know full well that almost all of it is fuelled by alcohol. It's the same discussion we've had time and again Rich. You accuse me of being dull and unadventurous, but you only need to look at the binge drinking and alcoholics. Salisbridge is only a tiny little city. This happens throughout the country night after night and frankly it's out of control. If I was on the dragon Council, it's one of the first things I'd try and change. I'm all for guiding the human race and letting them fulfil their potential, but on some issues we take a back seat when we know how damaging they are and this, I do believe, is one of them."

Peter stood on his doorstep, hoping that none of the neighbours had heard any of that, looking at his friends, both of whom carried expressions of complete and utter shock.

"Sorry, I didn't mean to go off on one... it's just that... ah... never mind. Let's just say it's something I have extremely strong views on and leave it at that. Forgiven?"

Tank and Richie both nodded in agreement, much to Peter's relief. Entering the house, all three were excited about watching their team compete in the semi final of the Global Cup.

13 NURSING A SEMI (FINAL, THAT IS)

Once inside, Tank got straight to work on the television, connecting the crystal and tuning it in. Peter and Richie headed into the kitchen to prepare some snacks. With his rant about alcohol over, the two friends soon started larking about, something that within minutes had turned into an almost full on food fight. Peter threw carrots, cucumbers and then celery at Richie, who in a blur, caught the aforementioned items and, at incredible speed, chopped them into edible slices to serve with a selection of dips. Halfway through the chopping, Richie stopped abruptly, wandered over to Peter and surprisingly pulled his shirt wide open at the neck. Gently, she placed her hand under the *alea*, making sure not to pull the chain onto which it was attached, too tight. More than a little gobsmacked, she leaned right into Peter's chest for a better view. After a silence that bordered on the uncomfortable, she finally spoke up.

"I've never seen anything like it. What is it?"

Peter looked anxiously at the door to the living room, hoping that Tank wouldn't come in.

"It's called an *alea*," he replied, smiling down at his friend's head nestled close to his chest.

"It's so... captivating."

Peter nodded his agreement.

"Yes it is."

"What's it for?" whispered Richie.

Over the course of the next few minutes, he explained how he'd inherited it from Mark Hiscock, how Gee Tee had told him what it was and in particular how Tank had no idea that Peter had been to see the old dragon on that very memorable night. All the time Richie couldn't take her eyes off the spectacular piece of jewellery.

"Name your price?"

"Huh?"

"Whatever you want, just name it."

Gently drawing his friend's fingers away from the *alea*, a very staggered Peter looked her straight in the eyes.

"I'm really sorry Rich," he said, meaning every word, "but I just don't want to part with it."

A millisecond's worth of angry scowl appeared and then disappeared on Richie's face.

"I understand," she whispered softly.

And then everything returned to normal. Richie threw two sticks of celery high into the air and in a dazzling display of dexterity proceeded to cut them into bite sized strips, before they hit the kitchen work surface. Peter joined in and the kitchen turned into a bizarre experiment that looked like someone had crossed two Gordon Ramsays with a circus act as knives and vegetables flew across the kitchen in a blur.

Just as the two vegetable jugglers had run out of ammunition and had decided to use the last carrot and cucumber as swords to fight like pirates, sideways on, with one hand each behind their backs, they heard Tank's voice from the living room, urging them to take a look at something. Sword fighting their way into the living room pirate style (Peter's carrot by this time had most certainly seen better days), the two friends entered to see Tank cross legged on the floor in front of the huge LCD television, gazing intently at the picture.

"It's even better than I imagined it would be," stated Tank, dreamily.

Peter and Richie stopped fighting and moved closer. Split into two, the screen had the view of the giant arena on the top half, and a close up picture of one of the goal mouths on the lower half.

"Is that live?" asked Richie.

Tank pulled his attention away from the screen, frowning at the battered and bruised cucumber in her hand.

"Sure is."

"The quality of the picture is incredible, despite the fact that it's in black and white."

"I think they must have integrated some of the latest film and broadcasting technology from the humans into it."

"It does look fantastic."

As they all looked on, the images changed. The upper image zoomed out to show the entire stadium, the cavern roof and the surface of the lava lake, while the lower view changed to show a rocky overhang on one side of the stadium. Concentrating on the bottom half of the screen, all three of the friends anticipated what would happen next. They weren't disappointed. With no sound available through the television, only their increased breathing could be heard as suddenly a triangular portion of rock face peeled back to reveal a hexagonal entrance with bright neon lights streaming out of it. Moments later, out flew two teams, the Gipsy Kings with their players surrounded by dark auras, and the Indigo Warriors surrounded by light. All three cheered on seeing their team enter the stadium.

*　　*　　*

Across town, it was a very different story. Manson sat at the bar of 'Ye Old Ale House', high up on a cherry red bar stool. Behind him, his fellow first team players were amusing themselves with a very silly drinking game about bunnies. Most of them were now very drunk indeed. Manson was not. That's not to say he hadn't been drinking, because, oh, he had. It was just that the drink, much like for Tank, had absolutely no effect on him at all.

He had, up until five minutes ago, joined in with all the different drinking games... the one with the matchbox, the one with the coins, the one about aliens, all of them, but now he sat, elbows propped on the dark wooden veneer of the bar itself, nursing a tankard of ale, consumed by anger, hate and rage. Mulling over events in his mind, blocking out the rowdy revelry that ensued behind him, loathing and disgust rolled off him like an angry sea in a violent storm.

'That sap Bentwhistle has no idea. No idea at all. His friends are just as clueless. Ohh... look at us, we're really useful little dragons doing just as the Council demand with our little human pets. Ohh... we're untouchable because we're smarter than all the humans. Ohh... the humans are our little darlings, we must look after them for the future of the planet. Huh! Boy, are you all in for a big surprise. Yes, that's right, not everything's gonna go your ever-so-laid-out dragon way. When the time comes, you're all gonna be punished for what you did, ohh and your little human pets are gonna suffer like they've never suffered before, while all of you stand by, helpless to intervene, you... smug... self righteous... sanctimonious... spineless... lackeys.'

Manson looked up from the beer-stained bar, straight into the terrified face of the bartender, a middle aged, bald, pot bellied, snivelling weasel, if appearances were anything to go by. He couldn't understand why the idiot of a man had such an expression on his face. He was certain he hadn't blurted any of that out loud. Looking down at his hands, however, he soon realised why. The metal tankard that he had been drinking from looked like a child had crafted it from play-doh. In his rage, his hands had quite literally squeezed it into something unrecognisable. Delving deep into his right pocket, he pulled out a crisp, clean fifty pound note and tossed it on to the bar in the direction of the tender.

"Sorry about that. Don't realise my own strength sometimes. I hope that about covers it."

Nodding frantically, the man nervously picked up the note and headed swiftly down the other end of the bar to continue polishing glasses. Manson shook his head and sneered as he did so.

'Another one for retribution,' he thought.

Looking around, he could see the drunken antics of the pesky humans he called teammates were getting more out of hand with each minute that passed. He even heard the word 'curry' being mentioned, and knew that it was time to make his excuses and leave. Dropping down off his stool, he added a slight wobble as he staggered to the nearest corner beside the dart board, dropping the misshapen tankard into a filthy looking bin that stood there. It made a resounding THUD as it skittered through all the crisp and cigarette packets, before hitting the bottom.

Adding a slight stagger to his limp, he carried on over to his teammates, walking stick in hand. Feigning a smile, he told them he had to go, using his age as an excuse for not being able to keep up. While everybody jeered and made sarcastic comments, nobody thought anything more about it as he was the oldest member of the squad by some way. After slurring his goodbyes, he gingerly walked to the door and headed out into the cold air. Turning left outside the main entrance to the pub, he walked along the badly paved footpath past the windows, all the time exchanging rude gestures with his teammates inside, while putting on another bout of staggering.

Once clear of the pub, he straightened up and walked briskly to the adjacent car park, where he promptly jumped into his black Mercedes. As he tossed his walking stick onto the back seat and settled back against the soft leather, he thought about what a day it had been. He'd been more than a little reckless. Deep down he knew he shouldn't have risked revealing himself like that to that berk Bentwhistle, but he was pretty sure he would end up having to deal with him one way or another, whatever happened, and he wasn't about to let a jumped up little jerk like that get the better of him at anything, let alone hockey. It wasn't just the fact that he couldn't have Bentwhistle, a bloody dragon, getting the better of him, he also needed to keep up the appearance of being a prolific hockey player for the other part of the plan to fall into place.

Turning the key in the ignition, it was only now, as the perfect purring engine thrummed into life, that he realised just how risky the day had been, vowing next time to be more... clinical and not let his emotions get in the way. What would the others say if they knew how... rashly he'd acted? Thoughts of terrible recriminations ran through his mind, that is until he forcibly pushed them away.

'Oh well', he thought, 'it's not like they're going to find out any time soon.'

*   *   *

Back at Peter's house, the three friends were glued excitedly to the mute television, an intriguing mixture of food and drink spread out on the living room floor. The dips that had been prepared in pirate style were strewn all over the place, accompanied by an assortment of bizarre additions. A large bottle of ketchup was the centrepiece, from which Tank periodically covered a carrot, stick of cucumber or massive stalk of celery, wolfing down the whole thing in one go, much to the revulsion of the other two. Beside the ketchup there were jars of mayonnaise, a bowl of coleslaw, pickled onions, strawberry jam, marmalade, chocolate and marshmallow spread, and a large jug of very cold gravy. Young dragons like to experiment with an array of tastes and these three were no different, especially in the privacy of Peter's home. As well as the vegetables being dipped, there were sponge fingers (Peter's favourite), bread sticks, iced buns, marshmallows and I kid you not... pencils. Oh yes... pencils, a dragon's staple snack when humans aren't looking. Most prefer the 2B or 3B variety because the darkness comes across as tangy when consumed.

You may think the food odd, but only as much as the drinks the three friends were downing. Peter had developed a taste for lime cordial... NEAT, straight from the bottle. Richie was on her third Baileys and lime (something known as a cement mixer), which it had to be said was more like a meal than a drink, while Tank was being the most conventional of the three by drinking a 'Mississippi Mud Pie' or orange juice, lemonade and coke.

In any other situation, Peter would have gone berserk, had any part of his house looked like his living room currently did, but he was far too interested in the match to care about anything else. They all were. Abruptly the split screen views that they were watching changed to one, showing both teams performing their fly pasts for the electrically charged crowd. Both teams were flying around the edge of the subterranean stadium in opposite directions, both at exactly the same height, so when they met, they curved in and out of each other at breakneck speed, almost faster than the watching crowd could comprehend, all to rapturous applause.

Two laps later, the teams broke off and headed towards the roof, directly in the middle of the stadium.

"Come on Warriors!" shouted Tank at the silent television, startling the other two.

"Kick their scaly asses!" joined in Peter.

Tank and Richie looked at each other in mock shock.

"Who rattled your cage?" teased Richie.

"Just getting into the spirit of things," Peter replied.

Tank let out a great big belly laugh, while at the same time tossing a ketchup covered carrot high into the air. Richie and Peter watched the orange vegetable turn end over end, before disappearing into their friend's gaping mouth.

All three returned their attention to the game, with the view having changed from both teams hovering in mid-air, to ten glowing crystals over one of the goal mouths. As the friends watched, one crystal winked out, and all at once the three said,

"Nine." One by one the crystals continued to wink out,

with the friends counting down as they did, knowing that the massive crowd in the stadium were no doubt all shouting their hearts out.

"Four... three... two... one..."

As the last crystal winked out, the view on the screen returned to both teams hovering high up in the centre. From out of a concealed hole in the roof shot the metallic laminium ball, almost faster than any of the dragons could see, bouncing off the chest of one of the Gipsy Kings players, winding him momentarily. With the ball in play, mayhem ensued. The three friends all unknowingly inched closer to the television, trying to make out what was going on in the mass of players and see just who had the laminium ball. Camera angles changed at random, making it hard to focus on any one thing. Both teams were still very much in the same area they'd been when the ball had come rocketing out, only now the action was frantic with tackles, raking talons, whipping tails and raging fiery breath. It was a sight to behold and looked very much like something from a prehistoric nightmare.

With both mouth guards having slipped out of the action to take up their normal positions, the melee in the middle became less of a jumble. Out of nowhere one of the Gipsy Kings players broke free, making a headlong dive for the lava, only pulling out at the last possible second, zooming inches above the smouldering surface, heading towards the Warriors' goal mouth. Players from both sides of the congested pack gave chase, with the Gipsy Kings players holding off the Indigo Warriors, one even dumping Barf unceremoniously into the lava.

The Gipsy Kings players had done a reasonable job in holding off their opponents, much to the dismay of the three friends at home, and had given the player now hurtling towards the goal with the laminium ball nestled on the end of his tail a free run at the Warriors' mouth. Although a good position for the Gipsy Kings, it was by no means a sure thing, because soaring in the players' way was a certain Silverbonce, the oldest player in the game and, most players and fans alike would agree, the craftiest and one of the most talented to ever grace the sport.

As the player with the ball rose from the surface of the bubbling lava, he slowed his ascent just slightly in an attempt to find the best position for a good shot. As he did so, Silverbonce drifted out of the mouth to narrow the angle. Only it appeared to everyone, including the player with the ball, that the old mouth guard had got his angles all wrong. A huge gap had opened up down Silverbonce's right hand side, leaving an easy shot for the eager Gipsy Kings' youngster. Grinning at the thought of the easiest goal he'd scored in a long time, the young player with the ball threw all of his momentum downwards and at the same time hurled the ball with his tail into the great big gap left by the Warriors' mouth guard. Not waiting to see what happened next, the relatively inexperienced dragon turned towards the fans, puffed out his chest, opened up his wings, all as if to say, "How great am I?" waiting for the inevitable applause.

It was a real shame he'd turned away, because if he hadn't, he would have seen a real master at work. As the ball left the young dragon's tail, bound for one of the teeth in the goal mouth through the gap that Silverbonce had deliberately left, the wily old mouth guard let out the most amazing jet of blue and orange tinged flame from his giant prehistoric jaw, with such precise timing that it hit the ball almost square on, deflecting it well away from the mouth, off into the side of the cavern. He coolly gathered it up with his tail, before playing a sublime pass out wide right to Flamer, who was just now picking it up with his tail. Meanwhile, the young Gipsy Kings forward, puzzled by the lack of appreciation, was still trying to get his head round the fact that the whole mouth was still intact and his teammates were expressing more than a reasonable amount of displeasure with him right at this very moment.

Flamer, having gathered the ball in, had taken flight

heading towards the lower right hand corner of the massive arena. Cheese and Barf were speedily heading in the same direction to help him. Steel, meanwhile, had sneakily lost his marker and was soaring along the upper left cavern wall, trying hard to be inconspicuous. The Gipsy Kings, with the exception of their young forward, were rallying their defence, getting players between the laminium ball and the goal mouth.

Peter, Tank and Richie sat mesmerised on the living room floor, munching on various combinations of food and guzzling down drinks, but not once taking their eyes off the action on the screen in front of them.

One of the Gipsy Kings' defenders thundered out towards Flamer, talons out, clearly hoping to dislodge the ball and inflict injury at the same time. But Flamer was having none of it. At the very last instant, a quick flick of his tail was enough to send the ball flying surely into the path of Cheese, who took it at speed and headed up in the direction of the mouth, partnered by Barf. Two more Gipsy Kings players drifted down into their way, with the mouth guard anxiously moving from side to side behind them. Still nobody had spotted Steel, who was by now only a few metres out from the mouth, but way out on the left hand side. Looking at each other after a telepathic agreement, the two Gipsy Kings players nodded, and then both drove towards Cheese and Barf as fast as they could. Both Warriors only had an instant in which to react, but that was all they needed. They knew where Steel was, it was just going to be a matter of getting him the ball. Cheese feinted right, bursting left at the last moment, doubling over into a sharp dive. Entering the dive, he gave a flick of his powerful tail, pushing the ball as hard as he could towards Barf.

Barf, meanwhile, wasn't quite as happy as he'd hoped to be. Having given everything he'd got in an effort to lose his Gipsy Kings marker, he'd only managed to gain a few metres on him rather than shed him altogether. Spotting the ball steaming towards him on one side and his challenger on the other, Barf realised there was only one thing to do. Pouring on as much speed as he could find, he surged towards the ball, knowing that he would get to it a fraction of a second before the player got him. On reaching the ball, instead of gathering it in, the expected course of action, he gently brushed it with the back of his right wing, ever so slightly changing its trajectory. Fans from all around the stadium let out a collective gasp, thinking that it was just poor play. As the ball left his wing, Barf closed his eyes and braced himself for the unavoidable. The Gipsy Kings player continued on his path, totally missing the ball but ploughing into Barf, sending him spiralling out of control towards the steaming red lava. All of this happened in a split second, and the only dragon in the stadium to have any idea about what had just happened was Steel, who, as he watched Barf plummet, sent his friend a telepathic 'thank you'.

You see, Steel was gliding in the same unmarked position that he'd been in for the last thirty seconds or so, and as the ball rocketed towards him, he knew that it was all that Barf could have done to deflect the ball in his direction because of the onrushing opponent, deliberately taking one for the team. With one giant flap of his wings, he sailed to meet the ball as it flew straight into his path. Because none of the Gipsy Kings had realised he was there, or that was where the ball was heading, the mouth was totally unguarded on the left hand side, leaving Steel with a clear shot. Not even bothering to collect the ball, even though he had plenty of time, Steel smashed the ball first time with his tail, destroying one of the teeth in the middle of the mouth. A resounding roar went up around the arena from all the Indigo Warriors fans. Flamer, Cheese and the worse for wear Barf all soared across the cavern to congratulate Steel, while Silverbonce remained guarding the mouth, pumping his wings in delight, trying to stir up the crowd even more.

Back at the house, the three friends were going wild. Jumping up, Tank knocked over his drink, Richie roared with delight, while Peter used some very colourful language to sum up his feelings, most unlike him.

"That was the best goal ever!" cried Tank.

"Did you see what Steel did?" bellowed Peter, "because clearly the Gipsy Kings didn't. He was amazing sneaking up like that. Who'd have thought that was even possible. He is a GOD!"

"Well... he's alright I suppose," mused Richie grinning, "but I could take him."

All three burst into a fit of laughter and it was only the sight of the restart taking place some thirty seconds later, that brought them out of it.

"Come on Warriors, make it to the final... pleeeaaasssssseeeee!" hollered Tank at the top of his voice as the action got underway.

Similar to the opening part of the match, punches, kicks, streams of flame were all being thrown in that very confined area, high up in the middle of the arena. Once again the Gipsy Kings took possession and pressed the attack. Unlike their previous offence, this one led to them knocking down a tooth and scoring a goal, and it was the young forward who'd failed so spectacularly last time, who'd got it. He scored from a long way out after a double tailed attack (very illegal) on Silverbonce, which the referee failed to spot, left the Indigo Warrior's mouth wide open. The crowd went ballistic, jeering and spitting flame in the direction of the harangued official. The players were up in wings about it, hovering around the referee, blowing smoke at him, the whole lot. He had no intention of changing his mind, however much his mistake was pointed out, so the match continued. 1-1.

If Peter's language had been colourful before, it was nothing to what Tank's was now. It was all Richie and Peter could do to get him to sit back down and watch the match restart once again. Peter looked over at his friend waving his oversized fist animatedly at the television, threatening the official, wondering how somebody as sensitive and caring as Tank, with not a selfish thought in his body, no matter what his form, could get so worked up about something like this.

'The humans,' he thought. 'We're all becoming more human. Is that even possible?' It was an odd thing to think, but something about it rang true. He vowed to give it more consideration at a quieter moment.

Gathering again in the centre of the stadium, waiting for that captivating ball to come shooting out, the dragons soared and rolled, drifted and dived. From the concentration on the faces of the Indigo Warriors players, it was clear they were discussing tactics telepathically. The young Gipsy Kings forward, pleased at having just scored the equaliser, was trying desperately to taunt the Warriors, but sensibly, they were ignoring him, or perhaps were just too busy planning their next attack.

As the ball shot out of the ceiling the Indigo Warriors, with the exception of Silverbonce, all grouped together and made for the ball. A Gipsy Kings player reached it first, but a split second after bringing the ball under control, he was hit full on with the concussive force of four dragons travelling at full tilt. The Warriors gained possession of the ball, while the surprised Gipsy Kings player tumbled clumsily towards the roiling surface of the lava, eventually hitting it head first. As the injured dragon floated on the surface, clearly unconscious, a small passageway opened in the middle of one side of the cavern, right above the lava. Out shot two medic dragons, dragging behind them a giant green net. Heading straight for the injured dragon, the two medics continued as the match became more frantic all around them.

The Warriors collective on the ball were lining up for a run at the Gipsy Kings' mouth. Their opposition, a dragon down, had got themselves between the Warriors and their mouth, but were a little unorganised. As the collective swooped towards the mouth, one by one Gipsy Kings players hurled themselves at the cluster. Although seemingly born of desperation, it was quite an effective tactic, taking out at least one of the Warrior players each time it happened.

With all this going on around them, the two medics had scooped up the Gipsy Kings dragon in their net, and were now flying with him in between them towards the opening from which they'd appeared. Now that the injured player had left the arena, the Gipsy Kings were finally able to bring on their substitute, albeit a little too late to help with the current action they were having to defend. All the Gipsy Kings players, with the exception of their mouth guard, had hurled themselves at the collection of Warriors players. Only Barf from the Warriors remained flying with the ball, after having been at the centre of the troop. As he zoomed towards the mouth with only the guard in the way, he looped the ball up and over the isolated mouth guard, while at the same time blasting him with a sustained stream of flame from his giant jaws. Momentarily disorientated, the guard could do nothing as Barf soared around behind him, gathered up the ball and shot at the undefended mouth.

On the edge of their seats, the crowd watched in anticipation at what would likely be just a tap in from a short way out, and one of the easiest shots Barf was ever likely to have, given that he had all the time in the world.

Inexplicably though, Barf had got all his bearings totally mixed up, whether from over confidence or maybe just nerves at the importance of the occasion. Unbelievably his shot sailed well wide of the exposed mouth, only to be picked up by a very surprised Gipsy Kings substitute in the corner of the arena. Roaring in disbelief, the crowd, along with the players and the referee, couldn't believe what they were seeing. Gipsy Kings fans cheered wildly, some hurling abuse at the distraught Barf.

Shock had overtaken the three friends as they sat

unmoving on the living room floor. Tank broke the deafening silence.

"I've seen eggs that haven't hatched that could have put that away," he suggested angrily.

Peter buried his head in his hands, feeling as though the chance had passed for his favourite team to take control of the game.

"Clearly... Barf is not a big game player," quipped Richie solemnly. "I say substitute him and get Zip on."

"Huh... like Zip's gonna do a better job," moaned Tank.

After a few seconds of his head spinning, and feeling more than a little sorry not only for himself, but for his friends and his team as well, Peter picked himself up and with a deep breath, and the belief that tonight was going to go his way, announced,

"Come on guys. We can still win. So Barf made a mistake. We've all done that."

Richie looked at him and raised her eyebrows.

"Most of us have done that," he amended. "The Warriors can still win. We just need to believe. It's not like we're even losing. It's still a draw and there's plenty of time left yet."

"Well... I hope they start pulling their wingtips out, that's all I can say," put in Tank, trying to pick up on Peter's optimism.

"I still say we need to bring on Zip... but I'm pretty sure we can still win," professed Richie, taking a long sip of her drink.

Back in the arena, the Indigo Warriors poured thoughts of confidence, understanding and support into their telepathic collectiveness, letting Barf know that the miss didn't matter, but it didn't seem to do the trick. He was utterly inconsolable as he flapped his wings dejectedly on his way back to defend.

Retaining possession, the Gipsy Kings had started to string two or three great passes together, the Warriors all the time chasing the ball and the players, without a great deal of success it must be said. The movement and co-ordination of the Gipsy Kings in this phase was very much reminiscent of two seasons previously, when they had gone on to become league champions for the second time in a row. Worryingly, the Warriors were barely able to get near the ball, let alone intercept it.

As the Gipsy Kings closed in on the Warriors' mouth, Steel made a last ditch attempt at a tackle, but missed quite spectacularly, tumbling into the side of the cavern, injuring himself badly in the process. The player with the ball wide on the right, about mouth height, had two players in the middle to pass to. Silverbonce, unusually for him, didn't know whether to come out to the player, or stay and defend the mouth. Just as he'd decided to come out, the wide player thrashed the ball across the middle towards his two waiting teammates. With such amazing speed and agility that it seemed almost impossible, Silverbonce changed direction in a flash, and was on top of the closest Gipsy Kings player in an instant. All of which would have been great if it weren't for the fact that this player, in all his wisdom, dummied the ball and let it fly right through the middle of his wings to the player behind him. Again it was the young forward, and as Silverbonce scrabbled about in an attempt to get over to him, the youngster, calmly as you like, gathered in the ball with his tail and hammered it aggressively into the mouth, turning one of the teeth at the end to dust.

Appearing to be in total disarray, the Warriors floated back towards the middle of the cavern to await yet another restart. Barf looked as though he just wanted to be somewhere else. Cheese and Silverbonce were arguing over some aspect of the previous attack that had led to the goal, while Steel just looked on, a cold, reflective expression on his face.

The mood back in Salisbridge wasn't that much better. Whereas only moments before it had been optimistic and full of hope, you could now have heard a pin drop as the friends studied the screen, willing their team to buck up their ideas and give the Gipsy Kings the damn good thrashing they deserved, but in their heart of hearts not truly believing it was possible. Historic game or not, it looked very much like the evening was over and that for this season at least, the Global Cup run had fizzled out like a damp squib. And much as the three friends hoped they would, the Warriors never really recovered from that particular moment. Almost straight from the restart, the Gipsy Kings scored another goal, shattering any small amount of confidence the Warriors retained. Shortly after that, Barf was substituted for Zip, much to the watching Richie's delight, but even though Zip had lots of energy, covering a massive amount of air, it didn't really impact on the match very much.

And so it was that with five minutes to go, a determined Steel had made a conscious decision to retrieve the ball and make a singular run on goal in one last concerted effort to get his team back into the match. However, his opponents though were currently playing the ball around for fun, just like they would in a training match, knowing that a 3-1 lead and such disorganised looking opposition meant all they had to do was keep possession for the match, and a place in the final, to be theirs.

Steel, in much the same way as his demoralised teammates, had spent most of the last half hour chasing the ball around without much success and was quite frankly getting more than a little bit fed up. But unlike the others, who seemed to have all given up on their hopeless situation, he believed implicitly that they could turn the game around and get through to the final. All they had to do was get two goals and they would go through, because in cup matches, whoever scores first will win the game should the match be drawn. As the Warriors scored the opening goal, they would win the match should the score be 3-3 at full time, something Steel thought the Gipsy Kings had realised, and knew they were not quite as safe as they evidently assumed, despite their current showboating.

Steel, while flying around chasing the ball, had hit on an idea about how to get it back from the Gipsy Kings. Their young forward had taken up a position low down, just above the surface of the toxic, bubbling lava, roughly in the centre of the arena. Every sixth or seventh pass would go to him, where he would just keep hold of the ball until one of the Warriors closed him down. If nobody from the Warriors managed that, he would just hover, keeping possession, running down the clock. Knowing he had to work quickly for his plan to work, Steel feigned an injured wing, acting as though he were in a fair amount of pain, and drifted over to the nearest rock ledge, far from the main action. All the time rotating his wing, he sent out a message to his teammates, telling them not to close down the young forward, but to stand off and be ready to attack when the time came.

Cheese and Zip were covering an enormous amount of air, chasing and harrying their opponents who were more than happy to keep hold of the ball in less dangerous parts of the arena, playing out time. While the Gipsy Kings had noticed Steel flying down to the ledge, supposedly injured, they didn't think much of it because the Warriors had already used their only substitute when they'd taken Barf off. Things continued much in the same vein, with Cheese and Zip following the ball around the cavern at top speed, closing down players, never actually getting near enough to intercept a pass. Meanwhile, if anyone had been paying attention, which they hadn't, they would have noticed that Steel was no longer on the ledge or, for that matter, anywhere to be seen.

Back at Peter's house, the friends had all but given up on winning the match and going through to the final. With the screen focusing solely on the ball and the players it was travelling between and with no commentary, the friends had no idea Steel had feigned injury or that he was on his way in a daring attempt to put things right.

Ticking down now, the clock showed that four minutes remained of the match. Dragon supporters of both teams had started exiting the arena, hoping to hop on the monorail and beat the crowds with the result already a foregone conclusion.

As the Gipsy Kings players passed the ball about with ease, the look on their faces said it all. They were already planning what they were going to do in the final. That's how confident they were that this game was already wrapped up. Cheese and Zip continued to chase the ball, that is until... the ball was passed to the young forward, hovering just above the lava.

From the look on HIS face, not only was he planning his moves in the final, but also rehearsing the speech he was going to give on raising aloft the Global Cup, having won it. With the ball nestling gently against the scales on the tip of his tail, the cocky smile on the young forward's face grew tenfold as both Cheese and Zip drew to a halt in mid-air. Cheese wiped his head in mock exhaustion, Zip just shook his downheartedly, looking as though he'd already given up. With his teammates encouraging him just to keep the ball, the youngster was happy to oblige with his opponents having already chucked in the towel.

Through the shimmering air, Zip and Cheese exchanged worried looks. Something must have gone wrong. Whatever Steel had planned had not come to pass and here they were, seconds slipping away, watching the opposition hold the ball and gloat. Even through their telepathic link, they could not sense him anywhere, which could mean only one thing... he was under the lava. Well under, for them not to be able to sense him. Diving beneath the lava in a laminium ball match is a risky business. Usually the lava is the hottest and most volatile found outside the Earth's core. Even a dragon's highly impervious scales can be susceptible to exceptionally high temperatures after a prolonged period of time. Because of this, dragons in a laminium ball match wouldn't last any longer than ten seconds beneath the surface. Steel had been missing for over thirty.

The extraordinarily large clock built into the ceiling of the arena clicked on to three minutes left, with the entire Gipsy Kings team drifting effortlessly in their own positions. Remaining in possession of the ball, the young forward held his position just above the lava, disgusted with his opposition for just giving up. Beneath the young forward, the orange and red lava hissed and spat, crackled and sizzled, all the time swirling around in mesmerising patterns as great plumes of steam rose into the humid air. Small bubbles broke the surface unnoticed. The rising panic asserting itself across the Indigo Warriors' telepathic collective turned to relief as the players suddenly felt the presence of Steel, heading upwards from well beneath the lava at quite a speed. Those small bubbles underneath the young dragon had turned into much bigger ones that were spluttering and bursting like bladders at an old people's home. A sense of disbelief and quiet anticipation ran through the crowd, who were aware, unlike the young forward, that something was about to happen. Before anyone could warn him... happen it did!

Like a fiery phoenix erupting through the gates of hell, Steel burst through the surface of the lava, huge streams of dazzling orange and red liquid exploding all around him. His naturally shiny scales were dull, some even black, and on fire. Appearing directly beneath the young forward, he flew straight into him, making sure to gather up the ball on the way. Dragon bones cracking and breaking echoed around the vast arena as the inevitable collision took place. Steel, of course, came away with the ball, the young broken forward falling unceremoniously into the steaming mass with a gigantic 'PLOP'. No surprise to anyone that the two medic dragons exited their hole at speed, just catching up with the injured dragon as the last vestiges of his body

310

dipped below the lava.

Having taken everyone by surprise and with the crowd roaring him on, Steel was winging his way towards the Gipsy Kings' mouth, smoke and lava pouring off his ravaged body. Two and a half minutes remained.

With almost every player caught by surprise at Steel's audacious move, only one Gipsy Kings player stood a chance at intercepting him before he reached the mouth and the very nervous mouth guard. In Steel's mind, there was no question about what had to happen. Only about two minutes remained, so he had to score immediately, without any fuss, and hope that some miracle opportunity presented itself to score again instantly after the restart. He cursed the fact that it had taken him so long to find the young forward from underneath the lava. He'd been submerged in different types of lava before, some for longer periods of time, but none had felt quite like this. Once under, he felt as though he were shrouded by a blanket of ice and not heat. Only a metre or so beneath the surface the lava had lost its warm kiss, to be replaced by a needle sharp darkness that had enveloped everything. Nothing was as it seemed, down and up were gone, his enhanced sense of direction nullified by his surroundings. What he knew to be his one shot was hanging by a thread. If he broke the surface at all, the game would be up. It took every ounce of courage and bravery he possessed to fight his body's urge to resurface, and stay under long enough to find the right route up to the surface directly below his young opponent. But he couldn't help wonder now, if having taken so long, it would all be for nothing.

Terror and alarm pulsed through what was left of the Gipsy Kings' telepathic bond at the surprise development of the last few seconds, even though they were still two goals ahead. As Steel closed in on the terrified Gipsy Kings mouth guard, the unthinkable happened. The only Gipsy Kings player close enough to get to Steel in time had done so, but had undoubtedly been consumed by the desperation and alarm through the telepathic bond. Instead of trying fairly to wrestle the ball from Steel, or even just slow him down, he had in fact come in jaws first, grabbing the Warriors captain by the throat. Growling in disbelief, both sides of the animated crowd couldn't believe what they were seeing. It was the worst kind of foul that any dragon could commit during a laminium ball match. Not only that, but it was taboo in the wider sense of the dragon community. It was a violation, an attack, one that was feared by every dragon on the planet, buried deep down in their very DNA. Even his own players were appalled. One dragon did not put its jaws anywhere near another dragon's throat... EVER! The referee stopped the match as the entire team of Warriors gathered around their stricken captain.

Even from their not so great angle on the television, the three friends could still make out the devastating damage to their team's captain, who it had to be said was in pretty bad shape. As well as the half a dozen puncture wounds on his neck oozing blood, about twenty percent of his body's scales were as black as night, most still smouldering. That trip beneath the lava looked as though it had really taken its toll.

"They should ban him for life for that!" screamed Tank at the television. "It's bloody disgraceful!"

"You're right of course," chipped in Richie. "But it was bloody clever on his part."

"WHAAAAAAATTTT!!!" screeched Peter.

"Think about it for a second," said Richie, all cool, calm and calculating. "If you were in his position and you knew that you could take out Steel, run down the clock and win the game for your team, and all that it would cost you would be a ban for the next match - wouldn't you do it? Wouldn't you take one for the team?"

"No I bloody wouldn't. Not like that!" objected Peter, furious. "I can't believe you would say such a thing."

"Calm down Peter. I'm not condoning what happened,

only saying that from his perspective he did the right thing to win his team the game."

"Yeah... well, it's not over yet, is it?" spluttered Peter, trying to rein in his temper.

"Oh that's right," replied Richie. "Tell me, just how are the Warriors going to win now?"

He turned away, returning his attention to the screen, knowing that she was right, it was all over. He just... didn't want it to be, that's all. As the three friends watched, the referee banished the Gipsy Kings player that had committed the foul, issuing him with a one match ban at the same time. The crowd roared with approval at the player missing the final.

Steel looked in slightly better shape than he had a few moments earlier, thanks in the main to his teammates. As he recovered from the brutal tackle (more like assault actually), the players around him helped lick his wounds, quite literally in fact. Flamer, Cheese and Silverbonce all attended to his smouldering scales, dabbing them with their own wings and giving them a good lick once they were fully extinguished. As the others did this, Zip concentrated on the puncture wounds around Steel's neck that had been inflicted by the Gypsy Kings player. Carefully licking Steel's neck, he made sure to leave a thick coating of saliva. Although this sounds kind of gross, dragon saliva contains a whole host of natural antibiotics, acting much quicker than any tablet a human would take. Even in their human disguises, dragon saliva still provides a potent form of healing, able to cure a wide range of ailments.

With Steel now compus mentus, the ref informed both teams that he had awarded a penalty to the Indigo Warriors. Cheers rose from the crowd, but only really from the Gipsy Kings supporters. They knew that with the clock almost run down, this would almost certainly be the last action of the match, meaning the best the Warriors would be able to do, was to lose 3-2. With realisation dawning on

Steel and his teammates, the depressing reality of having lost washed over all of them. Except Silverbonce, who looked... like he was up to something. Steel was the team's assigned penalty taker, so it was he who hovered with the ball, ready to strike on the referee's command.

But play hadn't started yet, and so when Silverbonce asked if he could recheck Steel's wounds to make sure he was fit to take the penalty, the ref gave a resounding yes. Flying over to Steel from off to one side, slowly circling him, Silverbonce made it look as if he were verifying his fitness. Steel had absolutely no idea what was going on, but the wily old mouth guard was clearly pitching an idea to his injured captain. This went on for a couple of minutes, until finally the referee lost patience with the two players who were, by now, quite animated. Calling both players over, the ref gave them both a verbal warning for time wasting and made it clear in no uncertain terms that he expected the penalty to be taken as soon as he restarted play.

Nobody had any idea what had gone on between the two players, but because one of them was Silverbonce, the Gipsy Kings players were all looking mighty nervous, even though they knew it was impossible for them to lose the match. The ball could only score one 'pure' hit. Even if it was played in such a way as to hit one tooth and then rebound and hit another, the second hit would not count because rebounds are illegal and don't count towards the goal tally. With the Gipsy Kings players all in the Indigo Warriors' half, Flamer, Cheese and Zip all drifted between them and the penalty area.

Hovering just outside the area, the referee was almost ready to restart play.

Unusually, Silverbonce remained by Steel's side as he prepared to take the penalty. There was no rule that said he couldn't do that, it was just... unheard of.

All glued to the television, Peter, Tank and Richie thought the last few minutes had been amazing. Even though their heads were telling them that the game was over and that their team had already lost, their hearts had been buoyed by Silverbonce's involvement in whatever was going on.

As everyone looked on, the referee started play. Steel drew back his immensely powerful tail, with the ball nestled on the very end, looking as though he were about to shoot. The Gipsy Kings mouth guard tensed, ready to try and save whatever was thrown at him. Powering his tail forward quickly, just as he was about to release the ball, Steel slowed his tail right down, and flipped the ball up in the air in front of Silverbonce.

You could have heard a pin drop in the stadium, that's how deathly quiet it had become, with almost everyone wondering what the hell was going on. It was the same back in Salisbridge, with the three friends sitting on the floor, gawping on an almost professional level, their mouths hanging open like tunnels awaiting the next train. Now that the ball had been played, the Gipsy Kings players on the half way point of the arena surged forward to try and get back and make a difference. It was a big ask. As the ball reached the apex of its trajectory, it started to fall. As it did so, Silverbonce started his forwards roll, bringing his tail up over the top of him, looking to make contact with the ball. For all intents and purposes, it looked as though he was going to slam the ball straight down into the lava. It was absolutely bizarre!

Just a split second before the flat, scaly, open side of Silverbonce's tail made contact with the ball, the cunning old mouth guard rolled his tail around, bringing the full force of the serrated edge down on to the middle of the laminium ball. Dragon eyes all around the arena nearly popped out as the shining silver ball split neatly into two, revealing the many layers inside that had gone into producing it.

As the two halves of the ball tumbled apart, Silverbonce ducked out of the way of Steel's onrushing tail, which even though he couldn't see, he knew was on its way, rushing towards the broken ball. A resounding 'THWACK' echoed around the stadium as the Warrior's captain made contact with the two halves, sending both spinning towards the Gipsy Kings' mouth, both on totally different courses. Rooted to the spot, the bemused Gipsy Kings mouth guard watched helplessly as the two laminium ball halves flew past either side of him, each hitting the outer tooth on either side of the goal mouth.

The giant scoreboard signalled two goals for the Indigo Warriors, making the score 3-3 flash up all along the side of the rocky wall below the spectators. The game was a draw. The Warriors had won.

The arena was still deathly silent. Crowd and players alike could not believe what they'd just witnessed. As the seconds passed, Warriors fans started to process exactly what had happened, and that their team had just made it through to the final. A muted round of applause and a little shouting started off in one corner, which slowly gathered momentum, eventually making its way to every other part of the stadium in only a matter of seconds. Unlike anything it had ever experienced, the rocky ceiling of the subterranean cavern started to shake and shed small rocks that plunged into the lava at high speed. Cheese, Flamer and Zip belted over to Steel and Silverbonce to celebrate the unlikeliest of victories. Gipsy Kings players surrounded the ref, pushing and shoving, complaining that the goals shouldn't stand. Ignoring the furore, the referee, from the look on his face, was clearly having another conversation with the match arbiter, who remained hidden in the depths of the stadium somewhere.

As both sets of fans and players realised that the referee had not signalled to end the game, the noise died down to virtually nothing. Crossing his wings in front of his body, and then sharply opening them out and pointing to the expired clock on the wall was what should have happened. It most certainly hadn't yet, with a telepathic discussion clearly still going on about the legality of the goals and whether or not the result should stand. Both teams drifted in separate huddles, waiting for over forty seconds, which seemed to the players like more than one lifetime. Finally the referee returned his attention to the present, finding the eyes of all the players and most of the seventy thousand strong crowd, fixed firmly in his direction. Steam rose from every part of his body as he realised the massive implications of the decision he was about to give. A massive expansion and constriction around the scales in his neck and throat seemed to indicate a massive 'GULP' on his part. Resigned to the fact that half the crowd was going to love him, with the other half wanting to lynch him, he turned towards both sets of players, crossed his wings in front of his body and pointed towards the clock. The double goal stood.

The boos were easily eclipsed by the roars that resounded around the stadium. Indigo Warriors players went mental. Flamer leapt backwards into the air, performing continuous loop the loops that seemed to go on forever. Cheese and Zip hurled themselves at each other, bouncing off one another's chests high up in the air. Steel grabbed Silverbonce's wing and raised it aloft for the fans. This got by far the biggest cheer of the night, almost quadruple anything else. Even the Gipsy Kings fans were cheering, knowing that they had all witnessed something that would go down in the history of the game. Gipsy Kings players had grudgingly accepted the referee's decision and had very slowly flown off to the exit tunnel that was now wide open and filled with journalists and photographers from all the telepathic papers. Now joined by the ecstatic Barf, the Indigo Warriors continued to enjoy their moment of glory, circling the stadium in a flying formation, waving their wings and shooting huge cones of fire from their mouths as they did so.

Peter's house was quite literally rocking from the noise the three friends were making. It was a good job the neighbours were away. Tank had been jumping up and down, using the full force of his very sizable bulk. Richie had been screaming in a very high pitched way, that is until Peter and Tank gave her quizzical looks, and when she realised she'd been doing it she stopped abruptly and began blowing intricate smoke rings with her mouth. Peter, when he'd seen the referee's signal that the Warriors had won, just pumped his arms in the air, mouthing the word 'yes' over and over again. The three of them were as happy as they'd ever been, with Tank vowing to get them all tickets to the final, no matter what the cost, even if he had to sell his own tail. As they watched their heroes circling the stadium, the television picture suddenly turned to static. Peter and Richie turned to Tank hopefully.

"I think that's it," said Tank, more than a little hoarse. "To be honest, I'm surprised they broadcast that much. I expected it to cut out as soon as the game finished. My best guess, is because of the controversial end of the game, they decided to keep on transmitting, but that's all we're gonna get. Looks like we'll have to wait for the papers in the morning to see anything else."

Peter sighed long and hard.

"That was one of the best nights of my life."

Tank and Richie nodded in agreement. After that, the three friends started going over the game again, re-living all the best bits and in particular THAT PENALTY. They stayed at Peter's house well into the early hours of the next day, celebrating.

14 A SPRINKLING OF MAGIC

When Peter eventually awoke, it was nearly lunchtime. His stomach rumbled, not only from hunger but almost certainly complaining about the near fatal combinations of food and drink that he'd consumed just a few hours earlier. Combinations that, while he was sleeping, had produced dragon like amounts of what can only be described as... aroma, challenged clouds of a gaseous nature that, with a will of their own, had floated throughout the house of their own accord, as he was now finding out.

Sitting down at the breakfast table, eyeing two of the aforementioned clouds in the far corner of the room, he sent out his consciousness and broke the habit of a lifetime by commanding it to return with more than one paper. After only four more mouthfuls of cornflakes, he found he had access to five of the most popular telepathic tabloids. Scanning the front and back pages really quickly, headlines such as 'Greatest Game Ever' and 'Controversial Penalty Sends Shockwaves Through The Sport' made him feel warm inside. He spent the next hour engrossed in various descriptions of the previous night's match.

That afternoon he cleaned his home, not something he looked forward to; however, he was something of a stickler for things being tidy and clean. After finishing the housework, he fancied going for a walk. Racking his brain for ten minutes, he couldn't come up with anywhere he fancied going and so after further consideration he decided, for a change, to venture below ground, deep into the dragon domain.

Making his way through the secret underground route from his house, he realised that it had never occurred to him to take a walk for no apparent reason, in the world below ground that he considered his home. Arriving at the monorail station, he'd already decided to catch the first carriage that arrived and follow it to its final destination, wherever that might be. Ambling onto the first silver carriage that presented itself without even looking at the LCD displays to see where it was headed, he watched the different rock formations pass by outside the window, stifling a grin as he did so, knowing that he was in fact heading for Purbeck Peninsula. Six minutes later, he faced out of the carriage as it pulled into the terminus at Purbeck. As the doors of the monorail carriage slid quietly aside, Peter felt the warm air from the concourse wash over him. Making his way through the surprisingly busy plaza, he caught the scent of something... ummm... delicious. Stopping in his tracks, he slowly turned, trying to find the source of the tantalising smell that was assaulting his nose. Looking around, first he ruled out the doughnuts, then the pancakes, then most of the other stalls that he could see. Just when he thought he must be imagining things, he caught sight of a tiny little alcove off to one side, which housed a vendor he was quite sure he had never seen before. Pushing his way through a whole host of dragons who were heading for the main exit, he eventually reached the secluded vendor.

"That smells amazing," announced Peter, licking his lips.

A dark blue dragon, with the most amazing mottled effect Peter had ever seen, looked up from a sizzling hot griddle.

"Can I interest you in one, sir?"

"What are they?" enquired Peter.

"I call them 'Charcoal Surprise'," said the vendor with a big toothy smile.

"And?" added Peter.

"That's all I'm saying."

Peter shook his head, wondering if it were some kind of scam. The vendor looked genuine, he thought, but it wouldn't be the first time some unscrupulous dragon had come along from elsewhere, selling something dubious. The 'Charcoal Surprise' did smell absolutely fantastic though, and he hadn't had anything to eat since his cereal earlier.

"Sure, I'll try one."

"You won't be disappointed I assure you sir," replied the dragon, boosting the heat on the griddle with a little of his own from between his jaws.

Watching intently as the vendor started to make the 'Charcoal Surprise', Peter was keen to know exactly what he'd purchased. Next to the griddle was a small clay oven that he'd neglected to notice up until now. Taking off its lid, the vendor tested the temperature before blowing a stream of bright orange flame into it, to warm it up. Finding it to his liking, the vendor pulled out a big lump of dough from beneath the counter. Placing the dough on the table next to the griddle, the blue dragon started to knead and shape the dough. As he did so, he grabbed a small container from beside the oven, from which he sprinkled out small dark lumps of something all over the dough.

Peter smiled.

'Hmmmm... there's the charcoal,' he thought.

Continuing to knead the dough, now speckled with charcoal, the vendor finished off by using the backs of his wings to roll the dough flat. He then cast the dough into the oven, sticking it to the curved side from what little Peter could actually see, before the lid went back on. With the griddle sizzling away nicely, again the vendor reached under the counter, this time pulling out two pink juicy fruits, that even the young dragon recognised.

"Oh my god," ventured Peter, astonished. "Are those what I think they are? Giant lau laus?"

The vendor answered with a deep throated chuckle.

"I suppose you thought the sprinkles of charcoal were the surprise?"

Peter gave the vendor a lopsided grin and said sheepishly,

"Maybe."

Expertly slicing the giant lau laus with a deadly knife

that looked more like a machete, the dragon continued to talk with Peter.

"Don't worry, most dragons are the same. Most are suspicious and used to the same old things. Pancakes with charcoal, doughnuts with charcoal, fajitas with charcoal. No offence to any of that, but it's all a bit bland for my liking. When I describe something I'm selling as 'Surprise', then I genuinely mean 'surprise', and only in a good way."

"But giant lau laus? They're a delicacy and so limited in supply. Where on earth do you get them? Umm... umm... if you don't mind me asking."

Slices of giant lau lau tumbled through the air on their way to the sizzling griddle, eliciting an unbelievable aroma. Peter's stomach churned and rumbled in anticipation. Pineapple, strawberries, bananas had all been added to the mix, along with the tangy juice of the biggest lime Peter had ever seen. It was a mouth watering cocktail of fruit, one that most sentient beings would have given their right arm just to taste.

"It's okay to ask. It's no big deal, not to me anyway. My grandfather owns and runs one of the biggest plantations in the South Pacific. He always supplies me with enough to be going on with. He's one of the most down to earth dragons you could ever wish to meet, and while you are right about the lau laus being considered a delicacy, in times gone by they were freely available to the likes of you and I. My grandfather keeps me supplied for that very reason, knowing that I can let ordinary dragons get a taste of these delightful fruits."

"Sounds like a top dragon... your grandfather."

A faraway look of days gone by came across the vendor's face as he tossed and turned the spluttering fruity mixture on the griddle.

"A top dragon... that would be an almost perfect description," agreed the vendor.

Taking a quick peek in the oven, the dragon quickly realised the bready concoction had finished cooking.

Pulling it out, he expertly sliced a huge hole in the middle. Peter thought the bread looked similar to naan bread that he had tasted on many outings with Tank and Richie to their favourite Indian restaurant in Salisbridge. Using the bread itself as a kind of shovel, the vendor scooped up the fruity ingredients into the hole, proceeding then to pour a white dressing all over it.

"There you go Sir. Hope you enjoy."

Peter could feel the heat of the bread and its contents almost burning the fake skin from his hands, but was only interested in the fastest way to get it into his aching stomach.

"Thank you very much. I hope to see you again," said Peter, momentarily looking up from the gorgeous smelling snack.

The vendor gave Peter another toothy grin and a short bow as he started to clean the griddle for the next customer.

Walking across the plaza, weaving in and out of commuters, Peter used his hands to lift the bread towards his mouth and gobble furiously on its contents. The 'Charcoal Surprise' was easily the most amazing thing he had ever tasted. Cooked to perfection, the fruit was so sweet and tangy, while the bread melted in his mouth as the occasional fizz of charcoal laid waste to his tongue, causing an almost perfect combination. Passersby in both forms were craning their small human and enormous dragon necks around to give him very curious looks. He didn't care one iota, imagining he looked a right sight at this very moment.

Leaving the monorail plaza, he headed towards the centre of Purbeck Peninsula. Halfway there, he stopped and sat on a seat carved into the dark brown rock. Expecting the feeling of cold, hard rock on his human shaped bum, it came as something of a surprise to get a surge of heat passed on to him by the seat. Examining the rock closely, he found tiny rivulets of molten lava running just beneath the surface, with little plumes of steam rising from the entire length of the seat, something he hadn't spotted before he'd sat down.

'Wow,' he thought, 'some fancy pants has designed the seats with built in heat from the lava running beneath the city. It's just one pleasant surprise after another today.'

Taking ten minutes or so to let his stomach soak up the delightful snack that he'd so greedily gobbled down, all the time making the most of the comfortably warm seat that just seemed to melt away his worries, eventually, and very reluctantly, he got up and continued heading into Purbeck. With his stomach content, his thoughts turned to where he should head next. He'd already had a great time, and didn't really have a destination in mind.

While trying to decide, he spotted an information terminal on one side of the path up ahead. Strolling purposefully over to it, he began to look at the display. Terminals like this can be found dotted around dragon communities all over the world. They can be used for very simple tasks such as looking up a dragon's address or getting directions, or more complex tasks such as contacting Council officials, checking on the latest construction work anywhere in the world, or if the area should allow it, boosting a mobile phone signal here underground. Found mainly in the more modern parts of the underground world, information terminals are commonplace in and around station plazas and the centre of towns and cities, unlike the area where the Mantra Emporium was located where the nearest would have been quite some way a way.

Looking at the different headings on the LCD touch screen, Peter stumbled across one entitled 'Purbeck and Surrounding Area Covert Entrances'. Scrolling down the screen, he looked at the information available. Basically it was a list of all the public surface access points into and out of Purbeck Peninsula. During their time in the nursery ring, young dragons learn all about how to access the surface discreetly and how to enter the dragon domain from any number of concealed entrances. While they aren't given the exact details of every entrance to the dragon world, they do have access to anything they want to know, either via the information terminals, the dragon libraries or telepathically.

A big grin spread across Peter's face. When this part of the curriculum had hit his nursery ring, he, Tank and Richie had developed a game that they had played for some weeks. It was all such a long time ago, but with his eidetic memory, he could remember it as though it were only yesterday. The idea of the game was to find all the concealed entrances in and around Purbeck Peninsula and use as many as possible, with the winner being the one who found either the most fun to use entrance, or the most bizarre. Tank and Peter had spent days at the library (unusually for Peter, not so much for Tank) looking up all the access points. All their hard work, however, turned out to be in vain. As was normally the case, Richie was way ahead of them both. Not only did she find the most bizarre entrance, but two others that were so much fun, the three of them constantly used them over and over again.

Located topside at a children's park right in the centre of Swanage, the bizarre entrance was perfect for a dead of night attempt in the middle of a very humid August. Most of the other entrances Peter had come across up until that point had seemed relatively simple to him, hence he was intrigued as to why they were skulking around in the pitch black. His opinion changed forever after that very night. All three friends sneaked into the park, easy really, with just a three foot fence surrounding it. After that, Richie showed them the sequence for unlocking the entrance. Peter and Tank were both blown away, not believing a word of it at first, assuming that it was one of her infamous practical jokes. However, she was telling the complete truth. Petals of four separate flowers in three separate flower beds all had to be folded so that they pointed down towards the ground. Finding the flowers was going to be impossible, or so Peter thought. Richie managed to find them all first time, without damaging any of the nearby blooms, even though they were surrounded by hundreds of flowers that looked exactly the same.

Next, three small children's spring mounted rides had to all be twisted around to face a northerly direction. As if that wasn't enough, the next stage of the operation was time dependant. The children's roundabout had to be spun at more than twenty revolutions a minute. After that it would be a case of sprinting to the far end of the playground to the giant yellow enclosed spiral slide. With the flowers and the rides in position, a small gap would open up about halfway down the slide, just above a wide metal support that held part of it in place, for only as long as the roundabout managed to stay turning faster than twenty revolutions a minute. Richie bounded up the yellow ladder, leaping feet first into the slide. Tank followed next, his gigantic frame a tight squeeze to say the least. Peter knew he had to hurry, because the roundabout was slowing down all the time. Grabbing the rail above his head, he hurled himself down into the dark after his friends. Turning one of the sharp corners in the dark, he suddenly felt the surface disappear beneath him. He fought the urge to scream, knowing that his friends before him hadn't made a sound. Almost as soon as the falling sensation had started, it stopped with a very wet THUMP.

In the pitch black, even with his enhanced dragon senses, he could still not see his friends, who he assumed were still somewhere in front of him. Sitting up to his tummy in freezing cold, flowing water, after only a few seconds he started getting swept along. He could feel the water behind him building up more and more, making him move faster and faster along the twisting and turning underground stream. Twice he banged his head on the ceiling as he was carried along, only just managing to hold back some very bad curses. Just as he was about to call out to his friends to make sure he was still travelling in the right direction, again the world beneath him fell away and he found himself falling in a shower of cold water in the pitch black. Tumbling wildly, he noticed a small cavern with a body of water rushing up to meet him. With a huge SPLASH he found himself dumped unceremoniously into the small, shallow lake. Sitting up, he was assaulted by roaring laughter from his friends that echoed around the cavern. Shaking themselves dry on the water's edge were Richie and Tank, curled up with mirth. Getting to his feet, Peter waded over to his friends, the smiles on their faces causing him to laugh, which in turn made the other two laugh again. All three of them looked a right sight, soaking wet, freezing cold, bursting with laughter. Peter couldn't recall that incident without chuckling out loud. To this day, it was still the most unusual entrance to the dragon domain that he'd ever come across.

Of the two fun entrances, one was a sinkhole, a little offshore from one of the beaches at Sandbanks, just East of Swanage. Hardly ever used as far as he could remember, it was designed to be accessed by boat, but it was possible to swim there, as it was only about three hundred yards from the shore. A discoloured old buoy marked the sinkhole's position. Had any humans dived in that particular area (they shouldn't have as it was marked out as being a site of special scientific interest), all they would have found was the wreck of a small ship, with absolutely no defining features. Something utterly uninteresting. However, a dragon would know that the sinkhole lies directly below the small wreck. He remembered fondly how Richie had led him and Tank out into the night, much in the same way as she had to the park in Swanage. Way too many people would have been here to do it any other time than late at night under the cover of darkness. Three swimmers going out that far and then not returning would definitely arouse suspicion in the daytime on the usually

327

crowded beach. Shrouded by the darkness, the three had a leisurely swim out to the wreck, changing into their dragon forms halfway, a new experience for Peter, having never done it underwater (steady!) before. He wanted to laugh madly at the overwhelming tickling sensation which was the only way to describe the very different experience, from his point of view anyway. Diving down to the bottom on occasion on the way, to swim among the delicate but stunningly beautiful seahorses and other marine life, the three weren't sure who was more surprised: the three of them to see the vast array of unusual aquatic creatures, or the creatures at seeing three prehistoric monsters larking about, blowing bubbles and just generally having a good time in the warm, late summer water. On reaching the wreck, Richie found an old steel bar lying on the bottom, no doubt part of some far reaching mantra, which she used to lever up the old ship's corpse from beneath. As she did so, water and sand started to disappear at a tremendous rate into the gap that she'd created. Richie indicated to Tank and Peter that they should dive through the narrow gap and into the darkness. Tank didn't need a second invitation and dived through, once again just making it due to his oversized dragon frame. Reluctant to throw himself into the darkness, Peter closed his eyes and propelled himself forward, knowing that Richie was becoming more and more impatient. Using his enhanced dragon senses, just like Richie and Tank, Peter was capable of holding his breath for more than half an hour, something he concentrated on now more than ever. Finding himself surrounded by a dizzying array of bubbles, suddenly something hard smashed into his shoulder, sending him tumbling head over tail. It was all he could do to keep holding his breath, as Richie's graceful form plummeted past him. Telepathically, she sent him a short apology for bumping into him, just managing a brief wave before a huge plume of bubbles engulfed her. For someone, or something, that was used to doing acrobatics (normally, of course, the aerial kind) he found himself having a great deal of trouble controlling his urge to throw up. He felt as though he'd been whisked up in a raging underwater vortex, spinning round and round at a positively dizzying rate. Imagine, if you will, the biggest, most amazing waterslide, only underwater and at the speed of a bullet. That's the only way he could think of the experience he was currently suffering. Still tumbling wildly out of control, concentrating on holding his breath and not throwing up (which in his mind only added to the building sense of panic, as he assumed that if he opened his mouth to throw up, then he would probably drown. No pressure then!) he could just make out Tank in the distance, being tossed around like a rag doll, seemingly loving every second of it. Richie had by now turned her uncontrollable descent into something of an art. Having stopped tumbling, she'd made her slim dragon form resemble a kind of torpedo shape, and was currently zipping in and out of the giant bubble columns at a jaw dropping angle. As he watched his friends, it dawned on him that just maybe he was approaching the journey all wrong.

'Perhaps enjoying the experience is key to surviving it,' he thought. With this in mind, he spread out both his wings in an attempt to gain more control over his ungainly drop. Rushing water and bouncing bubbles caressing the membranes in his wings made him want to... giggle. It tickled. It really, really tickled.

Not able to tell whether things had gotten better or worse, on the plus side he'd forgotten about wanting to throw up, but the desire to laugh out loud was overwhelming, which again made him think he might well drown, only this time from laughter. Panic once again started to rise from the pit of his stomach, but before it had a chance to take hold he found himself tangled up in a mass of slimy, dark green seaweed. It was everywhere, preventing him from moving, let alone getting himself untangled. He looked around for his friends, but they were nowhere in his eye line. Abruptly the seaweed contracted, nearly forcing open his clamped shut mouth. With a vice like grip on him, the seaweed spun him around and around, hurling him straight towards a bright orange, oversized starfish which, unbelievably, used one of its arms to bat him away in a totally different direction. Things were getting weird now, even for the dragon domain. Unable to change his trajectory even in the slightest, Peter now found himself heading for the wide open mouth of a monstrous giant clam. Looking back on it, he could certainly see the funny side, but at the time he had no idea if this was what was supposed to be happening. Hitting the back of the clam's mouth at considerable speed, its massive structure slammed shut, leaving him alone in the dark. Lying trapped, concentrating on holding his breath, he could feel everything all about him move, in an upwards direction he thought. After what seemed like an hour, but was actually only a few minutes, the clam's mouth opened, revealing the inside of a well lit chamber. Swimming gently out of the clam's mouth, careful not to touch the sides for fear of being swallowed again, he broke the surface to be greeted by his friends' laughter. Richie and Tank were desperate to go again, and come to think of it, now that Peter knew what to expect, so was he.

'The other fun entrance, well that's... that's... hmmm. That's only a short walk away,' he thought. Indecision set in, well at least for a split second. It was a bit childish to want to use the concealed entrance just for the fun of it, wasn't it? Especially as he was on his own.

'What the hell,' he thought, heading off in the direction of the nearest way to the surface.

It turned out the closest access point was only a few minutes' walk away and would bring him out in one of the arcades in Swanage itself. This worked out quite well because the 'fun' entrance he was planning to use to get back was only a little further along the seafront, in the guise of a beach hut.

Turning off the main walkway he'd been on since exiting the monorail station, he headed up a steep flight of rocky stairs. Climbing roughly three storeys, he turned a corner and found himself in a small circular chamber, entirely carved out of rock. In the middle of the chamber was a round glass cage with a circular metal pad at the base of it. Warning signs were plastered on either side of the cage's door. White writing on a red background warned 'ONLY USE IN HUMAN FORM' and 'NARROW IRIS IN USE. DRAGON BODIES WILL NOT FIT'.

Sliding the glass door aside, he stepped onto the metal pad. A tinny voice came out of a small speaker beside his head.

"Keep your body within the circumference of the pad. Be prepared for human interaction."

The glass door in front of him closed automatically, encasing him fully. Bending his knees slightly, he prepared to be shot upwards at high speed. The lights dimmed, before a staggeringly loud 'WHOOSH' sent him straight up into the air, through a hole in the top of the chamber and up into total darkness. Crouched ever so slightly, he could see the rock as it raced by only inches from his face. The noise from the ascent started to die off as the pad slowed. He craned his neck to look up. He was close enough now just to make out the metallic surface of the iris, able to make out the seams where it would split to let him through.

Only moving at about a metre a second now, Peter's eyes were suddenly dazzled by the bright light shining through the now open iris. Familiar sounds of arcade machines reverberated all around him as he came to rest in the middle of a group of slot machines. Having stopped moving, the pad looked just like any other part of the surrounding floor. Ducking down on coming through the iris, he was now looking for the opportunity to sneak through the very narrow gap between two of the machines. Right on cue, one of the two penny machines down at the far end of the arcade made a loud paying out kind of sound, followed by the ching-ching-ching of coins falling out of the bottom. With everybody's attention focused elsewhere, Peter squeezed through the gap and nonchalantly stood up.

Nobody in the arcade had witnessed his arrival, with the exception of the woman behind the change counter opposite: a seemingly middle aged woman with long, dark hair, part of which was tied back with a stripy bandana. She gave Peter a long stare, before breaking into a smile and giving him a surreptitious wink with her right eye. He returned the gesture before casually leaving by the seafront entrance.

The lady (or dragon) behind the counter was known as Madam Ladybird, and was renowned for the charity work she carried out not just in the human world up above, but also in the dragon domain down below. As well as working in the arcade, she was its owner and had been for some time.

Stepping out into the daylight, Peter found himself looking out across Swanage Bay, a sight he never got tired of, even on a chilly day like today. Much as the heat and warmth of the underground world he called home felt wonderful, there was something mesmerising about the sea, and this view in particular, that he found intoxicating. Whether it was the golden sand, the overpowering cliffs, the gentle sound of the waves lapping against the shore, just the right number of boats in the bay, the breathtaking view of the Isle of Wight and the Needles or the tummy rumbling smell of fish and chips, he just didn't know, but Peter felt this could well be his spiritual home, if such a thing existed.

Turning, he headed east along the seafront, past the three storey homes that were successfully rented to holiday makers throughout the year. In the distance he could just make out the shrill whistle of one of the steam trains that ran regularly on the celebrated railway. Walking towards the main stretch of beach, his attention was drawn to the waves rolling in and crashing on the sand only a few feet below the raised walkway he was on.

'The tide,' he thought, 'seems to be neither in nor out.'

Continuing past two bars and a couple of shops that sold all sorts of holiday stuff (inflatable boats, beach balls, boogie boards, buckets and spades, towels, swimwear, that kind of thing) he made it onto the road that ran behind the main expanse of beach, walking past another arcade, a fish and chip shop, the information centre and a newly designed toilet block. Set back from the road, past the aforementioned facilities, was a row of brightly coloured beach huts.

Bending down on the pavement, pretending to tie his shoelaces, he looked along the beach front to see if anyone was acting suspiciously or paying him any undue attention. He saw several couples with young children, a couple of groups of youths and numerous elderly people dotted about the place, taking in the brisk sea air, but nobody looking at him. Keeping his wits about him, he wandered down in front of all the beach huts. Being the end of October, none of them were in use. Probably luck more than anything, as he'd been here much later in the year and found huts with their doors open, with people sitting down inside, taking in the sights.

Eventually finding the hut he was looking for, he carefully placed one finger on the tip of a rusty old nail that poked ominously out of the door frame and using two fingers on his other hand, pulled out a small fragment of wood from the side of the hut, just a few inches. With the wood fragment pulled out as far as it would go, he pushed down on the tip of the nail until a satisfying 'click' could be heard as the door unlocked. All this happened in a split second. For a human to have witnessed it, there would have to have been an awful lot of luck involved. Checking quickly in the reflection of the hut's window, satisfied, he squeezed inside, silently shutting the door behind him. Looking out at the seafront through the once white, musty, net curtain, he once again checked that nobody had paid him any attention. Nobody had. Satisfied that he hadn't been seen, he turned his gaze to the interior of the hut. It was just as he'd remembered, right down to the ancient white gas stove that stood in the back right hand corner and the blue and white striped deck chair placed smack bang in the middle of the floor.

'I'm sure the deck chair had red stripes,' he thought, wondering if his eidetic memory was playing up in some way, shape or form. Half deflated beach balls and inflatable dinghies were all propped up in the other corner, along with an array of mismatched oars to heaven only knew what sort of boats. An old metallic white fridge stood at waist height next to the stove, a brown electric kettle straight out of the 1970's keeping it company. He wrinkled his nose as he took a step further into the hut. It smelt of old carpet, decaying mould and strangely... candy floss. Running his hand along the old worktop that the kettle sat on, he was rewarded with the thickest layer of dust he'd ever seen in his entire life, accumulating on the side of his fingers.

'Exactly as I remember it,' he thought, ignoring the OCD tidying instinct that threatened to overwhelm his body.

Jolted out of his daydreaming by the sound of small children running and laughing, he knew better than to hang around for no apparent reason. His body screamed at him to get on and activate the entrance as soon as possible. Racking his brain, for this was another puzzle activated entrance, just like the children's park, which ironically was only a stone's throw from where he now stood, he thought long and hard about exactly what to do. First, he took the lid off the dark brown kettle, checking first to make sure it was plugged into the dilapidated mains socket. Next, he opened the fridge door, while the light inside stuttered and flickered on, looking as though it was about to fail. Inside the fridge door, there were three bottles of ancient looking lemonade. Carefully taking out the first bottle, he poured its entire contents into the kettle, before putting the lid back on and flicking the switch to boil, whilst at the same time putting the empty bottle back in the fridge and shutting the door. All he had to do now, he knew, was sit back in the deck chair and wait for the kettle to boil. Slumping down in the deck chair, he looked at his watch. From what he could remember, the whole thing would take about three minutes. Desperate to keep his mind occupied in an attempt to ignore the urge that threatened to overcome him, he glanced around at the old junk. It was no good. He just had to look. Standing up, he paced over to the fridge and opened the door. Sure enough, all three bottles of lemonade were now full. Marvelling at the magic behind the mantra, only one thought shot through his head.

'It must be some sort of self replicating mantra,' he mused, vowing to ask his friend Gee Tee about it when their paths next crossed.

The sound of the kettle bubbling away made him leap back into the deck chair, ready for his journey below. Through the dirty net curtain that covered the window, he could just make out a brilliant luminescent rainbow that stretched from one end of the bay to the other, looking stunning against the back drop of the grey autumn sky. Abruptly, the floor beneath him opened up and swallowed the deck chair whole. Had anyone been in the hut watching, all they would have seen was a section of the dusty old floor rotate through one hundred and eighty degrees, with a new deck chair, this one red striped, appearing again in the middle of the hut.

Peter found himself zooming down a steep rocky slope mostly in the dark, occasionally lit by tiny patches of lava that he either zipped over or noticed low down to the side of the deck chair's crazy trajectory. Sparks flew from the metal feet on the bottom of the chair that constantly remained in contact with the twisting rocky path. Nothing short of exhilarating, the screeching ride with its sharp twists and turns in the near dark had his heart beating double time, especially on some of the steeper drops and the wicked hairpin bends. Speeding along at an unbelievable rate, he guessed he was travelling in excess of ninety miles an hour. Something he'd never been able to work out, in all the times he'd taken this journey, was whether or not he had any control over the ride. It always seemed as though he could affect the course of the chair by throwing his weight to one side, changing direction ever so slightly, but he always got the impression that the chair itself was almost... humouring him, if such a thing were even possible.

Without warning, the angle of descent increased dramatically, along with the speed, forcing him back in the chair as the screeching of metal on rock got louder and the sparks from the feet got wilder. Gripping the side of the chair for all he was worth, he prepared himself for what was to come.

Sure enough, it came. The excruciating drop changed in a split second, being replaced by a feeling of heading up a slope, and then... aaaahhhhhhhhhhh!

Even though he knew what to expect, the ferocity of it took him completely by surprise. The very first time he'd used this entrance with Tank and Richie, it had been explained to him that this section of the track was what can only be described as a 'loop the loop'. Used to 'G' forces of varying intensities, this was nothing new to dragons who regularly pulled more G's than most fighter pilots. This loop the loop though was something else. Maybe because the darkness didn't allow you to anticipate what was coming next, just the sheer speed, the enclosed space, or a combination of them all, the only thing that Peter knew was that this ride was like nothing else he'd ever experienced. It combined fear and excitement in equal measures, which certainly got his blood pumping.

Once through the loop the loop, he found himself back on a relatively gentle slope in the deck chair, but instead of facing forwards to travel down the slope, the chair itself was turning in circles, much like the Waltzers at the fun fair that comes to Salisbridge market place every year.

Just as he was regretting having eaten the scrummy 'Charcoal Surprise', the circles stopped and it slowed right down. Looking around, the faint light of liquid lava showed him that he'd come to a halt at a complete dead end. A solid rock face stood no more than three metres away, blocking the entire route. Peter sat tangled in the chair, legs almost around his ears, puzzled. For the life of him, he couldn't remember this part of the journey. As far as he could recall, the chair was supposed to cross paths with two underground streams, travelling down one for a short period, before hitting a tight spiral and ending up just on the outskirts of Purbeck Peninsula.

Grabbing the armrests of the chair to lift himself out, he decided to get up and look around. Halfway to a standing position the chair unexpectedly folded up on him, disappearing into a very small opening that had appeared beneath it. He couldn't move. Not an inch, with his knees firmly clamped against his chin, and no matter how hard he tried, he just couldn't force the chair any wider apart. Changing forms flicked briefly through his mind, but given the vice like grip the chair had on him, he wasn't so sure it was a good idea. All he knew was that he and the chair were falling fast now, very fast, and as far as he could remember this was not supposed to happen.

Suddenly, the speeding V shaped deck chair with Peter sandwiched in the middle, tore through a mass of thick roots and vines as it shot out into the top of a well lit cavern. Craning his neck to look back down the side of the chair, he could just make out dragons in natural and human form walking along a well worn path hundreds of metres below.

'Don't they realise I'm about to fall to my doom?' he thought, preparing to scream at the top of his voice in the hope that someone would come to his aid. Opening his mouth to do just that, he realised that his descent had started to slow. It was then that he noticed the roots of the plant, that he'd fallen through on entering the cavern, had in fact attached themselves to the deck chair and were responsible for slowing the fall. The roots and vines seemed to have an almost elastic quality, something Peter was only just noticing now that he was able to look back up towards the roof itself.

Still sandwiched in the V shape, instead of falling it was now more like being lowered. Half a metre from the ground, the roots let go of the chair, whipping back up through the air, no doubt waiting for the next poor sucker to use that particular entrance. Landing with the click of metal on rock, the deck chair sprang fully open, allowing Peter to bound out, to applause and laughter from smirking dragons all around. Trying hard to look casual, but not really pulling it off, he stepped through the gap in the short wall and onto the busy path. His legs felt like rubber. Deciding momentarily to sit down on the wall and regain his composure, he felt a giant hand slap him on the shoulder.

"Shook you up a bit did it, son?"

He turned round to find a tall, mature, spindly-looking dragon, munching on a stick of charcoal, looking down at him.

"It just wasn't quite as I remembered it," stammered Peter.

The dragon let out a high pitched giggle, and something of a splutter as a lump of charcoal seemed to stick in his jaws.

"They only changed it a week ago. It had to be closed off because part of the main shaft collapsed when a small tremor hit."

'Ahh,' thought Peter, 'it all makes sense now.

Emergency repair teams often come up with some ingenious solution to a critical problem, which would certainly explain the giant plant and its over-friendly roots.'

Peter gave the tall dragon a reluctant smile.

"Thanks for letting me know. I was starting to feel more than a little stupid."

"That's okay son. Most of the dragons walking along here are only doing so in the hope of seeing some unsuspecting traveller get a bit more than they bargained for. If you stick around long enough, someone else will come down."

With that, the dragon patted Peter on the shoulder, turned and walked slowly away. He stayed sitting on the squat stone wall, getting nods and smiles from those that had seen his fall in the deck chair. Sitting there, he suddenly felt his mobile phone vibrate in his pocket. Bemused, he took the phone out and had a look. At some point he'd received a text message.

'Must have happened while I was at the surface briefly,' he thought. Bringing the message up, he opened it, pleased to see it was from Tank. The message read:

Pete, what a night. Still can't believe it. Trying my best to get tickets to the final. Also got something for you from my boss. Will pop round Thursday night if that's okay. Let me know. Tank.

'What on earth can Gee Tee have given him?' Peter wondered, starting to reply. About halfway through, he heard an echoing scream from high above him. Those dragons around him all glanced up at the top of the cavern, where the thick rooted plant had taken hold. Sure enough, a small dark gap appeared in the middle of it, followed shortly by another unsuspecting victim, sandwiched in the middle of a deck chair, rocketing towards the ground.

'I was right,' he thought. 'There was a red and white striped deck chair.' Smiling and shaking his head as the plant's long roots locked themselves around the chair, gradually splaying out, slowing the fall and bringing the dragon, in the form of a rather stricken old lady, to a gradual halt, only metres away from him.

Finishing his text, remembering to mention the 'Charcoal Surprise', knowing his friend would like it as much as he had, he headed for home, having had enough excitement for one day, constantly thinking about what his friend had for him from the master mantra maker. Thursday evening couldn't come round fast enough as far as he was concerned.

Work was fairly routine, with absolutely no sign of Manson whatsoever. He didn't even appear to be in the grounds of Cropptech, with no one having seen hide nor hair of his black Mercedes. His armed guards, or as Peter like to think of them, gun toting goons, still patrolled certain areas of the facility, making him more than a little uncomfortable, but without Al Garrett's help, there was absolutely no way to remove them.

Using up a little of his accrued flexitime, he finished an hour early on Thursday, keen to meet up with Tank and find out what was going on. He didn't have to wait long before the doorbell of his house rang. He opened the door to be greeted by his friend's big toothy smile.

"Evening!" declared Tank, squeezing past Peter into the narrow hallway.

"Come on in, why don't you?" replied Peter jokingly, as Tank swept down the hall.

Sitting down opposite each other in the living room, Peter couldn't contain his eagerness any longer.

"Come on then... spill it. What's the old shopkeeper got for me?"

"First things first," interjected Tank. "Guess what I managed to get hold of?"

Peter just wanted whatever it was that Gee Tee had sent Tank to deliver. He wasn't in the mood to play guessing games. Shame. He'd have really liked this one.

"I don't know. Please can I have whatever it is that Gee

340

Tee's sent?"

Tank waved a finger at his friend, admonishing him for being so impatient.

"I have something way better than anything the old dragon's sent you. Three things in fact," he said raising his eyebrows.

Peter became suspicious.

'Three things', he thought. 'Hmmmm.' Then it dawned on him.

"NO WAY... YOU... YOU... HAVEN'T, HAVE YOU?"

"Yep," quipped Tank, pulling three large golden tickets from the inside of his jacket pocket. "Three tickets to the Grand Final of the Global Cup, to be held in Australia on Sunday the 6th of November."

Peter was flabbergasted. He took one of the tickets from Tank's mighty hand and gazed lovingly at it. It was genuine, all there in gold and white, tickets to the final of the Global Cup between the Flaming Fire Crackers and the Indigo Warriors. After a few seconds of worshipping the ticket, he leapt up in the air to celebrate and then, grabbing his friend's hand, shook it furiously.

"You are the absolute best, man. I can't thank you enough. What do I owe you?"

Tank shook off Peter's comparatively feeble grip and smiled.

"You don't owe me anything. The tickets are on me. Let's just all three of us go to the game and watch the Warriors become champions of the world."

"Agreed," Peter added, handing back his ticket to Tank. "Perhaps you'd better hold on to all the tickets, for safekeeping."

"Sure thing," said Tank, taking the ticket and putting all three back in the inside pocket of his jacket. Once the tickets were safely tucked away, he pulled out a leather bound parcel wrapped in delicate twine that was about the size of his fist. Gently, he passed it over to Peter. Holding it with both hands, Peter asked Tank,

"What is it?"

"Typically, I don't know. You'll have to open it to find out. Gee Tee said that it would help you wrestle back control of Cropptech."

Carefully, Peter untied the twine and then slowly unfolded the creased green leather. Inside lay a black fabric pouch, tied at the top, with a crinkled up note in the old dragon's handwriting beneath it. Holding up the pouch, he looked at it with one hand, while picking up the note and reading it with the other.

Peter,

Having applied my considerable brilliance and knowledge to your current predicament, I have used all the resources available to me to create a broad based multi-adaptive cure for the poison that you believe currently affects the owner of Cropptech based on the success of the mantra used to cleanse the house of the now deceased Mark Hiscock. The powder in the pouch stems from an ancient Egyptian antidote to an airborne plague. Combined with the mantra at the bottom of this sheet, the result should be an almost immediate reversal of the poison's effects. The powder has to be in the immediate vicinity of the individual concerned, i.e. on their clothes, hair, etc. Once the powder is dispersed the mantra should be chanted as powerfully as possible, out loud. As previously mentioned the reversal should be almost immediate. Please don't let this information fall into the wrong hands, as this powerful mantra in only known to a handful of dragons still in existence. Good luck with your task.

Your friend

Gee Tee

Poison and evil, out you shall seep,

The infections you caused while good people did sleep.

Purification, is nature's good way,

Of making sure, that gone you will stay.

Peter handed Tank the note, as he continued to study the fabric pouch, knowing that Gee Tee wouldn't mind his apprentice seeing what was written, in fact he was sure the old shopkeeper would count on that happening.

One of Tank's huge hands clasped onto Peter's shoulder, not quite surprising him enough to drop the fabric pouch, he was still holding on to.

"Well my friend, looks like all your problems might be solved by this," Tank commented, holding up the letter from his boss. "Douse Al Garrett with the powder, use the mantra and BANG, things are back to normal, Garrett can get rid of Manson and you'll be a big hero."

Taking the letter back from Tank, Peter carefully put it and the fabric pouch into the top drawer of the old wooden sideboard that stood along one side of the room, considering his friend's remark.

"The last thing I want to do is be a hero, as you well know," said Peter, clipping his friend playfully behind the ear. "I just hope though, it's as simple as you make out. Nothing would make me happier than curing Garrett and returning Cropptech back to the way it should be. Guards running around toting machine guns should be reserved for Hollywood, not Salisbridge."

"Perhaps you're letting your imagination run away with you, and just perhaps it will be as simple as all that. Don't over complicate things, and don't worry about things that haven't come to pass yet. Concentrate on the things YOU have control over. That's how you'll win, that's how things will get back to how they should be," urged Tank, getting up out of his chair. "Anyway, I have to go. I've got to pick up some coaching kit from the sports club as I'm coaching at one of the local schools tomorrow afternoon."

Peter shook his friend's hand on the way out, and they agreed to catch up later on in the week.

Drifting off to sleep that night, Peter's mind continued going over and over the eventual use of the mantra and powder on Garrett. Each time it ended with success, a fit and well Garrett once again controlling Cropptech, with Manson nowhere to be seen. It was all going to be soooooooo easy... at least in Peter's dreams.

He awoke the next morning, rested, more so than he had been in a little while, and vaguely able to remember snippets of his dreams, all of which centred around curing Garrett of the poison. During breakfast he toyed with the idea of taking Gee Tee's cure with him to work and keeping it there in his office, so that if an opportunity presented itself to get to Al Garrett without Manson around, he was fully equipped to go ahead with the plan. After much consideration, he decided that it was just too risky to keep it at work, and that he should concentrate on finding a way to track Manson's movements so that he could approach Garrett without fear of him getting in his way. So far he'd had little luck with the computer program he and Tank had developed, with Cropptech's mighty mainframe rebuffing it at every opportunity, but just maybe he could apply it in a different way to try and help keep tabs on the dreaded Major.

Over the next few working days he worked furiously to try and find a way to get to Garrett with Manson out of the way. Using the CCTV surveillance system seemed to be utterly useless, as his previous investigations had found out, and was no better at the moment with his nemesis popping up in unexplained places that he just shouldn't have been able to, bypassing some cameras while being caught by others. Speaking to the secretary in charge of the entire top floor, asking for a copy of Garrett's schedule, something he used to be given on a regular basis before Manson arrived, she told him in no uncertain terms that he did not need to know that particular information.

The break he was looking for only came late on a Friday afternoon. Having phoned across to the guard room to ask one of the managers for some much needed information regarding next week's duty roster, he'd been told by the lady on the phone that said manager was off the premises attending a meeting. She stated that had Peter checked the scheduling software that the company used on its main computer, he would have known that to be the case, and not be wasting her time. That's when it hit him. The scheduling software was the answer!

Over the moon, he apologised to the lady on the end of the phone, thanking her for helping him solve a much bigger problem, much to her bemusement. For the next hour, Peter busied himself on his computer, sifting through the scheduling software with a fine toothcomb, eventually coming to the conclusion that his program just might work, with just a little reconfiguring. Unlocking the drawer to his desk, he picked up the dark blue memory stick with the program on it and attached it to his key ring. Remembering to pick up his lunch and jacket, he headed home.

Friday night was spent in front of the computer, trying to put the finishing touches to his computer program. Not one to go out very much apart from with his friends or the hockey team, which normally meant a Saturday night, it was no different from what he normally did. Working well into the night, he finally stopped, pleased at his slow and steady efforts. His technical abilities were there, they were just more suited to taking the computer apart and putting it back together, rather than playing with lines of code. Letting out a series of yawns, he figured it was time to hit the sack, in the hope of getting some rest for his away game of hockey the following day.

The weekend didn't pan out quite the way he'd hoped. By his standards, he had a very poor game, with his side losing 4-1, their worst defeat of the season so far.

Monday came round, and as Peter drove through the security gate into Cropptech, he couldn't help feel a little guilty about the program contained within the memory stick attached to his key ring, even though he had the best interests of everyone in the company at heart.

Once in his office, he got on with all the relatively boring tasks associated with his job: emails, filling in log books, checking the CCTV system and its backups, were just a few of them. By late morning, most of the mundane tasks were out of the way, so he carefully uploaded his program. Almost instantly he knew it was going to work, because the mainframe hadn't blocked it in any way, shape or form. His alterations to the program now meant that it would only attach itself to the scheduling software, something the mainframe clearly considered little or no threat at all.

Feeling more than a little pleased with himself, he decided to treat himself to lunch in the staff canteen, something that had become a rarity since his little run in with Manson's gun toting maniacs.

Logging out of his workstation, he made sure to lock his office door, something he never usually did, before walking round to the other side of the building to see what was on offer for lunch. As soon as he caught sight of the decorative coloured writing on the giant chalk specials board, he knew exactly what he was going to have.

'Steak fajitas... ummmmm,' he thought, his stomach rumbling as he grabbed a tray and joined the back of the queue. With each step forward, the sound of the sizzling steak, onions and peppers became louder, the smell of the sumptuous dish more intoxicating. Eventually it was his turn. Smiling as the friendly staff gave him the fajitas and the sizzling hot skillet, he knew he'd made the right decision to come to the canteen. So pleased was he with his lunch, that he totally forgot all about the program left running on his computer. Leaving the canteen some forty five minutes or so later, he took a roundabout route back to his office, hoping he might bump into Richie, wary of meeting Manson. He didn't see either, but ended up having a leisurely stroll through the site, burning off just a little of his delicious lunch. Upon returning to his office, his thoughts turned to the computer, which he quickly logged back on to. He couldn't believe his eyes.

'Success!' he thought. His program had searched the entire scheduling database and had found exactly what he was looking for. On Friday 4th of November, just a little over three weeks away, Manson was scheduled to attend the Annual Security Awards of the Year dinner, on behalf of Cropptech, at a hotel in London. Starting mid-morning, the event was supposed to go on well into the evening. It was ideal.

'Maybe just a little too ideal,' he thought suspiciously.

Spending the next ten minutes on the internet double checking that the awards were genuine and were due to take place on the date that he'd seen in the scheduling software, he was delighted when it did indeed check out.

Over the next half hour he erased any trace of his program, tucking the memory stick back on his key ring before getting on with his mundane work, happy that everything was going to be cleared up and better within the month. Disappointment with just a hint of helplessness played on his mind at the fact that he had to wait so long to put his plan into action. Part of him wondered how much further downhill Garrett would go in that time. He had everything he needed, he just lacked the opportunity for three more weeks. Frustrated as he was, the more he pondered, the more it seemed clear that the best thing was to wait until 4th November when Manson wouldn't be in a position to ruin things.

* * *

Listening to the guards surrounding his truck bark out orders in a language he didn't understand, despite not being able to speak Russian, he knew from his many trips here that everyone was agitated. All the guards were alert, with most having at least one hand on the machine guns that they wore over their shoulders. None were smoking.

'That,' he thought, 'is a tell-tale sign that the tension is higher than normal.'

Once again, ice started to form on the inside of the windscreen. Reaching over, he turned the fan up to its most powerful setting, hoping against hope to keep the ice at bay. This was the part of the job he hated most... the waiting! In this most foreign of places, it wasn't just cold, it was absolutely FREEZING! When you mention Siberia to anyone, they immediately think of cold, snow, ice. But until you've actually been there you can't imagine how cold, desolate and bleak it really is. In some ways it's almost like another planet.

A quick glimpse in the side mirrors showed the forklift trucks, with their orange flashing lights, loading the cargo carefully into the back of his lorry. Soon, he told himself, soon he would be able to go. At least he would be away from those damn guards. No matter how many times he'd been here, they always gave him the creeps, regarding him with some degree of suspicion, even though he was almost a regular, having done this dozens of times before. He, on the other hand, thought they all looked the same, steely jawed, lean with just a hint of stubble around their faces, all seemingly smokers.

A sharp knock on the window jolted him out of his reverie. A guard waved a clipboard at him, with some documents on it. Instinctively he depressed the button to operate the electric window on the cab's door, but of course, it did nothing.

'Damn cold!' he thought.

Pulling up the hood on his jacket, he opened the door and grabbed the clipboard from the guard. The cold assaulted the inside of the cab, forcing all the warm air out after only a few seconds, the guard taking a perverse pleasure at this. Quickly he checked and signed the documents, waiting for the guard to give him his copy. Reluctantly the guard did so. Shutting the cab door, all the time watching the ice re-form on the inside of the windscreen, finally he heard the double doors of the container being slammed shut. From the side mirrors, he could see the forklift trucks retreat back into the warehouse, their jobs done. Once again the guard slammed his gloved fist onto the window, but this time indicated with a wave that he should get going. Not needing to be told twice, he engaged first gear and began crawling very slowly forward in the fresh snow. About halfway to the main gate of the facility, just when the heater had once again started to win the battle with the ice on the inside of the windscreen, his escorts appeared on either side of the snow laden track he found himself on. Nothing unusual there, apart from the fact that on previous trips there had only ever been one or two top of the line Range Rovers accompanying him. This time there were four, each full to the sunroof with guards.

'Wow,' he thought. 'Something must be going on.'

Holding the jinking steering wheel with one hand, he flicked on the interior light and pulled out his copy of the documents, giving it closer inspection. It took him a while to find what he was looking for. Once again he was transporting 'laminium', whatever that was. The only difference he could find this time was the fact that there appeared to be more than four times the amount of any of his previous trips.

'Come to think of it,' he mused, 'they were a long time loading up,' and the normally cooperative truck he was driving did seem a little more sluggish and unresponsive.

By now, the first Range Rover had reached the security barrier at the main entrance, and the driver showing his paperwork to the guards was waved through quite quickly, by Russian standards that is (about five minutes). As one, the convoy headed out, the snarl of the diesel engine just making itself heard over the howling wind, with two Range Rovers in front and two behind. As with the previous trips, the Range Rovers would shadow him from Magadan (his current location) through Siberia, beyond Moscow, leaving only at the Russian border with Belarus. From there another security contingent would accompany him through Belarus, Poland, the Czech Republic and on to Germany and France before the final leg to England, and then back to the processing plant at Salisbridge. All in all, the journey should take about three weeks, depending mainly on what sort of weather he encountered across Siberia.

'Oh well,' he thought, as snow started to pepper his windscreen, 'it may not be the Caribbean, but with the sort of money that Cropptech are paying me, at least I'll be able to afford to retire there.' The convoy disappeared into the snowy wilderness, carrying their rare and valuable cargo towards its final destination.

*　　*　　*

Back in Salisbridge, Peter was busy keeping his head down, doing his job and just trying to blend in. Secretly he couldn't wait for Friday 4th November to come round so that he could implement his plan to cure Al Garrett and return Cropptech back to normal. In everything that he did at the moment, he tried exceptionally hard to just look normal and not arouse anyone's suspicions, not wanting to do anything that would spook the ex-army Major and change his plans. Manson had to attend that awards ceremony. Everything depended on it. So here he was, resigned to all the new changes in the company and avoiding his nemesis like mad. He'd been doing this for the best part of a week now, and was quite sure he had perfected his 'I'm disappointed with the situation, but have agreed to accept it' face. It was, he was sure, the same face about ninety percent of the workforce wore as they got on with their daily business. Only a few people ever smiled in the complex, mostly visitors, or those gun toting maniacs armed with machine guns, who patrolled only certain parts of the facility. Theirs was more a psychotic grin than a smile though, as if they would really love to open fire on someone breaking in.

'Anyway,' he thought, 'all I have to do is blend in with the unhappy workers for two more weeks and then it will all be over, and everything will be back to normal.'

Later that week during breakfast, he sent out his consciousness to retrieve the latest edition of the Daily Telepath, as he hadn't seen one in a while and was behind on what was happening deep down in the dragon domain. As his mind reached its destination, he became aware of a message flagging itself up to draw his attention to it. Finding the paper, with his consciousness he grabbed hold of the message and the paper, and commanded them both to return. Storing the Daily Telepath to read later, he immediately took a look at the message. It was from Councillor Rosebloom, demanding an update on what was happening at Cropptech. Caught up in everything that was happening at the moment, he'd totally forgotten to keep in touch with the councillor about the situation.

'Damn!' he thought.

As he ran the message over and over again in his head, cursing the fact that he'd virtually forgotten all about the vengeful Rosebloom, he noticed that instead of the usual, basic message, this was one of the new fancy ones that he'd read about, that had an attachment to add a reply to, much in the same way as an email. Knowing that Rosebloom would be aware of him having picked the message up, he decided to make use of the new automatic reply function. Composing what he thought of as a proper reply, he checked it over one last time before adding it to the message. It read:

Councillor Rosebloom,

Thank you for your brief message. Rest assured I have been working tirelessly to resolve the issue at Cropptech that I mentioned to you when we met in your office. All is going well and on track. The whole issue should be resolved to a satisfactory conclusion on 4th of November and I would hope that Cropptech itself would be restored to its former glory very shortly after that.

Regards,

Peter Bentwhistle

Satisfied that it contained just the right amount of information, Peter used the automatic reply, keeping an eye on it until it was just out of range. Chucking his breakfast bowl in the sink, he grabbed his sandwiches and raced off to work, hoping his lateness wouldn't attract any unwanted attention.

Time passed slowly over the coming weeks. All he could think about was 4th November and getting everything right. It became something of an obsession, ruining his concentration and even the love of his life... hockey! Or for that matter, a once in a lifetime trip to Australia to see his team compete in the Global Cup Final. Not even the fireworks display which he'd agreed to go to with Tank and Richie at the Sports Club on Saturday 5th November could float his boat, even though the event itself sounded fantastic with a barbecue, fairground amusements, bonfire and well organised display of top notch fireworks. Normally he'd be looking forward to it a great deal, but nothing could distract him from this most important of tasks. Deep down inside himself he got the feeling that curing Garrett and returning Cropptech to normality was essential to... well, to... everything.

Eventually Thursday 3rd arrived, and as he'd done for weeks, he kept a low profile. Nothing extraordinary happened. On edge, he kept thinking he'd be found out. Nerves were getting to him, which in itself was unusual. It was the first time he'd ever really known what real pressure felt like. All that stuff back in the nursery ring was nothing compared with this. Lives depended on him, and he got the feeling that it wasn't just Garrett's. Continuing to tell himself that everything was going to go as planned, once or twice during the day he caught glimpses of Manson on the security cameras. Studying the pictures intensely, no matter how hard he tried, he couldn't find anything out of the ordinary. The ex-army Major seemed to be going about his business as he would on any other day. As well as the security footage, he also kept checking the scheduling software, checking that Manson's appointment at the awards dinner wasn't either cancelled or changed. Peter left at his normal time to head home, and as he drove under the barrier at the security check point and waved casually to the guard on duty, sweat poured down the back of his neck. He'd be glad when all this was over, and by this time tomorrow night, hopefully it would be.

After tea and one or two household chores, he packed Gee Tee's dust in his jacket pocket, so as not to forget to take it to work the following day. He was as restless as he'd ever been. Unable to concentrate, he tried reading a book, listening to music, watching the television, all with about the same success. Finally he switched off the lights and retired to bed, drifting off to sleep much as he normally would. However, his dreams were far from pleasant. They looped around into one, all featuring him trying to cure Garrett and failing miserably, whether it was because he was late, or had lost the dust or had used the dust and muttered the wrong mantra. His dreams pointed to failure, and when he awoke the following morning he was more tired than he could ever believe. As he sat bleary eyed, eating his breakfast, he kept telling himself that they were after all only dreams and that they meant nothing. Nothing at all.

Double checking everything, he set off earlier than usual, aiming to get there just before the first shift change at about seven thirty. Nobody would think it odd, as sometimes he was called in then anyway. Keen to get in early to make sure that if Manson had stayed overnight (which apparently he sometimes did, although where, Peter had absolutely no idea, despite his best efforts to find out) that he and his car left to go to the awards ceremony, knowing that once it had gone, it would be safe to approach Garrett in his office and administer the cure. Reaching Cropptech at twenty past seven, he parked in a very empty looking car park in which, of the five hundred spaces available, fewer than forty were currently occupied, due to the early hour. The reason he'd chosen this one was that Manson liked to park his black Mercedes in it and sure enough, not sixty yards away, that very car sat, parked all on its own, just a solitary street light illuminating it on this dark and frosty morning.

Peter shivered as he crossed the car park, not only because of the cold, but at the thought that his nemesis could be sitting in that darkened car, watching him right at this very moment. Had he misjudged things by parking here? Was it a dreadful mistake to alter his schedule and come in so early? As these and many other thoughts, all negative, raced around his head, his breath froze as he exhaled, sending a series of shivers down his back and along the tail he so often thought he still had in his human form. His office was toasty warm, so much so that he was able to dispense with his jacket and hang it on the back of the door, aware that the cure for the poison, his mobile phone and the *alea* which he had taken to keeping in a pocket or his car rather than attract undue attention by wearing it round his neck in plain sight, were all tucked away in the inside pocket. Getting on with some work, all the time keeping an eye on the security monitor that flicked between the different car parks, he hoped to see the exact moment Manson left. By his estimation, he would have to leave no later than half past ten to give himself enough time to get to the awards venue. Only when he was sure Manson was out of the way, would Peter put his plan into action.

Clock watching furiously all morning, by ten o'clock the Mercedes was still parked in the same place. Despair welled up inside him. What if Manson didn't go? What if Al Garrett went with him? What if Garrett was already off site somewhere? All this circled Peter's head as he sat at his desk, waiting for the monitor to flick back round to the car park with the Mercedes in it. He'd pinned all his hopes on this one opportunity. When the hell would he get another chance to get Garrett alone, without Manson anywhere to be seen?

Just as his hopes of Manson leaving the Cropptech site

looked to have been crushed, the monitor flicked back to the car park that held Peter and Manson's cars. Leaning in close, he could just make out the driver's door on Manson's black Mercedes being slammed shut as the camera tuned into that particular car park. A small puff of smoke coughed from the exhaust as the car speedily made its way to the front gate. Standing up from the bank of monitors, Peter bounded over to his window that looked out on the security lodge, eagerly watching the black Mercedes as it approached the security barrier. The guard on duty stood up straight, recognising the car, a good sign as far as Peter was concerned. After a few seconds the barrier was raised and the Mercedes shot off, turning out into the main road at speed, paying little attention to oncoming traffic from either direction, almost killing an unwary cyclist in the process. Peter let out a long sigh of relief. Everything, it seemed, was back on track, he thought to himself smugly.

Having decided days ago that it would be prudent to wait at least half an hour to be sure that Manson didn't come back, he spent the time mainly staring out of the window, peeking through the blinds at the main gate, hoping never again to see that black Mercedes. Every now and then he would glance at his watch, checking to see how much time had elapsed since Manson had left. Dialling down the control setting on the radiator; despite how chilly it was outside, he could feel himself getting hotter and hotter, due mainly to the anxiety of the situation. After half an hour had elapsed, he checked that he had the antidote and that he knew the mantra and, leaving his jacket with the *alea* and his phone hanging on the back of the door, started out towards the top floor.

With nothing to lose now, he took the most direct route to Al Garrett's office, slowing down for no one. Once in the lift, he checked his reflection in the its polished, mirrored walls. Sweating profusely under his arms, around his neck and, although he couldn't see it, he could feel the beads of sweat running down his back, almost as if they were competing in their own Olympics.

With a 'ding', the lift door jolted him back to the present. Stepping out onto the plush carpet, he smiled at Garrett's personal secretary. She reacted with surprise on seeing Peter. As he approached, the expression on her face turned from surprise to outrage.

"I'm afraid Mr Garrett is unavailable at the moment," she stated snootily. "My understanding, Mr Bentwhistle, is that you are no longer allowed on this floor."

Peter was prepared for this, thrusting a handful of papers in her direction.

"I'm afraid there's been some sort of error in the payroll department," he lied calmly. "My department's overtime for last month hasn't been sanctioned due to some kind of mistake on their part. I've spent all morning redoing the paperwork, and it just needs to be authorised so that I can get it to payroll before midday. If it misses the deadline, my staff will have to wait another month to get their money, not something most of them can afford to do in this financial climate, especially with it coming up towards Christmas, as I'm sure you can appreciate."

As Peter stood stock still, waiting patiently with a smile on his face, the secretary's face grew into a suspicious kind of frown, her eyebrows looking as though they were two caterpillars involved in some kind of secret mating ritual.

"I really am under strict instructions that Mr Garrett is not to be disturbed for the rest of the day," she said with a genuine hint of regret in her voice.

Like a well trained actor, Peter let out a long, deliberate sigh.

"All I need is Mr Garrett's signature. I won't be more than sixty seconds." Peter could see the secretary wavering and thought to himself,

'Gotcha!'

"Think of all those loyal Cropptech staff who would be short of money if this isn't done by midday." Leaning in close to the secretary, almost overwhelmed by the sickly smell of her overbearing perfume, he did his best to try and close the deal. "I'm sure you wouldn't want it known by the staff that it was your fault that they had to wait an extra month to get their hands on money that was rightfully theirs," he suggested menacingly.

Watching the conflicting emotions play across the secretary's pale face, he was sure he'd done just enough to get to see Garrett. After a few seconds of consideration, the pale face turned into a snarl.

'Oh no,' he thought. 'I've totally misjudged it.'

"You've got two minutes. Get his signature and get out," she countered forcefully, pointing her thumb towards the door of Al Garrett's office.

Peter nodded and smiled politely.

"Thank you," he said as he walked past her desk. She muttered something under her breath that even with his enhanced senses, he still couldn't quite pick up.

Reaching the solid oak door, he gave a short knock before going in. Once again the room was very dark. The overpowering smell of... evil, assaulted his nose in waves that made him feel physically sick. He knew there and then that it had to end now. And it would, in just a few more moments.

Approaching Garrett's desk, the 'bald eagle' was sitting in his high backed, black leather chair, taking little notice of anything going on around him. Peter shook his head in disgust.

'No one should be put through this,' he thought. 'I was willing to let Manson go his own way, but the more I see, the more I think he should be locked up for a very long time.'

Reaching the desk, he leant over towards Garrett. His boss's bloodshot eyes didn't move at all, even though he waved his hand in front of Garrett's face. Again, no reaction. Seeing him in this state sent spikes of anger surging up Peter's spine.

357

'How could anyone do this to another human being?' he thought. 'Well, no more. It ends now, once and for all.'

Walking around the desk until he stood behind Garrett's high backed chair, Peter slowly took out the pouch containing the powder, promising,

"It will soon all be back to normal," as he did so.

"Well, well, well, what do we have here?" asserted a low voice from the far corner of the room.

Peter nearly jumped out of his skin, that's how startled he was. Gripping the pouch tightly in one hand, he turned to face the darkened corner. From out of the darkness stepped his worst nightmare... MANSON, cane in one hand, drink in the other.

'What the... ?' thought Peter. 'I could have sworn this room was totally empty.'

Garrett's head swivelled at the sound of Manson's voice, his first discernible sign of movement since Peter had entered the office.

Pulse racing, a million questions fluttered through Peter's mind, all about how and why Manson was here. Pushing them away with a mighty effort, he focused fully on what needed to be done.

'Manson is over ten feet away,' he thought. 'All I have to do is cover Garrett in the powder, recite the mantra and it's all over.'

Poised to act, Peter took a deep breath. Suddenly the sound of a faint click resonated from the other side of the office. Peter turned to find that the huge book shelf that had covered all of one wall had slid back to reveal two of Manson's smirking guards, both toting machine guns in his direction.

'Oh crap!'

"No sudden moves now Bentwhistle," commanded Manson in a tone of pure evil. "It would be a crying shame if we had to fill you with holes."

Quickly reassessing his situation with the emergence of the guards, he knew he had little choice but to comply with the ex-army Major, at least for now. Even with his enhanced dragon abilities, he knew he would stand very little chance against two machine guns: maybe in dragon form he might fare better, but that was something that really wasn't going to happen, possibly ever again if he didn't keep his cool and use his head. So he stood totally and completely still behind Al Garrett's chair, holding the pouch with the antidote in it in one of his outstretched hands.

"Now you see, Mr Garrett, what has really been going on here. I told you I would get to the bottom of things and this I think you'll find is as far down the bottom, with all the scum and the slime, that it's possible to go."

Manson walked over and put his drink on Garrett's desk. The old man's head followed his every movement. Peter remained stock still, aware not only of the machine guns levelled at him, but also of the sweat once again racing down his back. Abruptly Manson slammed his fist down on the desk, causing even the very sedated Garrett to jump slightly in his chair. Peter remained motionless.

"This is the reason why you feel so ill," barked Manson, leaning down addressing Garrett, while at the same time pointing up towards Peter. "This... degenerate... is the reason you feel so overwhelmingly bad. He's been sneaking in here and poisoning you, day after day."

Peter wanted to protest. He wanted to grab his boss by his sagging shoulders and shake him until he could see what was really going on. But the two guards looked more nervous with every second that passed, as they continued to train their weapons on him. Manson continued.

"You still don't really trust me, do you Alan?" he scoffed. "Still in your poor health you think that I have something to do with all that."

BOOM. Manson slammed his fist down on the desk once again.

Peter closed his eyes, praying that the sudden shock wouldn't cause one of the two maniacs with the guns to open fire accidentally.

'Manson seems really out of it,' he thought. 'Not so much drunk, as... angry and obsessed with something.'

Manson grabbed Garrett's chin and forced the old man to look him in the eyes.

"I can prove it to you, you know. I can prove that it was this little worm that's been making you ill."

Still with a million things running through his head, Peter wondered exactly what Manson had in mind.

Stomping angrily around the desk until he stood in front of Peter, swiftly Manson grabbed the pouch from the young dragon's outstretched hand. All Peter could think was,

'Oh boy am I gonna get it for wasting Gee Tee's precious powder.'

Manson waved the pouch in front of Garrett's remarkably unresponsive face.

"This is what he's been poisoning you with. And I shall prove it."

Peter let out a very silent breath of air.

'At least this won't catch me out,' he thought, knowing that without the mantra, the powder was totally benign.

Marching over to the unoccupied area between Garrett's desk and the door, Manson pulled the drawstring loose. Suddenly he cast the contents into the air and to Peter's utter amazement, muttered the exact same mantra that he himself had memorised. Not knowing what to make of anything now that Manson had uttered those words, all that he could think was that without a dragon's magic, the words wouldn't mean a thing. Unfortunately he was more wrong than he could ever have believed possible. From out of nowhere the benign powder lit up like tiny fireflies as it wriggled and shimmied through the air, sparkling in almost every conceivable colour. It only lasted a few seconds but it was hypnotic. The damage had been done. From Garrett's worn and weary face, two bloodshot eyes turned and looked up at Peter with resentment and disbelief. The guards having also seemed a little sceptical before, now looked meaner than Peter could ever have thought possible. Part of him could understand that. If he'd thought that someone was poisoning his boss (and they were) he'd want to put a stop to it as fast as possible, with probably as much force as possible. He just couldn't get his head around what was happening. How did Manson know the mantra? More importantly, why did the mantra work? Did he have magic? Was he a dragon, or something else? What the hell did this mean for him? Nothing good, that was for sure. He reached one conclusion, very quickly. He needed help, and he needed it now. Richie! Of course, that was it. He could contact Richie telepathically and let her know what was going on. At the very least, he could get her to come up here and interrupt things.

Clearing his mind, he concentrated intently on his surroundings as he reached out, looking for one amongst hundreds in the throng of Cropptech workers. Abruptly, panic threatened to squeeze him into submission. Not only could he not sense Richie, but he couldn't sense anyone outside this room, despite knowing they were all there. Garrett's secretary was only twenty five feet away in the corridor, with forty or fifty other staff working on this level, let alone the hundreds of others that worked below them, but try as he might, he couldn't sense a single one of them. Concentrating again, pushing the panic aside, he felt the minds of the two guards, alert and deadly, having no hesitation about shooting him, should he warrant it. He sensed Garrett, weary, dejected and... dying. Letting his mind drift towards Manson, all he felt was a cold, dark void, filled with anger, despair, revenge and destruction. It was only then that he realised the trouble he was in.

As the remains of the powder drifted down onto the thick carpet, the shimmering finally fizzled out to nothing. Manson strode over to the front of Garrett's desk and looked straight into his bloodshot eyes.

"You see... it's true. He came here to poison you. What else could it be?"

Again, Peter found himself biting his tongue, desperately resisting the urge to try and tell Garrett everything. For his part, Garrett looked up into Manson's face and gave a small but telling nod. Things, it seemed, were about to get a lot worse.

Manson twirled round, arms open wide, a deeply disturbing smile etched onto his face.

"So now it would seem that everybody knows exactly what's been going on, what on earth are we going to do with you?" he chuckled, scratching his chin.

Peter knew better than to reply to Manson's rhetorical question. Whatever he had in mind, he was sure his fate had already been decided and wasn't about to give the goons an excuse to open fire.

Walking around Garrett's desk once more, Manson opened up the top drawer, pulling some plastic binders out from inside. Like big white cable ties, he proceeded to wrap them around Peter's wrists, after forcing his hands behind his back. Peter had no choice but to comply, with the machine guns firmly focused in his direction, instead he'd decided to wait for an opportunity, which he desperately hoped would come.

"There, that's better," bragged Manson, merrily, turning to address the guards with the machine guns. "Escort our ex employee off the premises immediately. Do not stop for anyone and only at the main gate can you cut the binders off him. Do not, and I repeat do not, take him to his office, and do not linger. Take him to the main gate by the most direct route. Get one of the plods from security to fetch his car."

"Yes sir," the guards said in unison, whilst both nodding at the same time. The meaner of the two grabbed the binders behind Peter's back, thrusting him forward towards the office door. Stumbling and nearly falling, he only just managing to regain his balance at the last moment.

"Well... it's been fun. Let's do this again sometime," Manson taunted from somewhere behind him as the guard opened the door to the corridor, the lift, and a very startled secretary who was surprised to see him in restraints being frogmarched out by two armed guards. Like him, she had assumed that only Garrett had been in the office.

Looking straight ahead as he walked past the secretary, he stopped in front of the silver lift doors as one of the guards pressed the button for the ground floor. Despite everything that had gone on in the previous few minutes, despite the dismal failure of what he'd been trying to do and the fact that he'd wasted Gee Tee's precious antidote and discovered that Manson was much more than he seemed, the only thing on Peter's mind right at this very moment was hoping beyond hope that he wasn't frogmarched by these goons past Richie at any point on their journey to the front gate. He didn't think he could face the shame of seeing his friend from this position.

Sliding silently open, the lift doors reminded him briefly of the monorail, as he stepped in, the guards hot on his heels. Travelling downwards, Peter noticed the guards' expressions in the mirrored surround... clearly they were enjoying every second.

Sliding effortlessly open on the ground floor to reveal a large office that was shared by the accounts and marketing departments, Peter stepped out of the lift, wrists bound, followed closely by the two guards, their guns pressed firmly into the small of his back. Looking down at the floor for the first few silent steps, he wondered how long it would take people to realise what was going on. As it happened, not long. Not long at all. About five paces into his walk through the open plan office, he heard the first gasp. It was very quickly followed by more and more, a whole lot of chattering and whispering echoing around in the background.

"Keep moving," grunted one of the guards, while at the

same time slapping Peter in the back with the butt of his gun. Clearly wanting to demonstrate the power he held, the move had the desired effect, as the whole office fell silent.

'You could hear two brain cells rub together,' Peter thought, continuing on his journey. 'Oh well, that counts out either of the two muppets behind me.'

Looking straight ahead, he recognised many faces, some that he'd come to think of as friends. Their expressions ripped his heart to shreds, with the looks of disgust and hatred seeming to penetrate his entire being.

'Please, please, please don't let Richie see me like this,' he thought, reaching the exit on the far side of the office.

The corridors that led towards the security gate were busy thoroughfares, and this morning was no different. Again Peter saw people that he knew, and again their faces registered much the same expressions. Ushered out into the cold November air, he was just glad not to have bumped into Richie. Crossing the road, he looked all around him. On all floors of the main building that he'd just exited, he could see people crowded at the windows, peeking through blinds, looking to see what was going on. Exactly the same thing seemed to be going on at the security gate, where people he'd been responsible for were scrabbling for a view through the vertically slanted blinds. Looking horrified at Peter being frogmarched towards them, the two guards on duty didn't know what to make of the machine guns pointed directly into his back. Peter shook his head trying to warn the men, who he knew reasonably well, not to make a fuss and just do as the goons asked.

"YOU," shouted one of the goons behind Peter. "Get his car keys from his pocket and bring his car round... NOW!"

"What the hell is going on?" demanded the guard on the gate that had just been spoken to.

Peter took a deep breath, and spoke just before the

goons could provoke the guards, his friends, any more.

"It's okay. Just do as he says. My keys are in my left trouser pocket."

Reluctantly the guard came over and took Peter's keys.

"It's parked in car park B," added the young dragon in disguise.

The guard nodded an acknowledgement and headed slowly off towards the car park, not really knowing what to make of events. Peter could see the other gate guard, a burly man called Owen, who he'd known since he'd started, was starting to get anxious. Mouthing to him to just calm down and not make a fuss, he hoped the goons behind him wouldn't notice.

"Raise the security barrier," one of the goons said bluntly to Owen, the remaining gate guard.

"Raise the security barrier... PLEASE," said Owen sarcastically.

It was all Peter could do not to laugh, despite the seriousness of the situation.

"Do it now!" demanded the other goon, waving his machine gun from side to side for effect.

Owen just stood there, arms crossed. In that moment, Peter gained a new found respect for his friend and colleague, vowing to himself that should things ever get back to the way they were meant to be, that is with Garrett back in charge and him returned to his old position, he would definitely make sure Owen got a well deserved promotion. With what felt like the whole world looking on, the tension of the situation was unbelievable, but eventually the goons decided, probably because of everyone watching, to accede to Owen's request.

"Raise the security barrier... please," mumbled one of the goons, giving Owen the eye.

After much consideration, Owen looked across to the gatehouse and gave the sign for the barrier to be raised. As the red and white striped barrier began its ascent, Peter was shoved forward so that he was on the other side of the barrier. Just then his car came around the corner, the other gate guard at the wheel. It slowed to a halt right beside Peter, with the guard leaving the engine running. In one swift motion, one of the gun toting lunatics reached down into his boot and pulled out a rather vicious looking knife. Putting his hands on the back of Peter's neck, the guard bent Peter forward and sliced through the binders, letting them drop to the floor in the middle of the road, before shoving Peter forward with his foot in the small of his back, hurling him towards the open car door.

"Don't come back if you know what's good for you," the goon spat as he and his mate turned and headed back towards the main building.

Feeling the gaze of hundreds of people on him all at once, he looked up, only one person catching his attention. There, at the top of the building was Manson, gazing down at him, looking oh so pleased with himself. Peter turned away and got in his car, tears by now, streaming down his face. Smashing his hand against the plastic dashboard angrily, he kept that picture of Manson in his mind.

'It's not over,' he vowed. 'It's soooooooo not over.'

15 FAWKING HELL!!!!!

It was raining, blowing a gale and even in the cab of his lorry his breath froze as he exhaled. But by goodness it was great to be back in England, even on this bleak November day. His truck trundled over the bumps in the ramp as he departed the ferry at Dover. Up until now, his journey had taken over three weeks, and even though he'd done the same trip at least a dozen times before, this one had been by far the most arduous. The Siberian weather had been unseasonably bad, even by Russian standards, which was really saying something. It was the first time on all his trips that he'd been thankful for the military style escort that he'd been given, as the guards in the convoy accompanying him had had to dig his truck out on more than one occasion during the trek across Russia. Heading out of Dover on the A20, he flicked the radio on to his favourite station, Radio 2, and looked forward to spending some quality time with his wife and two children. All he had to do now was negotiate the M20, M25, M3 and A303 and then he would be back at the Cropptech site in Salisbridge. With any luck he would be back there for six o'clock, an hour or so to unload his valuable cargo, and then he would be home in time to read his children a bedtime story. He couldn't wait.

* * *

Turning the key in the front door, Peter walked dejectedly through the hall and into the living room. Slumping down on the sofa, he felt more than a little sorry for himself, not even remembering having driven home. Oh, he knew that he'd done it, he was here of course, but he couldn't remember any of the details. It had all been done on autopilot. Holding his head in his hands, he wondered solemnly just where it had all gone so wrong.

He'd lost his job, blown the chance to save Garrett and restore Cropptech to its former glory, and wasted Gee Tee's rare and valuable antidote.

'At least things can't get any worse,' he thought.

After a few minutes, it might even have been half an hour, as time seemed to have lost significance, he turned on the television, choosing to watch the sports news, hoping to take his mind off things. It didn't work though. Unhappiness and the lack of a decent night's sleep the previous night seemed to hit, both at the same time, like a giant bulldozer on a building site. Before he knew it, he'd fallen asleep, television still blaring in the background, grey, dreary daylight shining in through the windows.

Much later, he awoke in a room lit only by images from the animated screen. It took him a few seconds to clear his head.

'Oh pants,' he thought. 'It wasn't just a dream after all.'

With the muscles in his neck and back sending waves of pain up and down his spine, he sat up. Falling asleep on the sofa wasn't the best way to catch up on sleep, he reflected, forcing his body to get up and turn the lights on. Pulling the curtains shut, the day's events came flooding back to him in a moment of crystal clear clarity. Shuffling into the kitchen, all the while rubbing his sore back, he closed the blinds and tried hard to ignore the grumbling noises his stomach was making. How could he eat at a time like this? But of course, he was deep down... a dragon. And that is one of their specialities, no matter what the circumstances.

With the events at Cropptech stuck in his head like pins in a pin cushion, he suddenly wondered why he hadn't heard from Richie. She was, after all, bound to have heard what happened even if she hadn't witnessed it firsthand. Odd! Then it dawned on him.

'Crap! I've left my jacket there. It's got my phone and the *alea* in it. Oh this is so bad.' No wonder he hadn't heard from Richie. She almost certainly would have tried to contact him on his mobile.

Returning to the living room, instead of sitting down he paced around the coffee table wondering what to do. Of course, he could ask Richie to get it for him, but she might get into trouble or worse, with Manson on the loose. Another option would be just to phone up and ask for it to be left at the gatehouse for him to pick up, but that would draw attention to it, something he desperately wanted to try and avoid given that the *alea* was in the jacket pocket.

'I could always go back there myself,' he mused. 'Yes, that would be incredibly bright after today's events.'

Sitting down, he leant forward, theatrically banging his head on the coffee table for effect. After a few seconds of intense pain and nothing becoming clearer, he sat up and thought,

'I really need to clear my head before I decide what to do next. Hmmm... time for something to eat methinks.'

With that, he perused his favourite takeaway menu, before phoning up the Indian restaurant and ordering some food. He loved Indian food, something he had developed a taste for long before taking up hockey, with it now having become so much more than that ever since. Nearly every other Saturday, one group or other from the sports club could be found heading for the local Indian restaurant for a curry. Having ended up tagging along on more than one occasion, he'd found the experience... well, memorable for more than a few reasons. The witty banter and drunken antics had opened his eyes quite a lot the first few times. Although he was over fifty years old, most of that time had been spent well below ground, hence in many ways he was still relatively naive when it came to many of the social aspects of human culture, but he did, however, really enjoy the post sport curry. He'd never really gotten into going around all the pubs and clubs just drinking until you passed out. That, to him, seemed a complete waste of time. But there was just something about sitting down and having a meal with your friends, no matter how intoxicated they were, that just really appealed to him. The last time he'd been dragged along for a curry, he'd been surprised to see Tank and Richie there, when entering with his teammates. Tank was there with his rugby team, and Richie, having nothing better to do, had got in on the action, which was something that happened on quite a regular basis, he'd subsequently found out.

That night had turned out to be one of the most memorable of his relatively (in dragon terms) short life. Hockey and rugby lads, plus Richie, had all joined tables, spending the entire night swapping drunken anecdotes and playing silly drinking games, much to the bemusement of the staff and other clientele. What made it really special though was the fact that he'd shared it with his two best friends.

Anyway, every couple of months or so he would treat himself to a takeaway, hence the menu. Forty minutes later the steaming hot food arrived, and after having paid, he wandered into the kitchen, inhaling deep breaths of the delicious smelling cuisine that he carried.

Unlike most, he found that his preferred options from the menu were usually those dishes without very much sauce, in particular, anything with Tandoori in the description. Having ordered chicken tikka, onion bhajis, keema naan with poppadoms and onion salad, he had to use two plates for the enormous feast. The next hour or so was spent chomping away in front of the repetitive sports news.

Some time much later he sat, bloated, on the sofa, full to the brim with delicious Indian food, contemplating what he should do next. With his mind whirring at full speed, he started to wonder how someone else in his position would handle things. Hindsight made him feel as though he'd been a bit of a pushover, having never really confronted Manson when maybe he should have. Perhaps Manson was just another school bully who needed to be met head-on, or to have his bluff called. Anyway, it was too late for that now. But just maybe it wasn't too late to stop being a pushover. Turning off the lights in the living room, he silently berated himself for not having done the washing up, vowing to himself that he would no longer be *that* pushover. And with that thought roaming around the empty space between his ears, he went to bed, hoping that a solution would present itself in the clear light of morning.

Waking up early, just after six, amazingly he felt bright, awake and full of energy, instead of the normal, sleepy, grumpy and reluctant to get up. Perhaps subconsciously his body knew it was November 5th because for weeks he'd been looking forward to going to the fireworks display at the sports club with Tank and Richie, despite the ongoing worries about Manson. Shooting downstairs, he switched on all the lights, deciding to keep the curtains closed in an attempt to ignore the cold and dark outside. Cleaning up all the mess from the night before, his thoughts turned to the Cropptech situation. He hadn't woken up with a solution buzzing around his brain, but things did seem a little clearer. He no longer felt the pressure and loneliness that had seemed to consume him up to and including yesterday. Up until now, he hadn't even realised that it had been affecting him so much. Only now could he see things for what they really were. He also felt renewed, invigorated and full of self confidence. His decision last night to no longer be pushed round must have had some deep down psychological effect.

Halfway through cleaning the plates, the weather forecast appeared on the television, so he stopped and watched, wanting to know if the hockey or the fireworks display were going to be affected. After a minute or so it became clear the weather man was stringing it out, with a ground frost the only thing to report, rain sleet or snow nowhere near a possibility for at least the next few days. 'Good news for the fireworks display' he thought, cheerily, continuing to tidy up.

Focusing his mind on what to do about losing his job and getting his jacket, phone and *alea* back, he was more than a little aware that he was supposed to be playing hockey and then meeting up with his friends. Buried at the back of his mind was a thought about contacting Councillor Rosebloom, to let him know what had happened, but that was something he wished to avoid like the plague for as long as dragonly possible.

By the time he'd finished breakfast, he'd decided what to do. He knew that if the right people were manning the security gate this morning, then getting his jacket back from his office, or ex-office now, would be relatively straight forward. Unfortunately it would be very difficult to find out who would be working without actually going there. So, he'd decided that his best course of action would be to drive his car to the nearby housing estate and then, in his running gear, go for a run along the main road that passes Cropptech's main entrance. If he wore a hooded top, nobody would know that it was him, and hopefully he would be able to get a good look at who was on gate duty.

Satisfied he was doing the right thing, he downloaded today's Daily Telepath, carefully reading all the stories on the front page:

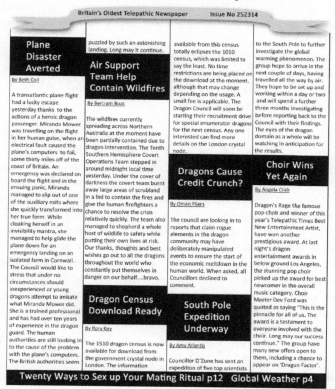

Brand New Delia Dragon's Delicious Charcoal Recipes Inside p8

The Daily Telepath

Britain's Oldest Telepathic Newspaper   Issue No 252314

Plane Disaster Averted

By Beth Coil

A transatlantic plane flight had a lucky escape yesterday thanks to the actions of a heroic dragon passenger. Miranda Mower was travelling on the flight in her human guise, when an electrical fault caused the plane's computers to fail, some thirty miles off of the coast of Britain. An emergency was declared on board the flight and in the ensuing panic, Miranda managed to slip out of one of the auxiliary exits where she quickly transformed into her true form. While cloaking herself in an invisibility mantra, she managed to help glide the plane down for an emergency landing on an isolated farm in Cornwall. The Council would like to stress that under no circumstances should inexperienced or young dragons attempt to imitate what Miranda Mower did. She is a trained professional and has had over ten years of experience in the dragon guard. The human authorities are still looking in to the cause of the problem with the plane's computers. The British authorities seem

puzzled by such an astonishing landing. Long may it continue.

Air Support Team Help Contain Wildfires

By Bertram Boat

The wildfires currently spreading across Northern Australia at the moment have been partially contained due to dragon intervention. The Tenth Southern Hemisphere Covert Operations Team stepped in around midnight local time yesterday. Under the cover of darkness the covert team burnt away large areas of scrubland in a bid to contain the fires and give the human firefighters a chance to resolve the crisis relatively quickly. The team also managed to shepherd a whole host of wildlife to safety while putting their own lives at risk. Our thanks, thoughts and best wishes go out to all the dragons throughout the world who constantly put themselves in danger on our behalf....bravo.

Dragon Census Download Ready

By Rory Key

The 1510 dragon census is now available for download from the government crystal node in London. The information

available from this census totally eclipses the 1010 census, which was limited to say the least. No time restrictions are being placed on the download at the moment, although that may change depending on the usage. A small fee is applicable. The Dragon Council will soon be starting their recruitment drive for special enumerator dragons for the next census. Any one interested can find more details on the London crystal node.

Dragons Cause Credit Crunch?

By Omen Pliers

The council are looking in to reports that claim rogue elements in the dragon community may have deliberately manipulated events to ensure the start of the economic meltdown in the human world. When asked, all Councillors declined to comment.

South Pole Expedition Underway

By Amy Atlantis

Councillor D'Zone has sent an expedition of five top scientists

to the South Pole to further investigate the global warming phenomenon. The group hope to arrive in the next couple of days, having travelled all the way by air. They hope to be set up and working within a day or two and will spend a further three months investigating before reporting back to the Council with their findings. The eyes of the dragon domain as a whole will be watching in anticipation for the results.

Choir Wins Yet Again

By Angela Crab

Dragon's Rage the famous pop choir and winner of this year's Telepathic Times Best New Entertainment Artist, have won another prestigious award. At last night's entertainment awards in below ground Los Angeles, the stunning pop choir picked up the award for best newcomer in the overall music category. Choir Master Dev Ford was quoted as saying "This is the pinnacle for all of us. The award is a testament to everyone involved with the choir. Long may our success continue." The group have many new offers open to them, including a chance to appear on 'Dragon Factor'.

Twenty Ways to Sex up Your Mating Ritual p12   Global Weather p4

Half an hour later he changed into his running gear, making sure to choose his hooded top. His new found confidence raging through him, he bounded out to his car, dressed to run. Driving to the housing estate that backed onto the Cropptech site, for the first time he could remember, he felt... carefree and happy.

Parking in one of the estate's small car parks and

making sure not to leave anything valuable in plain sight, he pulled on his hooded top, did a few calf stretches for effect and then set off towards the main road at a light jog. A couple of minutes later he found himself running alongside the road on a narrow strip of tarmac, grass and weeds on either side of him, most nearly coming up to his knees.

'Hmmm,' he reflected, 'only a madman would choose this route for a run. Oh well, with any luck nobody will know it's me and I can retrieve my jacket and be back in the car in quarter of an hour.'

Focused desperately hard on the tarmac in front of him, convinced that if he lost concentration for even a moment it would mean a twisted ankle or worse, something he most certainly could do without, the long curve in front of him opened out to reveal the turning into Cropptech in the distance. Twenty five yards further up that turning, the daunting red and white barrier that he'd associated with a peaceful work environment up until yesterday's cataclysmic meltdown, sat firmly in its down position, directly in front of the security gatehouse building. Glancing down at his watch, he pretended to be an ordinary runner, concerned with their time. As he got closer and closer, one thought in his head stood out above all others.

'Odd! Nobody manning the gate on the outside and although I can't be totally sure, it doesn't look as though there's anyone on the inside either.'

His pulse was racing, and it wasn't anything to do with the running that he'd done. Standing about on the corner of the turning, twenty five yards or so away, his face masked by his hooded top, he pretended to catch his breath and stretch out the muscles in his calf. Like a beautiful Italian fountain, his mind was overflowing, not with water but questions, ones that he could find no answers for.

'It could be a trap,' he thought, 'but nobody knows I'm

here. Why would the gatehouse be left unmanned? In all my time, I've never known that to happen, even if there's an emergency in another part of the facility, it should still under no circumstances be left unattended.'

His new found confidence wavering just a little, he thought back to last night and his vow not to be a pushover anymore. So straightening up, he walked briskly towards the open window of the gatehouse, adjacent to the security barrier. After a fleeting look to check that nobody was about, he stood on tiptoes and peeked through the open window. Able to see most of the open plan office, it looked as though nobody was there, but that didn't mean it was totally deserted. Someone could be in either of the toilets or the storage bay right at the back, all of which he couldn't currently see. As a shudder raced up the invisible tail that he always felt he had, he could only think that it was... very odd! Still worried that it might be a trap, but not really seeing how, he opened the white double glazed door and stepped inside. Looking past the water cooler and the hefty photocopier, the corridor was decidedly empty.

"HELLO!" he shouted. "Is there anyone there?"

No response. He did exactly the same thing again, with no reply. Cautiously, he edged his way down the corridor, pausing at the two toilet cubicles to check inside. They were both empty. Continuing up the corridor until it widened out into the office, it was clear there was nobody about. Odder than that though, was the fact that none of the office equipment was switched on. Computer screens were blank, printers silent, with the in tray beneath the fax machine full to overflowing with faxes that needed to be dealt with as a matter of urgency. Walking across to a secure metal door on the far side of the office, he stopped in front of it and once again knocked.

"Anyone there?"

Still no reply. Gingerly, he turned the handle, knowing that there was no way on earth that it would be unlocked. Much to his surprise... it opened. This in itself was enough to make the hairs on the back of his neck stand up. This door was always kept locked. Always! Something was desperately wrong here, he knew, but he had no idea what it was, or what to do next. Walking into the security bay, he inspected the bank of lockers that stood like soldiers at attention down one side of the room. Uniforms, handcuffs and truncheons all lay scattered on the cushioned benches that ran down the other side. The whole place was like a ghost town. What should he do?

Exiting the storage bay, he decided to head on over to the main building to see if anyone was over there. Providing there was, he could let them know about the situation here even, he supposed, if it meant revealing his identity to them.

'The security of this site is much more important than any one person,' he mused, as he started back up the corridor towards the double glazed doors. Just then, through the open window, he heard a large vehicle pull up outside the gatehouse.

'Great,' he thought. 'Just how am I going to explain this away?'

Through the window, Peter heard the vehicle switch off its engine. Prepared to go and meet the driver with a view to explaining the situation, suddenly he heard voices from outside. Instantly his blood, which in his true form was green, abruptly ran cold.

'Oh please no. Anything but this,' he thought, panic surging through his body, every last shred of confidence shattered like a mirror. It was MANSON!

Caught halfway along the corridor he froze, paralysed by fear, not knowing what to do, only able to listen to the voices coming from outside.

"You're late!" barked Manson.

"Only a few minutes," came the disinterested reply.

"I don't pay you the kind of money you're earning to be late," threatened Manson, with an edge like a razor to his voice.

"Lighten up will ya?"

"I'll lighten up when our business is concluded. I strongly suggest you concentrate on what it is that I'm paying you for, or not only will I see that you don't get the remaining fifty percent of your payment, but I will quite literally light a fire beneath your arse," spat Manson, leaving no one in any doubt about how he felt.

"Okay, okay... no need to get all silly about things. We'll just do what you say. No problem."

"Make sure you do," demanded Manson, with more venom than most deadly snakes.

"I'll raise the barrier. Take the trucks round to the loading bay. I want everything to run like clockwork from now on. Just think, in a matter of hours, you'll have been paid, and I'll be long gone."

Footsteps with a slight limp outside on the concrete, headed his way.

Stuck halfway down the corridor with few options, Peter slid into the nearest toilet, letting the door close gently behind him. As he did so, he heard the unmistakable sound of the double glazed doors opening up.

Cornered in the tiny toilet, he racked his brains for anything that would help his current situation. In a flash of brilliance like none he'd ever known before, it came to him. Silently, he put down the lid on the toilet itself and clambered on top of it. Reaching up, he slid one of the polystyrene ceiling tiles out of position. Through the gap where the tile had been, as he'd suspected, ran a series of thick pipes. Knowing that time was of the essence and that almost certainly he only had one shot, he closed his eyes, bent his knees, and with just a hint of extra dragon power, launched himself upwards through the hole, towards the pipes. Grabbing the largest with both hands, ignoring the searing heat, he swiftly pulled himself up so that he was crouching on a series of much smaller pipes. Leaning over as far as he dared, he pushed the polystyrene ceiling tile back into place. Just as it fell perfectly back, he caught a glimpse through the tiny, diminishing gap of somebody opening the door from the corridor. Refusing even to swallow, he remained totally still in the pitch black hidey hole that he found himself in.

'Whoever it is, they're still there,' he thought, as sweat poured down his back and neck, while he tried to remain silent.

Abruptly, a voice echoed down the corridor.

"What's the hold up? You alright in there?"

The toilet door swung closed. Peter could hear Manson on the other side of it.

"No hold up. Just checking the place is totally empty," he told the impatient truck driver. "I'm raising the barrier now."

From his hidden position in the ceiling, he could just make out the sound of two trucks starting their engines and then carefully moving off. A minute or so after that, he heard the outside door open once again and then close. With all his heart he hoped that Manson had now left the gatehouse, but having been deceived before, he was in no hurry to get down from where he was, just in case. As he remained precariously crouched on the pipework, a small smile crossed his face, despite his rather dire predicament.

He knew about the pipes running above the tiles in the toilets because of an incident that happened shortly after he joined Cropptech. To this day, he remembered it quite vividly. At the time, it was the talk of the security department. One of the most popular guards was on a nightshift during the week, who was renowned for his pranks and good natured practical jokes. With nearly all the security staff having a decent sense of humour, the guard in question found himself to be quite popular, people generally appreciating the stuff that he got up to. On the particular night in question, the prank playing guard found himself on duty with a colleague he'd worked with for years, and a trainee that had only started with the company two weeks earlier. As the night wore on, the prank playing guard plied his longstanding colleague with as much tea and coffee as he could. Just when his colleague was bursting to use the toilet, the prankster disappeared, supposedly to do his rounds. What he actually did was dive into the men's toilet, and do exactly what Peter had done. He removed the polystyrene ceiling tiles and hid above the toilet cubicle, waiting to surprise his friend, knowing it was only a matter of time before he would need the loo. As it turned out, he didn't have very long to wait at all. Barely a few minutes later, the toilet door opened and somebody entered. As the cubicle door closed and the lock slid shut, the prankster could barely contain his laughter at the thought of the surprise he was about to dish out. Hearing his friend below start his ablutions, the prankster slid back the tile, and in his loudest voice shouted "BOO!" The shock couldn't have been greater for both of them. It wasn't his friend that jumped up in fright, but the timid trainee. He had, quite literally, ... himself, a fact that everybody found amazingly funny when recounting the tale, some days later. Unfortunately for the prankster guard, the trainee had absolutely no sense of humour whatsoever, and despite many, many apologies about what had happened, he ended up leaving Cropptech shortly after, but not before making sure he got some compensation for his trouble. This in turn led to a company policy of no pranks, something rumoured to have displeased Al Garrett greatly, although he'd had little choice in the matter. After that, the prankster guard was never quite the same, and he left some months later to take up a new post at another company.

Crouching in the dark in that exact same spot, he found it hard not to laugh at the thought of the poor trainee being surprised.

'Just a shame that it couldn't be marketed as a laxative,' he thought, grinning.

The dim night light on his watch told him that nearly

an hour had passed, as he crouched for all he was worth on top of the array of pipes. Having been there so long, despite his dragon abilities he'd started to get cramp in his legs, something he couldn't use his magic to cure, which was proving to be particularly difficult in such a tight space.

Most young dragons naively believe that when they assume human form, they will be immune to such simple things as cramp, nose bleeds, headaches and dubious bowel movements, but it just isn't so. To create the kind of form that will withstand time and everything the human world has to throw at it, dragons have to manipulate their DNA to such an extreme that it is very difficult on first inspection to detect that they are anything other than human. Only a very experienced surgeon or a series of vastly complicated blood tests would confirm that the subject is something other than a human being, and even then, it would offer no clue as to what they actually were. Some dragons have been known to manipulate their DNA to fool all known blood tests, actually appearing one hundred percent human. Amazing really. So although Peter was struggling with cramp, it wasn't the first time, and he was pretty sure it wouldn't be the last.

'Hmmmm,' he wondered as the muscles in his legs convulsed with pain once again, 'whatever's waiting for me, whether a trap by Manson or an empty building, now's the time to find out.' Carefully sliding the ceiling tile back to reveal the cubicle below, he swung both legs over, ignoring the blistering pain, and jumped down onto the toilet itself, trying to make as little noise as possible, all the time expecting a dozen armed guards to burst through the door and do their worst. Needless to say that didn't happen, and after a few minutes of stretching, he felt much more confident about getting out in one piece.

Cautiously, he opened the door into the corridor. A wave of relief swept over him as he saw that it was deserted. His first instinct was to bolt for the door, and then run back to his car to get help. But what kind of help would he get? If he called the police, what would he tell them? That he was trespassing on private property and had seen the head of security letting two lorries into the site.

'Oh yes... very suspicious,' he thought sarcastically. He couldn't go to the authorities, he couldn't go to Garrett, and even if he knew exactly who to turn to in the dragon world, the chances were that Manson would be long gone by the time help arrived. What really didn't help matters in Peter's mind, was the fact that nobody knew where he was, and without his mobile phone he couldn't even call Tank and Richie to let them know what was going on, not that they'd necessarily believe him anyway. So for all intents and purposes, he was well and truly on his own. As he strolled back to the open plan offices in the hope of finding some security monitors that worked, he reflected on everything that had happened, coming to only one conclusion.

'If it means being on my own to take Manson down... then so be it.'

After two or three minutes of rooting around, it became clear that all the monitors had been sabotaged. Trying everything he knew and more, ten minutes later, he'd managed to get one meagre camera, showing different views of all the car parks, back online. Watching carefully, not noticing anything out of the ordinary at first, it was only after the third rotation that it became apparent something was going on at the distribution depot. Fork lift trucks were whizzing around, on a Saturday when the entire thing should have been locked up tight. On top of that, the whole area was littered with Manson's guards... the ones with the machine guns. Things had just got a lot more serious.

Heading back into the security bay at the back of the building, he picked up two pairs of handcuffs and a baton as well, just about all he could carry given he was still in his running kit. Not that it would do much good against a machine gun of course, but it was better than nothing at all.

Back in the open plan office, he stopped at the nearest desk, lifted the phone's handset and depressed the button for an outside line. Just as he suspected, there was no dial tone, just a long constant buzz.

'Oh well, figured as much,' he thought. 'Worth a try though. At least Richie and Tank would have known where I was.'

Strolling out of the gatehouse, heading for the entrance to the main building, the chilly November air battered his surprisingly underdressed body as he carefully circumvented each and every security camera, just in case someone somewhere was watching. It was unlikely given that the monitors in the gate house had been sabotaged, but not entirely out of the question. With the main doors firmly secured, he stealthily skirted the building looking for another way in, but was thwarted at every attempt. Everything had been locked down tight. In his wildest imagination he couldn't see how to get in, other than to transform into his natural shape and walk through a wall. It hadn't quite come to that yet, but he would bear it in mind for later on.

It had been worth a try to get into the main building, if only to get his phone and *alea* back, but with his options running out, he had little choice but to head for the distribution depot. Deciding on the long way round, hoping that the cameras and guards would be fewer and further between, he set off, using anything he could for cover, in an attempt to avoid confrontation wherever possible.

Avoiding the car park cameras proved more of a challenge than Peter would ever have thought, but thanks to some creative diving over ornamental hedgerows and a very long crawl beneath a series of portacabins, it wasn't long before he found himself concealed by an overhanging tree, overlooking the back of the distribution depot. The much smaller car park at the back of the depot was all but deserted, except for an unmarked, white van, its tailgate hanging down. No doubt the trucks he'd seen on the monitors were still around the front of the depot, the fork lifts continuing to load up. Deciding to wait and see if anyone was actually in the back of the van or whether it was being loaded up regularly like the trucks at the front, he knew he was going to have to cross the expansive car park in order to gain entrance to the back of the depot. If anyone at all was about, they would spot him immediately.

Waiting just over ten minutes before deciding it was clear, starting out at a sprint, he hoped his luck held. Zipping across the car park, he stopped at the side of the van, putting it between him and the back entrance. Breathing quietly, he listened carefully for any noises coming from inside, but it was totally silent. Gingerly, he slipped along the side until he stood right next to the lowered tailgate. Very slowly he peeked around the corner and peered into the back of the van. Lying inside was a massive leather... what could only be described as a harness. It looked as though it had been insulated against the cold, like a giant parka coat. Attached to the harness on either side, all folded up, were two gigantic nets. Instead of being made of rope, they appeared to be constructed of pliable metal. It was astonishing. Most astonishing though was the size. It was undeniably colossal.

'What the hell could carry a harness like that?' he thought, his brain a muddied mess.

His thoughts were abruptly interrupted by two figures from his past appearing from the other side of the van.

"Well... look who it isn't."

His stomach felt like he'd just jumped off the Empire state building and was currently in freefall. Temperature threatening to spiral out of control, his head felt like it was spinning faster than a fart in a hurricane. There, not three feet away, were two of the bullies from his nursery ring: Theobald and Fisher.

"So Benty, what would you be doing here on this cold, winter's day?" asked Theobald.

Trying desperately to focus his mind, he wondered what he was going to tell them. Would they even believe him? Had some help arrived, even if it was in this most unusual of forms? He felt so confused, so very light headed. He had to get them to help him; it was his only chance of bringing Manson to justice.

Turning towards the two of them, opening his arms wide in a show of friendship, he tried to appeal to their better nature.

"Guys, I know we've had our differences. But we really need to put them aside for the moment. There's something much more important going on here," he pleaded.

Theobald and Fisher frowned simultaneously.

"Such as?" prompted Fisher.

Putting his arm around the shoulders of them both, something that repulsed him deep down inside, he drew them back out of sight of the depot. Pulling them in close, he lowered his voice to a whisper.

"Something really bad is going on here. I'm not exactly sure what, and what I do know would take too long to explain, but I really need your help, both of you."

Fisher and Theobald both looked at each other, the same confused expression masking their faces.

"This is really, really big guys," continued Peter. "I'm sure the dragon Council will be very grateful for your help. VERY grateful," he added, hoping to appeal to their selfishness, knowing that if they helped him and thwarted whatever it was that Manson was up to, the Council would almost certainly reward their efforts in some way, shape or form. At this point, he was even willing to give them his share of anything that might come their way.

"Tttthhhheeee... the Council know you're here?" stammered Fisher nervously.

"Oh no," replied Peter without thinking, "nobody knows I'm here. All I was saying is that once the Council find out how much you've helped me with this, I'm sure they'll reward you both."

As he'd been speaking a strange, menacing look had formed on Theobald's face. Just a split second too late, he realised what he'd just told them. That nobody knew he was here, especially anyone from the dragon Council. Stepping back from the two of them, convinced he'd just made one of the biggest mistakes of his relatively short life, Theobald and Fisher stood and glared with evil intent. Preparing to turn and run for his life, without warning a sharp pain exploded on one side of his head and, as he started to fall to the ground, his last sight was the image of Theobald and Fisher both laughing, before darkness consumed him.

*   *   *

Cold gnawed at his very bones... it hurt everywhere. Summoning up every ounce of strength in his body, he rolled over onto his side. Slivers of light illuminated the dark space he found himself lying in. Trying to push the excruciating pain to one side, he attempted to recall what had happened. Moments later, it all came flooding back to him. Miserably, he let out a long breath, which immediately condensed in front of him. Fighting against the pain, he tried to sit up, only then realising his hands had been bound behind his back, presumably, he thought, with one of the pairs of handcuffs he'd procured from the security bay.

Flapping around like a stranded fish, eventually he managed to roll into a sitting position, his hands still behind his back. With adrenaline and fear trying to give the pain a run for its money, logically, he tried to take stock of his situation. It looked as though he was almost certainly in the back of the white van that he'd been standing by before being knocked out. He deduced this partly from the fact that he was definitely in some sort of van, but also because lying on the floor at the other end from where he was sitting, was the harness that he'd first noticed when he'd looked into the back of the white van. Apart from that the insides, lit only from the light shining through the gaps in the tiny rear doors, were totally bare. His head throbbed badly from whatever had hit him.

'Almost certainly Casey,' he thought to himself.

With hindsight, he could see that it was odd that it was just Theobald and Fisher, and couldn't remember a time when it wasn't the three of them.

'That would also explain why I didn't sense the presence of anyone. A human, I would have sensed, but a dragon, well... I should have sensed them, but if there was magic involved, it would have been all too easy for me to have been blindsided. I'm such a fool,' he thought, overcome with a sense of complete failure. It was so obvious looking back on it now. Of course, Theobald, Fisher and Casey were in league with Manson. It made sense on so many different levels. Those three idiots were always after a fast buck. It would also explain how Manson was able to perform some of his so called 'tricks'.

'It wasn't him doing it,' thought Peter, 'it was Theobald, Fisher and Casey. Manson himself must just be some low life, common criminal, who has just employed the three stooges to help out.'

Although this moment of clarity about what had really happened had washed away the feeling of failure somewhat, the physical pain he felt was starting to become unbearable. Giving his all, he tried in earnest to break free of the handcuffs, something which in normal circumstances would take little or no effort, even for a young dragon. The cold, though, was affecting him deeply. Looking down, he studied his legs. Still in the same shorts and hooded top he had been knocked out in, he was horrified to see the skin on his legs had turned a pale shade of blue from the excessively cool temperatures. He hadn't been put in a freezer or anything, just dumped here. If that was the case, the cold he was feeling was just due to the fact that it was a chilly November day, and he was dressed in very little, meaning that he'd been here a fair few hours.

Looking round, he tried to check his watch, but only succeeded in seeing that it had been removed from his wrist.

'That's how cold I am,' he thought, 'I can't even feel whether I'm wearing a watch or not.'

Leaning back against the inside of the van, he tried to think warm thoughts in the hope that it would clear his head, even a little. The problem was... the cold! There was just no way he could access any of his dragon abilities while his temperature was this low. So in effect he was stuck, at the mercy of Manson or his nursery ring bullies, or both. Not a pleasant thought either way. Determined not to give up, he forced himself to topple over onto his back so that his head was facing the harness. Tears rolled from his eyes as an agonizing pain ricocheted through the fingers of his right hand. Wiping the tears on the side of his top, slowly he used his feet to scoot along towards the harness. It was only eight or so feet away, but it seemed like a mile as his cold wrists and back dragged against the dirty, freezing floor of the van.

Eventually, after two or three minutes, he reached the edge of the harness. Pushing himself up against the side of the van once more, he leaned forward to have a good look at the harness and all its fittings. Metal filaments, flexible and very tough, made up the netting. Every last part of the harness itself, from the straps to the linkages, was made from the highest quality leather. Nestled underneath was a giant, insulated, cocoon-like enclosure, fashioned from a dozen different sized, shaped and coloured high quality thermal jackets, a huge patchwork of very desirable arctic protection gear.

'I'm not sure I want to meet whoever knitted that thing together, or more importantly, who, or whatever it was intended for,' he mused, trying keenly to rub back some heat in his wrists, aware that he could feel blood running through his fingers.

With a goal in mind, he figured that if he could open up the cocoon enough, he might be able to snuggle up inside and get warm enough to access his missing abilities, all of course providing he remained bad guy free for long enough. As he managed to wiggle across the metal netting, once again causing a great deal of pain to his hands and wrists, at the same time leaving a smudged trail of blood, he noticed that the small slivers of light coming into the van from outside were slowly getting dimmer.

'Oh great... it's getting dark outside.' The only consolation was that he now had a vague idea about what time of day it was, and just how long he'd been unconscious for. Knowing it was starting to get dark turned his thoughts towards the fireworks display that was due to start at the sports club in about two hours' time. At that precise moment he'd have given anything at all to be there with Tank and Richie.

After what seemed like three hours, but his best guess told him it was more like half an hour, he'd managed to rip enough of the thermal material to create a gap wide enough for him to wriggle inside. Of course, getting in there was a whole different matter. After another twenty minutes of trial and error in the pitch black, he'd managed to get as much of his body in the cocoon as he was going to get. Using his teeth to close it up as much as he could, he curled up against the material, trying again to think warm thoughts in the hope that it would speed the whole process along. The temptation now was to fall asleep, something he was focusing on avoiding at all costs. The moment he had enough strength to break out of the handcuffs, he wanted to be free from all of this, and planned to get out of here as soon as was physically possible, with a view to leaving whatever was going on at Cropptech, firmly to the dragon Council. He would contact them as a matter of urgency, and let them deal with it.

Trying to keep track of time proved of little success, but after a while he was sure things were starting to warm up, because he was becoming drowsy and could all but feel the metal of the handcuffs chafing his wrists. In the haziness of his mind, he started to imagine he could hear voices. Voices that were gradually getting louder, or closer.

Startled fully awake, he realised it wasn't his imagination. There really were voices emanating from somewhere outside the van and disappointingly they were most definitely getting closer. Concentrating like mad, he gave everything he had in an effort to bring forth his dragon abilities into his frail and human shaped body. Flexing his arms, he tried with all his might to break the handcuffs restraining his hands behind his back. After a few seconds, it was clear that he was still too cold. Silently, he swore to himself as he waited for whoever the voices belonged to, to open the van's tailgate.

Closer now, Peter couldn't make out the exact words, but it sounded as though they were in a rush. Two doors opening, one after the other, became clear, quickly followed by them closing again shortly afterwards. With a lacklustre rumble, the van's engine jolted into life.

'We're going somewhere,' he thought to himself. 'I've still got a chance, as long as the journey's a reasonably long one.'

Snuggled up as much as he could in the giant patchwork cocoon, Peter hoped that the journey, wherever they were headed, would give him enough time to warm up. Right about now he found himself getting a little bit mad about everything. So much so, he was even contemplating turning into his dragon form, if he ever got warm enough to do so. Very unlike him. But he kept telling himself that desperate times called for desperate measures and that the dragon Council would fully understand, once they found out the full circumstances; well, just maybe they would.

As the van started to twist and turn, he tried to imagine where they were headed, every left and right turn played out in his mind, but truth be told, he was lost long before they'd even left the Cropptech site.

Trying feverishly to warm himself up, not knowing when the unexpected journey would end, he struggled as the handcuffs would only allow him to rub the tips of his fingers together as he slid about in the back of the van. Rubbing his knees and legs together, while at the same time massaging both his feet, he tried to have a positive outlook.

'Another hour like this and things will most certainly be looking up.'

But did he have another hour? All too soon he would find out.

* * *

At the sports club, the evening's festivities were just kicking off. Outside, a third of the massive car park had been cordoned off for numerous attractions that had just finished setting up. Small fairground rides stood alongside candyfloss stalls, hook a duck booths, tombolas and all sorts of heavenly food outlets from hot dogs to hog roasts.

In the bar, the atmosphere had been fantastic all afternoon, maybe something to do with the fact that every home side in each sport had all been victorious. Some of the sports players from various sections still remained, propping up the bar, watching the football results. Most, however, had gone home to pick up the rest of their family, and were only now returning for the fireworks. Tank stood at the bar with Richie, mobile phone held firmly to his ear. After a few moments, he returned the phone to his right pocket and turned to his friend, a worried expression on his face.

"Still no response. All I get is his answer phone and I've left about a dozen messages already."

Richie leaned in close to her friend, primarily to make sure they couldn't be overheard.

"I've left messages as well. I'd like to think he's just sulking, but I have to say I'm really not sure now. It's so out of character for him to miss a hockey match, unheard of in fact. And I think however much he's sulking, I'm pretty sure he'd have the decency to phone that captain guy... Andy, and let him know he couldn't make it, even if he had to lie and say he was ill or something."

Tank nodded in agreement, whilst taking a giant slurp of his drink.

"I went round to his house on the way here today," ventured the strapping rugby player, "but nobody was there. There was no sign of his car. I just thought he'd left early to go to the hockey and that we'd meet up here after our matches. But since you told me about him being sacked and escorted off the premises yesterday, I'm not sure what the hell is going on."

Placing her empty glass softly onto one of the cardboard beer mats, the lacrosse playing dragon considered her friend's words.

"I only found out this morning when I ran into one of my training staff in town," whispered Richie, waving past Tank to one of her lacrosse teammates who had just come in with her husband and two children, both of whom were carrying the biggest sticks of pink and blue candy floss she'd ever seen. "I've been away at the Guildford site doing some in house training for two days. Apparently it was the talk of the entire complex yesterday. I'm staggered, and more than a little gutted that I wasn't there. You can be damn sure things would have played out differently had I been."

Tank shook his head, taking the final swig of his drink. He bent down low and put his head beside Richie's.

"I've even searched for him telepathically," he murmured, "using one of Gee Tee's old mantras that can treble the normal range, but still no luck. I don't know what else to do at the moment, Rich. There's still time for him to turn up tonight. Maybe you're right and he's just sulking. Wouldn't be too much of a surprise, would it?"

The two friends parted heads and nodded at each other, before looking down at their empty glasses.

"More?" enquired Tank, raising his empty glass.

"Ohh, go on then," said Richie, rolling her eyes. As Tank caught the eye of one of the bar staff, the two friends laughed, hoping that Peter would at any second walk through the door and complete their evening by coming to watch the much hyped fireworks display.

* * *

Although he had no idea where he was, he knew for certain that the van he was in had just turned off the main road and was now negotiating a very bumpy track full of potholes, every one of which he could feel.

'This,' he thought, 'does not bode well.' A track off the main road almost certainly meant he was very near his final destination, and he was not nearly warm enough yet. Once again he tugged frantically at the handcuffs that bound his hands, but he knew even before he did that it was doomed to fail. Still he hadn't recovered enough to break free.

Moments later the van stopped. Peter lay wrapped in all the layers, as frightened as he'd ever been. Voices from outside once again resounded through the thin van walls. They seemed impatient, edgy almost. A fierce rage started to burn at him from the inside, bubbling up out of nowhere, threatening to consume every last part of him. It was so overwhelming, that all he wanted to do was go and destroy these... criminals. How dare they imprison him?! Even with the help of Theobald, Casey and Fisher, he should not find himself in this situation. Dark, desperate thoughts of what he could do to these men if he managed to change into his dragon form engulfed his mind. One powerful swipe of his wings would trash their sorry van.

He'd scare the living daylights out of each and every one of them, so much so that all the therapy in the world during their prison stay would not be nearly enough to counter their fear of him.

A fresh sound jolted him out of his wishful thinking. Another vehicle had arrived. No, make that two other vehicles. As he waited for the tailgate to be lowered and the doors to burst open, more voices joined in outside. With the seconds turning into minutes, the doors did not open. A tiny ray of hope washed over him. All he needed was a bit more time. Clearly these humans knew nothing, otherwise they would have dealt with him whilst he was at his coldest, or when he was unconscious. Listening carefully, there was more talking, followed closely by a loud squeaking noise, a bit like a rusty gate creaking open. One by one, all the vehicles started up their engines, including the van that he was trapped in. As the van lurched forward, he found himself once again thinking of his friends, who by now would be waiting to see the fireworks. He would have given anything to be with them at that moment, that or any shred of warmth. Close, but no cigar.

Starting off, swaying from side to side as it dipped in and out of ever more potholes, the van, much to his surprise, went back to being on a perfectly flat surface again. If they were back on a main road, which clearly didn't make any sense at all, but if they were, that could only be a good thing, he mused optimistically. That thought, and any hope that remained, was shattered only a few seconds later when the van came to a halt and turned off its engine. The sound of doors being opened and closed again reverberated through the chilly air, but that wasn't what terrified him the most, giving his shivers shivers of their own. It was the tailgates on the other vehicles being lowered.

'This is it,' he thought. Mustering everything he had, and using thoughts of his friends as motivation in the hope that it might give him that bit extra, he fought to bring forth the magic that was rightfully his.

'Damn, still nothing.' Close, so close. He could feel his power bubbling just beneath the surface, soooo very close, but agonisingly out of reach.

'Just a few more minutes,' he mused. 'Please let them ignore me for just a few more minutes. That might be enough.'

With darkness surrounding him, he rubbed his limbs frantically, knowing that even a few seconds might make the difference. He could hear the voices again, and they weren't far away. It sounded as though there were at least six or seven of them. While he was listening intently, trying to glean anything that would help him later, he could just make out... something in the background. It sounded like a... concert or something like that, but try as he might, he couldn't fathom the exact content.

* * *

In an all but empty bar, Tank and Richie finished their drinks. Hundreds of people, young and old, packed the outside patio area and the lacrosse spectator zone, waiting in anticipation for the bonfire to be lit and for the fireworks to start. Grabbing their jackets from their respective bar stools, the two friends headed for the open doors that led outside.

As they did so, the reflection of dozens of different coloured sparklers twinkled off the adjoining windows. The children, Richie noted as she stepped outside just in front of Tank, were all having a whale of a time, creating different patterns with their mesmerising sticks of fire that cut finely through the air in front of them, each and every one of them laughing their little socks off. As she watched, a pang of sorrow swept over her, which came as something of a surprise once she recognised it for what it was. Slipping her coat over her shoulders to protect herself from the biting cold, something she and Tank were more aware of than most here, she tried to understand what had stirred such powerful feelings inside her.

They stood at the back of the crowd, gazing over people's heads, waiting for it all to start. Children on their parents' shoulders rubbed their hands excitedly, each dressed in colourful attire. Richie, searching inside herself for some answers to the sudden onslaught of emotion, abruptly had a moment of clarity when it all became clear. Children! It was because of the children. It was so obvious now that she thought about it. Like a startling revelation, she realised that she envied all the humans, because of their... children. She wanted what they had.

'Oh my God,' she thought, 'as if it isn't bad enough that I play lacrosse, spend nearly all my time amongst them and engage in arm wrestling contests, but now like them, I want to have... children.' In her mind she pictured the entire dragon Council toppling over like dominoes when it was announced that a certain lacrosse playing female dragon wanted to have children just as the humans did, and raise them that way. A huge contented grin crossed her face as she cuddled up to Tank for some extra warmth.

They stood alongside everybody else, waiting patiently for proceedings to begin. From the look of things, the chairman of the sports club would be taking hold of the microphone on the hastily erected stage to kick things off, just after the music being piped through the PA system finished. Both friends continued to gaze out over the darkened lacrosse pitch to the barely visible bonfire beyond, that was about to be lit. On one side of the lacrosse pitch lay the churned up, muddy rugby pitch with its big floodlights, now of course turned off. If you looked carefully in the dark, the giant H shaped posts could just be seen. Over on the other side of the lacrosse pitch sat the now deserted Astroturf hockey pitch. Like the rugby pitch, the floodlights were switched off, to give everyone a better view of the fireworks. Although the hockey pitch was only fifty or so yards away, because of the absolute darkness that enveloped it, it might as well have been on a different planet.

*   *   *

The tailgate handle of the van squeaked as it turned. Terror raced fear up Peter's spine to see which one would win as the doors whooshed open, letting in a different kind of darkness to the one that he had experienced in the last few hours.

"Ahhhh... look, he's cuddled up like a little fluffy bunny," claimed a voice sarcastically, as the light of a torch played across Peter's face.

Out of the darkness two pairs of hands appeared and began pulling the metal nets attached to the cocoon towards the back doors of the van.

"Sorry fluffy," mocked the sarcastic voice once again as Peter clumsily slid towards it, "but we can't have you missing the big show. Boss's orders I'm afraid."

Wrapped up in the cocoon, slowly sliding towards the open door at the back of the van and goodness knows what kind of fate, he made one last concerted effort to free his hands from the restraints. To his utter astonishment, it worked. His hands were free, without anyone else realising it. More confident now that he was unshackled, he decided to bide his time and wait for the right opportunity to present itself. Things were looking up.

The last part of his exit from the van was particularly unpleasant. Two large pairs of hands gave a huge yank on the netting, speeding him up, and as he reached the tailgate an enormous fist caught him fully in the middle of his stomach, knocking the wind straight out of him, before he was unceremoniously dumped on the freezing ground. Trying to adjust his eyes to the new environment, all he could tell at the moment was that he was somewhere outside, as the sound of the cocoon that had sheltered him being ripped open assaulted his frozen ears. He wriggled around, acting as frightened as he could, so that no one would realise his hands were free.

'The longer no one suspects,' he thought, 'the more time it buys me to find the right opportunity.'

As he was pulled free from the last shredded fragments of the patchwork of coats, a large hand grabbed his shoulder and sent him tumbling towards the floor, face first. Midway through his fall, he managed to spectacularly roll around, landing on his back, concealing the fact that his hands were no longer bound. Landing with a huge bump, his hands took the brunt of the impact. Pain scampered up both his arms, causing him to let out a little squeal, much to his captors' delight. However, it wasn't the pain up his arms that caused him the most concern. It was the fact that the skin on the back of both his hands had been burnt off quite badly as he'd landed. He recognised the sensation immediately; after all, he'd been experiencing it for nearly two whole years now on a regular basis. He was on an Astroturf pitch!

'What the hell is going on?' he wondered, through the pain and the cold biting at his body.

He wouldn't have to wait very long to find out.

* * *

Meanwhile, not a million miles away, Richie and Tank cuddled up to each other in their big thick coats, watching as the chairman of the sports club thanked the usual people for their help in making the display possible. Drifting on the cold, misty air, the aroma of sizzling hot food wafted over the crowd from the stalls at the front of the building. Stars lit up the sky like diamonds atop a black velvet cloak, with not a cloud in sight. Everyone's breath froze as they exhaled, most of the young children absolutely fascinated by it. For a dragon, even dressed from head to toe in warm clobber, none of this was particularly pleasant. Every time the two friends pulled in a deep breath, it felt like they were inhaling a swarm of hungry insects nipping away on everything on both inward and outward journeys. Dragons, you have to remember, are comfortable in exceedingly high temperatures, with their flames generally agreed to be somewhere in the region of 800 degrees, so by comparison it's quite understandable that a temperature in minus figures would cause very different effects in a multitude of different dragons. Some can withstand the cold, suffering only slight irritability, while others suffer extreme pain, in some cases passing out altogether. Tank and Richie both seemed to lie somewhere in between the two extremes.

Finishing his speech, the chairman started to count down on the microphone, the children all joining in as loudly as they could. Approaching five, more adults started to join in. 4... 3... 2... 1...

Exactly as planned, the bonfire erupted into life, clearly enhanced by something very flammable. A dreamy look crossed the two friends' faces at exactly the same time, as they both gazed lovingly at the bright yellow and orange twisting flames that danced and swirled in the distance.

* * *

As his eyes adjusted to the darkness he knew, however unlikely it was, that he was on the Astroturf pitch at the sports club. The noise that he hadn't been able to identify before, he now knew was music piped through a PA system not very far away, even though he struggled to make out the exact content. Pulled roughly to his feet, he tried desperately to keep his hands hidden, all the while taking in his surroundings to see exactly where he was. Dragged forward by two burly blokes, each digging into one of his biceps with their fingernails, Peter counted the number of people he could see on the Astroturf, by the corresponding number of torch beams.

'Six,' he thought, 'plus the two either side of me. 'Not as bad as it could be. I think I might have half a chance now that my hands are free.'

A sneaky look round confirmed his suspicions. It was the Astroturf at Salisbridge. He could just make out the side of the clubhouse, which was partially obscured by some kind of misty barrier that extended its way around the entire pitch. As if his suspicions needed confirmation, a giant bonfire blazed into life about three hundred yards away.

'My God, the fireworks display,' he thought. 'I really am here. Tank and Richie must be just over there. All I need to do is attract their attention. Things really are looking up.' A short, sharp punch in the back brought Peter to his knees, and back to the reality of the situation. Painfully he managed to lurch to his feet, all the time keeping his hands together, despite the muscles in his legs feeling as though they'd turned to jelly. Two of the torch lights broke off from the group and headed towards Peter and the two henchmen. It was hard to make out any detail in the darkness, but as the torches got closer, he could just make out two maniacal grins.

'Theobald and Casey.'

"Not getting a bit cold are you... Benty?"

Peter shook his head in disgust as he stood in the freezing cold in just his shorts and hooded top, all the warmth from his van ride already having dissipated.

"There's still time you know. I'll even speak up to the Council on your behalf if you stop this now and come peacefully."

Theobald and Casey both doubled up with laughter.

"Tell us Benty, do you really think you're in any position to speak to the Council?" mocked Casey, through the laughter.

"They'll find out," remarked Peter. "You know as well as I do that they will."

"Maybe so Benty. But do we look as though we give a

399

damn?" snarled Theobald menacingly, all signs of the laughter having disappeared.

Something about this caused a chill to run down Peter's spine, despite the fact he was barely dressed on a freezing Astroturf pitch on one of the coldest November evenings in living memory. It wasn't so much what was said, he thought as he faced the two bullies, it was the offhand manner in which they said it, almost as if the outcome had been predetermined, with Peter having absolutely no say at all in it.

Looking beyond his two tormentors, he could just see two other vans on what he guessed was about the middle of the synthetic pitch. With his eyesight adjusting all the time, he could just make out that the tailgates were open and the figures with the torches were unloading something onto the pitch. It was, however, impossible to see exactly what the cargo was. All he could gather was that it looked heavy, and there seemed to be a lot of it.

"Taking an interest in our little operation, eh Benty?" observed Theobald, having caught Peter looking over at the vans.

Deciding to remain silent, Peter was no longer sure he could hold his temper and wait for the right opportunity. With every second that passed he was getting colder and colder and with that, weaker and further away from accessing his dragon powers. Unlike both Casey and Theobald who were wrapped up in very flash looking outdoor weather gear.

'They could probably access their powers in an instant,' he thought, 'and tear me apart, no trouble at all.'

"Cat got your tongue... Benty?"

"Yeah, come on Benty, give your old nursery ring mates a smile will ya?"

Both goons squeezing Peter's biceps from behind swapped confused expressions at the mention of nursery rings. In fact much of the night's activities seemed beyond them. They only knew that they were getting paid mighty well for one night's work.

Peter remained silent.

"Ahh well, perhaps you'll be more talkative for the boss," taunted Theobald. Casey just stood there and sniggered.

"And look, here he comes now."

*   *   *

With the bonfire blazing in all its glory, the crowd, including Tank and Richie, were on their second countdown of the night, once again being led by the chairman of the sports club, who it had to be said, looked totally out of sorts. Despite missing Peter, the worry that entailed and the pain caused by inhaling the extremely cold air, both friends took great comfort from the giant bonfire, even though it was some distance away. Nobody seemed bored with yet another countdown, in fact the children, if anything, were more excited this time round, probably something to do with the impending FIREWORKS!

"6... 5... 4... 3... 2... 1..."

The squeal of rockets zooming into the air, followed by them bursting into supernovas, surrounded the crowd. That special firework smell that can only mean it's bonfire night, hung in the chilly air. Exploding arrays of colour lit up the sky above the lacrosse pitch and the bonfire on the ground beyond it. Bright blue, purple, orange, pink, green, yellow and red filled the air in almost every direction, thrilling not just the youngsters but the adults as well. Combined with that overwhelming sound, and the thick smell of cooked food, for most, it was the perfect winter's evening. As one, the crowd cheered, baying for more. Fireworks continued raining into the sky.

*   *   *

Peter froze as the fireworks beyond the Astroturf cut

through the air, lighting up the entire sky. It wasn't because he was so close to his friends that he could call out, no. It was because the stunning colours and bright lights had backlit the foreboding figure of Manson, stick in hand, skulking towards him. Whilst the sight of Manson was cause for alarm, he kept telling himself he was just a human and that there was nothing to fear.

'He may be running things,' he thought, 'but there's no way Casey and Theobald would murder me, another dragon. And that's what it would take.'

Manson, for all his show, was just a common criminal, alright, a pretty scary one at that, but still just a human. No match for a dragon. On his best day he couldn't hurt Peter; he would need the help of the bullies and although he despised them, he knew full well that they wouldn't be party to murder. So, as Manson approached, Peter felt confident enough to give him a big toothy smile, jutting out his jaw in defiance.

Manson rubbed his chin with his thumb and forefinger, inspecting the grinning Bentwhistle, before turning to Casey and Theobald.

"When you said you had a little surprise for me, I had no idea it would be this good," he crowed. "Where exactly did our cold little friend come from?"

Theobald took a step forward.

"He was sneaking around the distribution centre earlier. We took the liberty of capturing him, after he told us he was on his own and that nobody knew where he was."

Manson nodded, pleased, all the time circling Peter, inspecting him like a piece of meat.

"Very good, the two of you, very good." Turning away from his captured prize, the ex-army Major pointed his walking stick at Theobald and said,

"Just out of interest, I've seen no sign of Fisher tonight. Why is that? I thought the three of you were in this together."

Paying close attention, Peter picked up the fear and...

something else that passed across the faces of the two bullies.

Casey seemed too frightened to talk, barely able to look Manson in the eyes. It was Theobald who spoke up, albeit reluctantly.

"He... um... he... um... kind of had a... change of heart, about things."

"A change of heart?" growled Manson.

Theobald stammered on, looking straight down at the ground.

"Yes, a change of heart. After we captured... HIM," he spat, pointing at Peter, "Fisher began having second thoughts, wanting us all just to go to the Council and tell them everything."

"Did he now?" enquired Manson, a menacing glint in his eyes.

"He did."

"So where is Fisher now? Has he run off to warn the Council?"

Peter watched with interest and more than a little hope. If Fisher had warned the Council, the dragons would be here to free him any minute. It was odd though that Manson seemed to know all about the Council. What was that all about?

Theobald, head hunched over, staring straight down at the ground, started to shake uncontrollably as he began his reply.

"We took care of him," he managed to babble.

Manson opened his eyes wide and raised his eyebrows.

"Do tell," he demanded in a feigned posh accent.

Every cell in Peter's body screamed for him to make a run towards the crowd, just the other side of the fence, easily within throwing distance, to get away from the evil that currently surrounded him. Instead he remained rooted to the spot, as a tear creeping slowly down his cheek almost started to freeze.

Manson waited for the overcome Theobald to

continue. Although the air was filled with whooshes and bangs, whizzes and crackles from the fireworks above them, the silence surrounding the small group of beings gathered on the synthetic pitch was all consuming.

"C... c... c... c... Casey and I, w... w... we... took care of him, Sire," muttered Theobald, to no one in particular.

"For good?" asked Manson.

"Yes, Sire."

'Sire?' thought Peter, a steady stream of tears rolling down his cheeks at the thought of what his former classmates had done to their friend. 'What on Earth is all that about?'

Manson stalked forward towards Theobald and Casey who were standing side by side, shaking from their shoulders down. Stopping in front of them, he pulled their heads up to look him in the eye.

"If I wasn't sure of your loyal support, I am now. It wasn't the fault of either of you that Fisher was so weak willed and easily led. You did what you had to. You had no other choice."

The two bullies continued to shake, as they both nodded emphatically.

Manson grabbed both of them firmly by the shoulder, letting his walking stick drop to the frozen, sand covered pitch, which because of the freezing conditions was becoming reminiscent of an ice rink.

"When the time comes... and know this, it will... both of you will be part of the new order of things. You will have wealth, power and the rightful status that your belief and actions deserve. You will both be on the top tier, looking down at everyone and everything. The part you've played here will not be forgotten. Now... back to the matter at hand."

Both bullies nodded in agreement, buoyed at the thought of the wealth and power that had been promised them, as Manson turned away to pick up his stick. Casey sneakily wiped away a tear or two behind his back.

Walking straight up to Peter, Manson stood and looked him straight in the eyes. Peter matched his gaze, not flinching once. Staring deeply into Manson's dark forbidding eyes, a torrent of doubt rose up inside him. It all seemed to make sense that Manson was just a common human criminal, in league with Theobald, Casey and F... He'd started to think of Fisher. It was true that he'd never liked him very much, mainly because of the intense bullying he'd received from the three of them through pretty much his entire time at the nursery ring. But even Fisher didn't deserve this kind of sick fate. What on Earth was going on that would get one dragon murdered by his friends, both of whom were scared witless by a seemingly unimportant human criminal? Something was very wrong.

'I'm missing an important piece of the puzzle. Something I don't know, or haven't seen yet,' he thought, all the time keeping warm images in his head.

Abruptly Peter was startled out of his thoughts by Manson spitting in his face. It was a disgusting act, one which nearly lured him into trying to wipe his face, an action that might well have given away his one advantage. In any case, the two brutes still had a firm hold of his biceps, something that had helped stop his potentially reckless action.

"Look at you," sneered Manson, only a few centimetres from the young hockey playing dragon's face. "You think you're so superior. I bet even at this moment you're planning your escape, and just how you're going to contact your friends over there." Manson pointed towards where he knew the crowd watching the fireworks would be. Suddenly he let out a horrid laugh, more of a cross between a grunt and a giant snort.

Peter continued to gaze straight ahead, using all his focus to ignore the cold biting his body, and the spit running down his face.

"It's not going to happen you know. Your friends, I mean. You're not going to be able to reach them. They'll never know how you died, how much pain you suffered and why. Well, they won't know until it's too late."

Peter's heart (not his real one) was pounding so hard he thought it was going to jump right out of his chest. For the very first time in his life he was scared. Not just a little scared, but genuinely terrified that he was going to die. All along he'd thought he'd had some measure of control over what was happening, thinking that because he was a dragon, he was better than most, almost untouchable... that's what they were led to believe during their time in the nursery ring. Through everything, he always treated what was going on with... contempt. With hindsight, it was obvious now. Mark Hiscock's death should have been his biggest clue. It was his fault. He should have been more careful, looked at things in more detail, been more committed to finding answers, and less easily led. If he'd done all that, then just maybe he wouldn't now be at the mercy of someone who quite clearly didn't know the meaning of the word.

Weighing up everything, he decided in a split second that it was now or never, although he considered that the odds were not exactly great. But he couldn't see them getting any further in his favour. Things had gone rapidly downhill ever since he'd arrived on the synthetic pitch, and although he felt a bond to the pitch itself (you'd have to be a hockey player to understand) he couldn't see how that in itself was going to help him get out of the trouble he now understood he was in. That combined with the fact that Fisher had been killed by Theobald and Casey and also the odd way in which they'd both referred to Manson as 'Sire'. Firmly believing that Manson was not going to leave him here alive was enough to convince him it was time. Knowing all he had to do was reach the far edge of the Astroturf, right by the surrounding fence, that should put him close enough to the crowd watching the fireworks, from where he should easily be able to attract the attention of everyone, not least Tank and Richie. Yes, the dragon

Council would no doubt have to come in, erase a few memories and clean up a bit afterwards, but that would be a small price to pay to thwart whatever madness was going on here. Fisher's murder would be avenged, with those responsible facing the full force of dragon law. As he prepared to act, all he could think was that he really had no other choice.

With Manson's face hovering ever closer to his, he gave everything in an effort to look as though he'd given up and, in a gesture of submission, pulled his head back with a feigned sigh. When his head was back as far as it would go, he focused with everything he had and, after a deep breath, brought his head forward with as much power and strength as he could.

A resounding CRACK very much like a gunshot echoed across the pitch as Peter's head butt made contact with Manson's forehead. His nemesis hit the floor like a sack of potatoes. Knowing there was no time to waste, Peter shrugged off the two men holding his biceps, hitting them both with his opposing free hands as he spun round, his arms whirling like a windmill. The real worry, which he was constantly having to contain, was Theobald and Casey. Now that he knew what they'd done to Fisher, they couldn't afford to leave him alive, and with their dragon powers they would easily be a match for him individually, let alone together. In his heart he hoped they would take a few seconds, or more in the freezing conditions, to change into their natural forms because that just might buy him enough time to raise the alarm and get Tank and Richie firmly on his side, both of whom were more than a match for the two bullies. After dropping the two guards, he turned and, leaping over Manson's writhing body, ran off into the darkness, sprinting for all he was worth towards the nearest part of the fence with the fireworks display's spectators behind it, knowing that in only a few more seconds his fate would be decided.

Running for all he was worth, he could just see out of

the corner of his eye the hired help with flashlights had all stopped unloading and were starting to head in his direction. Pulling in a frozen breath, he put on one last burst of speed. There wasn't one part of him that didn't hurt from being in the van, being out in the cold, and from not having had anything to eat or drink for nearly half the day. Forcing the pain from his mind, he gave everything, not looking back over his shoulder for fear of what he would find. His imagination told him that both Theobald and Casey had already turned into their natural forms and were right at this very moment, swooping down behind him, talons outstretched, jaws opened wide, ready to tear him apart, followed closely by Manson and his goons. Two more steps his mind told him, and he was there. Smashing at speed into the wire meshed fence that surrounded the pitch, he opened his mouth ready to scream for help, and quite possibly, his life. As he did so, the stark realisation of something hit him like a prize fighter no longer pulling his punches. Although he could see the crowd and the fireworks display going on through the hazy mist that encompassed the pitch, he couldn't actually feel any of them with his dragon senses. Not as he should have been able to anyway. Shrugging it off and blaming it on the cold and his battered and beaten condition, only a few feet from the cheering crowd, he shook the fence with both his hands and let out the biggest scream of, "HELP" that he could muster. To his utter amazement, nobody paid him any attention at all, not even the young children that were standing no more than six feet away. Once again he banged on the fence with all his might and let out the mother of all screams. Still nothing.

'I know the fireworks are loud, but not nearly loud enough to prevent them from hearing me.'

From behind him came a huge, rumbling belly laugh (think Jabba the Hutt, only MORE!). Scared of what he might find, Peter found the courage to turn around, hoping against hope that it would be nothing like his imagination had pictured.

The sight that greeted him on turning around was strangely worse than anything his imagination could have mustered. Theobald and Casey hadn't moved at all. The flashlight goons had resumed their unloading. Only the enraged figure of Manson, blood gushing down the outside of his nose from two cuts above each eye, paid him any heed at all. It fact, it had been Manson's giant belly laugh from about twenty yards away that Peter had heard.

"So predictable and pathetic," Manson spat angrily, blood seeping down his face.

Peter still could not understand why the crowd behind him hadn't reacted to his screams for help.

'Surely they must have heard me,' he thought.

"Do you really think your annoying friends and those precious humans will come to your aid?" fumed Manson, wiping some of the blood from his face. "It's almost a shame that they can't. I would take great pleasure in killing them all. Hmmmm. Looks as though I'll have to make do with just you."

Still puzzled as to what was going on, there were just too many things for him that didn't add up. And just how was this misbegotten devil in charge of everything?

Manson stepped closer, the reflected light from the exploding fireworks accenting the features of his grizzled face.

"It's about time you learned exactly who you're dealing with," the ex-army Major bragged menacingly.

As the words finished coming out of his mouth, something incredible, deeply terrifying and completely unexpected happened. The blood from the gaping wounds that Peter had caused with his crushing head butt stopped running down the side of Manson's nose. Not only stopped, but actually started to move back up his face towards the source of the cuts. Once there, the blood withdrew into the cuts just before they healed over, leaving no visible sign that they'd ever even been there. Shocked, the hockey playing dragon had no idea of what to make of it. As if that weren't enough, a vaguely familiar transformation started to occur in Manson's midriff. It looked for all intents and purposes as if his body was folding in on itself, starting with a small part right in the middle of his stomach. Peter had seen this effect dozens of times, but not for many years. In the nursery ring, young dragons learning to take human form, were encouraged to practice in front of a series of mirrors, to try and help perfect their technique and the time it takes to change. He himself had done so hundreds of times and startlingly, the effect when he transformed as viewed from outside, was very similar to the transition that Manson was going through right now.

'Oh crap,' thought Peter. 'He's a flippin' dragon!'

As the cold from the chain link fence burnt into his back, Peter's senses became somehow heightened as time around him very much slowed. Exhaling, his frozen breath took an age to exit his mouth, as all the time in front of him Manson continued to transform, Peter only able to watch in horrified fascination as the edges around the ex-army Major's form started to fold out and gain more mass. With only a few seconds having passed, worryingly, in Peter's mind anyway, was the fact that the transformation was taking considerably longer than it would for most other dragons. Combine that with the size of the mass it seemed to be producing, which already appeared to be... huge. Way bigger than Tank was in dragon form, no mean feat in itself, with the really worrying aspect for Peter being that there was no sign of it abating.

Looking around, thinking about how to get away, his options seemed limited. It only now dawned on him that the hazy mist surrounding the synthetic pitch was clearly some kind of magical construct, created by Manson using whatever power he possessed, to prevent anyone from seeing or hearing what was happening within, as much as not letting any light or noise out. Without knowing much more about how it was created, there was almost zero chance that he could counteract it in the short space of time needed to. The emergency entrance that the vans had used to come in on the far side of the pitch from where he stood seemed to be the only way out, as surprisingly it was the only unlocked gate on the pitch, currently hanging open about halfway, revealing the bumpy, muddy track that connected it to the main road. What struck Peter as odd as he thought about the logistics of things was the fact that only two keys for that gate existed: one was kept behind the bar in the clubhouse, while the other one belonged to the chairman of the sports club.

Unfortunately for him, Peter's wandering mind returned to the nightmarish scene in front of him. The folding out from the middle had stopped, with the edges of the giant form starting to resolve neatly into place. Manson as a dragon was... MASSIVE! He must have been at least three times the size of Tank, who was easily the biggest dragon Peter knew personally. This, however, was not nearly the most frightening thing. Manson's whole body was entirely black. Peter had never seen a fully black dragon, in fact he'd only ever heard of them in stories as myths or make believe characters. Black was just such an uncommon colour throughout the dragon domain. Occasionally you would come across a dragon that had the odd patch of black on his or her body, like a black tail, underbelly, the odd stripe or marking on their head or back. But that was rare. And whoever they were, or wherever they were, they would always be stared at in the most uncomfortable of ways, much in the same way a human would if they had a visible, outlandish birthmark. But a huge dragon like that, totally black from the tip of its tail to the top of its ears was just... incredible!

The transformation had, by the look of things, finished. More like a dinosaur in some respects, the giant dragon looked unsteady on its feet as its head swayed from side to side, trying to get used to its new surroundings, scraping the tips of its giant wings through the frost that had now formed on the synthetic pitch. Peering beneath one of its wings, Peter could just make out Theobald and Casey still standing where they had been, totally unsurprised at the super-imposing dragon that towered over all of them.

'That's why they called him 'Sire'; they've known all along what he was. But why haven't any of us been able to sense him?' Peter wondered, as he legs threatened to give way from both fatigue and cold.

"Not so clever now, are you... little dragon?" Manson boomed groggily.

His voice was so loud that it almost knocked Peter off his feet. Optimistic, he glanced round at the crowd behind him on the other side of the fence, hoping that they might have heard it and be raising the alarm right at this very moment, but no, they were still all glued to the fireworks display. Manson eyed Peter, much as a human would an annoying fly, knowing full well he could swat it any time that he wanted to. And Peter knew that Manson was most definitely going to swat him, it was just a matter of... when.

Crazy as it may have seemed, Peter started to edge forward from the fence towards the black prehistoric beast, having realised that standing right up against it made him pretty much a sitting duck. At least if he moved out a little, he might have more room to manoeuvre or run away when the inevitable attack came. Also, he was, cunningly, on the lookout for Manson's weak spot, knowing if he got close enough, he should at least in theory be able to see it, not that it was going to help him in any significant way as he had no weapons, was seriously outnumbered, was too weak to transform into his natural state, and even if he could, Manson would still be way too powerful for him.

'Normally,' he thought, 'I can find something to smile about in almost any situation. Surprisingly, nothing springs to mind right now.'

Manson's jaws opened impossibly wide, almost akin to

a snake eating prey twice its size, giving the effect of a really disturbing smile.

"Coming to attack me little dragon?" he chortled. "Did you really think I didn't know that you had broken free of your handcuffs? I mean really, you are so naive, even for such a young dragon." Manson dragged one of his giant wings off the floor, pointing it in his direction. "You've been a permanent thorn in my side... little dragon. Our plans have constantly had to be readjusted because of you... and now... now you're going to pay the price for meddling in affairs that don't concern you. Don't worry though, you won't be alone. Your death will be the first of many to come. Your precious domain won't know what's hit it until it's way too late. Got any last words?"

Peter took a deep breath and calmed himself. With little alternative, he knew he would have to fight, something he was ill equipped and ill prepared to do. Nothing in the nursery ring had readied him to face a giant psychopathic dragon with nothing but murder on his mind. The best he could hope for was to buy himself enough time in the hope that some sort, any sort of opportunity presented itself, whether a chance to attack Manson or to run and escape intact.

Manson opened his jaws, imitating a big cheesy grin.

'Here it comes,' thought Peter. And sure enough, it did.

One of Manson's huge black scaly wings sliced through the air at speed. Peter desperately willed his body to move. Responding slower than normal because of the cold and fatigue, he jumped back and rolled sideways, feeling the air from the movement of the deadly wing just above his head. Gingerly, he straightened up, knowing he'd just burnt the skin off both his knees with his last ditch evasive exploits on the icy, sand encrusted ground.

A giant roar accompanied by a splutter of flame spewed forth from Manson's mouth as he stamped his feet in frustration, much like a petulant child not getting his own way, more than a little upset that Peter had avoided his well timed charge. With a prehistoric snarl buried into his face, Manson opened his mouth again, this time to much greater effect, having let rip with the biggest and hottest stream of flame Peter had ever seen. Caught off guard, the young dragon flung himself to the floor, trying to ignore the pain as he rolled over and over on the hard surface. Shooting pain down his arm, across his back and into his hand told him that his shoulder had been caught on the outer edges of the flame and badly burned. Scrambling along the ground as if completing an army assault course, he knew that ignoring the pain and surviving as long as possible was quite literally a matter of life and death. Rising up to a kneeling position to catch his breath and take stock of his wounds, he noticed the hired help that had been loading the vans had decided enough was enough. Despite what looked like strong threats from Theobald and Casey, the men had all run off towards the van that Peter had been trapped in, the one by the gate that remained open, and were now in the process of attempting to drive off at breakneck speed.

Manson, clearly distracted, had stopped heaving flame at Peter, the fleeing van more of a priority. Peter knew that he should use this fleeting opportunity to try and escape, but not only could he not see how, but some morbid fascination had taken over, forcing him to see what fate awaited the humans who, up until sixty seconds ago, had been part of Manson's force. Kneeling on one knee, forcing air back into his lungs, he watched powerlessly what he assumed would be the last few seconds of the human conspirators' lives.

Manson hated humans. Not hated them a bit, oh no... he really, really, really hated them. Hated them with every cell in his superior body. According to him, they stood for everything bad in this rotten and wrong world.

'Bentwhistle can sweat a bit more, while I take care of these lying, cheating, spineless... cowards,' he thought, assessing the entire situation all at once. Closing his eyes that were easily the size of beach balls, he rolled his huge head back as he concentrated on the open gate that the van was now heading for. Power and darkness surging through his body, he willed the gate to close and stay closed. Like a shot... it did! The massive gate slammed shut, mystically welded in place, as the driver of the approaching van slammed its brakes on, surprised to see the exit suddenly cut off. Confusion and panic erupted inside the van as they all argued about their next course of action.

Opening his eyes in a slow, sure, calculating way, Manson gave one flap of his gigantic wings, taking flight immediately, skimming low across the synthetic pitch on a collision course with the breakaway van that was now reversing away from the steadfast gate. Theobald and Casey watched as their 'master' raced by, a mixture of pride and obedience cut into their faces. The driver slammed the steering wheel round, shooting the van through one hundred and eighty degrees, looking for any other exit. But the sight that greeted him and the others crammed into the front of the van through the steamed up window was nothing other than gruesome, causing him to step on the breaks, bringing the vehicle to a sudden halt. Watching, Peter could just make out four petrified humans behind the windscreen, all frozen with fear like rabbits in a headlight, for which he really couldn't blame them. Manson was closing in, flying just above the pitch, frosty sand scattering through the air in his wake. One of the humans in the middle of the cab overcame his fear briefly, and tried to climb over his stunned friends to get out. He was too late.

Manson's entire being ploughed straight into the van, shredding it instantly. The noise of metal, flesh and bones all breaking, blocked out the sound of the fireworks that were going off overhead. Then came the blast. The whole van exploded in a shower of tiny, red hot, metal fragments, leaving a smoking and smouldering wreck that had melted a huge hole in the synthetic pitch, right in front of the locked gate. From out of the fire trudged Manson, using his wings to brush off tiny slivers of flame and red hot fragments from his chest and legs, all the while looking incredibly pleased with himself. If Peter hadn't recognised the trouble he'd been in before, he did now, particularly having witnessed the casual way in which Manson had just taken human lives. He knew that unless a miracle presented itself, he'd very likely be heading the same way.

From his position back near the fence, Peter surveyed the scene in an attempt to see if there was anything at all that might help him in his current predicament. The smouldering wreck of the van lay along one side of the pitch, blocking off the sealed gate. At one end, roughly in the centre, stood Theobald and Casey, taking in everything that had happened, looking more than a little shaky. Right in the middle of the pitch, strewn across the frozen ground, was another giant harness like the one in the van Peter had been trapped in. Amazingly, this one looked even bigger, as it lay flat on the cold, icy surface, with the large metallic nets either side. One of the nets had been pulled open, and some of the contents of the two vans which surrounded it had been piled in. Wooden boxes and pallets with smaller packages on were spread out amongst the vans, and had clearly been in the middle of being unloaded when the humans had tried to make a run for it.

'What on earth is in the boxes, and why are the contents being loaded into the nets attached to the giant harness?' Peter wondered.

Manson, still ever so slightly on fire, motioned to Theobald and Casey to join him. They did.

"Start loading all the cargo into the harness, ready for departure," he ordered, his breath forming a massive white cloud in the chilly night air.

Theobald and Casey headed quickly towards the centre of the pitch, but not before they'd stopped to bow to their 'master'. Manson, knowing that his harness was once again being loaded up, turned his attention back to Bentwhistle.

Watching everything at a distance, it seemed to Peter that whatever was being loaded up in the harness must be extremely important to Manson. Briefly he wondered if he'd ever find out what it was.

Turning his huge, prehistoric body towards Peter, Manson's head swayed from side to side almost as if enquiring what the young dragon was up to.

Standing up from his kneeling position, a wave of pain from the burns on his knees ran up Peter's legs, nearly forcing him to scream out. But not quite. Managing to ignore it with only a small grimace, he found that despite the cold, he was actually starting to warm up.

'It must be something to do with the rush of adrenaline, and being near Manson's scorching flame that he let out,' he thought. 'I'm still a long way off being able to turn back into a dragon, or use any of my key abilities to raise the alarm though.'

Manson couldn't help but notice Peter's interest in the harness and its contents.

"Still not clever enough to understand what's going... little dragon?" he sneered as he plodded over.

Peter ignored the jibe, knowing full well the giant, menacing dragon was trying to bait him. Keeping his temper in order to seize that one miracle opportunity should it arise, was his priority.

"Not even a little interested... little dragon?" taunted Manson.

'Obviously he needs to feel superior by instilling fear in others and flaunting his power by bragging about his plan. Well, if he wants to brag, then maybe I should give him the chance..

"The dragon Council and I know all about your plan," lied Peter, hoping his bluff would at least keep Manson a little off balance.

"Haaa haaaaaaa haaaaaaaaaaaaaaa! Then why aren't they here to stop me eh? You know nothing about what's going on here. Even now, your feeble little mind isn't smart enough to put the pieces of the puzzle together. You look at the boxes over there," Manson pointed to the harness that was slowly being filled by Theobald and Casey, "and you have absolutely no idea of their contents."

Peter crossed his arms in front of his chest and put on his most determined expression, which under the circumstances (standing in the frozen night air in just shorts and a hooded top) seemed utterly ridiculous, but it was all he could think to do. If he could somehow raise some sort of doubt in Manson, then he just might get to live just that little bit longer.

The giant black dragon took a couple of massive strides towards Peter, shaking the ground and raking the ice on the surface of the pitch with his sharp talons as he did so.

"I know everything you're thinking... insignificant little dragon. You're so predictable, with your schemes and plans of how to get out of all of this in one piece."

A quivering shudder ran through Peter. Manson didn't appear to be buying any of it. Using all his strength and courage, he maintained the defiant expression, hoping that his opponent might give something else away.

"But since you're going to die anyway, I might as well put you out of your misery, before I put you out of your misery." Manson clapped his huge wings together in front of him, before blowing out a short jet of flame on to them. Peter wished with all his heart to feel the warmth contained within the flame. Manson shot him a knowing look, fully aware that Peter was freezing and longing for the heat that he so brazenly showed off.

Stamping around in a semicircle some thirty or so feet away, every now and then Manson blew out a jet of flame to ward off the cold. As he did so, he turned towards Peter, looking like some kind of prehistoric predator teasing its prey.

"You see, my... associates and I have a rather different long term view of how the planet should be governed.

While we've had little choice but to bide our time in the past, we now find ourselves with a real opportunity to bring our plans to fruition, helped in no small part by some resources from... Cropptech," Manson quipped, pointing towards the boxes and pallets scattered about.

Alarm bells started going off in Peter's head.

'Oh my God,' he thought, 'he's stealing the laminium!'

A big, smug, evil grin crossed Manson's scaly face, as his bloodshot eyes focused intently on Peter.

"At last you've managed to work it out. Good for you," he laughed. "Where in the world would we as a group find enough laminium for our goals? Where in the world would we find enough laminium, unguarded and free for taking? Ha ha ha! Here of course. With only a couple of pathetic dragons watching over things, one hopelessly inadequate, the other... fresh out of the nursery ring, with absolutely no idea how things work in the real world." Manson shook his head as he laughed. "Easier than taking charcoal from a hatchling," he goaded.

Images of what Manson and his cohorts might do with that amount of laminium flashed through Peter's mind as he stood in the cold, trying desperately hard to look confident. His imagination pictured a world ruled ruthlessly by dragons. Humans decimated by cruelty and sport for the ruling class. Other species wiped out on a whim, by neglect and misuse.

'Everything would revert to how the world was hundreds of thousands of years ago,' he thought, terrified at the prospect.

It was the first time that day that his death, a very realistic possibility, was put into perspective. If he didn't stop Manson getting away with all the laminium, then the world might never be the same again. Everything he loved, his friends, Cropptech, the dragon world, Gee Tee, the nursery ring... hockey, it would all be destroyed. There and then he vowed to himself that he would not let Manson leave with the precious metal, even if it meant sacrificing his own life. In fact, he would gladly give his own life to stop the evil monster's terrifying plot right now. In Peter's mind, things had changed. It wasn't so much: how could he survive and even get away? It was more: how could he use his own life to take Manson's and thwart him in the process? A loud growling voice brought him back to the present, more determined than ever.

"So you see it was never about Garrett or Cropptech. They were just a means to an end so that we could liberate the laminium," barked Manson loudly, now flicking out small streams of flame to keep himself warm, much to Peter's consternation.

Finally understanding the overall scheme of things, Peter nodded. He'd never even come close to suspecting what it was all about, having always been too concerned with the people involved, that is Garrett and Hiscock, when in fact he should have been paying attention to the bigger picture, in particular the... laminium. That was, after all, the primary reason he'd been put there by dragon society and should have been his top priority, even if it had meant that the humans paid for it with their lives. If he'd thought his cold, numb legs would have felt it, he would have kicked himself.

'Stupid, stupid, stupid,' he thought as he gazed across at Manson's infuriating smile.

As the mammoth black dragon gazed over its shoulder to see how Theobald and Casey were getting on with loading up the harness, Peter couldn't resist a look and followed Manson's example. The two bullies had, from what Peter could see, loaded nearly all of the contents into the nets attached to the enormous harness. Each metallic net was so full that the harness itself now stood a good four metres off the ground, supported only by the full nets either side of it. Empty pallets and wooden boxes lay dispersed around both vehicles, both of which had been left with their rear doors open, revealing total emptiness inside.

Only then did Peter really get it.

'That's how he plans to escape,' he thought, looking over at the giant harness. 'It would fit him like a glove, and if he can reproduce the masking effect that's encasing the pitch while he's flying, he'll get away scot free.'

Manson's interest returned to Peter, now that he was sure the harness was loaded and ready to go.

"I'm afraid it's nearly time for me to depart," he gloated. "And unfortunately that means the end of the road for you, although I can't really say I'm that sorry. You've blundered about and got in the way enough to cause serious disruptions. At least after your death I'll have the satisfaction of knowing all the workers at Cropptech will think you died a traitor, having attempted to poison Al Garrett, only to be stopped at the last minute by... ME! Think of the irony of it. Even your friends will have their doubts about you."

Peter's temper started to rise. He knew only too well that he should ignore Manson's taunting, but believing that everyone would think badly of him stung him more than he thought possible. Surprisingly, he stepped forward, a rather stupid thing to do under the circumstances.

"You wouldn't know true friendship if it jumped up and bit you on the tail," he spat furiously. "No matter what the situation or circumstances, my friends would never think badly of me. They'd know that whatever I did, however odd it looked, I did it with the best of intentions. They'd have faith that I would do the right thing, no matter what the situation. You probably don't have a real friend in the entire world," he raved, letting his temper get the better of him. "The only thing I feel for you is... PITY! What's it like to be alone, and afraid? I'll take comfort in the fact that when the dragon Council catch up with you, and they will, you'll die all alone, with absolutely nobody to mourn you."

Peter evidently hadn't noticed Manson getting angrier as his tirade went on. The gigantic matt black dragon had a

421

look of murder in his eyes as his huge head swayed from side to side in a deranged sort of fashion.

Rant over, Peter took a breath, only then realising quite how much he'd provoked the dark scaled beast. The two, a bedraggled looking human, barely dressed, and a menacingly colossal, black-as-the-night-sky dragon stood on the synthetic pitch, staring at each other as the fireworks raged overhead, with a crowd numbering in their hundreds standing off to one side, blissfully unaware of what was happening. Hate and rage inside Peter threatened to gobble him up. He wanted to hurt Manson... badly, but had no idea how to do it. More than anything, he wanted to kill him. For Mark Hiscock, whom Manson had killed. For Al Garrett and the staff at Cropptech, all of whom had been misled, none of whom were safe. And for the human accomplices that Manson had murdered right in front of him only minutes ago. He wanted to do if for Fisher, who had been slaughtered by Theobald and Casey for not wanting to take part in Manson's scheme any longer. His hatred for Fisher was immense because of his part in the bullying that had gone on for decades during his time in the nursery ring, but nobody, human or dragon, deserved to die like that. Most of all, he wanted to do it for... himself! Manson had made his life a misery for the last seven months and he was planning to change the world beyond recognition. For that, Peter decided, he deserved to die.

Manson had rolled his head away from Peter. It looked innocent enough, but was in fact designed to lure his prey into a false sense of security. In an instant, he struck. The one thing it wasn't, was subtle. Manson launched himself like a jet plane towards Peter. The young dragon used up all his luck in moving off to one side as fast as he could, and then at the moment the dark dragon's hooked talons came screeching towards him, he dived head first with all the speed he could muster into a forward roll, carrying all his momentum as far as he could. Scrambling to his feet, he was grateful that his tactics had worked, albeit at a cost. He'd got out of the way of Manson, and now found himself some thirty or so feet away from the unhinged dragon, who was now over by the fence, with him off to one side. The cost of this had become apparent when he'd turned to inspect his right shoulder, which was throbbing slightly from the impact of the forward roll, or so he thought. It turned out he was mistaken slightly. Manson's razor sharp talons had caught his shoulder on the way past, slicing into the flesh from shoulder to bicep, with the torn skin hanging off, like meat on a butcher's hook.

Flashing Peter one of his deranged smiles, Manson stood confidently baring his talons and teeth, not far enough away on the synthetic pitch. Lifting his right arm into the air, just enough for the messy flap of skin to sit back down on his arm, he closed his eyes for a split second, and, using all his concentration, channelled what little magic he had available into the wound in the hope that it would heal. Under normal circumstances, an injury like this would be fully healed in about an hour. Unfortunately his circumstances now were far from normal. He figured the best he could hope for was for the skin to knit together slightly, and for some of the pain to be relieved. That was assuming he didn't have to move or receive any other injuries in the immediate future.

'Fat chance of that,' he thought.

All the time watching Manson, waiting for another ferocious attack, from out of the corner of his eye Peter could just make out Theobald and Casey putting the last of the laminium into the metallic nets attached to the giant harness. It looked now as if it was ready to go.

'Somehow,' he thought, 'I have to stop that cargo from leaving here.'

The ex-army Major, if that's what he really was, caught Peter looking at the two bullies putting the finishing touches to the cargo. Done with insults and taunting, he just wanted to get on with the mission, leave this human infested hell hole and head back south to the others. Pulling in a deep breath, he instantly expelled a terrific cone of fire that burned blue in the middle as it arced towards Peter. Immediately the young dragon threw himself to the ground once again, but on peering up, and with the crackling cone of fire above him, he had no idea which way to roll to get free of the threat. That was partly because Manson continued to turn his head from side to side, causing the giant arc of flame to continually move back and forth, trapping Peter beneath it. From his position, it was impossible to gauge exactly where Manson was. So he had to gamble, as the intense heat started to become unbearable, affecting not only his movement but his breathing as well. One positive to come out of this surprising attack though, was that he was now warm enough to access a vast array of his dragon abilities, something Manson had clearly not bargained on. Putting on a burst of dragon speed, he gambled and rolled right, hoping that the frenzied dragon had gone the other way. A treble roll later and Peter had his answer. He'd gambled wrong, and smashed clumsily into one of Manson's tree trunk thick legs as he rolled out from the massive arc of rainbow coloured flame. Manson had been counting on his nemesis appearing here and for the first time in the battle he'd got his wish.

Knowing instantly that he had to act, Peter jumped back, trying to perform an audacious back flip, throwing as much of his dragon power into it as he dared, in the hope that it would get him out of the psychotic dragon's reach. A resounding SMACK boomed across the Astroturf, like a plane breaking the sound barrier as the air and everything around it shook. Still the humans watching the fireworks were totally oblivious to the battle taking place in their midst. Every atom in Peter's body screamed out in pain as he flew unceremoniously into the air. His eardrums felt as if they'd imploded, while horrific pain tore out from the left side of his ribs, which if he were able to turn his aching head to look at, he would have done. After a journey that felt as if it had taken months, he landed with a sickening CRUNCH, his fall broken by something very solid indeed. Barely clinging onto consciousness as the awesome pain assaulted his body in waves, he knew something extremely bad had happened to his ribs; he just couldn't seem to clear his head, or move his tangled body enough to look and see exactly what.

Glaring across the icy pitch at the crumpled form of the annoying dragon in human form, Manson could sense that there was something different about this one. Not able to quite put his talon on it, it was almost as if he preferred to be human shaped, which repulsed him to his very core, and would even be something all the other dragons hiding away in the domain deep beneath their feet would find hard to understand. Humans were weak, feeble, lazy and second class, no more than pets at best. They were imposters, thinking themselves top of the planet's food chain, when quite obviously they were not. They shouldn't be allowed to go on deluding themselves. In no short time at all, they would, to a man and a woman... know the truth!

By now a thin layer of mist had settled just above the surface of the synthetic pitch. It was clear to Manson that he'd already won and completed the mission he'd been sent on, something that pleased him no end. Bentwhistle's mangled body lay smashed against the now ruined, green metal fence that would normally have separated spectators from the playing surface. From where he stood, it was difficult to separate Bentwhistle's body from the twisted metal wreckage of the sturdy fence, the damage had been so bad. Manson smiled, pleased with himself.

'I must have thrown him nearly sixty yards,' he thought proudly. 'Perhaps when I'm in charge and the new regime begins, we could make this some kind of regular event... toss a human. Sounds quite catchy.'

With the evil Manson already celebrating his hard

earned victory on one side of the pitch, an altogether different battle was taking place on the other. A battle to stave off pain, to remain conscious and in the end... to stay alive.

Quite a feat really, considering the scale of his injuries, he'd managed to sit himself up. The part of him made to look like human blood was leaking all over the frozen pitch, from the injury to his shoulder that had reopened and from the gaping wound around his ribs. Likely he'd broken at least three of them, as well as badly bruising some of his internal organs. He was a mess. Trying as hard as he could in the state that he was in, he tapped into all his dragon magic and attempted to heal some of the damage he'd taken. Realistically he knew that he had neither the time nor the limitless energy required to achieve such a thing.

Fireworks still exploding overhead, for the first time he could hear music from the speakers that accompanied them. From the sound of it, the spectacle was just reaching its finale. As mind crushing pain threatened to overwhelm his false form, he managed to chuckle.

'How fitting that our finales seem to be occurring at the same time. As if it wasn't enough that it would end here for me... on the Astroturf.' Strange as it may seem, and despite being an inanimate object, Peter had come to regard that synthetic pitch as his... FRIEND! Having shared sweat, blood, anger and passion on it as well as performing many outlandish hockey feats alongside his teammates, if he had to die somewhere, on the pitch that meant so much to him was as good as anywhere.

Like puddles of oil beneath a very old car, the blood from his wounds pooled and congealed, leaving bright red frozen ponds all around him. In his confused state he briefly wondered why it was red and not the normal green. Turning his head as far as he could without passing out or being sick, he hoped against hope to see a wave of dragon guards hurtling through the sky, on their way to give

Manson the fate he so deserved. All he could see though was the clear dark sky, pierced by tiny pinpricks of light. At that moment, he accepted that he would die here and very soon. Mixed with pain and nausea, regret washed over him. His friends would probably never know his true fate. He'd never get to play hockey again, although it was fitting that he should die here on the pitch that he loved so much. Regret also at never having mated, thus ending his birth line. Instantly his thoughts turned to Richie. More than once in his relatively short life span, he'd imagined mating with her, producing an entire hockey team (well, a seven a side one) of gorgeous dragonlings. In his heart of hearts though, he knew that she was way out of his league and that it would never happen in a million years. But it hadn't stopped him thinking about it from time to time. Just recently however, he'd found himself thinking more and more about the idea. Oddly enough, whenever he thought about Richie and the idea of mating, he somehow got the impression that she would rather mate in human form, possibly even with a human, although he had no idea why this occurred to him. In the here and now, it was quite possible his injuries had taken too much of a toll on him because in the extreme, it was a very daft idea, not least because the coupling of dragons and humans had been strictly forbidden by the dragon Council for over two thousand years.

As the cold bit at his body and hazy sleep threatened to take him forever, a memory slipped into his mind and shook him awake.

'I know where it is,' he thought, suddenly alert. The memory, from a split second before Manson had hit him halfway across the pitch with one gigantic scaled wing, focused in on the wing bearing down on him, just before impact. In that moment he could vividly remember seeing a brilliant yellow patch, covering a couple of Manson's scales protruding from the right hand side of his underbelly. It was his weak spot!

Every dragon ever born had a weak spot: an area of vulnerability visible only to other dragons, which if pierced will cause unbelievable pain and will very often lead to death. Covered extensively throughout the nursery curriculum, young dragons were all taught to find each other's weak spots and the weak spots of various different dragons who came to lecture them. In his confused state, Peter's mind wandered to his favourite tale, that of George and the Dragon. George had managed to take down the evil dragon Troydenn against all odds by knowing where his weak spot was and hammering a sword down into that exact area. With all this running through his mind, his entire body screamed at him to get up.

'We still have a chance,' it said. 'We know where his weak spot is. We can stop him.'

His head swimming all over the place, he could just make out the music accompanying the fireworks and see the rockets in all their multicoloured glory exploding overhead. More than anything, he just wanted to throw up, or at least that's what his cold, numb body told him.

'Why me?' he wondered. 'Why has all of this happened to me? I'm simply not cut out to be a hero.'

Looking back, he could easily think of several dragons from the nursery ring who all had the attributes of readymade heroes. But not him. He was the last dragon on the planet who should be fighting the forces of evil. As far as he was concerned, there wasn't a heroic bone in his body (dragon or human).

'Why couldn't this have happened to somebody else?'

As his head flopped back against what was left of the separating fence that had so graciously broken his fall from sixty or so yards away, he spotted something out of the corner of his eye. Only a few metres away from where he found himself propped up was the olive green light box containing the controls for the floodlights that surrounded the pitch. Straight away he thought about turning them on.

'That,' he thought, 'would surely get the crowd's

attention.' Immediately he dismissed the idea, as the box itself was locked and at the moment he didn't have enough strength to pull a cracker, let alone break into the control box. What did catch his attention though, was a rather large, lethal looking icicle dangling down from the underside of the box. It had to have been there for a few days at least, judging by the size of the thing. More than a foot long, it had a diameter of a couple of inches, with the point looking sharper than one of Gordon Ramsay's kitchen knives. Hope, and a plan, welled up inside him.

Tentatively, he pulled himself up against the twisted metal, all the time fighting off the desire to sleep. Glaring across the cold, mist enshrouded pitch, he could just make out Manson talking to Theobald and Casey next to the fully laden harness.

'Perhaps he thinks I'm already dead,' mused Peter. He considered this for a few moments. 'If Manson thought I was already dead, he would just strap on the harness and fly out of here, in which case I've already lost. No,' he concluded, 'it isn't Manson's style. He's going to come across and finish the job, knowing full well I'm in no condition to go anywhere and that he can take his time. Well... let's see if I can surprise Mister All-Knowing, shall we?'

Using his arms to pull himself up into a sitting position, he immediately wished he hadn't when bright spots flickered before his eyes and the pain made him retch. Gritting his teeth, he tried to stand up. His legs were having none of that and instantly gave way, causing him to fall back onto the icy ground with a THUD. Standing, clearly wasn't going to be an option, he thought, looking across to make sure Manson wasn't on his way over yet. Sure enough, the ferocious looking matt black dragon was still confidently dishing out instructions to Theobald and Casey.

Taking in a long, deep breath that seared his throat and the inside of his lungs, he plucked up all his courage and

PAUL CUDE

began pulling his battered body towards the control box for the floodlights. It was slow going, with his hands and fingers taking a hell of a beating not just from the constant icy cold, but from the scattered metal shards that had not long ago made up the metal fence. They constantly pierced the palms of his hands and sliced open his fingers as he moved. Doing his best to ignore it, he told himself that at least it was taking his mind off his other more serious injuries.

After a couple of minutes he'd dragged himself about halfway to the control box. Manson had glanced over a couple of times, but continued speaking with the two nursery ring bullies, very much confirming what Peter had suspected, that in fact the murderous shadowy monster regarded him as no threat at all and would come over to finish him off when it suited him.

Continuing on, leaving a thick red trail of frozen blood in his wake, he tried desperately to ignore the incredible waves of pain that parts of his body were generating. Focused on his friends, knowing they were nearby, hoping that would inspire him enough to drag himself to the control box, he thought back to all the good times they'd shared, from their many years in the nursery ring to their relatively short time above ground in the human world. As he crawled painfully towards his goal, images of Tank, Richie, Gee Tee, the nursery ring, hockey, laminium ball matches, everything that he'd enjoyed in his scaly and not so scaly life, flew past.

Before he knew it, he'd determinedly made it to the control box. With his last ounce of strength, he ripped the glistening icicle from the underside of the box with his right hand, gripping it firmly behind his back, while with his left hand he began to scrabble at the locked part of the box, making it look to Manson as though he were making an attempt to turn the floodlights on. This, interestingly, got the evil black dragon's attention. Instantly he strode meaningfully away from Theobald and Casey, eyeing Peter

430

with suspicion. Fumbling with the looked door on the box, making it look as though he knew it was his last chance to save himself, Peter turned to face the fast approaching Manson, immediately recognising the mad, deranged look in his eyes for what it was.

'Here he comes,' he thought, as once again time seemed to be measured in units so small it was impossible to even begin to quantify them.

Halfway between the two bullies and the control box, Manson launched himself forward with one powerful flap of his massive wings. The low lying mist on the pitch around him was suddenly sucked up in his wake, forming tiny circular vortices behind the tips of his wings and the end of his tail as he closed in on his prey.

Peter's face became racked with fear as the impressive homicidal black dragon zoomed towards him with only one thing on his mind. His grip on the icicle behind his back increased, the frozen cold stinging his hand beyond belief as he prepared to strike. Clearing his mind, he urged his body to provide him with the strength he needed for this one last attack, knowing full well that one way or another, the welcome relief of death was not far away. Feeling the brush of air wash over his face as Manson approached at full speed, he knew what he had to do. It was now or never.

Manson opened his huge slavering jaws as he approached the raggedy human form of the irritating pest that was Bentwhistle. So close he could almost feel his razor sharp teeth closing around the battered body in front of him, savouring the delight of flesh and bones crunching in his prehistoric jaw.

Leaving it to the last one hundredth of a second, Peter moved with a speed that betrayed his life threatening injuries. It wasn't the fastest he'd ever moved, that was for sure, but not far off, and an absolute miracle given what his body had already been through. Able to see straight down the black dragon's throat as the open jaws sped towards him, horror still etched on his face, he threw himself forward, diving beneath the terrifying chops that wanted nothing more than to chomp on him, looking more frightening than any crocodile or shark he'd ever seen on the television. As he dived, he willed his body to turn over mid flight. Reluctantly it did so, inflicting even more pain, which Peter wouldn't have believed possible. Even so, he maintained his focus and while twisting over in full flight, below the fast moving scaly body of his nemesis, he brought round the glistening icicle that he'd been concealing behind his back. In the almost total darkness of the underside of Manson's huge frame, he found what he was looking for, a distinctive area covering two of the evil dragon's tiny dark scales. It stood out like a beacon in the blackness, drawing Peter's every action towards it. Having fully turned over during his daring dive beneath, and knowing that he'd caught Manson totally off guard, he used every last bit of strength that he had to thrust the transparent crystalline form of the icicle into the dragon's heavily shielded body. As the icicle tore into Manson, Peter could feel the satisfactory yielding of dragon flesh, followed by what can only be described as the sound of a huge SQUELCH.

Peter thumped to the hard icy surface on his back, his body riddled with pain and numbness. As his head cracked back onto the synthetic pitch, he watched the fireworks light up the sky beyond the black outline of Manson, relief and regret washing over him one last time. Without turning his head, he watched out of the corner of his eyes as Manson tried frantically to compensate for overshooting his target, only to be struck by the realisation that he himself had been dealt a fatal blow. The fearsome, homicidal dragon wheeled around in the air one last time, not knowing what to do at first. Peter watched, captivated, as Manson flapped his wings in panic and let out the most undragon-like scream he'd ever heard in his life.

As he hovered to the ground, one of his giant legs gave

way, causing the huge black dragon to topple over to his left. Collapsing to the ground, the entire Astroturf shook, causing even more ripples of pain up Peter's now useless back.

Tears began to flow like a raging river down Peter's cheeks, most freezing before they hit his chin. Every emotion he'd ever known swirled around inside him, alongside the pain and numbness. Bizarrely, he started to laugh hysterically.

'I've done it,' he thought, feeling an immeasurable pride well up inside his chest. 'I've saved them all.' He'd known that he wasn't cut out to be a hero, but when it counted, when it really mattered, he'd stepped up and given his life to stop Manson and had thwarted his twisted plans for the entire planet.

As he lay there, unable to move at all on the bone chillingly cold synthetic pitch, waiting to depart for good, his mind began to wander.

'Strange,' he thought to himself as he looked towards the edge of the pitch nearest to him, 'I'd have thought with Manson's downfall, the mystical haze surrounding the pitch would have dissipated totally. It definitely faded momentarily when I thrust that icicle into him, but why hasn't it gone altogether? The crowd should be rushing in from the fireworks display to see what's been going on.'

Over the sound of the very best fireworks launched so far, a soft ringing laughter echoed subtly across the misty pitch. It was the kind of laughter that could turn a being's blood cold, or even still a beating heart. Peter had thought he couldn't get any colder. It turns out he was wrong. As his goose bumps got goose bumps and the fear inside him threw itself off the nearest tall building in fright, he just managed to turn his head in the direction of the dreaded mirth.

The sight that greeted him washed away all his hopes and pride. It felt as though all the remaining intact bones in his body had all been broken at once. Wetting himself straight away, he was amazed that he hadn't done so before now, given everything that had gone on. His hope lay shattered, his pride shredded and any dignity he had was long gone. Worst of all was the fact that he knew in the not too distant future his friends' lives would be destroyed and they might well face the same fate.

Manson plodded towards him, clutching the icicle he'd ripped out of his underbelly. He tossed it towards Peter for dramatic effect, not wanting to end things just yet.

"You showed more courage than I ever could have expected... impressive. It's almost a shame things have to end this way; you might have made a welcome addition to our... cause."

Peter spat a huge gob full of blood as far as he could in the vile dragon's direction.

"Yes, I thought that would be your response. Shame really, you certainly seem to have more backbone than those two," he said, pointing in the direction of Theobald and Casey. "Still... never mind."

Lying on the ground, wondering how the hell Manson wasn't dead, or at least near death, Peter was sure he'd hit the right spot, and had damn well thrust the icicle in with enough power to finish the dark dragon for good. What he was seeing was just not possible.

Manson watched the helpless young dragon as he lay near death in front of him, knowing exactly what was he was thinking.

"Would you like me to put your mind at rest?"

Once again Peter spat in Manson's direction, but only the tiniest of globules came out.

Prehistoric evil chuckled at the pathetic attempt and, turning just slightly, pointed to the spot on his belly where Peter had so carefully thrust in the icicle.

"Unlike the poor deluded, weak and pitiful dragons you serve, I belong to a much stronger, smarter breed. You all loll round with your weak spots showing to everybody so that they can all see where to deliver the fatal blow. How sporting," he boomed sarcastically. "That will be the undoing of your dragon community. By the time they realise, it will be too late. You see, the breed of dragon that I belong to would never dream of showing another dragon its weak spot, not when we can mask our weak spots and replicate them on a much stronger part of our body. You see, much as I admire your one last attempt at taking me down, you never really had any real chance. The spot you saw isn't my weak spot, and when my associates and I take on your dragon community in the very near future, they'll find that out the hard way. Anyway, much as this has been... a nice little workout," he bragged, flexing the muscles in both wings, "it really is time for me to go. And I'm afraid, for you, it's time to die."

Lying on the cold surface, covered in blood and urine, determined to face whatever was coming head on, he knew it would be more painful than anything he'd experienced so far that evening, something he found hard to imagine, but steeled himself for anyway. Craning his neck to look at Manson, he waited for the deranged dragon to leap forward and deliver the killer blow. That murder-in-his-eyes look crossed Manson's face once again as he hungrily anticipated delivering death to the already expiring body strewn out in front of him.

As the muscles in Manson's legs tightened, he prepared to swoop forward and end it all.

And then, the most amazing thing in the world happened.

From out of nowhere, it started to snow. Not just a little bit of snow either. Huge, intricate flakes the size of tennis balls rained out of the dark sky, like comets having a race. It was so dense that at first Peter couldn't quite believe what he was seeing. Looking up, although he could hear the last of the fireworks exploding above him, he could see nothing but a thick white apron of snowflakes heading his way. The mighty flakes settled all over his body, burning fiercely as they touched his exposed flesh, of which there was quite a lot. This, however, was nothing compared with what the supremely confident, homicidal, deranged Manson was going through. One of the first things to be drilled into young dragons at the nursery ring is the need to avoid all forms of cold, particularly in their natural state. One thing worse than the cold for dragons in their prehistoric, dinosaur like natural state, is... snow. The impact of snow on a dragon's unshielded body has been described by historian dragons as akin to a human being branded with a red hot poker, over and over again, stung by a thousand jellyfish, while at the same time being flogged by a cat o' nine tails. Not very pleasant you could say, something Manson was proving right at this very moment. He'd thought that the dark dragon's earlier screams, which he now knew to be fake, were as bad as anything could sound. Boy was he wrong. The huge evil dragon was screaming and writhing around in absolute agony, trying desperately to bat away the snowflakes as the incredible flurry continued to strike his body.

Despite the burning of the snow, Peter let out a little chuckle at the sight of Manson in so much pain. From his prone position, he could just make out the foggy haze that encircled the pitch start to flicker.

'He must be in so much pain that he can't maintain his concentration,' Peter thought to himself. Through the occasional gap in the endless stream of snowflakes, he once again caught sight of the floodlight control box, not three metres away. He had nothing left to give. Most of his bodily fluids were strewn across the sand encrusted, icy pitch, which now had about two inches of snow covering it. He really didn't have anything else to give... honest! At least that's what his body kept saying. His mind, however, had other ideas. With the sound of the climactic fireworks and Manson's howls of agony pounding his besieged eardrums, his body made one last heroic attempt to get to its feet. He wasn't quite sure how it was happening, but unbelievably he had got up, in a very wobbly sort of way.

Swaying from side to side and being pelted at the same time by the torrent of burning snowflakes, he shuffled his feet through the deepening snow towards the control box.

Mind screaming in pain constantly from the injuries he'd already sustained and from the never ending flurries of snow, as if on some kind of autopilot, his legs continued shuffling along, determined to get to their destination. Only the thought of death offering a swift release played through the insanity that was now his mind, almost lost forever. But before madness could consume him fully, some tiny part of his consciousness recognised the object that stood before him... the green box had a covering of snow, nearly four inches deep and getting thicker with every second that passed. It was a thing of beauty he thought, as he stretched out his deeply cut and burned hands. Ignoring the pain and the noise, he gripped the locked cover and with the strength of someone else, casually ripped it off, tossing it to one side, where it landed with a THUD in the soft, thick snow. His vision started to fade as his body gave up, but he knew now that there was no chance of failure. Before him in the box lay four bright red buttons, the buttons that would each turn on a bank of two floodlights. When all were depressed, all eight of the giant lights would burst into life, illuminating the pitch for miles around. Reaching out with his right hand, he depressed all four buttons. In doing so, the pain became too much. As his battered legs gave out, he fell gracelessly into the snow, satisfaction sweeping over him from knowing that he'd switched all the lights on. He just hoped it would be enough.

Slumped below the control box, covered in snow, his life ebbing away, snowflakes still bombarding him, Peter's mind fed him what limited information it could. Through the barrage of now illuminated snow, he could just make out two human shaped silhouettes clambering over the still burning wreckage of the van by the blocked gate on the far side of the synthetic pitch. In the furthest corner of the pitch, it looked as though a giant figure of something with wings was trying frantically to take to the sky. That was the last thing he saw before everything turned black.

Flying through the open sky was the polar opposite of everything he'd recently felt. All he'd known was the biting pain of constant cold and chilling ice. But here he was now soaring through the sky, the radiant yellow sun beating down on his back as he cut through the air, executing perfect loop the loops. Sometimes he heard voices, carried on the soft breeze, some that even sounded like his friends, Richie and Tank. It was difficult to understand exactly what they were saying, but occasionally he could just make out the odd phrase, such as, "Hold on," and "It'll be okay, help's coming," but in the main, it just seemed like gibberish. Continuing on with his flying, occasionally he felt the odd burning sensation on his... hmmm. It felt like arms, but he was here, flying. So it had to be... .wings, didn't it?

'How odd,' he thought to himself, as he continued, getting ever closer to the scorching sun, feeling its warm embrace all over.

16 A KING SIZED SURPRISE

Brilliant light pierced his pupils as his eyes fluttered open. A clean, white, bright room swam slowly into view. Combing his memory, he searched for any clues as to where he was. Frustrated at coming up empty, he sunk his head back into the big squashy pillow and looked up at the bright ceiling lights. It was only then that he heard it: the sound of shallow breathing from somewhere off to his right. Trying to sit upright, he immediately wished he hadn't, as a wave of what can only be described as 'pain masked by strong medication' washed from his head to his toes. Closing his eyes momentarily, hearing the screech of a chair on the mezzanine floor as he did so, he felt a comforting hand gently squeeze his shoulder.

"Easy son, you've been through one hell of an ordeal," a soft, reassuring voice whispered.

Allowing the hand to guide him back down to a prone position, once again he found the comfort of the squashy pillow as it engulfed his head. After a few moments he opened his eyes, staring up at the ceiling, past the bright white lights. White polystyrene tiles with tiny holes in covered the whole ceiling. Something deep inside him screamed. Slowly at first, but it quickly turned into an unstoppable freight train as all the memories started to return, triggered by the innocuous ceiling tiles. Distinctly remembering hiding behind some, not that long ago, after that, the thoughts came thick and fast, overwhelming him. Fear coursed through him, quickly followed by panic. Ignoring the pain, he sat bolt upright. Knowing he'd felt worse made it much easier to ignore. Once again the hand landed gently on his shoulder, urging him to lie back. Ignoring it, he instead focused on who the hand belonged to. As the man's features materialised through the bright light, all he could think of was,

'YOU!'

The man nodded, offering a sympathetic smile, his long, unkempt, grey hair framed a hardened face that looked sad and happy in equal measures, a face that Peter had seen on many different occasions and in many different locations. Never though, had he seen him looking so serious. With his memories returned, he looked the old man in the eyes, and urgently said,

"I need to speak to the Council... now!"

"It's alright son," came the reply, "you are."

"You're part of the Council?" asked Peter wide eyed.

The old man's long grey hair bobbed around his shoulders as he nodded his reply.

Peter scratched his chin in thought, and for the very first time noticed the array of bandages covering his body.

"You need to know what happened. There was this... this... this... dragon... called Manson. He was, he was... after the laminium. Oh God, the laminium. Did he take it? Please tell me he didn't manage to take it."

Standing up, the old man walked to the head of the bed, behind Peter, and adjusted the pillows, so that the young dragon would be sitting up properly, before wearily slumping down in the chair beside the bed.

"He didn't take the laminium," he recounted, "well, not the bulk of it anyway."

Peter frowned as he sat propped up.

"Not the bulk of it?"

"There was close to two tonnes of raw laminium stolen from the Cropptech site. The amount recovered from the Astroturf, thanks to your intervention, matched that almost exactly. A discrepancy arises because, through intensive research, it appears that before the laminium was loaded onto the trucks, a small amount seems to already have been taken. As far as we can tell, about fifteen small chunks, roughly ring sized, weighing no more than six or seven grams each, were cut out of a much larger chunk of ore. How, we don't know. Our belief is that the rogue dragon Manson did this some time ago, without the assistance of anyone else, using the advanced technology at Cropptech. Still... no easy task to do on your own. Why he did this, we still don't know. As to where the missing laminium is, we have no idea about that either, but we do have agents working hard to try and find out. You interrupted a very sophisticated operation here, son."

Peter took in all the information, trying to piece it together in his mind. A question popped into his head as if from nowhere.

"Just how long have I been here?" he croaked, his mouth feeling like the eye of a sandstorm in the middle of the Sahara.

The old man got up and poured Peter a glass of water from the jug on the table beside his bed. Peter gulped it down pretty much in one go, not realising it was possible for water to taste that good.

"You were in a really bad way when you got here. By all accounts you should have been dead."

"Just where is here?" Peter interrupted.

"Salisbridge district hospital, where else? You're in one of the advanced treatment rooms secluded in the basement of the hospital. The emergency dragon plan was set into motion as soon as they were aware that you were on your way."

Nodding, he knew all about dragon plans from his lessons at the nursery ring. In time of great emergency, dragon wise, it should be possible in most major facilities to instigate a change of procedure that in effect subtly moves humans out of the way of what is really happening. In a hospital, for example, dragons in their human form hold posts that would allow them, in a catastrophe, to change shift and rota patterns unexpectedly and commandeer rooms and equipment without causing suspicion or alarm amongst the humans. Staff such as nurses, doctors and consultants, who may through their specific training recognise inconsistencies in the medical data and results from a patient that looks human but is in actual fact a dragon, would be casually relocated until such a time as the patient can either be found somewhere more private to be tended to, in or out of hospital, or has in fact recovered enough to hide their true identity and return to the dragon realm. Peter now knew that he was in the depths of Salisbridge hospital, hidden away, known only to a few, all of whom were dragons.

The old man continued.

"They say the only reason you survived was because someone at the scene applied a very fancy mantra, ancient in design, but incredibly effective. It stopped your body bleeding in an instant and then slowed your metabolism, effectively putting you in a coma, buying enough time for you to get here and be treated by the best we have. If it weren't for that mantra, you would have died."

Peter thought carefully about what he'd just been told. He couldn't recall any of it.

"Do you have any idea who would have done such a thing?"

He nodded, knowing straight away that it could only have been one person...

"Tank."

"Ahhh... your friend, the big dragon with a love of plants and animals."

"That's right," ventured Peter, suspiciously. "How do you know that?"

Abruptly, the old man (well... dragon) burst into a fit of laughter, the first time Peter had seen anything but seriousness since he'd woken up. After the laughter had died down, the old man wiped his eyes and turned to look at Peter.

"It's my job to know."

He nodded, not entirely convinced.

"Anyway, to answer your question. You've been here for six days."

"SIX DAYS!" exclaimed Peter. "And I'm still in this state, with all the bandages and everything."

"Your injuries were substantial. For some reason you don't seem to be healing as quickly as would normally be expected. Many different mantras have been used to try and heal your injuries, but alas, most have had little or no effect. We think that the particular dragon you came up against has some special abilities that might be contributing to how long it's taking you to heal. Perhaps if you're up to it, you could give me a more detailed description of what happened."

He felt truly terrible. In some respects it felt as though he was back on the chilly Astroturf, taking the beating of his life. But he didn't want to let anyone down, not least the dragon Council. So, taking a small sip of his water, he replied,

"Of course. Where would you like to start?"

"At the beginning," coaxed the old man, settling into his chair.

That's where Peter began and over the course of two hours, told the old man everything he could remember. Occasionally the old man would interrupt him and ask a question, but for the most part he just sat in his chair and listened.

Having finished reciting his account of the events of the last few months, he lay back in the hospital bed and closed his eyes, grateful not to have to think about it anymore. In silence, the old man considered everything he'd heard. Eventually he spoke up.

"Thank you for your frank and honest account of what happened. It's pretty much as the Council assumed," he said seriously. "There are one or two more details that we were unaware of, but the bulk of it we'd managed to piece together over the last few days."

Lying there with his eyes closed, hoping not to come across as rude, he nodded at what the old man had said.

"I'm guessing there are questions you'd like answered?"

Opening his eyes, Peter nodded eagerly, ready to risk his somewhat croaky voice. Before he got the chance, the old man held up one hand to stop him.

"How about I tell you as much as I can, and then if you have any questions, we can deal with them at the end?"

Peter smiled and nodded, knowing a good compromise when he saw one.

"First things first," announced the old man. "You will no doubt be pleased to hear that Al Garrett has made a full recovery, and with the exception of feeling a little fatigued, is back to his normal, chirpy self, well on his way to reversing everything Manson did at Cropptech, including re-employing everyone who had been fired."

The thought of Garrett once again in charge, and the company pretty much back to the way it had been, forced him to smile.

"He also knows that it was you that took Manson down and recovered the stolen laminium. At the moment everyone thinks you're in intensive care, which in a way you are," smiled the old man. "So I'm sure Garrett and his staff will want to congratulate you when you're well enough to return."

Peter raised his eyebrows at this.

"You were always going to get your job back, it's only a matter of when you're fit enough to return. As far as everyone at Cropptech knows, you had your suspicions about Manson some time ago, you were just biding your time to gather enough evidence against him. They all know you got badly hurt in getting the laminium back. There's a warrant out for Manson's arrest... the human Manson, obviously. Don't worry though, the humans have strict instructions not to approach him. Dragon infiltrators are on the case. Not that anyone expects him to show up in his human form. Personally I think he's long gone."

A crazy picture of human police officers looking at a wanted picture of a gigantic matt black dragon ran through Peter's head, causing him to spill a little of his drink in his lap.

The old man gave him a curious look.

"Events at the Astroturf have all been resolved successfully, mainly due to the quick thinking of the dragons present at the fireworks display. They managed to alert us to the situation very quickly, and a squad of our finest recovery dragons were able to attend the scene within a matter of minutes. None of the humans had left, thank goodness. Posing as police officers, the recovery squad applied a blanket mantra, making everyone think they'd seen the same thing... a lightning strike. While the humans had their memories adjusted, a cleanup squad worked hard on the synthetic pitch itself. Before daylight the next morning, you'll be pleased to know the Astroturf, its fences and floodlights had all been repaired after the damage caused the night before. Apparently it looks as good as new, only with a large smattering of sand in the hope that nobody would look too closely at the surface."

This news pleased Peter almost as much as hearing that Al Garrett had fully recovered. Strange really, but the pitch itself seemed very much like an old friend after all the games of hockey he'd played on it. It was hard to explain, even to himself. At least none of his human friends, or more importantly their children, would be scarred by what they'd seen. He'd had visions of children seeing a big dragon flying over them in the night sky, or the burning remains of a van full of dead bodies. Although he was one of the many dragons that didn't approve of mantras that adjusted human memories as a rule (something that wasn't done that often anyway, and when it was, there were strict guidelines and regulations controlling it,) in this instance, he was glad it had been done, and felt happy in the knowledge that his friends, teammates and their families would remember nothing more than having an enjoyable evening watching the fireworks.

"You will also be pleased to know that your car has been recovered from... " the old man pulled out a sheet of paper from the top pocket of his white linen shirt and studied it, "ah yes, from the housing estate beside the

Cropptech site. It's very handy having dragons in high places in most of the country's police forces. Your car is now back outside your house. Speaking of which, we have two dragons looking after your house at the moment. Posing as your aunt and her best friend, they'll remain there for as long as it takes you to fully recover. They look completely innocuous to the neighbours who have been more than a little curious, but are in fact elite members of the King's Guard. We've put them there just in case Manson or one of his associates should try to come back and finish things off. We don't have any reason to believe he will, particularly with both the dragon and human world on such a high alert because of him, but we thought it prudent to do so for at least a few weeks."

Once again, Peter nodded, taking it all in. He hadn't even considered that Manson would come back for him, but the more his mind dwelled on it now, the more uncomfortable he felt about the whole thing.

As if reading Peter's mind, the old man interrupted his chain of thought.

"Don't worry son, we're having a few modifications made to your house, just in case you should get such a visit. Undoubtedly things will never be quite the same, for either you or dragonkind in general. But the one thing that will happen, mark my words, is that we all, including you, will be prepared."

As the words left the old man's mouth, a feeling of hope ran through Peter. If anyone else had told him that the dragon world would be ready to take on Manson and his associates, he would probably have laughed in their face. But there was something about this guy, something about the way he talked, carried himself, spoke, the way he looked into your eyes... Peter had no doubt at all that if the old man told him to run up the stairs to the top of the hospital and fight Manson all over again, he would, here and now, even though he wouldn't want to of course. This old man seemed so ordinary and yet, Peter decided, he would follow him into battle at a moment's notice.

"As well, your phone and that very fancy necklace that I saw you wearing the last time we met on the monorail station, have both been recovered and are now in the drawers beside your bed. And that my young friend, is all that I have to tell you. Do you have any other questions at all?"

"One thing that really bothers me," Peter croaked, taking a small sip of his drink, "is the matter of how Manson knew I was going to try and cure Garrett on that particular Friday. I'd worked so hard and planned it all out to the very last detail. I even watched as his car left the facility to go to the awards ceremony."

"Are you sure you didn't tell anyone?"

Concentrating as much as he could, he thought back to the events leading up to all that.

"I'm sure I didn't tell anyone my intentions. Tank delivered the cure to me, but had no idea what I was planning to do or when." Suddenly, he remembered.

"I do recall sending a brief communication to Councillor Rosebloom though. He sent me a message asking for an update on my progress, as I hadn't been keeping him informed about what was going on," recounted Peter, more than a little guiltily.

"Did you tell him about your plan?"

Peter thought for a moment.

"No, no I didn't. I sent him a quick message telling him when the whole thing would be resolved by, but I didn't give him any details."

The old man twiddled the ends of his unkempt hair in thought.

"What I tell you next must be in absolute secrecy, between you and me. Do you understand?"

"Of course."

"I and some of the other members of the Council have had doubts about Rosebloom for some time. A number of his actions in the past have seemed dubious to say the

least, but nothing has ever been proved against him."
Revealing all this, the old man looked deeply troubled.
"He's also related to a rather treacherous fellow from very
far back in the past. A person called... Osvaldo."

Peter vaguely recognised the name, but maybe because
of the drugs, or the fact that his body was still recovering
from the beating it had taken, he couldn't quite put his
finger on it. The old man continued.

"Osvaldo cost the lives of many good dragons, a long
time ago. It's been generally believed that he's been dead a
very long time, but every now and then something comes
up that has all the hallmarks of Osvaldo. I don't believe for
one second that he's dead. What I do believe is that he is
in some way connected to Councillor Rosebloom. I don't
know how, and more importantly, I can't prove anything,
but I would stake my life on it. While you've done the right
thing Peter, I think it's best and also safest for you if you
give Councillor Rosebloom a very wide berth. If he or
anyone else asks, you're to say that I've asked you to report
directly to me. Is that okay?"

Peter stared wide eyed at the old man, barely able to
believe anything he'd heard.

"Of course, of course," he croaked in reply.

Though tired, drugged, bruised, battered and
overwhelmed, he mulled over everything in his mind,
unable to think of anything else he wanted to say, which
was just as well because once again the old man spoke up.

"Oh... the one thing I didn't tell you, but you've
probably figured out already, is that you're being guarded
by a whole host of police down here. All of them are
dragons, along with all the medical staff of course. You
haven't been allowed any visitors I'm afraid, due to the
seriousness of the situation, but I've a funny feeling that
there might just be some waiting to see you right now."

Feeling exhausted, just the thought of any visitors
threatened to send him to sleep, but before he had a
chance to say anything, the old man closed his eyes and

whispered,

"Send them in."

Stretching out with his dragon senses, which were limited at the moment due to his injuries, he could just about sense the guards who manned the corridor, two of whom he felt hiding in the recesses of the ceiling. Just as he felt his strength waning, right at the limit of his ability, he felt a familiar presence, no make that two familiar presences. HIS FRIENDS!!!

Mere seconds later Richie and Tank burst through the door like a raging river, grinning like Cheshire cats. Both ran straight to Peter's bedside, crowding him for all he was worth.

"You had us so worried," announced Richie, bending forward and kissing him on the forehead.

Peter smiled, squeezing Richie's hand tight. Tank leant in close and said,

"Yes so worried," and puckered up, ready to kiss Peter too.

Peter burst into a fit of laughter, something it seemed he hadn't done in an absolute age, his injuries flaring up with pain. Both friends followed suit with the laughter, almost as though the three of them were back in the nursery ring. As the hilarity came to a gradual halt, the friends noticed they were not alone in the room. Silence overtook what should have been a joyous reunion. Tank and Richie stared at the old man. Peter couldn't comprehend exactly what was going on, but joined his friends anyway. He wanted to tell them that they had nothing to worry about as this was one of the Council members. Joining his friends in looking over the old man, he was drawn for the very first time to the stunning looking cane that the old man always kept with him. Something at the back of him mind nagged at him, but for the life of him he couldn't work out what it was.

Tank reacted first, shooting down on one knee faster than a bullet from a gun. Unusual for Richie not to be first on the uptake, she too dropped to one knee, as quick as a flash, right behind the strapping rugby player. Peter sat up as far as he was able to without passing out. Leaning over the side of the bed, watching his friends both on one knee, their heads bowed, he wondered briefly if they'd both gone mad.

"What's going on?" he whispered in Tank's direction.

Tank curled his head round slightly, rolling his eyes in the direction of the old man. Peter had absolutely no idea what was happening.

"Enough!" commanded the old man sternly. "You may both get up."

Peter was stunned to see both of his friends obey immediately.

Both Tank and Richie glanced at Peter, who it had to be said, had the most confused expression ever, almost as if someone were trying to explain football's offside rule.

Eventually, he had no choice but to ask,

"What the hell is going on?"

Tank turned to face his friend and mouthed just one word.

"King."

Totally baffled, Peter mouthed back the same word to his friend.

Tank shook his head in disbelief.

"What he's trying to tell you," laughed the old man, grinning from ear to ear, "is that I'm the... KING!"

Peter gulped as his stomach did a somersault that any Olympic gymnast would have been proud of.

"The king?" he said sceptically.

"That's right," replied the king, smiling.

"But you said you were from the Council?" ventured Peter.

"Well, technically, I am," answered the king, standing up. As he did so, he pulled his cane out from behind the chair, moving closer to the bed, alongside Tank and Richie.

Looking magnificent, the cane reflected the bright white light from the ceiling in a kind of purple hue, whilst continually looking flexible and strong, both at the same time. Two thirds of the way up its hilt, a sparkling purple trident carved into it glowed, occasionally pulsing on and off. Raising his head, he followed the entire length of the cane, stopping only when he reached the top, and the old man's hand.

'I can't believe it,' he thought to himself. 'It's so obvious now.' As the old man's hand rested on the cane, it wasn't its top which caught Peter's attention. It was the ring on the middle finger of the old man's hand. Not just any ring, but the most famous and recognisable ring in the kingdom. How on earth had he not spotted it before? Silently, Peter berated himself.

The old man, no, the king, spotted Peter gazing intently at the ring.

"Mesmerising isn't it?"

"It certainly is," replied Peter, not taking his eyes off it for one moment.

"When I first joined the Council, hundreds of years ago, I was but a lowly knight, easily the youngest dragon there," the king continued, starry eyed. "I attended Council meetings whenever my knight's duties allowed, and also had private audiences with the king on a regular basis. Years passed, and not once did I notice this," he declared, holding up his hand, indicating the spectacular ring.

Each of the three friends let out a long breath.

Holding up his hand to stop the inevitable question being asked, the king continued.

"You see, the ring itself, as well as containing an almost limitless supply of... how would you put it... mana, magic, mantra enhancing energy, has a sentience of its own, a mind if you like. It can sense those all about it, good, bad, indifferent. And for some peculiar reason, which to this day isn't known even to me, it chooses not to show itself to certain individuals. Ever since we first met Peter, you've never been able to see the ring, not before just now when your friends pointed out to you who I am, even when others around you can."

"Why has it always been concealed from me, up until now I mean?"

"That's what I've been trying to tell you. I have absolutely no idea. The crazy band has a mind of its own. I can use its power and enhance mantras and spells at will, whenever I like, although I wouldn't be surprised to learn that actually it's humouring me in some way, shape or form, but I have no control over who it shows itself to."

Off to one side, Tank began to open his mouth to ask a question. Before he could do so, he was stopped once again by the king.

"And before you ask, hardly anyone knows what I've just told you, and I'd like it to remain that way, our little secret."

The three friends nodded eagerly in unison. Well, you would wouldn't you... for the king.

"Good. I know I can trust each and every one of you," declared the king, stepping back a little from the bed, so that he could take in Tank and Richie.

Richie bowed her head as the king stared straight at her. She didn't want to appear rude. In truth, she didn't know what to do.

Taking a couple of paces forward, the king reached out and gently tilted her head by the chin, so that they could look into each other's eyes.

"No need to be shy, child," he whispered softly, all the time taking her in. It wasn't often Richie was lost for words, but she was most certainly speechless now. Peter and Tank exchanged a little glance, knowing that in any other situation, they'd probably be laughing their socks off at their friend's dilemma.

"You would be Richie Rump. Am I correct?" asked the king.

She blushed as she nodded a response.

"Hmmmm...," uttered the king, studying Richie carefully. "So much paperwork comes my way that it's often hard to pick out the wood from the trees. So many individuals, it's almost impossible, even with an eidetic memory to remember, but you... hmmmm... I seem to recall."

Worried expressions developed on both Tank and Peter's faces simultaneously, knowing all about Richie's antics, standing up for everyone all the time, showing off, arm wrestling rugby players, that sort of thing. It looked as though it was all going to come back and bite her in the ass in the biggest possible way.

Richie's blushing disappeared, a much more defiant expression taking its place. The two friends looked on in horror.

"Yes, that's right," said the king, suddenly seeming to remember something.

"The last report with your name on it mentioned something about... what was it again... arm wrestling big, bulky sportsmen of some sort. Would that be correct?"

Jutting out her chin, her expression remaining defiant, she looked the king firmly in the eyes and answered,

"Yes."

'This is it,' thought Peter. 'Richie's going to get carted off and be forced to remain underground, with little or no chance of ever getting to see the planet's surface or the humans ever again. Perhaps', he thought, 'if I could just beg forgiveness on her behalf, then just maybe she'll be allowed to stay.'

Before he had a chance to act, the king burst into the biggest, rambunctious belly laugh that he'd ever heard in his entire life, bewildering all three friends. After thirty seconds or so, the king managed to regain his composure.

Peter had no idea what was going to happen next. Unexpectedly, the monarch put his arm around Richie's shoulders in a fatherly sort of way.

"Save the defiance for somebody else, my dear," he

said, plainly amused. "It's wasted on me. I know about most of the things you get up to. I've followed your career with interest ever since I presented you with your prize for winning the 553rd History Fest Face-Off nearly fifty years ago in Bath. Ever since you graduated from the nursery ring, I've been getting reports with your name on them. Of course some of my advisors frown upon your actions, but then most of them are pushing three hundred years old and have never even visited the surface, let alone lived amongst the humans. Much the same can be said for some of the other dragons living in Salisbridge, I'm afraid, which is why I see so many reports linked to your good self. In all honesty, they'd like to see me give you some sort of reprimand or dressing down, I'm sure. But you remind me of..." A thoughtful expression crossed his weathered face. "Let's just say another dragon I once knew. He acted in much the same way and although many frowned upon his actions, his heart was in the right place, wanting only the best for the humans."

A little smile broke the steely facade of Richie's face momentarily, as she remembered that day in Bath when she'd been given her full name.

"That's not to say that I'm giving you some sort of permission to embarrass and ridicule human kind on a regular basis, you understand," voiced the king sternly.

Richie's smile disappeared faster than a rat out of an aqueduct.

"But, and if you tell anyone outside this room that I said this, ohhhh they'll be trouble," said the king, now smiling, "I trust you to keep the humans on their toes, and bring the ones that get too big for their boots, down to Earth once in a while." The king held out his hand for Richie to shake, before adding, "Deal?"

Richie grasped the outstretched hand, her confidence restored. Instead of shaking it, she walked right up to him and planted a soft kiss on his weathered right cheek.

Peter and Tank both winced as she did so. They were

pretty sure that kissing the monarch without permission wasn't royal protocol. However, the king just let out a raucous cackle, much to the friends' relief.

Having finished laughing, the king turned to study Tank. Unlike Richie, Tank carried himself as always, with a cheerful expression and a larger degree of modesty. He stood happily as the king approached him and gazed into his large, smiling face.

"And you would be... Tank?" suggested the king.

"That's right," replied Tank, offering out his hand. "Pleased to meet you, Your Majesty."

A sudden frown crept over the monarch's face.

"What... no kiss?"

For a split second Tank's face was an absolute picture. Richie burst into laughter first, followed swiftly by the king and then Peter. Tank soon saw the funny side and joined in, always able to appreciate a joke at his own expense.

"Sorry, son," chuckled the king, when the guffaws died down. "Couldn't resist I'm afraid."

"No problem," countered Tank, meaning every word.

"You're the one that nearly became a laminium ball player, is that right?"

"Yes, Your Majesty."

Peter and Richie shared a momentary look of astonishment. That was news to them.

"And now you work for... Gee Tee?"

"Yes, Majesty."

"Less of the majesty," ordered the king. "We're all friends here."

Tank nodded his big head in agreement.

"How do you like working for the master mantra maker, son?"

"It's fascinating," Tank asserted wistfully. "I had no idea that so many different types of mantras and magical artefacts existed. I've only seen a fraction of what's in the shop itself, but those that I have would make most dragons' eyes pop out."

This time it was the king's turn to nod in agreement.

"Not to mentions the things Gee Tee himself knows," continued the rugby playing dragon. "Some of it's mind boggling, it really is, but mostly it's just absolutely brilliant. I'm sure with more time and research, the mantras, combined with Gee Tee's breadth of knowledge could have astounding beneficial effects on human civilisation."

About to go off on one as Peter liked to describe it, the king stopped the young dragon before he could go any further, having already got the impression that the youngster could talk about his work for a whole day or more.

Peter smiled on noting how quick the king was on the uptake. Clearly one of the attributes of being the monarch was to be able to distinguish somebody that could talk at great length and know just when, and how, to stop them.

"I do hope that before you use any of your newfound knowledge topside that you'll run it by the planetary development department at the Council."

"Of course, Majesty."

"You could also perform a small act for me," stated the king, "and don't worry, there's no kissing involved."

All three of them smiled at the king's joke as Tank replied,

"Anything, Your Majesty."

"You could thank your employer for helping out in this instance, from me personally. Also, perhaps you'd be good enough to tell him that I'm sorry it's been so long, but I will pop in as soon as I get the chance. I look forward to examining some of his... mantra ink again."

Taking a sip of water just as the king uttered those last few words, on hearing "mantra ink", Peter sprayed the entire length of the bed with the contents of his mouth, then went on to have the mother of all coughing fits. Richie patted him hard on the back, so hard in fact that his internal organs felt it. The king, meanwhile, gave him a knowing look.

"You do know Peter, that certain mantra ink has an age requirement before you can use it?" declared the monarch, in a tone that could have been either very serious or a little light hearted. Finished with his coughing, Peter pretended not to know what the king was talking about, while it was abundantly clear that neither Richie or Tank needed to pretend. The king turned his attention back to Tank.

"I'll certainly pass the message on, Majesty," said Tank, letting all the stuff about the mantra ink go over his head.

"Good dragon," remarked the king, slapping Tank hard on the shoulder.

"You know Gee Tee?" enquired Peter from his hospital bed.

"Who doesn't?" replied the king quickly.

Peter eyed him suspiciously, suspecting there was more to it than that.

"Truth be told," added the king, looking around cautiously, "the old shopkeeper has helped me in much the same way he's helped you, on more than one occasion. In fact, I'm pretty sure that I wouldn't be standing here if not for his help. I owe him my life many times over, as I'm sure many other adventuring dragons down the ages do. Once again, I feel I'm trusting the three of you with one of my innermost secrets."

"We won't say a thing," the three of them replied, almost in unison.

Nodding, the king acknowledged that he could trust them, and then stepped back so that he could address all of them at once.

"I think now might be a good time to take my leave and let the three of you catch up."

Relief ran through Tank and Richie. Although honoured and gobsmacked in equal measures to meet the king in person, something very few dragons ever got to do, they were also more than a little unsure of how to act and behave in front of him. Peter, on the other hand, was very nearly overwhelmed by panic. At first he wasn't quite sure why, but a split second later he knew. He wanted answers, answers that perhaps he would never have the chance to get again. Quickly swinging his legs down to the floor from the bed, ignoring the searing pain, he stood up, and despite the fact that his head spun more than a little, he wobbled over towards the king. Tank and Richie rushed to his aid, but he waved both of them away and stood firmly in front of the monarch on his own two feet. The king looked at him bemused.

"Please don't go just yet," he pleaded.

"I'm afraid I have some very important unfinished business to attend to," answered the king.

"I... I... I... I have some more questions," stuttered Peter, gazing straight down at the floor.

"Okay," agreed the king, picking up on just how important this seemed to the young dragon. "What's on your mind, son?"

With the undivided attention of the dragon king, in this small hospital room, suddenly Peter felt under extreme pressure, almost wishing he'd kept his mouth shut.

"Don't be shy son. You can ask me anything you like."

Feeling the steam rising off him, much in the same way it did off his favourite steam trains in Swanage, nerves caused his stomach to rumble and tumble, while his legs wobbled like jelly. Grabbing his arm, the king led him back to the bed. Peter gratefully sat down on the edge of it.

"Is it something you'd rather not have your friends hear?" asked the king, glancing over at Tank and Richie.

"No... no... no... not at all."

"Then ask," said the king. "I don't bite, well... not in this form anyway."

Peter managed to smile at the king's attempt to put him at ease.

"It's just that... it's just that... why me?"

The king looked questioningly back at him. Peter knew he hadn't made himself clear.

"I understand the whole Cropptech, Manson thing... he

458

was after the laminium and I was just in his way. Wrong place, wrong time and all that. It's just, well... I was wondering why you sought me out all those times in the past? Do you do that for everybody or is there some sort of reason?"

"Ahhh," sighed the king. "I did wonder if you would ask."

Peter lifted his head expectantly.

"Perhaps the three of you should sit," suggested the king, motioning towards the bed.

Tank and Richie perched down on the edge, one either side of Peter. The king in the meantime looked as though he was doing some serious thinking, deciding no doubt just how much he could tell the three friends.

After pacing the length of the room twice, the monarch stood in front of the trio and began.

"I haven't always been king, as I'm sure you're all aware. I've already mentioned that at the start of my career on the Council, I was also a knight. What you probably don't know, and only a few do, is that I wasn't just any knight. In fact, I'm guessing with a little help, Peter can tell the two of you exactly who I once was, before I became king."

Tank and Richie turned towards Peter, waiting for him to work it out.

Feeling the pressure and expectation on him mount, Peter didn't care for it very much, and had no idea how he was supposed to work out the king's puzzle. He'd never met a genuine knight, only heard the stories like so many of the other dragonlings. Noting the youngster's creased face, the king took pity on him, giving him the clue that he so needed.

"What would be the most ironic thing, bearing in mind your favourite nursery ring tale?"

Racking his brains, he tried desperately hard to think what the king meant. No good at quizzes at the best of times, he felt this most certainly wasn't one of those. As the breath from each of his friends caressed either cheek and steam rose steadily from beneath his dark, curly locks, he gazed up into the king's worn, but kindly face. In that moment, it looked as though it had seen terrible tragedies and remarkable sorrow.

'What would be ironic?' he thought over and over to himself. His favourite tale with or without a knight was of course George and the Dragon. He'd heard it so many times that he knew it off by heart, but ironic?

Abruptly, the light bulb moment in his mind arrived.

'You've got to be kidding me!' he thought, smiling at the king, trying to gauge if it could be true. The old man persona had a perfect poker face and gave nothing away.

"Are you really him?" Peter asked quietly.

The king gave a gentle nod in return.

"I've always thought it ironic that your favourite tale was that particular one."

Richie and Tank were frantic, bursting to know what was going on.

"Is anyone going to let us in on the little secret?" requested Tank, feigning annoyance.

The king smiled at them all.

"As a knight, I believe you would have known me as... George. You might even remember a little encounter I had with a... dragon."

It took a couple of seconds for the penny to drop, but for anyone who was watching, the wait would have been thoroughly worth it. Richie's eyes were as wide as dinner plates, while at the same time Tank's jaw nearly hit the floor.

"*The* George, from George and the Dragon," the two friends said as one.

Once again the king nodded, remembering fondly his time as the knight, George.

'So long ago,' he thought, 'far simpler times.'

"All my secrets are coming out today, it would seem. You may all address me as George in private. Otherwise you'll have to stick to Your Majesty."

All three friends nodded at once.

"The reason that I've followed you with interest, Peter, is that your grandfather, your mother's father, was one of my most trusted comrades. We fought side by side for decades and developed something of a friendship."

Peter's face had gone totally ashen. He'd never met his grandfather, but had inherited the house in Salisbridge and all its contents from him, never really knowing what had become of him.

The king, glancing over at Peter's face, decided to press on.

"I first met your grandfather the day after the battle with Troydenn. He was one of the first to arrive in the city. Although already a seasoned warrior, what impressed me most about him was his ability to recognise what needed to be done, and then to get on and do it. Immediately he helped set up the first of the emergency hospitals... no more really than a large hall with an array of tables and a primitive grasp of medicine. But straight away he mucked in, organising triage, making use of everything available in an effort to save as many humans as possible. They were desperate and dark times. While others slept from exhaustion, he'd wander the wreckage of the beleaguered city looking for anything that had been missed. Most thought him mad, myself included at the time. However, we were all proved wrong when, on the second night, he was heard shouting out for help. For a moment we all thought our worst nightmares had sprung back into life and that Troydenn had escaped. Not so. Your grandfather had moved a huge amount of rubble on his own and found a pregnant woman trapped in a hole about thirty feet deep, still alive. She was only moments away from giving birth. With the surrounding area unstable and ready to collapse, and with the child about to spring into this world, your grandfather, with absolutely no thought for his own safety, tossed me the end of a rope, and then clambered down into the hole, gripping the rope with one hand, carrying a lamp in the other. While I and a few others watched from atop the rubble, your grandfather safely delivered the baby, a girl if memory serves me correctly. He then, calmly as you like, tied the baby to the rope, wrapped in his own clothing and let us bring her out, doing the same with the mother shortly after. Only after they were safe did he come out himself. I've fought battles against some of the harshest monsters this planet has to offer, but I can honestly say that incident was one of the bravest things I've ever witnessed."

Peter couldn't hide the stream of tears that gushed down his cheeks from his friends sitting either side of him, listening intently.

"After that night, I made a point of finding out about your grandfather. He was the kind of dragon I wanted by my side. Brave, fearless, inventive, he possessed all those qualities and more. During that damned episode he helped transport Troydenn back underground and but for a quirk of fate would have been one of the guards that accompanied the conspirators on that fateful journey to the South Pole. The king at the time had heard about his heroics in the city, mainly from me but from others as well, and rather than let him go to Antarctica, instead promoted him and assigned him to partner me. And the rest, as they say, is history. He stayed, avoided death at the Pole, got promoted, we worked together and became the best of friends."

Stopping all of a sudden, the king rubbed his forehead, looking as sombre as any of the friends had seen him that afternoon. Tears continued to stream down Peter's face at the thought of the valiant and heroic deeds his grandfather had performed alongside George, all those years ago.

Continuing where he left off, the king started pacing again.

"As the years went by, I became enthralled by and embedded in the politics of the dragon kingdom, looking to make an impact and shape the world in that particular forum. Your grandfather had little time for politics and especially politicians. He thought them time wasters and frauds. Many a night we would down an ale together and nibble on some charcoal, putting the world to rights, fighting like cat and dog about how best to serve the world. God I miss those nights so much," sighed the king. "Although our careers kept us apart for long periods of time, we always reunited wherever possible. The bond of friendship between us remained strong. Eventually I was crowned king, not in the most pleasant of circumstances, but something I'd worked towards for a very long time. One of my first acts as the new monarch was to recall your grandfather from the mission he was on. When he arrived in my chambers, he was livid, raging on about how important the mission was and how I had wrecked everything, calling him back at a moment's notice. It took some time, and many broken relics, for him to calm down. Those chambers were never quite the same after that. In due course, he listened to what I had to say. Most rulers have their own emissaries, right hand dragons, call them what you will. I explained to your grandfather that I wanted him to be mine. He scoffed and laughed at me for quite some time. Finally, however, after I explained to him that he was the only dragon on the entire planet that I trusted completely and utterly, he started to listen. I explained that not only would it be diplomatic matters that he would deal with, but also delicate matters that might require a more... covert approach. This got his attention, and somewhat reluctantly he agreed to take up the position. From my point of view, I never looked back. Despite his reservations, he was a wonderful diplomat: courteous, understanding, intelligent and tough as nails when he had to be. Carrying out covert operations with such cunning, skill and guile, he undoubtedly saved tens of thousands of lives, both human and dragon, most certainly making the world a much better and more civilised place.

Pacing across the hospital room quickly now, the king's

bottom lip began to quiver just a little, as Peter wiped away the tears, determined to hear the rest of the story. He'd always felt a connection with his grandfather, even though he'd never known him. Everything he'd heard here today made him so proud.

"About seventy or so years ago," began the king, threatening to become overwhelmed by the situation, "I sent your grandfather on one of those missions. At the time it didn't seem like anything too special; neither of us had any major concerns about the outcome or indeed how it would be carried out. The danger was minimal. Or so we thought. Anyhow, that fateful mission went wrong. To this day, I'm not quite sure how, but it did. Neither your grandfather nor any of the dragons with him have been heard from to this very day. I sent other teams to search for them, but all to no avail."

Wandering around to the other side of Peter's bed, the king slumped in the chair, eyes closed, running his hands through his long grey hair.

"I wish to God that I'd never sent him on that blasted assignment," he ranted angrily. "There were others that could have gone in his place, but none were as good as he was. No matter what, he always got the job done. I still have no idea to this very day what happened to him and his team. I've done everything I can think of to find out. I'd give everything I have just to know."

Richie and Tank sat rigid on the edge of the bed, the quiet, out of the way hospital room punctuated by only the sounds of the king and Peter sobbing.

Moments passed, seconds turned into minutes, and the crying stopped. To his credit the king, although upset, was determined to carry on and finish off the story.

"Some time before all that, a few years earlier in fact, your grandfather had taken me to the Purbeck nursery ring to see you. We travelled incognito, not wanting to be recognised. It was difficult not to recognise you with that bent whistle marking that, even as a young dragon, stood out very clearly. While we were there, perched on the wall by the side of the walkway, watching you listen intently to your *tor*, he asked a great favour of me. He asked that I look out for you, should anything happen to him. Telling me that he'd left you his house and all the belongings inside it, he was very serious about making sure you were looked after. How could I possibly refuse?

The other thing he went on to mention was the fact that he'd fallen out with your parents. I have no specific details as to why, but something very bad happened between them. So much so, that when they deposited your egg at the nursery ring before they disappeared, they left explicit instructions not to let your grandfather have anything to do with you, for as long as you were there. As you are aware, those instructions have to be followed to the letter. And so it was they upped and left as many parents do."

Peter covered his eyes with his hand, thinking that he might cry again. It was all too much to take in. He felt sad that his parents had left him without so much as a thought. Why couldn't he have grown up in their company? Where had they gone? He'd known their names on leaving the nursery ring, and had looked them up on the dragon register. But there was no sign of either of them anywhere. They seemed to have abandoned him and disappeared into thin air.

Despite his disappointment at a life without his parents, he felt great pride and love for the grandfather he'd never known. From what he'd heard this afternoon, his mother's father sounded like such a decent dragon, making sure his house and its contents were passed down and that his best friend (the king) kept an eye on him. Through watery eyes and snot filled nostrils, he desperately wished he could have met him, just once. As he delved deeper into his thoughts, anger leapt up to the forefront, threatening to consume him.

'Why would they not want my grandfather to come

near me? What did they fall out over? It must have been something really bad to cause all that. Did it have something to do with them leaving?'

Startled back to the present by the sound of the king clearing his throat, Peter continued listening.

"Despite the instructions that he wasn't allowed to have anything to do with you, I know for a fact that your grandfather would spend most of his time when he wasn't working for me, sitting alone on that wall next to the nursery ring, watching your development, looking over you in his own special way."

On hearing this, Peter's head fell into his hands, the tears readily flowing down both cheeks again, dropping onto the polished white floor.

"Only a month or so after he took me to see you at the nursery ring, your grandfather left a large trunk with me (not the grey sort with the meanest wakeup call in the world) to be given to you when I thought you were ready for it. To this day, it remains untouched in my home, waiting for you. Perhaps when you've fully recovered you can come and claim it; your friends would be welcome too."

Continuing to cry, Peter gave a large sniff as he nodded in reply.

The king's mood lightened a little, a weight lifted from his shoulders.

"Have you ever wondered why your grandfather's house is in Salisbridge?" he asked cheerily.

Peter shook his head, as both Tank and Richie looked on.

"It seems he fell in love with the place while working there. I bet you can't guess when that was?"

With Peter still distraught, Tank thought he'd try and break the silence that was becoming more awkward by the second, so he replied, trying to lighten the mood,

"During your fight with Troydenn... you know, George and the Dragon and all that."

466

"Exactly!" roared the king, much to Tank's astonishment. All three of them looked up at the monarch, thinking that perhaps he was building up to one of his jokes.

"It's true," exclaimed the king. History books only ever mention that I battled Troydenn in some rural part of England. They never actually say where, but it was in fact Salisbridge. Your grandfather once told me that from the moment he arrived there as part of the aid effort, he felt a connection of some sort, not just to the people, but to the city itself. Throughout the years, whenever he was off duty or recovering from one of the missions that I'd sent him on, he could always be found in Salisbridge. Eventually he bought his own human house there around the turn of the century I believe," said the king wistfully. "And he remained in love with the place right up until he... until the day he left on that fateful mission."

Peter's head sprang up, looking the king right in the eyes.

"Can I ask what the mission he set out to do was... please?"

This clearly caught the king off guard. He hadn't for the life of him been prepared for this, but perhaps he should have been. Wandering over to Peter, the monarch crouched down in front of him.

"I'm afraid it's not quite that simple, my young friend. You see, the mission and all information pertaining to it is top secret. And while I would be quite happy to tell you and trust you with that information, if it ever got out that I did so without the permission of the Council itself, my political enemies would use it against me. I can, however, put in a request to the Council on your behalf, asking for the details to be shared with you, so that you may put to rest the memory of your grandfather. Would you like me to do that?"

Peter nodded vigorously.

"Yes please."

"Okay son, I'll do that for you. Hopefully by the time you're well enough to come to visit me and pick up your grandfather's belongings, I'll have some sort of decision as to whether or not the details can be revealed to you."

With the king looking as though he was about to make his excuses and leave, Tank raised his hand to ask a question about something that had been bugging him for a little while now.

Smiling at Tank's manners, the monarch asked,

"What's on your mind, big fella?"

Tilting his head to one side, giving the king one of his lopsided grins, Tank asked,

"We were always taught in the nursery ring that the dragon king wasn't allowed on the surface of the planet... ever! If that's so, how is it that you're here?"

"And I thought it was this young lady here, who was the smarty pants of the group," laughed the king, gazing at Richie.

Richie blushed, lost for words once again.

"It would appear that I've been... busted!" announced the monarch, opening his arms wide, whilst whirling around in a circle. "Guards, guards, guards, come and arrest me!"

Tank perched on the hospital bed, wishing he'd never asked.

"Let me share something else with all three of you. I'm not supposed to be on the surface," whispered the king, tapping his nose. "But I figure since I'm the king, I'll do as I damn well please."

All three friends chuckled at his attitude.

"And let me tell you another thing. I haven't been above ground in over a hundred years and I'm not sure I care for it too much. It's all so... fast. Everyone's in a hurry... cars, people, even the hospital porters, dragging patients at top speed everywhere, and driving those damned little trucks. Five times I was nearly run over by them on my way here. Five times!"

The friends were beside themselves with laughter at this, tears, for very different reasons, racing down their cheeks.

"It's all true," cried the king indignantly. "Seriously though, Tank, you're right. I'm not supposed to be here. However, at this present moment, as well as the seventy or so dragons hidden throughout the hospital, I would guess that within a five mile radius of where I'm standing, there are at least another five hundred or so dragons, ready to come to my aid at a moment's notice."

Tank whistled to himself, impressed.

"So you see my young friends, I always think of myself as the knight I once was. And while, at this present time, we as a community face a very real threat, part of which you all thwarted, I will never be afraid to go anywhere or do anything that I have to ask other dragons to do."

Sighing profoundly, the king rolled his head around his shoulders in an attempt to loosen up the muscles that had tightened since he'd been at the hospital.

"I'm sorry, but I really do have to go now. There are some pressing issues that have developed in the South Pole that I have to go and sign off on. No doubt you will all learn about them soon enough, through the telepathic papers. Another of our expeditions there has gone missing, the second in a row. The first was very low key, with hardly anyone knowing. This time, however, it's much more serious. I bid you all farewell and look forward to meeting you again. Your friends are welcome to accompany you when you come to pick up your grandfather's belongings, Peter. For that matter, you may extend the invitation to Gee Tee as well. I can only imagine how long he's had to wait. As a whole, the domain owes you a debt of gratitude for what you've done in stopping the dragon Manson. On their behalf I thank all three of you." Turning to leave, the king bowed and said,

"Farewell."

The scuffed wooden door closed silently after him, as

the three friends sat in silence, barely able to believe what had gone on. To have caught a glimpse of the king through a crowd was one thing; this was something else altogether. Tank spoke first.

"Your grandfather sounds like one hell of a guy."

"That he does," replied Peter, a hint of sadness in his voice.

"Fancy having the king looking out for you," teased Richie. "What's that all about?"

Tank smacked his friend playfully in the arm.

"Do we have to bow now? I'm not quite sure what the protocol is," he scoffed.

Peter shook his head, smiling as he did so.

"There's going to be no end to this, is there?"

"Whatever do you mean... majesty?" chuckled Richie.

"Sire?" mocked Tank, grinning.

"Bugger!" quipped Peter loudly.

Richie and Tank both burst out laughing.

Sitting on the bed contemplating the months of abuse just like this that he had to look forward to, realisation dawned on him.

"Hang on a minute," he cried. "What happened in the final?" he asked excitedly. "Did they win... ohhhhh... tell me they won, pleeeaaassseee tell me they won."

Richie and Tank shared a look, their smiles slowly disappearing. In unison they shook their heads in answer to Peter's question.

"They lost!" Peter exclaimed, heartbroken.

"Afraid so," mused Tank.

"Did you... did you... got to the match?"

Richie stifled a laugh.

"What do you think?"

"We've been here all the time," added Tank. "All the time."

Peter hung his head in shame.

"Sorry, I should have known. I would have done the same for either of you."

"You know I do believe his majesty would have attended the match," mimicked Richie in a pretend posh voice.

"I'm pretty sure you're right. Sire would have gone to the final of the Global Cup."

"Oh right... very funny," observed Peter.

"We did at least get to hear a live running commentary though," sighed Tank.

"No way!"

Tank and Richie both nodded.

"The brother of one of your guards was at the match. His brother phoned him and we all got to listen in live. Don't worry, from the sounds of it we didn't miss very much as Indigo Warriors fans. They got their asses kicked."

"Oh well... there's always next year," said Peter hopefully.

"Yeah right," said Tank. "Do you have any idea what the likelihood is of the Warriors getting to the final two years in a row?"

"Yeah," said Richie, "you've got a better chance of sprouting wings and flying out of here."

The three friends laughed their socks off.

The adventure continues in book 2, A Chilling Revelation. An epic page turner not to be missed. Read on for an extract...

"Something's not quite right here. I'm not sure what, but we should proceed with caution." Peter nodded, and with a sweep of his arm indicated that perhaps Flash should go first. Flash duly obliged.

Creeping stealthily towards the front of the shop, the two friends rounded the last of the tall bookcases. Out of nowhere shot a giant blur, smashing them both into one of the dust covered shelves, causing them to roll back up the aisle from which they'd both come. With the massive weight of the blur crushing his chest, Peter was pinned helplessly to the ground. Flash, not so much. His body had gone onto autopilot and his combat training was a fraction of a second from kicking in. It was only then that Flash's brilliant mind recalled that he'd heard a shout of, "DOWN!" as the speeding blur had crashed into them... odd, he thought, as he started to slide out from under the breath sapping weight on top of him. Just as it looked as though things couldn't get any weirder, three deadly thick needles of ice shot into the bookcase, behind where they'd been standing only a split second before, quivering there like frosted little arrows. The speeding blur had just saved their lives. Both Flash and Peter craned their necks at the same time, trying to get a glimpse of who, or what, had landed on them. As they did so, a thick neck full of muscle swung round above them. On it was a familiar head, with the same inane smile that Peter had come to know and love.

"Sorry about that," whispered Tank. "We've got something of a situation here," he added quietly, nodding towards the icy bolts embedded in the bookcase.

Flash smiled as Tank rolled off the two visitors, and added,

"Do tell."

As the three of them sat on the floor, backs against the shelves on the opposite side of the aisle to the ones with the ice bolts in them, Tank began to explain what had happened.

"Gee Tee and I were working our way through a set of old mantras, trying to determine what they were, if they worked and if they were worth saving. We were employing all the usual safeguards, morphic shields, phase resonators, blanket containment mantras, the lot. Well, after working our way through five or six in quick succession, we came across a most unusual one written in Inuit. I had no idea what any of it said, and although Gee Tee claimed he knew, I could sense a lot of nervousness in the old dragon, something very rare indeed. Anyway, against MY better judgement, he pressed on and cast the mantra, resulting in something akin to one of my nightmares, something that is currently residing round the corner there, near the front desk."

"Let me guess," ventured Flash. "An ice salamander?"

Tank nodded his head.

"And not just any ice salamander. I've seen them before, and yes, they can be a little bit tricky to handle. But this thing is like the queen of all ice salamanders. She's huge, and you've seen the things she's been firing at us. Gee Tee's trapped in the back of the workshop, where he fled as soon as we realised what happened. I've been out here trying to keep her occupied in the hope that the old dragon will find a way to reverse what he's done. This all started about three hours ago, and we've been doing this ever since, with no luck whatsoever."

"Three hours!" exclaimed Peter incredulously.

Flash's forehead creased deep in concentration, as he considered the sticky circumstances that they all found themselves in.

"Why not simply banish it back to where it came from?" he asked, puzzled.

"That was my thought originally," huffed Tank, looking absolutely shattered. "The problem is that the ice salamander seems to be guarding the scroll with the mantra on it, and is currently curled up atop it, making it all but impossible to banish it. I've spent nearly two hours trying to draw it away from the front desk, in the hope that Gee Tee might sneak out, get the scroll, and... waheyyy... banish it. But it's not happening. It will not leave that scroll. It's almost as if it knows what it is and where it's come from."

"That, Tank," said Peter, "is simply not possible."

Tank sighed deeply, wishing that his tired body could go home and curl up in bed.

"It's not quite as impossible as you seem to think Peter," interrupted Flash, eyes closed, leaning his head back against the dust encrusted book shelves. "In ages past, mantras that summoned creatures with a better understanding of exactly what they were, were almost commonplace. I'm talking of course about a time many, many thousands of years ago, but it did happen. What I struggle to understand is how a mantra could have lasted so long, and ended up here. Still... at this moment it's a moot point. We need to banish the ice salamander back to where it came from. If it does have any sort of understanding of what it is, the longer we wait, the harder all this is going to be."

"Uhhh, there's something else as well," whispered Tank nervously. "The shields on the building are weaker than they've ever been. Gee Tee's known this for some time, but hasn't got round to having them reenergised."

"Exactly how weak are the shields?" demanded Flash, quietly. "Weak enough for that thing to make a break for it?""

Rather sheepishly, Tank nodded his head.

"And you haven't called the King's Guard?"

Tank shook his head.

"If the King's Guard come, they'll shut the whole place

474

down for good. This will be the end of it all. They'll do it, and Rosebloom will make sure that it stays shut," added Tank, trying desperately to hold back tears. "I know they should have been called, and I realise the danger if that thing gets out... but I just couldn't do it. If they closed this place down, it would finish him off. I thought I could distract it and together we could undo everything... oh I can't believe this is happening. What a day!"

Flash slapped Tank playfully on the shoulder.

"Well... now that the cavalry has arrived, there's nothing to worry about is there? I'll create a distraction worthy of note, and you two can get the mantra back to Gee Tee. How does that sound?"

Tank's inane smile reappeared immediately.

"That sounds great. But are you sure you can do it?"

"Do dragons pee in the air?" (And if you'd ever been hit by flying dragon pee, boy you'd know it. Not just hospitalisation, but decontamination as well.) "I'm not called Flash for nothing you know. One very important thing to remember though guys."

"What's that?" mumbled Peter.

"We must avoid those ice bolts at all costs. If one of those hits a dragon, no matter what their form, I think it would be safe to say that the only thing you'd be seeing after that is a great big lake of lava."

Peter and Tank both understood his meaning. It brought home to Tank just how much danger he'd been in over the last few hours. Numerous times he'd felt the cold chill of an ice bolt skimming within inches of a limb or two. Momentarily, his large, powerful legs wobbled a little at the thought of what could have happened.

"Now," whispered Flash, finally seeing what he needed on a belt strapped around Tank's waist. "I need that mantra scalpel Tank, please, and Peter, I need your mobile phone."

Tank drew out the sharp blade that was used to repair and reconfigure broken mantras. The tip had a brilliant green glow to it. Peter handed over his mobile phone. Flash took the touch screen phone and held it up in the air so that a tiny part of it poked around the end of the bookcase. Glancing into the reflection on the screen, Flash gauged exactly where the deadly ice salamander was. After a few moments, he pulled the phone back and crouched down with his friends.

"Okay, get as near as you can on the southern side, nearest to the workshop. I'll approach from the north and attempt to lead her out into the depths of the shop that way. When you get the mantra... don't hang about. I'm guessing she's going to be rather mad at me, and I'm not going to have very long. Good luck!"

With that, Flash turned and headed back up the aisle, in the direction of the front door. Meanwhile, Peter had the startled expression of a bunny caught in the headlights of an onrushing car.

"Come on Pete," whispered Tank, slapping his friend on the back. "What could possibly go wrong?"

Ducking down, Tank and Peter shuffled silently along the exposed cross section of the aisle on all fours. Reaching the welcome cover of the bookcases on the other side, both stood up, relieved that no ice bolts had been fired in their direction. Before Tank could go any further, Peter put a hand on his shoulder to stop him.

"Do you think he's going to be alright?"

"He'll be fine," replied Tank quietly. "Besides, he's got more experience at this stuff than we'll ever have."

"I know," mouthed Peter. "But he's not done anything like this, since... you know... since he got stuck in human form."

"He'll be fine Pete. If we work as a team, this will all be over shortly. That's the key to it all... combining our strengths and working together. You should know that better than most."

Momentarily Peter's mind flashed back to the hockey, and as it did so, a dreamy smile crept across his face. The mere thought of working as a team sent goose bumps up his arms, at the same time filling him with confidence. Normal service resumed, the two friends made their way past the bookcases, aiming to get as close as possible to the front counter without being spotted by the ice salamander queen.

Meanwhile, Flash had been crawling commando style along the grubby stone floor, with only Peter's phone and Tank's mantra blade for company, knowing he was uncomfortably close to the ice salamander queen's position, the humming coming from only a few feet away, the smell of her icy cold breath being expelled every few seconds assaulting his nose. Lying on his side, snuggled up to one of the small, half yard bookcases, he very patiently and very quietly sat up. Slowly, he raised Peter's phone above the parapet, eyes glued firmly to the reflection on the screen. Nearly frozen with fear at the sight that greeted him, whipping the phone back down, his hands and fingers started shaking with fright as he realised the ice salamander queen was considerably bigger than he'd first thought. Not only that, but she looked... tough, strong... scary even. Unable to remember a time when he'd felt so afraid, even his recent adventures in Antarctica hadn't elicited the same terror that he was experiencing right at this very moment. Quietly, he took a few deep breaths to calm himself, knowing that, despite the fear, the butterflies zipping around in his stomach, the shakiness of his legs, he was going to do what was necessary, because... because he wasn't going to let his friends down. Peter, Tank... Gee Tee. Yes, even the old shopkeeper, he regarded as his friend. Now that he thought about it, he realised that he'd never really had any friends. Ohhh, he'd thought he had... in the Crimson Guards, but looking back on it now, he realised they were only really colleagues, most only associating themselves with him because of his talent and reputation, and because he was well thought of by the dragons in charge.

Exhaling the last deep breath, he knew now was the time to act. Using the silent touch screen on Peter's phone, he quickly set the alarm to go off after one minute, while counting down the remaining time in his head. On reaching ten seconds, Flash slid the phone along the floor of the aisle, its dark black shell contrasting harshly with the light coloured floor as it silently spun out of sight. Flash tensed himself, ready to act, the mantra blade gripped firmly in his right hand. Immediately a loud, telephone style shrill emanated from the direction he'd flung the phone in only moments earlier. Counting to two, he hoped that the deadly head part of the ice salamander had fallen for the distraction and gone to investigate. As his mouth finished whispering the word, "Two," in a fluid motion, he leapt over the small bookcase he'd been hiding behind and headed at speed towards the front desk, knowing as he leapt that if he'd miscalculated and the salamander hadn't moved from its position, then he was almost certainly dead. It wasn't the first time he'd found himself in this kind of situation, but it had been a little while and he'd forgotten the unmistakable thrill that ran through him at times like this. Counteracting this, somewhere at the back of his mind, a little voice gently whispered,

"One day you're going to do this and it will go horribly wrong... and you'll die."

But not today, at least... not yet. The ice salamander had indeed gone to investigate the shrill noise of the phone, well, the front half of it had anyway with the remaining half of the salamander curled tightly around itself atop the front desk, wisps of cold infusing the air all around it. No time to lose, Flash pulled back his right arm and, with all his might, buried the mantra blade into the nearest part of the ice salamander's tail. An ungodly screech echoed from the direction of the phone, as the huge tail started to jump and flail about. Suddenly the top half of the salamander whipped round the corner of a giant bookcase, its dull white eyes filled with hatred, anger and... revenge. Knowing he'd outstayed his welcome, Flash was already moving in the opposite direction to where he hoped Tank and Peter were hidden, desperately trying to find some sort of cover from what he knew would be an imminent attack. As he hurdled an untidy pile of tomes, the sound of multiple projectiles cutting through the air and heading in his direction assaulted his very sensitive ears. Maybe the little voice in his head had been right after all.

Tank and Peter were as close as they dared get when the phone's alarm had gone off. Peter's reaction had been to try and look over the top of the counter behind which they were hidden. Tank had known better and had used one of his giant arms to anchor Peter to the floor, having a fair idea of what was coming next, and wasn't surprised when the hideous screech echoed around the shop. Waiting for a split second after the haunting sound, Gee Tee's young partner popped his head over the parapet of the counter to see the ice salamander, only a few yards away, sitting up like a cobra, firing a seemingly endless bout of ice bolts, then slithering off in the opposite direction after Flash, its long tail uncurling from the top of the counter, freezing cold vapour evaporating into the air all around it. As the last of the tail slithered off in chase of its body, Tank spotted what he was looking for... the scroll with the mantra on it. Ordering Peter to keep an eye out, Tank dashed over to the counter and grabbed the scroll, causing waves of pain to shoot through his fingers and up his arm, forcing him to drop the scroll. Shaking his hand to try and get rid of the pain, Tank examined the scroll closely. An icy blue grain had formed on the parchment, accompanied by a similarly icy blue mist, something he was quite sure hadn't been there originally. This, he thought, was far from good. With the crashing of bookcases and the sound of books and ice bolts flying indiscriminately somewhere off in another part of the shop, Tank knew he had to act.

"PETER," he shouted, "open the door to the workshop and then get the hell out of the way."

Although Peter couldn't quite understand what was going on, he did at least recognise the command and urgency in Tank's tone of voice. Running over to the door, he slid to a halt. Giving it a sharp yank, he continued to hold it open for whatever his friend had in mind. As he stood holding the door, a smooth whisper drifted in his direction.

"Hello Child. Come to join in the fun?"

It took Peter over a second to find the source of the voice, but when he did he found himself smiling. There, poking out from behind one of the oversized dragon chairs, were the distinct, square glasses that could only belong to one being... Gee Tee! With the smile still on his face, he gave the old shopkeeper a 'pleased to see you' nod, and turned back round to see what Tank was doing.

Tank, by now, had decided on a course of action. With his friend holding the workshop door open, he grabbed the mantra and began tossing it from one hand to the other as if it were a hot potato, all the time heading for the workshop at speed. Positively flying past Peter by the door he then threw the scroll down onto the nearest workbench, all the time trying to ignore the burning pain running up his hands and arms. Gee Tee stood up, giving his former apprentice a puzzled look. Making to pick up the scroll, one of Tank's powerful arms shot out to stop the master mantra maker.

"There's something wrong with it," Tank spluttered painfully. "It seems to be imbued with cold."

Shuffling his glasses back along his nose towards his eyes, the shopkeeper leant over to get a better look.

"Fascinating!"

A deafening crash followed by a rumble and a bump, reverberated throughout the shop.

"I don't mean to hurry you, or anything," exclaimed Peter, "but Flash is being chased by that thing, and I'm not

480

sure exactly how long he can last."

Gee Tee glared across at the two friends.

"Why on earth didn't you say so?" With that, he grabbed a couple of mantra pens from a pile on the desk and proceeded to use them to fully unfurl the scroll.

*   *   *

All he could feel was his heart pounding in his chest. It was so loud, he thought he might die. Sprinting around another corner, he grabbed books from bookcases on either side of him and flung them as hard as he could back over his shoulder. Sweat dribbled down from behind his ears, racing down his neck, flooding his T-shirt with moisture. Instinctively he pushed the top half of his body forward, forcing himself into a roll just as two more deadly ice bolts carved through the air where his head had been only a split second before. Feeling exhausted and somehow... different, whether it was something to do with his transformation and being stuck in this ridiculous human form he didn't know, but he did know that he couldn't go on for much longer. It felt almost as if his human fuel tank was running on empty. Even in his most desperate state after being attacked by the naga's poison, he'd never once felt like this. With no time to think, he came to a T junction and without knowing any different, turned right... skidding straight into a dead end. His first thought was to clamber up the bookcase he was facing and jump down on the other side. But the bookcases he found himself enclosed by were at least fifty feet high, and he knew that the salamander would be on him before he could even get half way up. Turning round, he wondered if he had time to cross over to the aisle that lay directly opposite him in the distance.

Before he could take a step, he had his answer. Steaming with cold and pure, unadulterated rage, the giant ice salamander queen slithered into view, her vicious fangs

481

bared, her scales bristling. Flash instinctively threw some more books at her from the shelves, despite the futility of it. Her snarl turned to more of a smile as she realised that her prey had nowhere else to go. Backing up the aisle as far as he could go, Flash only stopped when his back rested against one of the giant bookcases. She followed him, her head swaying from side to side, powered by her injured tail. For his part, the former Crimson Guard racked his brain for anything that would help him out, but nothing sprang to mind. Having done all he could, he hoped, with what he supposed was one of his last thoughts, that he'd bought his friends enough time for them to get out of this safely. As the frosty queen pulled back her head, baring her icy-white, needle sharp fangs, ready to strike, Flash looked on determinedly, facing his death with strength, pride, dignity and courage. Just as the queen's head darted forward, a look of shock and confusion rippled across her face, before the loudest POP in the world sounded and her whole body disappeared for good. Slumping down against the bookcase, sweat racing down his arms and legs, Flash had never felt so relieved in his entire life.

Seconds later, two sets of footsteps closed in on the aisle's dead end. Tank and Peter skidded round the corner, both coming to a direct halt right in front of the glittering puddle that only moments earlier had been the ice salamander queen. Both friends had exactly the same thought at exactly the same time... that Flash looked an absolute mess. Both had the forethought not to say it out loud.

"Somehow I imagined you'd be a bit fitter," Tank deadpanned.

Flash looked up from his sitting position on the floor.

"You're kidding me... right?"

"Well... you know... all that training and everything... seems to have been wasted, if you ask me."

Not able to contain himself, Peter burst into a fit of

laughter as Flash hurled two dust laden tomes in Tank's direction with the very last of his energy. Tank dodged out of the way with much more agility than most people, or dragons, would have given him credit for.

Sidestepping the puddle, Peter and Tank each offered Flash a hand. Gratefully accepting, Flash let himself be pulled up by his friends. Tank slapped the exhausted ex-Crimson Guard on the back in admiration.

"Sorry it took so long," quipped Tank, "but you know what he's like... can't be rushed and all that, even when someone's life's on the line."

Flash just shrugged his shoulders in acceptance. It wasn't the first time he'd been a bedbug's eyelash away from death and he was pretty sure, the way things were going, that it wouldn't be the last.

Making their way back through the maze of bookcases, stepping over the wreckage as they did so, Tank already had a pretty good idea as to who would be tidying up the shop, and as usual, he was pretty sure it wouldn't be the old shopkeeper. Striding through the gap in the counter, the three of them sauntered into the workshop, just as Gee Tee appeared from behind one of the huge filing cabinets.

"I'm so glad you're okay," he whispered huskily, patting Flash gently on the head. "I would never have forgiven myself if anything had happened to you."

"It was a close run thing," gulped Flash, "but you just managed to reverse the mantra in time. Thanks."

"You're welcome youngster, but it is I who should be thanking you... what happened was a whole lot more than we'd bargained for... and yes, before you say it app... Tank, I've learned a valuable lesson today."

Tank nearly fainted in disbelief. In all the time he'd worked for the shopkeeper, hardly ever had he heard him apologise, let alone in the manner he just had.

'Who's stolen Gee Tee, and what have they done with him?' he thought, only half jokingly.

"I think it might just be about time for a drink, don't

you?" announced Gee Tee.

"I'll put us all on some hot charcoal," declared Peter, looking to be helpful.

"That wasn't quite what I had in mind, child," purred the master mantra maker, a mischievous glint in his eye.

Understanding immediately, Peter wondered just how Tank might react to what was about to happen. Dragging his tail in the direction of the nearest filing cabinet, Gee Tee was about to try and reach up when in one leap, Tank jumped and grabbed something long and silver off the top. Slamming back down onto the floor, Tank held out the dusty, silver cylinder towards the old shopkeeper.

"Would this be what you're after, by any chance?"

Gritting his teeth, Peter held his breath. Flash stood, bemused by what was going on. Gee Tee turned his head back over his shoulder, giving Peter an icy glare, not realising that he hadn't revealed the old shopkeeper's secret.

"It might be," replied the master mantra maker.

"Hmmm," voiced Tank, clearly enjoying every second of the Emporium owner's discomfort. "I have to ask why you would want some..." Tank took a deep breath and blew off part of the thick layer of dust, "Peruvian Mantra Ink."

As a single thought circled throughout his head, Peter's lips creased into a tiny smile. Tank knew about the ink, and what it really was. The follow on thought was: how? Most certainly, he himself had never even so much as hinted at its existence.

"Might I ask how you know?"

"No... you might not," countered Tank, grinning from ear to ear. "But you should know two things. One... Peter didn't tell me, as I assume from your little glance at him, that he knew. And two... you're not nearly as sneaky or clever as you seem to think you are." And with that, in one fluid motion, Tank whipped the cap off the cylinder and let a small sip run gently down his throat. Peter, Gee Tee, and in particular Flash, who had no idea what was going on, all looked on in anticipation. Rolling his head and neck from side to side, seemingly swirling the liquid round and round inside him, Tank's face changed in an instant, but not how Peter pictured it would. A dreamy quality etched itself across the rugby playing dragon's bold, rugged features. Peter could almost see the liquid making its way up inside his friend's neck. Effortlessly, Tank opened his mouth just slightly and exhaled. A long, drawn out, blue flame, tinged around the edges with red and orange, snaked out across the room. Gee Tee, Peter and Flash all looked on in awe. Just when Peter thought it couldn't get any more amazing, the flame started to curl up in the air and form a shape. The line of flame cut off and then started again, in much the same way. All the time the room's occupants stared in disbelief. Four separate lines of flame hung in the air on the far side of the room, as Tank stood making tiny motions with his fingers. Ever so slowly, the flames twisted and turned and... changed. Changed into four separate letters, spelling out the word... T... A... N... K.

Surprisingly, Gee Tee was the first to react.

"Very good. I'm... impressed. Some of my tutoring must have rubbed off after all." Tank grinned and shook his head.

Peter patted his friend on the back gently to get his attention.

"How did you get it to do that?" he asked. "When I had a go, it was like a raging tempest that I couldn't control."

"The raging tempest responsible for that slag heap of a filing cabinet that I spent most of one morning cleaning up?"

"Uhhh... yeah, sorry about that," replied Peter sheepishly.

"You two must think I've got the brains of a politician," ventured Tank, offering the silver cylinder to Flash.

Still a little behind on the conversation, his experience had enabled him to catch up on a few things. Gripping the dusty cylinder, he put his nose directly above the top and sniffed.

"If I'm not mistaken... *'igneus saevio'*... very impressive."

"Igneus saevio?" questioned Peter, just beating Tank and Gee Tee to it.

"Yeah, means... 'fiery rage'," remarked Flash thoughtfully, "from my least favourite beings on the whole planet... the nagas. Although, to give them credit, this was one of the best things they've ever produced and if memory serves me correctly, it was specially concocted for one of the dragon kings, a gift for the aid he rendered them in some kind of battle they were losing. A gift that incorporates all their renowned alchemy skills, I might add."

The three others all looked on in astonishment.

"Anyway... bums in the air," Flash announced, taking a slightly bigger sip than Tank had.

"I think you mean... bottoms up," corrected Peter, in a voice that sounded very much like that of a teacher.

"I know what I meant," gurgled Flash, much to Peter's chagrin.

ABOUT THE AUTHOR

Paul Cude is a husband, father, field hockey player and aspiring photographer. Lost without his hockey stick, he can often be found in between writing and chauffeuring children, reading anything from comics to sci-fi, fantasy to thrillers. Too often found chained to his computer, it would be little surprise to find him, in his free time, somewhere on the Dorset coastline, chasing over rocks and sand in an effort to capture his wonderful wife and lovely kids with his camera. Paul Cude is also the author of the Bentwhistle the Dragon series of books.

Thank you for reading.....

If you could take a couple of moments to write a review, it would be much appreciated.

CONNECT WITH PAUL ONLINE:
www.paulcude.com
Twitter: @paul_cude
Facebook: Paul Cude
Instagram: paulcude

OTHER BOOKS IN THE SERIES:
A Threat from the Past
A Chilling Revelation
A Twisted Prophecy
Earth's Custodians
A Right Royal Rumpus